Twin Faces
Shadow's Patience

How To Experience The All Of You!

Other Works by H. T. Manogue

Poetry

Short Sleeves: A Book for Friends 2006 Children's Collection
Short Sleeves: A Book for Friends 2007 Children's Collection
Short Sleeves Spirit Songs 2008 Collection
Echoes From The Wind 2020 Collection
(Reader Views Bronze Poetry Award)

Award-Winning Novels

Living Behind the Beauty Shop
2011
The Butterfly Ball
2012
Bed Bosh & Beyond
2013–2014
Black Orchid Night
2015
Pine Cone Pandemic
2019

Essay And Art Collection
Just An Old Fashioned Love Song Meets Stoic Man
2021
The Lawn Party And Everyone's Invited
2023
— Short Sleeves Insights: 2010 Collection — Out of Print

Thanks To These Publishers
For Their Artistic Contributions:

All works are available from your book source.

New Awareness Network Inc., Manhasset, NY

The Seth Material Seth, Dreams And Projections of Consciousness Seth

Quotes By Jane Roberts and Robert F. Butts © Laurel Davies

Amber-Allen Publishing Inc., San Rafael, CA

The Unknown Reality Volume One

The Unknown Reality Volume Two

The Nature of the Psyche

Dreams, "Evolution," and Value Fulfillment, Vol. 1

Seth Speaks The Way Toward Health. The Nature Of Personal Reality

Seth Quotes By Jane Roberts and Robert F. Butts © Laurel Davies

Conversations With Seth: The Story of Jane Roberts ESP Class,
Combined Volumes 1 and 2

Seth Audio Collection #41 December 12, 1972

Conversations with Seth, 25th Anniversary Edition, book one,
chapter one, by Susan M

Watkins. (C)

The Seth ESP Class

*Original Book Location appears at the end of the Seth posts.

Special Thanks

Members Of Facebook's The Seth House Group

Members Of The Fans Of The Seth Material (Jane Roberts)

Members Of Other Facebook Seth Groups

And Especially

Major Seth Internet Contributors:

Laurel Davies

Barrie Gellis

Ivan Kelly

Ron H. Card

Oshara Waago

Lynda English

Chiron O'Keefe

Rick Scott

Rachel Enevoldsen

John Blair

Front & Back Cover Art

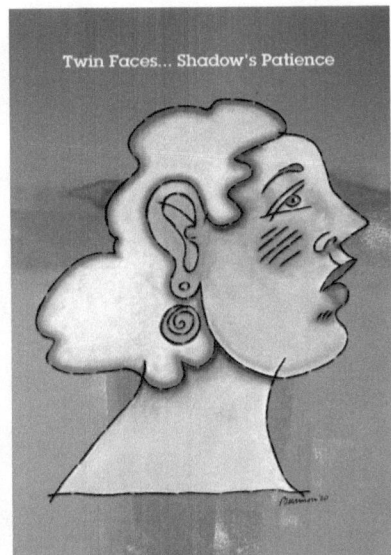

Paul Harmon, one of the 21st Century's prominent artists, gives this book its identity.

Front Cover: Monaco Odalisque, Oil & Acrylic on Paper. 46 X 34". 2019.

Back Cover: Springtime Adelaide, Oil & Acrylic on Paper. 46 X 34". 2019

Mr. Harmon provided paintings for the front and back cover, and he also adjusted the graphics so they would flow smoothly with the book's format and accompanying text.

paulharmon.com

To: Perceptions

Certificate of Registration

This Certificate issued under the seal of the Copyright Office in accordance with title 17 United States Code, attests that registration has been made for the work identified below. The information on this certificate has been made a part of the Copyright Office records.

Shira Perlmutter
United States Register of Copyrights and Director

Registration Number
TXu 2-478-945
Effective Date of Registration:
March 08, 2025
Registration Decision Date:
April 04, 2025

Title _____
Title of Work: Twin Faces Shadow's Presence

Completion/Publication _____
Year of Completion: 2025

Author _____
Author: Howard Thomas Matregue
Author Created: text, compilation of text of from other sources
Work made for hire: No
Domiciled in: United States

Copyright Claimant _____
Copyright Claimant: Howard Thomas Matregue
408 Brentwood Pl, Brentwood, TN, 37027, United States

mitation of copyright claim _____
Material excluded from this claim: text from other sources
New material included in claim: text, compilation of text of from other sources

Rights and Permissions _____
Name: Howard Thomas Matregue
Email: hal9 shontalavya.net
Telephone: (615)400-0431
Address: 408 Brentwood Pl.

From The Author

Let's Face It. We all have at least two faces. Quantum Physics tells us we have more faces than we realize. Understanding why we have all these faces can be challenging.

In the 1950s, author and Professor Joseph Campbell wrote the Book *The Hero With A Thousand Faces*. The book describes the many faces in the human psyche. Theorist and author Ken Wilber explained what our faces look like in his 20th-century book *Spectrum of Consciousness*.

Recognizing our multiplicity is an avenue for our minds to explore.

Even though we do not realize it, we try to be true to our Twin Faces. Those faces have several names, personality traits, influences, and associations.

Associations we brought with us at birth and some we developed physically. We then deposit them in our core belief system.

Blending the face we show to the world and the face hidden underneath can be challenging. We feel like auto mechanics who know something needs attention. But we lack the tools to make us aware of who we are.

Allowing the ego to stop and listen to that inner face (inner self) takes work. And we only have partial or unassembled tools to hear it.

We do not know how to use our inner senses. And we rarely listen to our intuition and impulses.

We hide our inner face with egocentric thoughts that put roadblocks between our ego face and our subjective one.

We let that inner self sit on a shaky physical bench filled with religious answers that require something from us.

Religion is one of our current sources of core beliefs. If new information does not conform to the associations and influences that concur with the laws of religion, we have a hard time accepting our inner self.

Core beliefs develop from those influencing voices, and they direct our perceptions and the choices we make from those perceptions.

Everything in this physical reality is subjective or non-physical before it manifests. Everything we know and see is our consciousness manifested in various objective forms to expand our entities consciousness and the universal consciousness.

But Know.

You have non-physical faces waiting for discovery

H.T. Manogue

September 2025

Now, About The Book:

Twin Faces has Forty-Three Chapter Descriptions that describe the content in a way that kick-starts imagination. Other thoughts in each chapter could belong somewhere else in the book, but they play an incredible part in their current chapter. These thoughts have a way of repeating themselves in a non-physical consciousness pattern.

The answers to questions that religion does not give us about the nature of subjective reality are in this book.

The answers are not new. People around the world receive messages like these from their non-physical entities daily.

The words from non-physical Seth and Elias are physical links to understanding the non-physical side of us. All consciousness connects to itself in some way or ways. We feel is connection from our non-physical version of Seth and Elias but we don't acknowledge it.

My world changed when I started reading the Seth books. That was in the 1990s. When I found Facebook Seth Groups on the Internet, this book became a daily project. I put it together as a personal dictionary of thoughts. Seth Cliff-Notes — internal thoughts I could continue to study.

Elias came along in the early 2000s via Facebook. Elias uses a woman named Mary Ennis. (Michael) Ennis currently lives in New England, to express his knowledge.

Seth used Jane Roberts (Rupurt) and Rob Butts (Joseph) in Elmira, NY. They wrote more than thirty books using the Seth material.

This book contains original posts from Facebook Groups and Elias Group emails. The posts are in what I call Chapter Description (CD) order.

Feel free to pick a chapter of interest and start there. As Seth said, there is no beginning or end. And the same for this work. None of the original words changed, but the manuscript experienced a slight punctuation proofreading process. The original punctuation did not change in the quotes, except for the omission of quotation marks used by some posters. So, there are punctuation distortions.

Each chapter explains how interwoven non-physical consciousness is in our lives. Knowing and believing we create our reality is the key to moving out of the negative field of thought and into some other world of experiences.

That is the message.

This book is a stepping stone in the quest to boost our connection to that Twin Face that dwells in the nuclei of every one of our cells. Call that Shadow Face what it is.

It Is A Huge Part Of You.

Chapter Descriptions

Names Used In The Book

Seth Calls Author Jane Roberts, "Ruburt"

Because Of Other Incarnational Relationships

Experienced In The Past Lives Together.

Seth Also Calls Artist Robert Butts (Jane's
Husband) "Joseph" For The Same Reasons.

Robert Butts was the Scribe
During Seth's Non-Physical Appearances Through Jane.
Elias Uses the "Michael" when referring to Marry Ennis.

Jane and Rob Wrote More Than Thirty Books in Their Modest
Elmira, New York home.

I read most of those books during the 1990s. My old books contain
Post-It Notes that seem to grow out of the pages. They are filled
with pertinent stuff I randomly wrote down.

I intended to reread the paperback editions, but that never happened.

Instead, I found the Seth groups online and began to save the
quotes I remembered from the books. This book represents a lot
of the quotes I wrote down. I read the online Seth posts daily.
The ones I picked came in the order written.

That process started several years ago. Then, I found Elias online
and noticed his thoughts felt like Seth's material.

After reading the thoughts of Seth and Elias, it's easier to
understand why both energy personalities say:

"You create your reality using thoughts, emotions, and beliefs."

Seth's Explanation For His Non-Physical Communication Mode

"You could not understand us if we did not speak through one of your kind. We try to give you information for your benefit and that of your world.

It is necessary that we rely upon the mental equipment of the person through whom we speak,

And at times we are able to activate the intellectual capacities many times above normal, in order that certain concepts be given.

But we must still rely upon the mental structure of the person through whom we speak.

This has disadvantages but without the method such communications would not be possible."

The Early Sessions: Book 9 of The Seth Material; Session 464 February 10, 1969, Jane Roberts © 2014
Laurel Davies-Butts

What's It Take To Be Human?

The atoms that compose the fetus have their own kind of consciousness.

The volatile awareness-consciousnesses that exist independently of matter,

Formulates matter according to their ability and degree.

It also seems that each fetus must naturally desire to grow, emerge whole from its mother's womb,

And develop into a natural childhood and adulthood.

However, in those terms JUST AS MANY fetuses want the experience of being fetuses without following through on other stages.

They have no intention of growing into complete human development.

In fact, many fetuses explore THAT ELEMENT of existence numberless times

Before deciding to go on still further, and emerge normally from the womb.

Those fetuses that do not develop still contribute to the body's overall experience,

And they feel themselves successful in their own existences.

An understanding of these issues can greatly help throw light on the question of early deaths and diseases, and spontaneous abortions.

This is not AN UNCARING UNIVERSE OR NATURE OPERATING,
portions of consciousness who choose at whatever levels certain
experiences that nourish the living environment,

And bring satisfactions that may never show on life's surface.

The Way Toward Health, Chapter 12, June 15, 1984

The fetus, therefore, has its own consciousness.

The simple component consciousness made up of the atoms that
compose it.

This exists before any reincarnating personality enters it.

The consciousness of matter is present in any matter –

A fetus, a rock, a blade of grass, a nail.

The reincarnating personality enters the new fetus according
to its own inclinations, desires, and characteristics, with some
built-in safeguards.

However, there is no rule, then, saying that the reincarnating
personality must take over the new form prepared for it either at
the point of conception,

In the very earliest months of the fetus's growth,

Or even at the point of birth.

The process is gradual, individual and determined by experience
in other lives.

It is particularly dependent upon emotional characteristics —

Not necessarily of the last incarnated self,

But the emotional tensions present as a result of a group of past existences.

Various methods of entry are adopted.

If there is a strong relationship between the parents and the child-to-be,

Then the personality may enter at the point of conception if he is extremely anxious to rejoin them.

Even here, however, large portions of self-awareness continue to operate in the between-life dimension.

In the beginning, the womb state under these conditions is a dreamlike one, with the personality still focused mainly in the between-life existence.

Gradually the situation reverses, until it becomes more difficult to retain clear concentration in the between-life situation.

In these circumstances, when the personality attaches itself at conception, there is almost without exception strong past-life connections between parents and child,

Or there is an unceasing and almost obsessional desire to return to the earthly situation—

Either for a specific purpose, or because the reincarnating personality is presently obsessed with earthly existence.

This is not necessarily detrimental.

The personality can simply realize what it takes to physically experience well,

It is presently earth-oriented and finds the earthly atmosphere a rich dimension for the growth of its own abilities.

Some personalities are drawn to enter at conception as a result of seemingly less worthy motives

Greed, for example, or an obsessional desire that is partially composed of unresolved experiences

Propensity is a selection of significance, an inclination toward the formation of a selected experience.

This applies on all levels — atomic and psychological — and to biological stimulus and mental intent.

Hell is being blocked and knowing you're being blocked from using your abilities;

Your abilities of creativity.

Now. There can be a hell—
I've been there several times—
And there can be a limbo.
But these are not places.

They are spiritual states, and even in those terms, hell is not eternal.

They are the results of ignorance.

Hell, for example, could not exist unless you have the concept of a heaven.

There would be nothing to compare it with.

The Early Class Sessions: Book 2 Sessions 1/6/70 to 12/29/70; ESP Class Session, May 5, 1970,

Jane Roberts © 2008 Laurel Davies-Butts

Other personalities who never completely take to earthly existence may hold off full entry for some time and even then, always remain at a certain distance from the body.

At the other end of the scale, before death, the same applies, where some individuals remove their focus from physical life, leaving the body consciousness alone.

Others stay with the body until the last moment.

In the early days of infancy, there is not a steady focus of the personality in the body in any case.

Now:
In all cases the decisions have been made ahead of time, as I told you.

The reincarnating personality is aware, therefore, when the conception for which it has been waiting takes place.

And while it may or may not choose to enter at that point,

It is drawn irresistibly to that time and point in space and flesh. On occasion, long before conception takes place,

The personality who will end up as the future child will visit that environment of both parents-to-be, drawn again.

This is quite natural.

Between lives an individual may see flashes of the future existence, not necessarily of particular events,

But experience the essence of the new relationship and in expectation remind himself of the challenge he has set.

In these terms, the ghosts of the future are as real in your homes as the ghosts of the past.

You do not have completely empty shells of matter about to be filled, in that the new personality hovers in and about, particularly after conception and with greater frequency and intensity thereafter.

The shock of birth has several consequences, however, that usually draw the personality full blast, so to speak, into physical reality.

Before this, the conditions are fairly uniform. The body consciousness is nurtured almost automatically, reacting strongly but under highly controlled conditions.

At birth, all of this is suddenly over, and [new] stimuli [are] introduced with a rapidity that the body consciousness has never to that point experienced.

It greatly needs a stabilizing factor.

Previously the body consciousness has been enriched and supported by deep biological and telepathic identification with the mother.

The communication of the living cells is far more profound than you imagine.

The identification is almost complete before birth as far as body consciousness alone is concerned.

Until the new personality enters, the fetus regards itself as a part of the organism of the mother.

This support is suddenly denied at birth.

If the new personality has not entered earlier to any full extent, it usually does so at birth, in order to stabilize the new organism.

It comforts the new organism, in other words.

The new personality, therefore, will experience birth to varying degrees according to when it has entered this dimension.

When it enters at the point of birth, it is fairly independent, not yet identified with the form it has entered, and acting in a supportive role.

If the personality entered at conception or sometime before birth, then it has to some extent identified with the body consciousness, with the fetus.

It has already begun to direct perception –

Though perception has begun whether or not it is so directed –

And it will experience the shock of birth in immediate, direct terms.

There will be no distance between the personality and the experience of birth, then.

The newly entered personality, as a consciousness, flickers, in that there is a while before stabilization takes place.

When the child, particularly the young child, is sleeping, for example, the personality often simply vacates the body.

Gradually the identification with the between-life situation dwindles until nearly full focus resides in the physical body.

Seth Speaks by Jane Roberts. Session 557, October 28, 1970

No course is irrevocably set or beyond change.

Within the limited framework of your usual operations, however, so-called predictions may be made. They will be workable to some degree.

In deeper terms however, no action is set beyond alteration.

The unknown reality is the source for the known one.

If you want to "discover" how things work, then your journey must eventually lead you into the dimensions that lie within the world you know.

You must therefore explore the psyche, the living consciousness.

It will lead you to the within-ness.

This is not an impractical, but very practical, endeavor in all areas.

Scientifically, such studies would vastly enlarge your concepts so that a loving technology could follow the most beautiful contours of the mind,

Rising on the natural mountains of human abilities and then more easily into fulfillment.

The "Unknown" Reality Volume 1, Jane Roberts Copyright L. Davies

The rules are that you create your universe—

That you create within the system that you know the world that you know.

The rules are that within you there is knowledge. . .

And that you must look inward, not outward, to find it.

The rules are that this universe is created by the thoughts that exist within each of your minds.

And that these thoughts are materialized outward.

And that if your body becomes ill, it is because of an inner disease and again, there are no exceptions.

There are no exceptions.

And these are the only rules,
for you have been given what you always say you want—

Your desires— for what you think of is materialized.

And when thoughts of resentment and hatred are materialized, you end up with wars.

I have said this many times the condition of your physical world is the result of your mass inner thoughts and desires.

And your physical environments, your personal physical environments, are the results of your inner materialized thoughts. And there are no exceptions.

You are responsible for the sunrise—you are responsible for the tides— you are responsible for the wars and the starvation.

Your experience follows your expectations.

Now, the same applies to after-death experience and to out-of-body encounters.

If you are obsessed with the idea of evil, then you will meet evil conditions. If you believe in devils, then you will encounter these.

As I mentioned earlier, there is greater freedom when consciousness is not physically directed. Thoughts and emotions are constructed, again, into reality without the physical time lapse.

So if you believe you will be met by a demon, you will create your own thought-form of one, not realizing that it is of your own creation.

Seth Speaks: The Eternal Validity of the Soul; Part Two: Chapter 10: Session 538, June 29, 1970, Jane Roberts © 2012 Laurel Davies-Butts

Your impulses are your closest communication with your inner self, because in the waking state they are the spontaneous urgings toward action,

Rising from that deep inner knowledge of yourself that you have in dreams.

You were born because you had the impulse to be. The urge to be came from within.

And, that urge is repeated to some extent in each impulse, each urge toward action on the part of man or molecule.

If you do not trust the nature of your impulses, then you do not trust the nature of your life,

The nature of the universe, or the nature of your own being.

The Individual and the Nature of Mass Events by Jane Roberts Session 870 © Laurel Davies

At one time or another all of us on my plane give such lessons,

But psychic bonds between teacher and pupils are necessary,

Which means that we must wait until personalities on your plane have progressed sufficiently for lessons to begin.

To explain more clearly, lessons are conducted with those who are psychically bound to us, although reason is extremely important and I do not mean to minimize its value.

Nevertheless, what you call emotion or feeling is the connective between us, and it is the connective that most clearly represents the life force on any plane and under any circumstances.

Your plane could be likened to a small position between four very spindly and thin wires,

And my plane could be likened to the small position in the neighboring wires on the other side.

Yet not only are we on different sides of the same wires, but we are at the same time either above or below, according to your viewpoint,

And if you consider the wires as forming cubes—this is for you, Joseph, with your love of images—then the cubes could also fit one within the other without disturbing the inhabitants of either cube one iota;

And these cubes are also within cubes, which are themselves within cubes, and I am speaking now of only the small particle of space taken up by your plane and mine.

The Early Sessions: Book 1 of The Seth Material; Session 12 January 2, 1964, Jane Roberts © 2012

Laurel Davies-Butts

Open your eyes and look about you. You are now in a projection.

You have projected yourself to this room, in your terms, from other times and other places.

You belong in this room at this moment of your time because you have projected yourselves into it.

Around you there are friends and strangers, and you have always been friends and strangers to each other.

Now look closely about you. How real is the room? How much do you know of the selves you think you are?

Now I want you to try something with me. As you have projected yourselves here, then give yourselves the freedom to project yourselves elsewhere.

You may close your eyes or leave them open, as you prefer, but sense within yourselves your own inner identity.

Travel through the personality that you call yourself.

Do not take it at face value but feel within yourself for the hidden self that is within.

Feel also within you the tremendous energy and vitality that gives existence to your physical image and propels the reality of your thoughts and images and gives any kind of reality to your dreams.

Get a hold of this energy within yourselves and feel it as your own for you are this energy, and you are within it and a part of it.

Now you may each interpret your experiences in your own way but feel the independence of yourself from this room and from this time and from this existence. It is, indeed, real and so are dreams real.

Pretend then that the room itself is a dream from which you are almost about to awaken,

And with your eyes closed still, you will awaken from this room into another place and another time. And with your eyes closed you will awaken to another reality as valid and legitimate as this one.

A reality in which you are intimately concerned and feel within yourselves the inner identity recognizing that which it now sees and perceives.

You may, again, interpret the experience in whatever terms you choose. If you hear voices, then listen to what they say.

The voices of strangers and beloved ones are often the same voices, and the scenes that you see often, you have seen before.

But the vitality that draws you, and the vitality that is within each of you is the same vitality

That changes the seasons that you know and that gives your physical existence its meaning that insures the survival of your identity.

And within this energy have you your independent existence.

Climb up my words then, rush up the vowels and the syllables and let them form for you a ladder of energy by which you can send.

And let them form a foundation upon which you can climb to find your own reality and your own existence

That is in itself independent, both of my words and even of the room in which now your bodies sit,

For that independent inner self wanders through all existences that you have known, in your terms, has a wisdom and knowledge that you can use.

And each of you in a greater sense knows the nature of your own vitality, and none of you are alone or have ever been alone for within you is the knowledge of all the personalities that you are, and within you are those abilities to be used and tapped.

Now feel, again within yourself, the birth and emergence of ever new energy so that it pulses within all the reality that you know.

Let it sustain you, let it carry you again safely back to the hallucination of the physical room and the projection that you now accept.

And let all of you remember what you have learned, and where you have been.

TECS3 ESP Class Session, May 11, 1971

The body is a highly energized gestalt of intelligent processes

The body is composed of organs, physical parts, living matter —

But the body is also composed of processes, relationships that exist on all levels between various portions of the body and between the body and its environment.

All processes in nature are intelligent.

They may involve a different kind of consciousness and intelligence than your own.

But there are no unintelligent processes. There are no closed processes.

There is no process that is not in one way or another related to others.

In a fashion, any one natural process carries within it the implied existence of all others.

The body is in that regard a highly energized gestalt of intelligent processes.

These include emotional processes, of course, mental ones, emotional ones, and constant transformation of energy from one form into another.

The Unknown Reality, Volume 1, Section 1: Session 682 February 13, 1974 - by Jane Robert

Your stomach cannot read.

What you read, however, is in one way or another translated into other terms,

So that for example your stomach reacts in its way to your reading matter, as the visual information is translated into other terms.

In ways really difficult to describe, your bodily processes, and what you think of as, say, cultural or national events, are highly connected and a part of each other.

Events are indeed also processes, partially physical and partially not physical.

It is as if bits and pieces of any and all probable events exist in a jigsaw-like fashion throughout the minds of men, throughout the consciousness's of plants and all natural things, wanting to be put together —

And each individual consciousness has its part to play in directing which of those events occur or do not occur —

But the processes involve in the formation of those events are hidden from the conscious mind.

The Personal Sessions, Book 5, by Jane Roberts Session November 19, 1980 © Laurel Davies

As a child forms mud pies from dirt, so you form your civilization out of thoughts and emotions,

And then see what you have created, and you must deal with it on its terms.

In other systems, energy is more directly felt, more extensive.

Consciousness has much more freedom in its utilization.

The lessons must be properly learned before such responsibility.

There are other training systems, each dealing with various aspects of such understanding and discipline.

You cannot do any basic harm. When you act within your system however you act within others.

When you leave the physical system after reincarnations, you have learned the lessons,

And you are literally no longer a member of the human race in those terms, for you elect to leave it.

Only the conscious self dwells within it in any case, and it is other portions of your personality who simultaneously dwell within the other training systems.

In other more advanced systems, thoughts and emotions are automatically and immediately translated into action, into camouflage, into whatever approximation of matter there exists.

Therefore, the lessons must be taught and learned well.

The responsibility for creation must be clearly understood. You cannot hurt others within your system.

To some extent you are, comparatively speaking, in a soundproof and isolated room.

Hate creates destruction and in that room, until the lesson is learned, destruction follows destruction.

The ideals are like instructions on a blackboard that will not be erased.

When you have learned the lesson you realize that the ideals were not necessary, but until you learn the lesson they are all you have as guidelines.

The ideals are mere shadows of instructions.

They are however your own translations of truths as nearly as you can comprehend them within the system.

The training gained in your system then will serve you for existence in a variety of interrelated systems.

If the sorrows and agonies within your system were not felt as real, the lessons would not be learned.

The teachers within the system are those who are in their last reincarnation, and other personalities who have left the system but have been assigned to help those still within it.

You are dealing with the transformation of emotional energy into action and form.

You then manipulate within the system which you have yourselves created, and by its effects learn where you have succeeded and where you have failed.

The system always includes some fragments who are entering for the first time, as well as individuals in their third or fourth reincarnations.

Problems leading to world wars also cause worldwide natural disasters.

These are merely another materialization of energy projected by those who have not learned how to handle it.

Such reactions fire through the dream universe also, and are reflected through all phases of your activity.

The whole self compares the performance of various portions of itself in physical reality and in dream reality, and draws its own conclusions.

The Early Sessions Book 9 Session 446 November 6, 1968

Now the weapons and the destruction are the obvious things that you see.

The counterparts are not so evident, and yet it is the counterparts that are important.

The self-discipline learned, the control, the compassion that finally is aroused,

And the final and last lesson learned—the positive desire for creativity and love over destruction and hatred.

When this is learned the reincarnation cycle is finished.

Now there is a reason why these lessons must be learned in just this way.

Elementally there is only creativity.

Destruction is merely the changing of form.

A cloudburst or a tornado knows nothing of destruction.

This same energy encased within a human form is something else.

There are different kinds of creativity, then, to learn,

And a specialization in energy is focus and feelings that emerge;

Elemental energy becoming conscious of itself, and aware of issues that did not exist for it earlier;

Millions of molecules momentarily united with the living consciousness (pause), filled with primal energy,

Now learning love, and forming highly sensitive psychic patterns, electrical charges that now form emotions instead of clouds;

The innocent chaos of undifferentiated personality that exists behind the highly specified and truly sophisticated mechanism of one thought—

And all of this before an individual is born within your system. In terms of time this is behind us all.

Little wonder that psychic battles wage, and yet beyond your system there are refinements impossible to describe, and further developments more miraculous than those that have gone before.

And through all of this, the entity formed from that massive chaos retains its identity and the knowledge of its pasts, and continues to grow in creativity.

This is some of the most important material that I have given you, for you have wondered about the purpose, and have been able often to see but one small speck of time and space.

The Early Sessions Book 9 Session 452, December 2, 1968

By Jane Roberts and Robert F. But© Laurel Davies

A Heavy Dose Of Consciousness

Give us a moment.

You identify a highly evolved self-consciousness with your own
species development, and with your own kind of perceptive
mechanisms.

You apply these as rules or conditions whenever you examine
any other kind of life.

In your system of probabilities there are no reptilian men or
women, yet in other probabilities they do indeed exist.

I mention this only to show you that the evolutionary system you
recognize is but one such system.

The physical basis rests latently within your own cellular
structure, however.

You think that evolution is finished. Its impetus, however, comes
from within the nature of consciousness itself. It always has.

In some quarters it is fashionable these days to say that man's
consciousness is now an element in a new kind of evolution — but
that "new consciousness" has always been inherent.
You are only now beginning to recognize its existence.

Every consciousness is aware of itself as itself.

Each consciousness, then, is self-aware. It may not be self-aware
in the same way that you are. It may not reflect upon its own
condition. On the other hand, it may have no need to.

The "Unknown" Reality: Volume Two; Section 4: Session 705 June 24, 1974,

Jane Roberts © 2012 Laurel Davies-Butts

Consciousness, seeking to know itself, therefore knows you.

You as a consciousness, seek to know yourself, and to some extent or other, you become aware of yourself as a distinct and individual portion of All That Is.

You not only draw upon this overall energy, but you do so automatically, for your existence is dependent upon it.

The extent of your realization of this fact is the extent of your freedom or vitality, fulfillment and power.

It should not be forgotten, however, that the ego is also a portion of All That Is, a highly specialized portion, enabling the inner self to manipulate and interpret particular conditions.

If the ego considers itself as the only self, then you are cut off to a large degree from the vitality and energy available.

The ego's false ideas prevent it from accepting this energy, but once the ego is aware of its position as a portion of the self, then it should not be shunted aside, but can take its place.

It is sometimes referred to almost as if it stood entirely outside of basic reality. It is, of course, within it also.

The ego, as you now know it, will not always be necessary, you see, but a type of ego is a basis for individuality and will always be necessary.

An inner ego, of course, that contains various egos that have been or will be a portion of any given self—

These egos and any ego organizes experience along various lines and ties experience together within meaningful pattern.

The inner self or the whole personality consists of many such egos, as you know, but the inner self is also aware of itself as something more than the sum of its parts.

Now this something more than the sum of its parts is a curious phrase, but within it lies a key that can give you some small understanding of what God may be.

Again, the term God is used simply because it is an accepted term for the reality we are discussing.

That which knows itself, which experiences itself within many forms and yet knows itself as something apart from the total of its sums, that left-over, unexplainable remnant you see, can be thought of as original action, original consciousness, prime mover, or consciousness as distinct from its own creations, of which it is also part.

You are yourself obviously an energy gestalt; as you become more fully conscious of reality your sense of identity will contain larger and larger aspects of reality.

Biologically all human beings, as you know them, have existed as the various cells of which a human image is composed.

This is very difficult to explain clearly.

I do not mean to imply, necessarily, progression here.

Theoretically, you see, you will one day be a fully conscious portion of the personal god to whom you may now pray.

By then, you see, you will be aware of further gestalts. Do you see?

All portions of All That Is do not recognize themselves consciously as All That Is.

But know themselves mainly as individuals, not as the prime gestalt individual.

When realization is reached at the highest level, then All That Is instantly creates new realities,

And to some extent, you see, loses the conscious knowledge of its own identity.

The loss is always temporary and self-generated.

This is quite enough on a difficult subject this evening.

The Early Sessions", Book 7, Session 311, January 11, 1967, by Jane Roberts Laurel Davies
1999 by Robert Butts

What you call God is the primary, omnipotent, electromagnetic energy force - source from which all creation springs.

The energy that holds all existence in perfect harmony, symmetry, balance and order.

Thus, God is ALL THAT IS.

The electricity that is perceivable within the physical plane or field is merely a projection of a vast electrical system that you cannot perceive because of the nature and construction of the physical system itself.

The electrical system possesses many dimensions of reality that cannot be perceived within the physical system.

So far scientists have only been able to study electricity by observing the projections of it that are perceivable within their frames of reference.

As their physical instruments become more sophisticated they will be able to glimpse more of this reality,

But since they will not be able to explain it within their known system of references, many curious and distorted explanations of reported phenomena will be given.

I mentioned that the electrical universe is composed of electricity that is far different from your idea of it.

Electricity as you perceive it within your field, is merely an echo emanation,

Or a sort of shadow image of these infinite varieties of pulsations,

Which give reality an actuality to many phenomena with which you are familiar,

But which do not appear as tangible objects within the physical system.

Now, there are some philosophical matters that I would like to clear.

Ruburt has been somewhat confused concerning some of these matters.

The conventional Christian concept of God has been in many ways a convenient one, and it carries with it many truths.

It is true, you see, while it is not true.

When you realize that this is a symbol only then you begin to see more and come closer to an understanding, not further away from an understanding.

There is no personal god-individual in Christian terms

And yet you do have access to a portion of All That Is, that is highly attuned to you only above all others.

In this respect, you see, there is a personal god, if those are the words you use.

There is a portion of All That Is, that is directed and focused upon every individual consciousness.

A portion of All That Is resides within and is a part of every consciousness.

Every consciousness is therefore cherished and protected individually.

There are automatic electromagnetic connections that exist here.

One portion of All That Is, is instantly aware, for example of your most insignificant and significant problems—of yours and yours alone.

This portion of overall consciousness is the portion that is individualized within you.

Now there is even something like the idea of a personality god, but hardly in the terms used by theologians.

The personality of God, as it is generally conceived is again a one-dimensional concept based upon man's small knowledge of his own psychology.

Many of the old ideas of pre-civilization come closer to anything near the truth.

What you prefer to think of as God is basically and above all, indeed as I have said, an infinite energy gestalt: or pyramid consciousness.

It is aware of itself as being, for example, you, Joseph (Rob). It is aware of itself as what seems to you as your own future and past selves.

It is aware of itself as the smallest seed, both those that grow and those that do not grow.

The personality of this gestalt is beyond comprehension at this point. It is both demanding and compassionate.

The word, justice, is a human one, always implying punishment.

And it has nothing to do with the God concept.

While there is a portion of All That Is, that is aware of itself as you, for example,

A portion that is indeed focused within your existence, whose energy is directed within you, and to whom you can call for help when necessary,

There is also an overall god-personality that is aware of itself also as something that is more than the sum of its creations.

This is All That Is, in the deepest sense.

I am trying to make this as simple as possible.

The part of All That Is, that is aware of itself as you, is also aware of itself as something more than you.

This portion that knows itself as you and as more than you is the personal god, you see.

Again: This gestalt, this portion of All That Is, looks out for your interests and may be called upon in a personality manner.

But this portion is only a part, itself, of All That Is.

But, you see, even this overall pyramid gestalt is not static.

All or most concepts of a god deal with a static god and herein lies the main theological difficulties.

The awareness and experience of this overall gestalt constantly change and grow.

Again, there is no static god.

When you say, "This is God", then God is already something else.

I am using the term God for simplicity's sake.

All portions of All That Is are constantly changing and enfolding and unfolding.

All That Is, seeking to know itself, constantly creates new versions of itself.

For this seeking itself is a creative activity, and the core of all action.

Consciousness, seeking to know itself, therefore knows you.

You as a consciousness, seek to know yourself, and to some extent or other, you become aware of yourself as a distinct and individual portion of All That Is.

You not only draw upon this overall energy, but you do so automatically, for your existence is dependent upon it.

The Early Sessions", Book 7, Session 311, January 11, 1967, by Jane Roberts 1999 by Robert Butts
Laurel Davies Seth and his Christ story; S591, Part 1 of 4.

Therefore, as always, make of this voice what you choose to make of it.

Make of me what you choose to make of me, but recognize within yourselves the vitality of your being.

And look to no man or no idea or no woman or no dogma, but the vitality of your own being, and trust it.

And that which offends your soul, turn away from, but trust yourself.

Jane Roberts, The God of Jane: A Psychic Manifesto - (C) Laurel Davies

Climb up my words then, rush up the vowels and the syllables and let them form for you a ladder of energy by which you can ascend.

And let them form a foundation upon which you can climb to find your own reality and your own existence that is in itself independent,

Both of my words and even of the room in which now your bodies sit,

For that independent inner self wanders through all existences that you have known, in your terms, has a wisdom and knowledge that you can use.

And each of you in a greater sense knows the nature of your own vitality,

And none of you are alone or have ever been alone

For within you is the knowledge of all the personalities that you are, and within you are those abilities to be used and tapped.

The Early Class Sessions Book 3 by Jane Roberts: ESP Class Session, May 11, 1971

The fear that blocks [positive] energy can indeed be dissipated if new beliefs are inserted for old ones —

So again we return to those emotional attitudes and ideas that automatically promote health and healing.

Each individual is a good person, an individualized portion of universal energy itself.

Each person is meant to express his or her own characteristics and abilities.

Life means energy, power, and expression.

Again, we cannot generalize overmuch, but many persons know quite well that they are not sure whether they want to live or die.

The overabundance of cancer cells represents nevertheless the need for expression and expansion — the only arena left open — or so it would seem.

Consciously you might want to express certain abilities, while unconsciously you are afraid of doing so.

The unconscious beliefs are not really unconscious, however.

You are simply not as aware of them as you are of normally conscious ones.

Negative beliefs can block the passageways between Framework 1 and Framework 2.

It is an excellent idea for those in any kind of difficulty to do the following simple exercise.

Gently remind yourself again: I am an excellent person,

Adding: It is good and safe for me to express my own abilities, for in doing so I express the energy of the universe itself.

In all such cases, you are opening the doors of Framework 2, clearing your channels of communication.

Since your physical body itself is composed of the very energy that drives the universe, then there is nothing about you which that energy is unaware of.

Simply repeating these ideas to yourself can result in release of tension, and an acceleration of the healing process.

The Way Toward Health Part Two: Chapter 11: June 12, 1984,

Jane Roberts Copyright L. Davies

The patterns for the earth and for its creatures were as real before their physical appearances, and far more real than, say, the plan for a painting that you might have in your mind.

The universe always was innately objective in your terms, with its planets and creatures.

The patterns for all of the species always existed without any before or after arrangement.

I am not pleased with those analogies,

But sometimes they are all I can use to express issues so outside of normal channels of knowledge.

It is as if, then, the earth, with all of its species, existed in complete form as a fully dimensioned cosmic underpainting, which gradually came alive all at once.

Birds did not come from reptiles. They were always birds.

They expressed a certain kind of consciousness that sought a certain kind of form.

Physically the species appeared — all species appeared — in the same way that you might imagine all of the elements of a highly complicated dream suddenly coming alive with physical properties.

Mental images — in those terms, now — existed that "in a flash of cosmic inspiration" were suddenly endowed with full physical manifestation.

To that extent, the Bible's interpretation is correct.

Life was given, was free to develop according to its characteristic conditions.

The planet was prepared, and endowed with life.

Consciousness built the forms, so life existed within consciousness for all eternity.

There was no point in which chemicals or atoms suddenly acquired life, for they always possessed consciousness, which is life's requirement.

I understand that it appears that species have vanished, but again you must remember probabilities, and that those species simply "developed" along the patterns of probable earths.

You are not just dealing with a one-line development of matter, but of an unimaginable creativity, in which all versions of your physical world exist, each one quite convinced of its physical nature.

There are ramifications quite unspeakable,

Although in certain states of trance, or with the aid of educated dreaming, you might be able to glimpse the inner complications,

The web-works of communications connect your official earth with other probable ones.

You choose your time and focus in physical reality again and again, and the mind holds an inner comprehension of many seemingly mysterious developments involving the species.

Even the c-e-l-l-s (spelled) are free enough of time and space to hold an intimate framework of being within the present,

While being surrounded by this greater knowledge of what you think of as the earth's past.

In greater terms, the earth and all of its species are created in each moment.

You wonder what gave life to the first egg or seed, or whatever,

And think that an answer to that question would answer most others; for life, you say, was simply passed on from that point.

What gives life to chemicals now?

That is the more proper question.

All energy is not only aware-ized but the source of all organizations of consciousness, and all physical forms.

These represent frameworks of consciousness.

There was a day when the dreaming world, in your terms, suddenly awakened to full reality as far as physical materialization is concerned.

The planet was visited by desire.

There were ghost excursions there — mental buildings, dream civilizations which then became actualized.

NoME Part Four: Chapter 10: Session 872, August 8, 1979

Excellence! There are no standards but your own!

You cannot compare yourself against others.

For your own abilities are like no others, and dimensions of your own greatness cannot fit in the standards of others.

But you know what excellence means within yourself, and it means truth to the heart of yourself.

There are some things that you know it means.

It means not lying.

It means not lying to yourself; not being afraid to use your own abilities;

Not being afraid to be the excellent self that you are.

Excellence does not mean false humility.

It does not mean inflated, artificial pride that sets you apart from all others, for you cannot set yourselves apart from all others.

You are, because of your nature, apart from all others, and everlastingly unique—

While everlastingly a part of all others.

In the terms that you understand, excellence means not lying to yourself.

It means do not shop-lift [which a few class members had been joking about]—it is not funny.

It means when you steal objects, you steal ideas, and you do not know what belongs to you and what does not.

It means you are playing around with other peoples' integrity instead of your own, and you are not willing to stand there and say, "This is mine!

Excellence means that in your relationships, you face each other honestly, and do not pretend.

It means that you do not use excuses. It means that you do not hide your abilities from yourself.

[It] means that you take advantage of your abilities, and do not deny them,

And that you expect things of yourself, and do not look to others for their answers; that you do not dribble away your energy.

The [Iranian] hostage crisis was a materialized mass dream.

Now, the year 1980 exists in all of its potential versions, now in this moment.

Because mass events are concerned, there is not a completely different year, of course, for each individual on the face of the planet.

But, there are literally an endless number of mass-shared worlds of 1980 "in the wings", so to speak.

It is not quite as simple a matter as just deciding what events you want to materialize as reality,

Since you have, in your terms, a body of probabilities of one kind or another already established as the raw materials for the coming year.

It would be quite improbable for you, Joseph [as Seth calls me], to suddenly turn into a tailor, for example, for none of your choices with probabilities have led toward such an action.

In like manner, England, in all probability, next year will not suddenly turn into a Mohammedan nation.

But, within the range of workable probabilities, private and mass choices, the people of the world are choosing their probable 1980s.

I am taking my time here, for there are some issues that I would like to clear up, that are difficult to explain.

Any of the probable actions that a person considers are a part of that person's conscious thought.

Just underneath, however, people also consider other sets of probabilities that may or may not reach conscious level, simply because they are shunted aside or because they seem to meet with no conscious recognition.

I want you to try and imagine actual events, as you think of them, to be the vitalized representations of probabilities,

That is, as the physical versions of mental probabilities.

The probabilities with which you are not consciously concerned remain psychologically peripheral.

They are there but not there, so to speak.

Your conscious mind can only accept a certain sequence of probabilities as recognized experience.

As I have said, the choices among probabilities go on constantly, both on conscious and unconscious levels.

Events that you do not perceive as conscious experience are a part of your unconscious experience, however, to some extent.

This applies to the individual. And, of course, en masse the same applies to world events.

Each action seeks all of its own possible fulfillments.

All-That-Is seeks all possible experience.

But in such a larger framework, in this case, that questions of, say, pain or death simply do not apply, though [certainly] they do on the physical level.

Great expectations, basically, have nothing to do with degree, for a grass blade is filled with great expectations.

Great expectations are built upon a faith in the nature of reality, a faith in nature itself, a faith in the life you are given, whatever its degree.

And, all children, for example, are born with those expectations.

Fairy tales are, indeed, often (though not always) carriers of a kind of underground knowledge, as per your discussion about Cinderella.

And, the greatest fairy tales are always those in which the greatest expectations win out:

The elements of the physical world that are unfortunate can be changed in the twinkling of an eye through great expectations.

Your education tells you that all of that is nonsense, that the world is defined by its physical aspects alone.

When you think of power, you think of, say, nuclear energy or solar energy.

But, power is the creative energy within men's minds that allows them to use such powers, such energies, such forces.

The true power is in the imagination which dares to speculate upon that which is not yet.

The imagination, backed by great expectations, can bring about almost any reality within the range of probabilities.

All of the possible versions of 1980 will happen. Except for those you settle upon,

All of the others will remain psychologically peripheral, in the background of your conscious experience.

But, all of those possible versions will be connected in one way or another.

The important lessons have never really appeared in your societies:

The most beneficial use of the directed will, with great expectations, and that coupled with the knowledge of Framework 1 and 2 activities.

Very simply: You want something, you dwell upon it consciously for a while,

You consciously imagine it coming to the forefront of probabilities, closer to your actuality.

Then you drop it like a pebble into Framework 2, forget about it as much as possible for a fortnight.

And, do this in a certain rhythm.

Now, in our book, I will be doing my best to explain the origin of your universe and in such a way that most of the pertinent questions are answered.

But, man's present concept of reality is so limited that I must often resort to analogies.

In the most basic of terms, as 1980 happens,

The energy that comes into your universe is as new as if (in your terms) the world was created yesterday,

A point that will be rather difficult to explain.

All of the probable versions of 1980 spin off their own probable pasts as well as their own probable futures.

And, any consciousness that exists in 1980 was (again in those terms) a part of what you think of as the beginning of the world.

Like the entire American hostage affair [in Iran], any physical event serves as a focus that attracts all of its probable versions and outcomes.

The hostage situation is a materialized mass dream,

Meant to be important and vital on political and religious platforms of reality,

Meant to dramatize a conflict of beliefs, and to project that conflict outward into the realm of public knowledge.

Everyone involved was consciously and unconsciously a willing participant at the most basic levels of human behavior.

And, it is, of course, no coincidence that 1980 is immediately foreshadowed by that event.

What will the world do with it?

Your TV and news systems of communication are a part of the event itself, of course.

It is in a way far better that these events occurred now and in the way that they have, so that the problems appear clearly in the world arena.

They are actually thus of a far less violent nature than they might otherwise have been.

Religious beliefs will be examined as they have not been before and their connections and political affiliations.

The Arab world still needs the West.

And, again, it is better that those issues come to light now, while they must to some extent consider the rest of the world.

Do not personally give any more conscious consideration, either of you, to events that you do not want to happen.

Any such concentration, to whatever degree, ties you in with those probabilities.

So, concentrate upon what you want.

And, as far as public events are concerned, take it for granted that sometimes even men are wiser than they know.

Imagine the psyche again as some multidimensional living television set.

In what seems to be the small space of the screen many programs are going on, though you can tune in to only one at a time.

The Unknown Reality, Volume 2, Session 713, Page 357 - by Jane Roberts (C) L. Davies Butts

I am speaking here in more or less historic terms for you.

You must realize that the process has nothing to do with time as you know it, however.

This particular kind of adventure in consciousness has occurred before, and in our terms will again.

Perception of the exterior universe then changed, however, and it seemed to be alien and apart from the individual who perceived it.

God, therefore, became an idea projected outward, independent of the individual, divorced from nature.

He became the reflection of man's emerging ego, with all of its brilliance, savagery, power, and intent for mastery.

The adventure was a highly creative one despite the obvious disadvantages and represented an "evolution" of consciousness that enriched man's subjective experience, and indeed added to the dimensions of reality itself.

To be effectively organized, however, inner and outer experiences had to appear as separate, disconnected events.

Historically the characteristics of God changed as man's ego changed.

These characteristics of the ego, however, were supported by strong inner changes.

The original propulsion of inner characteristics outward into the formation of the ego could be compared with the birth of innumerable stars –

An event of immeasurable consequences that originated on a subjective level and within inner reality.

The [outer] ego, having its birth from within, therefore, must always boast of its independence while maintaining the nagging certainty of its inner origin. SS 587

Religion Is The Band And We March On

You are the power of God manifested

You are not powerless.

To the contrary, through your being, the power of God is strengthened, for you are a portion of what He is.

You are not simply an insignificant, innocuous clump of clay through which He decides to show Himself.

You are he manifesting as you.

You are as legitimate as He is.

If you are a part of God, then He is also a part of you.

And, in denying your own worth, you end up denying His as well.

I do not like to use the term "He", meaning God, since All-That-Is is the origin of not only all sexes but of all realities, in some of which sex, as you think of it, does not exist.

Affirmation is in the spontaneous motion of the body as it dances.

Many churchgoers who consider themselves quite religious do not understand the nature of love or affirmation as much as some bar patrons,

Who celebrate the nature of their bodies and enjoy the spontaneous transcendence as they let themselves go with the motion of their beings.

True religion is not repressive, as life itself is not.

Excerpted from the book, The Nature of Personal Reality, by Jane Roberts

Session 674 © Laurel Davies

Obviously there are objects of all sizes, durability, and weight.

There are private objects and public ones.

There are also 'vast psychological objects,' then, sweeping mass events, for example, in which whole countries might be involved.

There are also mass natural events of varying degrees, as say, the flooding of large areas.

Such events involve psychological configurations on the part of all those involved,

So that the inner individual patterns of those lives touched by each such event have in one way or another a common purpose that at the same time serves the overall reality on a natural planetary basis.

In order to endure, the planet itself must be involved in constant change and instability.

I know this is difficult to comprehend, but every object that you perceive—

Grass or rock or stone—even ocean waves or clouds—ANY physical phenomenon—

Has its own invisible consciousness, its own intent and emotional coloration.

The Individual and the Nature of Mass Events, Session 826

You share an existence with others who are experiencing their own journeys in their own ways, and you have journeying in common, then.

Be kind to yourself and to your companions.

NoPR Part Two: Chapter 22: Session 677, July 11, 1973

I would like each of my readers to be a practicing idealist, and, if you are then you will automatically be tolerant of the beliefs of others.

You will not be unkind in the pursuit of your own ideals.

You will look upon the world with a sane compassion, with some humor, and you will look for man's basic good intent.

You will find it. It has always been there.

You will discover your own basic good intent, and see that it has always been behind all of your actions —

Even in those least fitted to the pursuit of your private ideals.

NoME Part Four: Chapter 10: Session 873, August 15, 1979

It is quite proper for Ruburt's intellect to understand this, and to say, simply now, "That is not my realm."

I will leave the solution to that problem where it belongs.
We will use the magical approach here.

This will allow you to include the feeling of inner, magical "work" into your calculations.

It would also BEGIN to give you a feeling for the magical support that upholds you both, and your lives —

The support that Ruburt can count upon, and that can bring about the solution to his physical difficulties.

Here, again, the vital word is ease or effortlessness.

If you want to feed a dog in the physical world —

And he is on the other side of the door —

You must open it.

In the inner world you or the dog can walk through the door without effort, because desire is action.

Desire is action. The Magical Approach Session Four August 18, 1980

Fanatics certainly serve a purpose, and actually they help maintain overall equilibrium of society

By serving as examples to others, who often have some of the same beliefs but are of a less explosive nature.

By going to extremes fanatics point out to others the virtue of more moderate ways,

And their actions actually make others with the same kind of persuasion evaluate their own beliefs.

I realize the impracticality of asking anyone in physical life to bear no human rancor. It is futile.

On the other hand, when you look at your fellows, try to see them as they are in all respects —

As you would, say, a group of individual animals.

Do not always compare them against any ideals —

Ideals superimposed by you, or anyone, upon others.

Though the fanatic may make much noise in the world, he is actually isolated from all of the world's ideas except his own.

Anything else is seen as a threat.

He does not allow the development of his concepts or beliefs, for example.

They stop at one particular point —

And at that point he wages his battle against reality.

So even the fanatic serves good purposes.

And I will tell you that no one and no fanatic leads masses of people.

People follow because they want to and no one leads them.

And if you think you are a leader you misunderstand the people,

For they are taking you where they want you to go.

Only you are taking the responsibility and not they.

Conversations With Seth, vol. 2 - chapter 9, by Susan M. Watkins (C)

The varying and various fanatical groups, such as, for example, the anti-homosexual

Florida contingent, are in a way quite natural and necessary in your country.

They serve as focus points for others who have the same ideas

But are afraid to really face them or admit their beliefs.

TPS3 Deleted Sessions July 9, 1977

Your idea of time is false.

Time as you experience it is an illusion caused by your own physical senses.

Your physical senses force you to perceive action in certain terms, but this is not the nature of action.

You must perceive what you do of reality through your physical senses,

But your physical senses distort reality.

They present reality to you in their own way.

The physical senses can only perceive reality a little bit at a time,

And so it seems to you that one moment exists, and is gone forever,

And the next moment comes, and like the one before it disappears.

But everything in the universe exists at one time, simultaneously,

And the first words ever spoken still ring throughout the universe;

And in your terms, the last words ever spoken have been said time and time again,

For there is no ending and no beginning. It is only your perception that is limited.

Reality is not limited. There is no past, present and future.

These only appear to those who exist within three-dimensional reality.

Since I am no longer within it, I can perceive what you do not see.

But there is a part of you that is not imprisoned within three-dimensional reality,

And that part of you knows that there is no time, that there is only an eternal now;

And that part of you that knows is the whole self, the inner personality that knows all of your lives.

When I tell you that you have lived for example in 1936,

I say this because it makes sense to you now;

But you live all of your reincarnations at once.

Only you are not aware,

And you cannot understand within the framework of three-dimensional reality.

Pretend that you have seven dreams at once and you the dreamer know that you are dreaming.

Within each dream 100 earthly years may pass —

But to you the dreamer no time has passed,

And there is no time to pass, for you are free of the dimension in which time exists.

The time you seem to spend within the dream, within each life, is only an illusion,

And to the inner self no moment has passed, and to the inner self there is no time.

ECS1 ESP Class Session, February 8, 1968

Transposed into religious terms, then, we are each continuous with what 'God' is,

And any 'prayer' travels through dimensions of psychological validity

That connect us with those portions of our own consciousness' that are aware of that added identification.

Now. Prayer once enabled the intelligent man to focus his psychic abilities,

Because the hard fact, taken for granted by all in Western civilization, was the belief in such a God.

The so-called hard fact has changed.

The truth behind the myth still exists.

Mankind has been engrossed in dreams of a god who is like himself,

Except that he was considered to be superior and possessed of the highest qualities that man admires in himself.

I am not going to keep you much longer.

Nor have I any intentions of starting a new religion.

I am, however, trying to tell you the truth, and this material is perhaps the most important of any so far,

In that comprehension of it will allow the intelligent man to avail himself of energies and abilities once utilized in prayer.

Prayer is now shunned. Why pray if there is no one to listen?

The prayer contains within it its own answer, and if there is no white-haired, kind old

Father God to hear,

Then there is instead the initial and ever-expanding energy that forms everything that is,

And of which every human being is a part.

This psychic gestalt may sound to you impersonal, but since ITS ENERGY FORMS YOUR PERSON, how can this be?

If you prefer to call this supreme and absolute psychic gestalt God,

Then you must not attempt to objectify him in terms of material,

For he is the nuclei of your cells, and more intimate than your breath.

The Early Sessions, Book 2, Session 81

A sudden but intense feeling of hatred or resentment or fear may cause tragic physical circumstances, for example.

A sudden and intense exaltation, however, will have the same immediate and literally astounding but opposite physical effect.

That is, pure joy, even of brief duration, can literally change the direction of a life.

Between these extremes lie all the other colors and hues of inner feeling.

A variety of poor or negative feelings, however, of fairly low intensity, can add up to a general negative emotional climate,

Which projects itself outward into physical reality.

These negative feelings will be translated in physical terms.

It does you little good to know that physical symptoms or inadequate physical surroundings are symbolic

Unless you realize that the inner situation can be changed.

Now it APPEARS to you that a difference is worked when you exchange a poor physical symbol for a constructive one.

The change of course comes before this in the inner self.

The physical being simply uses the physical system as a checking board.

It must be realized that the physical conditions are NOT permanent, but ever changing.

To imagine otherwise is to become hypnotized by the physical symbols.

Each day should be considered a new day.

Ruburt should not think for example:

'I have had these symptoms for such and such a time.'

This reinforces the idea of permanency.

The day should be considered as a psychic rebirth.

The Early Sessions, Book 8, Session 334

Once you understand the symbolic nature of physical reality, then you will no longer feel entrapped by it.

You have formed the symbols, and therefore you can change them.

You must learn, of course, what the various symbols mean in your own life, and how to translate their meaning.

To do so, you must first of all remind yourself frequently that the physical condition IS symbolic—not a permanent condition.

Then you must look within yourself for the inner actuality represented by the symbol.

This same process can be followed regardless of the nature of the problem, or of your challenge.

If, however, you imagine that the environment or physical condition is the reality,

Then you can feel trapped by it, and spend your efforts fighting a paper dragon.

The environment is always altered from the inside.

The entire framework of your existence is constantly flowing from within outward,

And being projected into those physical symbols that you mistake, then, for reality.

Seth Speaks, Session 594

Fear is always future-based. It's always an anticipation.

And what you're doing now is giving yourself that opportunity to know that,

And to choose intentionally, rather than avoiding because it's automatic

And because that's what you know.

Elias
I speak to those who believe in a god,

And those who do not,

To those who believe that science will find all answers as to the nature of reality, and to those who do not.

I hope to give you clues that will enable you to study the nature of reality for yourself as you have never studied it before.

There are several things that I shall ask you to understand.

You are not stuck in time like a fly in a closed bottle, whose wings are therefore useless.

You cannot trust your physical senses to give you a true picture of reality.

They are lovely liars, with such a fantastic tale to tell that you believe it without question.

You are sometimes wiser, more creative, and far more knowledgeable when you are dreaming than when you are awake.

I am primarily a teacher, but I have not been a man of letters per se.

I am primarily a personality with a message:

You create the world that you know.

You have been given perhaps the most awesome gift of all:

The ability to project your thoughts outward into physical form.

The gift brings a responsibility,

And many of you are tempted to congratulate yourselves on the success of your lives,

And blame God, fate, and society for your failures.

In like manner, mankind has a tendency to project his own guilt and his own errors upon a father-god image, who it seems must grow weary of so many complaints.

The fact is that each of you creates your own physical reality; and en masse,

You create both the glories and the terrors that exist within your earthly experience.

Until you realize that you are the creators, you will refuse to accept this responsibility.

Nor can you blame a devil for the world's misfortunes.

You have grown sophisticated enough to realize that the Devil is a projection of your own psyche,

But you have not grown wise enough to learn how to use your creativity constructively.

Most of my readers are familiar with the term, 'muscle bound.'

As a race you have grown 'ego bound' instead, held in a spiritual rigidity,

With the intuitive portions of the self either denied or distorted beyond any recognition.

When man realizes that he creates his own image now, he will not find it so startling to believe that he creates other images in other times.

Only after such a basis will the idea of reincarnation achieve its natural validity,

And only when it is understood that the subconscious,

Certain layers of it, is a link between the present personality and past ones,

Will the theory of reincarnation be accepted as fact.

The Early Sessions, book 2, Session 82 August 27, 1964

Few beliefs are intellectual alone.

When you are examining the contents of your conscious mind,

You must learn, or recognize, the emotional and imaginative connotations that are connected with a given idea.

There are various ways of altering the belief by substituting its opposite.

One particular method is three-pronged.

You generate the emotion opposite the one that arises from the belief you want to change,

And you turn your imagination in the opposite direction from the one dictated by the belief.

At the same time, you consciously assure yourself that the unsatisfactory belief is an idea about reality and not an aspect of reality itself.

You realize that ideas are not stationary.

Emotions and imagination move them in one direction or the other, reinforce them or negate them.

Quite deliberately you use your conscious mind playfully, creating a game as children do,

In which for a time you completely ignore what seems to be in physical terms and "pretend" that what you really want is real.

If you are poor, you purposely pretend that you have all you need financially.

Imagine how you will spend your money.

If you are ill, imagine playfully that you are cured.

See yourself doing what you would do.

If you cannot communicate with others, imagine yourself doing so easily.

If you feel your days dark and pointless, then imagine them filled and joyful.

Now this may sound impractical, yet in your daily life you use your imagination and your emotions often at the service of far less worthy beliefs;

And the results are quite clear — and let me add, unfortunately practical.

As it took a while for the unsatisfactory beliefs to become materialized,

So it may be a time before you see physical results;

But the new ideas will take growth and change your experience as certainly as the old ones did.

Ego We Go

The body is a highly energized gestalt of intelligent processes.
The body is composed of organs, physical parts, living matter —
But the body is also composed of processes, relationships that
exist on all levels

Between various portions of the body and between the body and
its environment.

All processes in nature are intelligent.

They may involve a different kind of consciousness and intelligence
than your own

But there are no unintelligent processes.

There are no closed processes.

There is no process that is not in one way or another related to
others.

In a fashion, any one natural process carries within it the implied
existence of all others.

The body is in that regard a highly energized gestalt of intelligent
processes.

These include emotional processes,

Of course, mental ones, emotional ones, and constant transformation
of energy from one form into another.

Your stomach cannot read

What you read, however, but in one way or another it is translated into other terms,

So that for example your stomach reacts in its way to your reading matter, as the visual information is translated into other terms.

In ways really difficult to describe, your bodily processes, and what you think of as, say, cultural or national events,

Are highly connected and a part of each other.

Events are indeed also processes, partially physical and partially not physical.

It is as if bits and pieces of any and all probable events exist in a jigsaw -like fashion throughout the minds of men,

Throughout the consciousness's of plants and all natural things, wanting to be put together—

And each individual consciousness has its part to play in directing which of those events occur or do not occur—

But the processes involved in the formation of those events are hidden from the conscious mind.

November 19, 1980, The Personal Sessions, Book 5

The ego does not exist within the electrical field.

The ego is a product of the physical field, formed from physical birth on.

The inner identity and individuality, as you know, has its origins long before this.

The inner self adopts an ego in order to allow manipulation within the physical universe,

And yet part of the ego is composed of portions from the inner self,

While the bulk of the ego is allowed to develop through physical heredity and environment.

The breath of life, so to speak, is breathed into the ego by the inner self,

But from that point on the ego is independent.

All of these influences have a part in the formation of the physical individual, and his existence is dependent upon a balance being maintained.

In some instances, to use an analogy, serious short circuits do occur, intensities of power accumulate.

The dream universe, for example, may intrude with unusual sharpness.

The systems lose complementary balance, but on the whole the systems operate together most efficiently.

Even the electric reality of a dream is decoded,

So that its effects are experienced not only by the brain, but in the furthest reaches of the most minute cells in the human body.

Dream experiences long forgotten are forever contained as electrically coded within the cells of the physical body.

If an effect is felt in any one portion of human experience,

Then you can be sure that such an effect is felt in all other possible ways,

Whether or not such an effect is immediately obvious.

This is also an extremely important point to remember.

Every effect of any kind, experienced by the human being, exists as a series of electrical signals and codes,

That in themselves form a pattern that is an electrical pattern.

They exist within the cells, or I should more properly say that the cells form about them.

These electric coded signals then form electric counterparts of complete experience, as it has been felt by any given individual.

It is, the pattern is, then independent of the physical system, while residing within it.

In other words, each individual from birth on forms his own counterpart from built up, individual, continuous electric signals.

At physical death his personality then exists in its complete form,

And of course escapes the sort of ending that it would suffer if it were an integral part of the physical system.

This electrical pattern is the personality, with all the experiences of its earthly time.

It then can join or partake of the inner self.

In other words, though the ego was adopted originally by the inner self, and was a product of physical heredity and environment,

It does not die;

But its existence is changed from physical reality into electrical reality.

It is still individual.

No individuality is lost, but it becomes a part of the inner self,

And its experiences are added to the total experience of the many personalities that have composed the inner self.

The Early Sessions Book 3 of the Seth Material Session 126, January 27, 1965

Jane Roberts © L. Davies

With greater practice, the contents of your own mind will become as readily available.

You will see your thoughts as clearly as your inner organs.

In this case you may perceive them symbolically through symbols you will recognize, seeing jumbled thoughts for example as weeds, which you can then simply discard.

You can request that the thought content of your mind be translated into an intense image, symbolically representing individual thoughts and the overall mental landscape, Then take out what you do not like and replace it with more positive images.

This does not mean that this inner landscape must always be completely sunny,

But it does mean that it should be well balanced.

A dark and largely brooding inner landscape should alert you, so that you begin immediately to change it.

None of these accomplishments are beyond my readers, though

anyone may find any one given feat more difficult than another.

You must also realize that I am speaking in practical terms.

You can correct a physical condition for example, in the manner just given.

If so, however, by examining the inner landscape of thoughts, you would find the source here that initially brought about the physical ailment.

Feelings can be examined in the same way.

They will appear differently, with much greater mobility.

Thoughts, for example, may appear as stationary structures, as flowers or trees, houses or landscapes.

Feelings will appear more often in the changing mobility of water, wind, weather, skies and changing color.

Any physical ailment, then, can be perceived in this state by looking inward into the body and discovering it;

Then by changing what you see

You may find yourself entering your body or another's as a very small miniature,

Or as a point of light, or simply without any substance, yet aware of the inner body environment.

You change what needs to be changed in whatever way occurs to you, then

By directing the body's energy in that direction,

By entering the flesh and bringing certain portions together that need this adjustment, by manipulating areas of the spine.

Then from this adjacent platform of A-1 consciousness, you perceive the mental thought patterns of yourself

Or the other person in whatever way you find characteristic of you.

You may perceive the thought patterns as quickly flashing sentences

Or words that are usually seen within your mind or within the other mind,

Or as black letters that form words.

Or you may hear the words and thoughts being expressed,

Or you may see the earlier mentioned 'landscape' in which the thoughts symbolically form into a picture.

This will show you how the thoughts brought about the physical malady,

And which ones were involved.

The same thing should then be done with the feeling pattern.

This may be perceived as bursts of dark or light colors in motion, or simply one particular emotion of great force may be felt.

If it is very strong, one emotion may be felt in many such guises.

In the case of both thoughts and emotions, with great confidence you pluck out those that are connected with the malady.

In such a manner you have made adjustments on three levels.

Session 574. 'Seth Speaks: The Eternal Validity of the Soul' by Jane Roberts.

Down The Rabbit Hole Of Thoughts

Now, when you allow negative thoughts to predominate in your conscious mind you then become more open to the negative thoughts of others.

You are given a natural protection but you weaken this protection when your conscious thoughts are negative.

This not only happens in the waking state,

But you also become more open in the dreaming state to telepathic communications from others of a negative pattern.

It is you who open these channels through your thoughts, a sort of psychic contagion in which you are the agent.

You not only attract negative conditions therefore in the physical world that you know, but you open yourselves up to these in the dream reality.

As you all know, and this is not new, your pitiful body changes with each thought that you have and with each emotion.

If you luxuriate in self-pity and feelings of chaos, then you have yourselves to blame.

There is no other place where you can lay the blame and it is up to you, to each of you individually,

To watch the nature of your thoughts for with your thoughts you created the body that you have,

And the individual realities that you know.

You create your little toe and your elbow and the pupil of your eye and your legs.

When you allow your thoughts to run riot then your life runs riot.

Now, there is no contradiction here with what I have said about spontaneity.

When you have allowed negative habits, however, to take over,

Then somewhere you must draw the line for the negative habits knock away the discipline.

The negative habits knock away even spontaneity for all thoughts of good will and health and vitality disappear beneath these thoughts

That you are handing yourself every day like poison upon the spoon, whether the spoon be wooden or tarnished or silver.

A negative thought alone would be followed by a more positive one.

Remember what you were saying earlier about cycles.

Thought patterns and emotional patterns, left alone, would change one into the other as stormy weather changes into sunny.

It is only when strong negative patterns are allowed to flow unrestrained

And indulged in so that they become a barrier holding back positive thoughts that you run into difficulty.

You get into a habit and you do not realize that you have done

So, where predominately your thoughts about yourselves and others are all negative with very few positive ones in between and then the positive ones have no chance to grow.

This is where the difficulty comes in.

I am not telling you to be so frightened of a negative thought that you want to run into a corner or hide under the bed or say "Oh, this is a negative thought, I must change it at once" and half-terrify yourselves to death.

I am telling you that when you indulge in such thoughts for a period of time so that they become habitual then you must change them and no one can do this but yourself.

There is no one else that has control over your own thought patterns and you would be very upset, indeed, if anyone else did.

The Early Class Sessions Book 2 ESP Class Session, July 21, 1970, Jane Roberts Copyright L. Davies

You are individuals, yet each of you forms a part of the world's reality.

Consciously, you are usually aware only of your own thoughts, but those thoughts merge with the thoughts of all others in the world.

You understand what television is. At other levels, however, you carry a picture of the world's news, [one] that is "picked up" by signals transmitted by the c-e-l-l-s (spelled) that compose all living matter.

When you have an impulse to act, it is your own impulse, yet it is also a part of the world's action.

In those terms, there are inner neurological-like systems that provide constant communication through all of the world's parts.

If you accept the fact that man is basically a good creature, then you allow free, natural motions of your own psychic nature —

And that nature springs from your impulses, and not in opposition
to them.

Your thoughts and beliefs and desires form the events that you
view on television.

If you want to change your world, you must first change your
thoughts, expectations, and beliefs.

If every reader of this book changed his or her attitudes, even
though not one law was rewritten,

Tomorrow the world would have changed for the better. The new
laws would follow.

The Individual and the Nature of Mass Events Part Four: Chapter 10: Session 873, August 15, 1979, Jane
Roberts Copyright L. Davie

Now:
You cannot prove scientifically that [your] world was created
(pause) by a god who set it into motion,

But remained outside of its dominion.
Nor can you prove scientifically that the creation of the world
was the result of a chance occurrence—

So you will not be able to prove what I am going to tell you either.

Not in usual terms.

I hope however to present, along with my explanations, certain
hints and clues that will show you where to look for subjective
evidence.

You live your lives through your own subjective knowing, to
begin with,

And I will try to arouse within your own consciousness's memories
of events

With which your own inner psyches were intimately involved as
the world was formed—

And though these may appear to be past events, they are even
now occurring.

All That Is, before the beginning contained within itself the
infinite thrust of all possible creations.

All That Is possessed a creativity of such magnificence

That its slightest imaginings, dreams, thoughts, feelings or
moods attained a kind of reality, a vividness,

An intensity, that almost demanded freedom.

Freedom from what? Freedom to do what? Freedom to be what?

The experience, the subjective universe, the "mind" of All That

Is, was so brilliant,

So distinct, that All That Is almost became lost, mentally wandering
within this ever-flourishing, ever-growing interior landscape.

Each thought, feeling, dream, or mood was itself indelibly
marked with all of the attributes of this infinite subjectivity.

Each glowed and quivered with its own creativity, its own desire
to create as it had been created.

Before the beginning there existed an interior universe that had
no beginning or ending,

For I am using the term "before the beginning" to make matters easier for you to assimilate. (That same infinite interior universe exists now, for example.)

All That Is contained within itself the knowledge of all existences, with their infinite probabilities,

And "as soon as" All That Is imagined those numberless circumstances, they existed in what I will call divine fact.

All That Is knew of itself only.

It was engrossed with its own subjective experiences, even divinely astonished as its own thoughts and imaginings attained their own vitality,

And inherited the creativity of their subjective creator.

[Those thoughts and imaginings] began to have a dialogue with their "Maker".

Thoughts of such magnificent vigor began to think their own thoughts—

And their thoughts thought thoughts.

As if in divine astonishment and surprise, All That Is began to listen,

And began to respond to these "generations" of thoughts and dreams,

For the thoughts and dreams related to each other also.

There was no time, so all of this "was happening" simultaneously.

The order of events is being simplified.

In the meantime, then, in your terms, All That Is spontaneously thought new thoughts and dreamed new dreams, and became involved in new imaginings—

And all of these also related to those now-infinite generations of interweaving and interrelating thoughts and dreams that "already" existed.

So beside this spontaneous creation, this simultaneous "stream" of divine rousing,

All That Is began to watch the inter-actions that occurred among his own subjective progeny.

He listened, began to respond and to answer a thought or a dream.

He began to purposefully bring about those mental conditions that were requested by these generations of mental progeny.

If he had been lonely before, he was no longer.

Your language causes some difficulty here, so please accept the pronoun "he" as innocuously as possible.

"It" sounds too neutral for my purpose, and I want to reserve the pronoun "she" for some later differentiations.

In basic terms, of course, All That Is is quite beyond any designations having to do with any one species or sex.

All That Is, then, began to feel a growing sense of pressure as it realized that its own ever-multiplying thoughts and dreams

Themselves yearned to enjoy those greater gifts of creativity with which they were innately endowed.

It is very difficult to try to assign anything like human motivation to All That Is.

I can only say that it is possessed by "the need" to lovingly create from its own being;

To lovingly transform its own reality in such a way that each slightest probable consciousness can come to be (long pause);

And with the need to see that any and all possible orchestrations of consciousness have the chance to emerge, to perceive and to love.

We will later discuss the fuller connotations of the word "love" as it is meant here,

But this chapter is a kind of outline of other material to come.

All That Is, then, became aware of a kind of creative tumult as each of its superlative thoughts and dreams, moods and feelings, strained at the very edges of their beings,

Looking for some then-unknown, undiscovered, as of then unthought-of release.

I am saying that this mental progeny included all of the consciousnesses that [have] ever appeared or will appear upon your earth—

All tenderly couched: the first human being, the first insect—each with an inner knowledge of the possibilities of its development.

All That Is, loving its own progeny, sought within itself the answer to this divine dilemma.

When that answer came, it involved previously unimaginable leaps of divine inspiration, and it occurred thusly:

All That Is searched through the truly infinite assortment of its incredible progeny to see what conditions were needed for this even more magnificent dream, this dream of a freedom of objectivity.

What door could open to let physical reality emerge from such an inner realm?

When All That Is, in your terms, put all of those conditions together it saw, of course, in a flash, the mental creation of those objective worlds that would be needed—

And as it imagined those worlds, in your terms, they were physically created.

[All That Is] did not separate itself from those worlds, however, for they were created from its thoughts, and each one has divine content.

The worlds are all created by that divine content,

So that while they are on the one hand exterior,

They are on the other also made of divine stuff,

And each hypothetical point in your universe is in direct contact with All That Is in the most basic terms.

The knowledge of the whole is within all of its parts—
And yet All That Is is more than its parts.

Divine subjectivity is indeed infinite.

It can never be entirely objectified.

When the worlds, yours and others, were thus created,

There was indeed an explosion of unimaginable proportions, as the divine spark of inspiration exploded into objectivity.

The first "object" was an almost unendurable mass, though it
had no weight,

And it exploded, instantaneously beginning processes that
formed the universe—

But no time was involved.

The process that you might imagine took up eons occurred in the
twinkling of an eye,

And the initial objective materialization of the massive thought
of All That Is burst into reality.

In your terms this was a physical explosion—

But in the terms of the consciousnesses involved in that
breakthrough,

This was experienced as a triumphant "first" inspirational frenzy,
a breakthrough into another kind of being (most intently).

The earth then appeared as consciousness transformed itself into
the many facets of nature.

The atoms and molecules were alive, aware—

They were no longer simply a part of a divine syntax, but they
spoke themselves through the very nature of their being (gesturing).

They became the living, aware vowels and syllables through
which consciousness could form matter.

But in your terms this was still largely a dream world, though it was fully fashioned.

It had, generally speaking, all of the species that you now know.

These all correlated with the multitudinous kinds of consciousness's that had clamored for release,

And that consciousness's were spontaneously endowed by All

That Is with those forms that fit their requirements.

You had the birth of individualized consciousness as you think of it into physical context.

That consciousnesses were individualized before the beginning,

But not manifest.

But individualized consciousness was not quite all that bold.

It did not attach itself completely to its earthly forms at the start, but rested often within its "ancient" divine heritage.

In your terms, it is as if the earth and all of its creatures were partially dreaming,

And not as focused within physical reality as they are now.

For one thing, while individualized consciousness was within the massive subjectivity of All That Is,

It enjoyed, beside its own uniqueness, a feeling of supporting unity, a comforting knowledge that it was one with its source.

So in the beginning of [your] world, consciousness fluctuated greatly, focusing gently at the start,

But not quite as willing to be as fully independent as its first intent might seem.

You had the sleepwalkers, early members of your species,

Whose main concentration was still veiled in that earlier subjectivity,

And they were your true ancestors, in those terms.

For one thing, early man needed to rely upon his great inner knowledge.

All of the species began by emphasizing a great subjective orientation

That was most necessary as they learned to manipulate within the new physical environment.

Dreams Evolution and Volume Fulfillment Volume 1 by Jane Roberts. Session 883, October 1, 1979

Before physical construction can occur therefore,

Psychological perception, manipulation and construction of inner data or inner structures must be performed.

These psychological structures and constructions are the basis for material construction,

And therefore this inner manipulation of psychological structures is extremely important.

No Pr Part One: Chapter 4: Session 619, October 9, 1972

We will take as an example hatred. Hatred does not exist as a basic psychological structure.

It is, however, the result of psychological manipulation of fear, and fear is not a basic psychological structure.

Survival IS a basic psychological structure.

Consciousness survival:

Construction of this basic psychological structure of consciousness survival must be interpreted,

Or projected or constructed in terms of physical survival within your physical field.

Inadequate perception, manipulation, or construction in the psychological structure of consciousness survival

Leads to the psychological creation of fear and hatred.

The individual then constructs fear and hatred into physical construction, giving fear and hatred definite physical form.

The error is in the original inability to perceive the correct inner data, the basic underlying psychological structure of consciousness survival.

This error may become habitual, coloring all other psychological structures, and resulting in unfortunate and dangerous physical constructions.

They are extremely destructive errors and have many causes.

The physical construction is then perceived by the outer senses as threatening and fearful,

And influences through the outer senses the inner individual,

So that he begins a vicious circle in an attempt to form further, more threatening physical constructions to combat the earlier ones.

And the greater the number of such destructive physical constructions, the greater his expectation of further fear.

I have hinted at the reasons for such errors.

Habitual errors become part of the psychological perspective.

Communication between individuals in any psychological perspective is almost exclusively telepathic,

And is picked up early by the young from their parents, at the same time that they learn their own manipulation in the psychological perspective.

Using the analogy of consciousness survival and its distortion into fear and hatred,

I have given you but one of the ways in which basic psychological structures are misinterpreted with unfortunate results.

I am leading up to the part that expectation plays in the construction of your physical environment,

But you can see now why it was necessary that I explain the psychological perspective to you beforehand.

The Early Sessions book 2, session 75, pages 271-272, by Jane Roberts © L. Davies Butts

The process of imagining will also bring you face to face with other subsidiary ideas that may momentarily bring you up short.

You may see where you held two quite conflicting ideas simultaneously, and with equal vigor.

In such a case, you stalemated yourself.

You may believe that you have a right to health, and yet with equal intensity believe that the human condition is by nature tainted.

So you will try to be healthy and not healthy at the same time, or successful and not successful, according to your individual system of beliefs—

For later in the book you will see how your beliefs will generally fall into a system of related ideas.

This is the end for the evening. I bid you a fond good evening, and a hearty introduction to good beliefs.

The Nature of Personal Reality, Session 619

The body exists in the world of space and time.

The experiences you may encounter in your sixties are as necessary as those in your twenties.

Your changing image is supposed to tell you something.

When you pretend alterations do not occur you block both biological and spiritual messages.

In old age the organism is, in certain terms, preparing for a new birth.

The combined events of spirit, mind and body involve not only the passing of one season but preparation for the beginning of another.

The situation includes all of those supports necessary to carry you through,

Not only with acceptance but with the great aggressive drive toward new experience.

To refute your reality in time, therefore, results in your being stuck in time and obsessed by it.

Accepting your integrity in time allows the body to function until its natural end, in good condition, free from those distorted, invisible concepts about age.

If you believe that youth is the ideal and struggle for it while simultaneously believing that old age must involve infirmities, then you cause an unnecessary dilemma,

And hasten aging according to the negative aspects of your mind.

Each individual must examine his or her individual beliefs, or begin with feelings which will inevitably lead to them.

In this area, as in all others, those of you who are proficient verbally might use the method of writing.

Either write down your beliefs as they come to you, or make lists of your intellectual and emotional assumptions.

You may find that they are quite different.

If you have a physical symptom, do not run away from it.

Feel its reality in your body.

Let the emotions follow freely.

These will lead you, if you allow them to flow, to the beliefs that cause the difficulty.

They will take you through many aspects of your own reality that you must face and explore.

These methods release your withheld natural aggressiveness.

You may feel that you are swamped by emotion, but trust it —

Again, it is the motion of your being, and it arouses your own creativity.

Followed, it will seek the answers to your problems.

The Nature of Personal Reality Part Two Chapter 11: Session 644, February 28, 1973

Now:

Only out of unpredictability can an infinite number of orders, or ordered systems, arise.

Anything less than complete unpredictability will ultimately result in stagnation, or orders of existence that in the long run are self-defeating. Only from unpredictability can any system emerge that can be predictable within itself.

Only within complete freedom of motion is any "ordered" motion truly possible.

From the "chaotic" bed of your dreams springs your ordered daily organized action.

In your reality, the behavior of your consciousness and of your molecules are highly connected.

Your type of consciousness presupposes a molecular consciousness,

And your kind of consciousness is inherent in molecular consciousness –

Inherent within your system, but not basically predictable.

Predictability is simply another word for significance.

Unpredictability looks at itself in a variety of different fashions,

Finds certain points of itself significant, and forms certain orders, or ordered sequences, about itself.

In one of our very early sessions, I told you that you perceive from a vast field only certain data that you find meaningful.

That data could only arise from the bed of unpredictability.

Only unpredictability can provide the greatest source of probable orders.

Your cells are quite able to handle different orders of events, therefore,

In the dream state they are able, in their individual ways, to perceive your experience,

And from it to choose those actualities you want made real in your terms.

In dreams you are acquainted with probable events, from which you then choose. [to Rob:]

So before you died as a child, you knew that you could pick or choose that death.

In greater terms you chose both life and death,

And the picture of you at the age of 16 was never taken in one reality.

UR1 681

Consciousness: The One In The Many

Each individual is a universe in a small package.

As the physical planets move in order while being individual, so there can be a social order that is based upon the integrity of the individual.

But that order would recognize the inner validity that is within the self.

And the inner order unseen, that forms the integrity of the physical body likewise would form the integrity of the social body.

The self, the individual, being its Fulfilled self, would automatically function for the good of itself and for the good of society.

The individual's good, therefore, is the society's good, and represents spiritual and physical fulfillment.

This presupposes, however, an understanding of the inner self

And an exploration into the unknown reality of the individual psyche.

Seth, Session 704, The Unknown Reality, Volume One. Jane Roberts.

Your experience in the world of physical matter flows outward from the center of your inner psyche.

Then you perceive this experience.

Exterior events, circumstances and conditions are meant as a kind of 'living" feedback.

Altering the state of the psyche automatically alters the physical circumstances.

There is no other valid way of changing physical events.

It might help if you imagine an inner living dimension within yourself, in which you create, in miniature psychic form, all the exterior conditions that you know.

Simply put, you do exactly this.

The Nature of Personal Reality by Jane Roberts, Chapter 1, Where You and the World Meet.

True spirituality is a thing of joy and of the earth, and has nothing to do with fake adult dignity.

It has nothing to do with long words and sorrowful faces.

It has to do with the dance of consciousness that is within you,

And with the sense of spiritual adventure that is within your hearts.

That is the meaning of spirituality;

And as I have told you before, if I could I would do a merry dance about the room to show you that your vitality is not dependent upon a physical image.

It is not dependent upon your youth it is not dependent upon your body.

It rings and sings through the universe, and through your entire personality.

It is a sense of joy that makes all creativity probable.

So do not think you are being spiritual when you are being long-faced,

And do not think you are being spiritual when you berate

yourself for your sins.

The seasons within your system come and go.

The sun falls upon your face whether you think you are a sinner or a saint.

The vitality of the universe is creativity and joy and love, and that is spirituality.

And that is what I shall tell the readers of my book.
(Seth Speaks - Appendix) ESP CLASS SESSION: BEFORE JUNE 23. 1970

ELIAS: But the one piece that is also significant:

You will hear and listen to people that move in the direction of transgender

Or people that move in the direction genuinely of being homosexual

Not any of the other identities, but simply homosexual, male or female.

They identify with their gender.

When you speak with most of these individuals,

They will make statements that they have had inklings or have somewhat known that they were either in the direction of transgendered

Or in the direction of homosexuality from very young ages,

That they knew that they could feel that when they were very young.

Now; an individual that is "other," from very young ages, again, they will have had a sense of not being either.

From very young ages they will have accepted that they were partially male or female,

But that they don't actually think of themselves as a boy or a girl.

That they will move in the direction of compliance,

Because they're young and because they don't perceive they have any other choice,

But inwardly they don't actually view themselves as being a boy OR a girl.

They view themselves as being neither, that they aren't both, but they're not one or the other.

This is something that is very similar to these other expressions.

Humans know intrinsically from the time they are very young in age.

They simply have a sense of themself. Now, THAT is more of the identity.

Now, there are definitely humans that from the time they are very small children know they are boys, know they are girls,

And they are very rooted in that and they're very happy in that.

That's the difference, that they're very rooted in it, and children that are "other" are not rooted in either.

ELIAS: Now; what I would say to you is, when I began my conversations with all of you, I did identify three genders.

People have speculated about that and misunderstood that from the beginning.

Now you're beginning to see the evidence of it.

What does it mean? You don't only have two genders in your reality.

You do have three.
One of them is not actually male or female.
It's something else.

And it doesn't fall into the role of male and female.

Male and female are very clearly defined in relation to reproduction.

These individuals are not moving in that direction.

Reproduction doesn't factor into their identity.

And in keeping with development, not all of them know in a clear capacity that they may not necessarily fall into the category of male or female until they are slightly older.

Meaning some of them may be aware of that around the age of twelve moving into adolescence.

Some of them might not recognize that until they are fully into adolescence

And they may not express anything about it because they're afraid, because there are still many, many, many, many, many people in your world that are confused and oppositional.

And there are many individuals that perceive this situation in a very similar manner to yourself, which is tremendously discounting,

And it's discounting because it's uninformed.

And it's uninformed because you're not asking questions.

THAT is your responsibility.

In this, there are as many individuals in your world that are of the third gender as there are of the other two.

That's a lot.

Therefore, what I would say is in actuality, if everyone was allowed to express themselves freely,

This situation of being presented with that third gender would likely touch every single family. That that's how prevalent it is.

Now; it doesn't touch every single family because it's still in its infancy of being able to be expressed.

But I would also say that moving in the direction of physically altering their physical bodies is not extreme, and it's something that is not inappropriate.

As I said, this is not a situation of simply individuals moving in the direction of becoming what you identify as trans-gendered.

Trans-gendered individuals, generally speaking, although it's not a rule,

But generally these are individuals that know at very young ages that the physical form that they inhabit doesn't match their identity.

Generally, individuals know as young or even younger than primary school.

They're already expressing in capacities that are different from their physical gender.

What we are speaking of isn't that black and white.

Because those individuals are still moving in the direction of the two main genders.

Through these consciousness units, consciousness makes its mark, and not one scribble is ever annihilated.

The experience of any given unit, constantly changing, affects all other units. Give us time.

It is difficult to explain because your concepts of selfhood are so limited.

These units contain within themselves, in your terms, all "latent" identities, but not in a predetermined fashion.

Selves may be quite independent within the framework of their own reality,

While still being a part of a larger reality in which their independence works not only for their own benefit,

But for the sake of a greater structure.

Within these units, there is, again, a propensity for growth and organization.

Within a literally infinite field of activity, meaningful order arose out of the propensity for significance.

Briefly, certain units would settle upon various kinds of organization, find these significant,

Then build upon them and attract others of the same nature.

So were various systems of reality formed.

The particular kind of significance settled upon would act both as a directive for experience

And as a method of erecting effective boundaries, within which the selected kind of behavior would continue.

The [consciousness] units can and do intermix, yet because of the propensity for selectivity and significance, whole groups of them will "repel" other whole groups,

Thus providing a protective inner system of interactions.

The units form themselves into the various systems that they have themselves initiated.

They transform themselves, therefore, into the structured reality that they then become.

Ruburt is quite correct in his supposition of what he calls "multi-personhood" in

Adventures in Consciousness. UR1 683

Units of consciousness (CU's) move faster than the speed of light, then

But that statement itself is meaningless in a way, since the units exist outside as well as inside in which light itself has meaning.

As these units approach physical structure, however, they do slowdown in your terms.

Electrons, for example, are slow dullards in comparison with EE units.

It goes without saying that the units of consciousness are "mental," or if you prefer, disembodied, though from their inner organization all physical forms emerge.

Certain intensities are built up of unit organization even before the smallest physical particle, or even invisible "physical" particle, exists.

These units form what you think of as the mind, around which the structure of the brain is formulated.

The units permeate the brain.

The great communication system within the body itself is dependent, then, upon the constant inner flux and flow of these units.

On one level the body's very survival is largely determined by the units' propensities for selectivity and significance. Also, however, the body's physical reality is a seeming constant in a seemingly constant physical existence.

UR1 684

There is no authority but the authority that is within your own consciousness –

The legitimate reality that is your own! Follow the wisdom that is within yourself.

Distrust easy answers (even from counselors)

There is no authority but the authority that is within your own consciousness –

The legitimate reality that is your own!

When it seems to you that you are powerless, it is because you
are denying the authority that lies within yourself,

Closing your mind to the answers that are as free as air.

You are not here to accept ready answers.

You are here to use your abilities, to consider your problems as
challenges and to work them out.

You must first of all realize that within you there is somewhere
the miraculous knowledge that keeps your body alive.

You can draw upon this knowledge to solve your problems.

If you accept answers from others,

You will simply run into the same problem again and again, and
you will have solved nothing. **ESP CLASS** March 17, 1970

You can understand what is meant by saying that your
consciousness fluctuates –

For each individual is aware of various intensities and
concentrations.

You are more alert, or, in your terms, more conscious on some
occasions than others.

Now, the same applies to these units of consciousness –

And to atoms, molecules, electrons, and other such phenomena.

The world literally blinks off and on.

This reality of fluctuation in no way bothers your own feeling of consistency, however.

The "holes of nonexistence" are plugged up by the process of selectivity.

This process chooses significances then, again, around which experience is built, and around which "life" is felt.

The very sensations of one kind of life then automatically set up barriers against other such "world-schemes"

That do not correlate with their own.

It is impossible for you to examine an atom, a cell, or anything else except in your now.

Period.

Because your sense experience follows a time pattern that you can understand,

Then you take it for granted that a cell, for example, is the result of its past,

And that its present condition arises from the past.

The fetus grows into an adult, not because it is programmed from the past,

But because it is to some extent pre-cognitively aware of its probabilities,

And from the "future" then imprints this information into the past structure.

The beginning of your physical universe occurred when
conscious energy directed enough of its attention

In what was generalized dimension, to spark the formation of
physical properties.

The creation was just that.

The first explosion of psychic energy in an un-generalized
dimension sparked the birth of specifics.

Before this the generalized dimension was simply nonexistent,
a vacuum, which consciousness had not yet filled.

Since consciousness or action can never fully materialize itself,

There are literally infinities of such nonexistent areas from
which new dimensions can spring.

Consciousness or action forms all realities.

What is not simply represents a possibility which consciousness
may bring to life. (Long pause.)

Consciousness then formed out of itself a new dimension which
was the physical one.

The formation, the explosion, of energy, shattered consciousness
into an infinity of parts,

Each with all the abilities in here within consciousness itself.

From itself, therefore, and of itself, consciousness gave birth to
its new dimension of experience,

And then experienced what it had created, further extending
itself

And in turn bringing forth further possibilities of development.

Consciousness therefore continually creates and maintains itself,

And this includes the physical materialization,

The properties of the dimension,

And yet basically there is no difference between the creator in
these terms and the created.

Nor between inner reality, which forms physical matter, and
physical objects themselves,

For the atoms which are manipulated to form objects are themselves
a portion of consciousness, and alive in those terms.

They respond to emotional and psychic directives as the physical
body responds to light.

TES8 Session 338 May 1, 1967

You cannot separate your beliefs about reality from the reality
that you experience.

That is, your beliefs about reality form it.

Your ideas about what is possible and what is not possible are
reflected in all areas.

It is almost impossible to begin with concepts of one isolated
universe,

One self at the mercy of the past, one-time sequence,

And end up with any acceptable theory of a multidimensional soul

Or godhead that is anything else

But a glorified personified concept of what you think man is.

Not only do your metaphysics and sciences suffer,

But your daily experience as a human being is far less than it could be.

There are, then, probabilities quite present,

And for that matter biologically practical, that would allow you a change in individual consciousness

So great as literally to propel the race into another level of experience entirely.

As in your terms the caveman ventured out into the daylight of the earth,

There is a time for man to venture out into a greater knowledge of his subjective reality,

To explore the dimensions of selfhood,

And go beyond the small areas of himself in which he has thus far found shelter.

UR1 684

In terms of history as you understand it,

Man felt safe and secure as a prime species under one sun,

imagining that all else revolved about his being.

This provided, in that framework, a stability that was dispensed with as

Man allowed his consciousness other freedoms.

So he must now come to realize that he himself chooses from a myriad of probabilities the one that he now encounters.

The one self that he recognizes is the only part of himself of which he is presently aware.

Other facets of consciousness available to him, and a part of his greater nature, appear foreign, or "not-self," or "beyond self,"

Because of the focus of selectivity as it now operates.

We will return to the subject of war later on.

UR1 Section 1: Session 684 February 20, 1974

Religion Is A Sly Devil

I want to mention here, however, that man is not basically endowed with "warlike characteristics.

He does not naturally murder.

He does not naturally seek to destroy his own life or [the lives of] others.

There is no battle for survival—

But while you project such an idea upon natural reality, then you will read nature, and your own experiences with it, in that fashion.

Dreams Evolution and Value Fulfillment Volume 1 by Jane Roberts. Session 901, February 18, 1980

The rules are that you create your universe—that you create within the system that you know the world that you know.

The rules are that within you there is knowledge.

And that you must look inward, not outward, to find it.

The rules are that this universe is created by the thoughts that exist within each of your minds.

And that these thoughts are materialized outward.

And that if your body becomes ill, it is because of an inner disease.

And again, there are no exceptions.

Ruburt is no exception, you are no exception, no one within your system is an exception.

There are no exceptions.

And these are the only rules, for you have been given what you always say you want, your desires—

For what you think of is materialized.

And when thoughts of resentment and hatred are materialized, you end up with wars.

I have said this many times.

The condition of your physical world is the result of your mass inner thoughts and desires.

And your physical environments, your personal physical environments, are the results of your inner materialized thoughts.

And there are no exceptions.

You are responsible for the sunrise.

You are responsible for the tides.

You are responsible for the wars and the starvation.

The Early Class Sessions Book 2 ESP Class Session January 13, 1970

The past, in the preset, would appear so brilliantly that man could not react adequately in circumstances of time that he had himself created.

The future was blocked, practically speaking, to preserve freedom of action

And to encourage physical exploration, curiosity, and creativity.

With memory, however, mental projections into the future were of course also possible

So that man could plan his activities in time and for see probable results:

"Ghost image" of the future probabilities always acted as mental stimuli for physical explorations in all areas, and of all kinds.

The race was dealing with the creation of a new world of physical experience.

To do this particular kind of experiment, it was necessary that physical manipulation be concentrated upon.

Ghost images from the future were one thing, inspiring mankind. Had such data instantly appeared before him, howe er, man would have been deprived of the physical joys, endeavors, and challenges that were so basic to the experiment itself.

It would have been quite possible for you as a race to have chosen any other "series" of neurological pulses, or messages, as the "real" ones, and to structure your experience along different lines.

The biological structure and the mental consciousness together, however, chose the most comfortable sequence in which a present area of activity, brought about by neurological recognition, would be backed up by unconscious mental knowledge and other biologically invisible neurological connections.

UR1 686

Now: You may be quite able to see through the distortions of conventional Christianity.

You may have changed your ideas to such an extent that you can see little similarity between your current ones and those of the past.

Now you may believe in the theories of Buddhism, for example, or of another Eastern philosophy.

The differences between any of those systems of thought and Christianity may be so apparent that the similarities escape you.

You may follow one of the schools of Buddhism in which great stress is laid upon the denial of the body, discipline of the flesh, and the avoidance of desire.

These elements are quite characteristic of Christianity also, of course,

But they may appear more palatable, exotic, or reasonable coming from a source foreign to your childhood education.

So you may leap from one to the other, shouting emancipation and feeling yourself quite free of old limiting ideas.

Philosophies that teach denial of the flesh MUST ultimately end up preaching a denial of the self and building a contempt for it,

Because even though the soul is couched in muscle and bone it is MEANT to experience that reality, not to refute it.

All such dogmas use artificial guilt, and natural guilt is distorted to serve those ends.

In whatever terms, the devotee is told that there is something wrong with earthly experience.

You are, therefore, considered evil as a self in flesh by virtue of your very existence.

This alone will cause adverse experience, making you reject the very basis of your own framework of experience.

You will consider the body as a thing, a fine vehicle but not in itself the natural LIVING expression of your being in material form.

Many such Eastern schools also stress — as do numerous spiritualistic schools —

The importance of the "unconscious levels of the self," and teach you to mistrust the conscious mind.

The concept of nirvana (see the 637th session in Chapter Nine) and the idea of heaven are two versions of the same picture,

The former being one in which individuality is lost in the bliss of undifferentiated consciousness,

And the latter one in which still-conscious individuals perform mindless adoration.

Neither theory contains an understanding of the functions of the conscious mind, or the evolution of consciousness —

Or, for that matter, certain aspects of greater physics.
No energy is ever lost.

The expanding universe theory* applies to the mind as well as to the universe.

However, these philosophies CAN lead you to a deep mistrust of both your body and mind.

You are told that the spirit is perfect, and so you can try to live up to standards of perfection quite impossible to achieve.

The failure adds to the sense of guilt.

You attempt then to further banish the characteristic enjoyment of your own creature-hood,

Denying the lusty spirituality of your flesh and the strong present corporeal leanings of your soul.

You will try to rid yourself of very natural emotions, and so be cheated of their great spiritual and physical motion.

On the other hand, some leaders may give little consideration to such issues,

But still be deeply convinced of the misery of the human condition, focusing upon all the "darker" elements, seeing the world's destruction ever closer to hand

Without really examining the beliefs that arouse such constant feelings.

They may find it easy to cluck their tongues at obvious fanatics who cry out for God's vengeance, and speak about the world's end in brimstone and ashes.

They may be as equally convinced, however, of man's basic unworthiness, and so of course of their own.

In daily life such people will concentrate upon negative events, store them up, and unfortunately cause personal experience that will seem to quite reinforce the basic ideas.

Here in different context is the same denial of the worth and integrity of earth experience.

In some such cases, all of the desirable human attributes are magnified and projected outward into a god or super-consciousness,

While all the less admirable characteristics are left to the race and the individual.

The individual therefore deprives himself of the use of much of his ability. He does not consider it his own, and is astounded when any others of his race display such superior qualities.

The Nature of Personal Reality, Chapter 12: Session 647, March 12, 1973 - by Jane Roberts © L. Davies Butts

How can the well-meaning idealist know whether or not his good intent will lead to some actualization?

How can HE know, or how can SHE know, whether or not this good intent might in fact lead to disastrous conditions?

Look at it this way: If someone tells you that pleasure is wrong and tolerance is weakness,

And that you must follow this or that dogma blindly in obedience,

And that if you are told this is the only right road toward the idealized good,

Then most likely you are dealing with a fanatic.

If you are told that the end justifies any means, you are dealing with a fanatic.

If you are told to kill for the sake of peace,

You are dealing with someone who does not understand peace or justice.

If you are told to give up your free will, you are dealing with a fanatic.

The Individual and the Nature of Mass Events, Session 856

OPEN UP THE GATES OF YOUR CONSCIOUSNESS WHILE YOU SLEEP!

You know you are more than what you refer to as your conscious I.

But you should know it through EXPERIENCE!

Open up the barriers in your daily lives.

Step outside of the self that you know –

AND YOU WILL SOLVE YOUR DIFFICULTIES!

YOU will solve them and you will KNOW that you have done so.

You will know that the ability is within yourself and you have used it –

THEN you may hit me over the head with your crutches and I will laugh!

ECS1 ESP Class Session, May 20, 1969 - by Jane Roberts © L.Davies Butts

Such "new truths" can still be very ancient indeed,

But truth is not a thing that must always have the same appearance, shape, form or dimension.

Those who persist, therefore, in shielding their truths from questions threaten to destroy the validity of their knowledge.

Again, those who are so certain of their answers will lack that need to know that can lead them into still greater dimensions of understanding.

And valid expansion of consciousness is itself, of course, a part of the message.

The personality finds itself encountering living truth and knows
that truth only exists in those terms.

Seth Speaks The Eternal Validity of the Soul APPENDIX: Session 596

It's a matter of paying attention to HOW you flow, and how
another individual flows with you and how YOU flow with them.

Because it's not one way, it's both ways.

And therefore in that, it's a matter of recognizing that it's not
only how the other individual flows with you or complements you,

But how do you complement them also?

And it's the same process of evaluation.

Therefore in that, what I would say to you is that it isn't difficult
to discern all of this.

It's simply a matter of paying attention.

It actually isn't difficult to see, because it's all about whether you flow

Or whether your movement at times seems fragmented or jerking,
rather than flowing.

Let me express in this manner.

Either you would be flowing and in that, seeming as if you would
be a stream that has a constant, steady, even flow to the water

OR you might be being the stream and there are many rocks and
boulders in the stream.

And what does that create?

As the stream flows, it creates rapids.

It creates a choppiness with the water.

The water isn't smooth in its flow.

It's choppy and fragmented because it's flowing over and around
a lot of obstacles.

Therefore, it's a matter of looking at your life and whatever it is
that you're doing in your daily life,

And are you flowing and can you flow with another individual?

And do they appear to be flowing also? Or are you creating
whitecaps?

Elias

And in that, there are many people that may be aware of certain
aspects of their own trauma that they have experienced,

But what they're paying attention to is what they define as being
triggered.

Therefore, they're more paying attention to triggers than they
are to their own behaviors

And how their trauma has influenced their own behaviors, their
own choices.

And in that, they're more paying attention to everyone around
them

And then moving in the direction of paying attention to everyone
else's behavior

And expressing that other people's behaviors are triggering of them.

That's a very common theme in your present time framework.

Therefore what I'm saying to you is you're correct, it's not unusual to be engaged with an individual that has trauma or has had trauma in their life.

That's something that is very common,

But yes it should be raising a red flag for you.

Because in that, it should alert you to pay attention to what the individual is doing with that trauma.

The race also realizes well the advantages and disadvantages of the physical reality it has adopted.

It knows for example that there is a tendency to go to extremes.

I mentioned earlier that the rewards, the challenges and the dangers exist precisely because so much freedom is allowed.

Those within the system know this.

Regardless of what you may think of their present performance at any given 'time' in quotes,

It is from this system that the greatest potentials emerge;

For having dealt with it, consciousness undergoes one of the severest tests in learning to handle its own energy.

The horror and the results of mismanagement, and the vulnerability, are the teaching methods

That each consciousness has accepted before entering your system.

There is no way out but to learn or to ruin the entire system.

In no other field of reality are the terms so drastic. For this reason, the inner self withholds much of its knowledge.

There must be no leaning upon the very basic fact that behind and within the system there is relief.

You must believe in the physical reality and accept the vulnerability.

The Early Sessions, Book 9, Session 498

My purpose is not to solve your problems for you,

But to put you in touch with your own power.

My purpose is not to come between you and your own freedom by giving you 'answers,' even to the most tragic of problems.

My purpose is to reinforce your own strength, for ultimately the magic of your being is well equipped to help you find fulfillment, understanding, exuberance, and peace.

Your problems are caused by your own doubts.

These doubts arise because you have been out of touch with the validity of your own existence.

Let me here reinforce that validity.

Let me reinforce my faith in your innate ability to find joyful acquiescence, and to rise above any problems that you have.

If I presume to solve problems for you,

Then I deny you your own power, and further reinforce any feelings of powerlessness that you have.

I know that you can grow tired, however, and that sometimes a
gift of energy can be quite a boost;

So, again, with this I send my joyful recognition of YOUR existence—
And energy that you can use to reinforce your own vitality and
strength.

The "Unknown Reality, Vol 1, Introductory Note

Now:

You use atoms and molecules in a strange way.

You transpose your ideas upon them.

You perceive them in a certain fashion.

I am not blaming you.

I have done it too, in my time, and there is good reason for it.

But the fact is that physical matter is not solid except when you
believe that it is,

And that organization is transposed from within upon the without.

It is not transposed from the without upon you.

You form the reality that you know,

And even though the table holds up your arms and you may lean
upon it and write,

I still tell you that the table is not solid.

This makes little difference as long as you can write upon it.

It makes little difference as long as you can sit upon your blue couch.

But when you leave your physical system and when physical
perception is no longer the rule,

Then you must learn new root assumptions.

Seth Speaks The Eternal Validity of the Soul
APPENDIX: ESP CLASS SESSION 6/23/1970

You must return, wiser creatures, to the nature that spawned you—

Not only as loving caretakers

But as partners with the other species of the earth.

You must discover once again the spirituality of your biological
heritage.

The majority of accepted beliefs—religious, scientific, and cultural—
Have tended to stress a sense of powerlessness, impotence, and
impending doom—

A picture in which man and his world is an accidental production

With little meaning, isolated yet seemingly ruled by a capricious God.

Life is seen as 'a valley of tears'—

Almost as a low-grade infection from which the soul can be
cured only by death.

Religious, scientific, medical, and cultural communications
stress the existence of danger,

Minimize the purpose of the species or of any individual member of it

Or see mankind as the one erratic, half-insane member of an otherwise orderly realm.

Any or all of the above beliefs are held by various systems of thought.

All of these, however, strain the individual's biological sense of integrity,

Reinforce ideas of danger, and shrink the area of psychological safety that is necessary to maintain the QUALITY possible in life.

Body Consciousness Is The Bomb

Your body consciousness is like the consciousness of ANY animal.

Animals enjoy being petted, stroked, and loved.

They react in their own ways to suggestion,

And in that regard your body consciousness responds to your
CONSCIOUS TREATMENT of it.

Think of your body as a healthy animal.

Animals and your own body consciousness HAVE LITTLE
CONCEPT OF AGE.

In a fashion almost impossible to describe, those consciousnesses—

Of the body and the animals—are 'young' in each moment of
their existence.

I am taking it for granted that you understand that I am referring
to the 'mental attitude' of animals and of the body consciousness,

For they do possess their own mental attributes—psychological
colorations—and above all, emotional states.

Dreams, "Evolution," and Value Fulfillment, Vol. 1, Session 898, Note

Now if there is good communication between the self,

That is the inner self and the outer ego,

Then the ego begins to understand what it is,

And also to realize that it has greater capacities than it can realize
by continued reincarnations, upon one plane.

If the ego is exceptional it may take one of two courses.

It may choose to return to the same plane as a great originator,

Using knowledge that it receives from the inner self to make lasting and original innovations upon that plane,

According to its interests, abilities and capacity.

It will therefore become a Buddha, a Christ, a Michelangelo, a hero in one field or another,

An ego who changes the physical world completely in untold manners by the mere fact of its existence.

It then does not reincarnate again upon that plane.

However, because of its own extraordinary nature, it itself forms with the inner self in an added gestalt,

Adding to the energy and ability of the inner self;

And in a manner which I cannot yet explain to you,

It voluntarily may give up its ego identification to a large degree for the purpose of giving its full energies to the store of the inner self.

That is one possibility.

It is followed by egos who have actually worn out not this energy, which is tremendous, but their desires.

Other egos choose instead to become entities of their own, in which case this magnificent outer ego becomes in turn an inner ego,

Which then from its own unfulfilled desires, abilities and initiatives are formed new outer egos which once again seek fulfillment.

Such an outer ego turned inner ego, has only experienced existence then upon a particular plane.

It is therefore filled with impatience as far as existence upon other planes are concerned;

And therefore if it developed upon your plane initially,

It will not choose to initiate anew there, but will choose other planes of activity.

It does therefore contain within it the knowledge of its experiences upon your plane,

Though such an entity can spring from any plane.

This of course represents the most extraordinary possibility,

And such an entity can, if it is so propelled by its own strength, exist upon a variety of planes,

Carrying along with it knowledge of all previous planes;

And each of its outer egos have the same opportunities.

This is important.

The choice is always made by the particular ego, and we are speaking here of outer egos, remember.

Many are content to continue indefinitely along the same plane, having almost endless incarnations

And in contact more or less with the inner self.

TES2 Session 58 June 1, 1964

It is only because you have a highly limited conception of your own entity

That you insist upon its being almost sterile in its singularity.

There are millions of cells within your body, but you call your body a unit, and consider it your own.

You do form it, from the inside out, and yet you form it from living substance,

And each smallest particle has its own living consciousness.

There are clumps of matter, and in that respect, there are clumps of consciousness, each individual, with their own destiny and abilities and potentials.

There are no limitations to your own entity:

Therefore, how can your entity or soul have boundaries, for boundaries would enclose it and deny it freedom.

In many philosophies, this sort of idea is retained —

The soul being returned to a primal giver,

Or being dissolved in a nebulous state somewhere between being and non-being.

The soul is, however, first of all creative.

It can be discussed from many viewpoints.

Its characteristics can be given to some degree,

And indeed most of my readers could find out these characteristics for themselves if they were highly enough motivated, and if this was their main concern.

The soul or entity is itself the most highly motivated, most highly energized,

And most potent consciousness-unit known in any universe.

It is energy concentrated to a degree quite unbelievable to you.

It contains potentials unlimited, but it must work out its own identity and form its own worlds.

It carries within it the burden of all being.

Within it are personality potentials beyond your comprehension.

Remember, this is your own soul or entity I am speaking of, as well as soul or entity in general.

You are one manifestation of your own soul.

How many of you would want to limit your reality, your entire reality, to the experience you now know?

You do this when you imagine that your present self is your entire personality,

Or insist that your identity be maintained unchanged through an endless eternity.

Such an eternity would be dead indeed. In many ways, the soul is an incipient god, and later in this book, we will discuss the "god concept."

For now, however, we will simply be concerned with the entity or soul,

The larger self that whispers even now in the hidden recesses of each reader's experience.

I hope in this book not only to assure you of the eternal validity of your soul or entity

But to help you sense its vital reality within yourself.

First of all, however, you must have some idea of your own psychological and psychic structure.

When you understand to some extent who and what you are,

Then I can explain more clearly who and what I am.

I hope to acquaint you with those deeply creative aspects of your own being,

So that you can use these to extend and expand your entire experience.

Seth Speaks Part One: Chapter 6: Session 526, May 4, 1970

Seth on the Doer, the Mover, the Breather & the Dreamer

No one, I am sure, denies the existence of air because ordinarily you do not see it.

No one denies the existence of air because they do not understand the method by which their own lungs breathe.

Yet they know that they breathe,

And they know that without breath death is inevitable.

To deny the existence of air would seem ridiculous.

Some part of the individual is aware of the most minute portions of breath,

Some part of the individual knows immediately of the most minute particle of oxygen and components that enters the lung.

The thinking mind, or I had better say the thinking brain, does not know. Your all-important "I" does not know.

In actuality, my dear friends, the all-important "I" does know.

You do not know the all-important "I", and therein lies your difficulty.

It is fashionable in your time to consider man, or man's "I",

As the product of the brain

And an isolated bit of the subconscious, with a few odds and ends thrown in for good measure.

Therefore, with such an unnatural division it seems to man that he does not knowhimself.

He says "I breathe, but who breathes, since consciously I cannot tell myself to breathe or not to breathe?"

He says "I dream, but who dreams? I cannot tell myself to dream or not to dream."

He cuts himself in half, then wonders why he is not whole.

Even in my own lifetimes on your plane I sensed this basic contradiction.

Man has consistently admitted to the evidence only those things he could see, smell, touch or hear,

And in so doing he could only appreciate half of himself.

And when I say half of himself I exaggerate.

He is aware of only a third of himself, because two-thirds of himself exists in that realm to which he will not admit.

If man does not know who breathes within him,

And if man does not know who dreams within him,

It is not because there is one who acts in the physical world and one completely separate who dreams and breathes.

It is because he has buried the part of himself which breathes and dreams.

If these functions seem so automatic as to be performed by someone completely divorced from himself, it is because he has done the divorcing.

It is not in any manner inevitable or a law of the universe.

Far from it.

For some reason mankind as a species on your plane has become much more attached to its camouflage patterns

Than most other kinds of consciousness.

It is on your part more than anything else, a simple refusal to admit into existence anything that is not a camouflage pattern.

The part of you who dreams is the "I" as much as the part of you that operates in any other manner.

The part of you who dreams is the part of you who breathes.

And this part is certainly as legitimate and actually more necessary to you as a whole unit,

As far as survival on your physical plane is concerned,

Than the part that also plays bridge or Scrabble.

The facts are simply that you yourselves form these camouflage patterns, and I repeat this simple statement:

You form the camouflage world of appearances with the same part of you that breathes.

You do not admit the breather as really being a part of yourselves,

Nor do you admit the creator of the camouflaged physical world as being part of yourselves.

Now when I speak to you I very seldom use such words as "love."

I do not tell you that a God is waiting for you on the other side of a golden door.

I do not reassure you by telling you that when you are dead,

God will be waiting for you in all his majestic mercy,

And that that will be the end of your responsibility.

And so as I said last evening, in my latest chapter,

I offer no hope for the lazy, for they will not find eternal rest.

However, through traveling within yourselves, you will discover the unity of your consciousness with other consciousnesses.

You will discover the multidimensional love and energy that gives consciousness to all things.

This will not lead you to want to rest upon the proverbial blessed bosom.

It will instead inspire you to take a better hand in the job of creation;

And that feeling of divine presence you will find indeed, and feel indeed,

For you will sense it behind the dance of the molecules,

And in yourselves and in your neighbors.

What so many want is a God who walks down the street and says, Happy Sunday, I am I, follow me.

But God is hidden craftily in his creations,

So that he is what they are

And they are what he is;

And in knowing them, you know him.

Seth Speaks The Eternal Validity of the Soul APPENDIX: ESP CLASS SESSION 6/23/1970

Now: There are many words for psychological time.

I do not mean my method of meditation alone.

I do mean subjective activity on your part, and exploration.

Do you follow me? I am glad!

Actually, you are with God now.

It is you who do not realize this.

You see, you have believed many tales, and symbolically they were very important.

As was mentioned earlier, they have their place in your lives and your development,

But there are times when you must leave them behind, and you may feel lonesome for a while without them.

Question: *"Then we need those beliefs as part of development, even though we cast them off later?"*

Existence on your plane or any other plane is merely self-hypnosis.

As far as an analogy is concerned, this one is very nearly perfect. Your existence, and mine for that matter, on any particular level is predetermined

By complete concentration or focus of inner selves upon the particular universe in question.

And your camouflage patterns can most aptly be compared to the

HALLUCINARY effects created by the hypnotist upon his subject.

Only in this case the hallucinary effects are actual constructions upon the plane in question, and involve problems that must be worked out.

The hallucinations appear more or less consistent merely because everyone on that particular level is under the effects of self-hypnosis,

And because they have already constructed hallucinary senses, the outer senses, in order to perceive the hallucinary world that they have created.

This is not meant to deny the importance or the value of the particular hallucinary universe in any way.

It has a definite purpose.

But the analogy holds, and is more valid than you might think.

Complete concentration and focus is your answer.

When this focus is finished, when the subject tells himself 'Now I will come to,

Now I have solved the problems that I set out to solve,' then what happens is the withdrawal of the self from the plane.

The construction vanishes

And is heir to the materials which compose the particular universe.

The Early Sessions, Book 1, Session 37

Yes, even though someone like myself will come along and take off the comfort blankets

—For after a while they hamper your development, where earlier they helped you grow.

The fact remains, however:

You do not have to die to find God.

All That Is, is now, and you are a part of All That Is now.

As I have told you often, you are a spirit now.

The avenues for development are open now.

You can, now, set out to explore environments that are not physical if you want to,

But I do not see any rush of students at that invisible door!

Now I am going to close our session, but I would like you all to read carefully a copy of what I have said.

And now and then, when you have nothing else to do —

Nothing better to do —

Then try, try to sense that lapse in the pulsation of your consciousness.

Try to leap that gap!

Seth Speaks The Eternal Validity of the Soul APPENDIX: ESP CLASS SESSION 6/23/1970

Because you know that somehow you breathe, without consciously being aware of the actual mechanics being involved,

You are forced despite your inclinations to admit that you do do your own breathing.

When you cross a room you are forced to admit that you have caused yourself to cross the room,

Even though consciously you have no idea of willing the muscles to move or of stimulating one muscle or another;

And yet even there, though you admit these things, you do not believe them.

In your quiet unguarded moments, you still say who breathes, who dreams, and even who moves?

How much easier it would be to admit freely and wholeheartedly the simple fact that you are not consciously aware of important vital parts of yourself,

And that you are more than you know you are.

But since it is so difficult for man to even recognize the self that moves his own muscles and breathes his own breath,

Then I suppose it should not be startling that he cannot realize that this whole self also forms the camouflage world of physical appearance,

In almost the same manner that he forms a pattern with his breath upon a glass pane.

There is no reason why mankind cannot be aware of this transformation,

If once he admits into existence the whole self which makes this possible.

As I mentioned earlier the process of breathing seems automatic,

And yet some part of you is aware of the most minute portions of air that inflate the lungs.

You, or the part of you that you are pleased to call yourself, refuse to admit as part of yourself the "I"

That is aware of every breath you breathe, every move you make, and every dream that you dream.

In other words, breathing and dreaming are not automatic, nor do they operate without your knowledge.

Mankind simply refuses to admit the breather and the dreamer.

In many cases he refuses to admit the mover.

He trusts himself much more when he says "I will read," and then he reads, than he does when he says "I will see," and then he sees.

He remembers having learned consciously to read, but he does not remember consciously having learned to see.

And what he cannot remember consciously he fears, and what he fears he simply denies existence to.

The fact is, he sees although no one taught him how to see.

And the part of himself that did teach him to see still guides his movements,

Still moves the muscles of his eyes, still becomes conscious despite him when he sleeps, still breathes for him without thanks, without recognition,

And still carries on his task of transforming energy from an inner reality to an outer camouflage.

He becomes trapped by his own artificially-divided self.

He looks for gods, anything at all, to explain perfectly natural functions that belong to him.

This beautifully absolves him in his own eyes from all responsibility,

But it does not.

I have been speaking here only, if you will believe it, of personalities in their particular lives as they operate on your plane, and I have much to say.

It is true that as a rule you are not aware of your whole entity, which as a rule does not reside within your boundaries.

But there is no reason why you must be blind to the whole self of your present personality,

Which is part of your entity, and which can be glimpsed on your plane in terms of the breathing and dreaming self of which I have spoken.

TES1 Session 23 February 5, 1964

When I speak of the whole self I am of course referring to the personality as it exists in its entirety,

Having at its command use of both the inner and outer senses.

That is, I speak of the doer, the mover, the breather

And the dreamer as all belonging to one whole self.

This designation does not include the entity as a whole, however.

The personality does have access to the entity,

But the personality does not contain the entity.

In other words, the whole self as it exists on your plane does not contain the entity,

Although communication between the entity and the whole self can and does take place by means of the inner senses.

TES1 Session 25 February 12, 1964

Beliefs Spill The Beans

In Seth Speaks I tried to describe certain extensions of your own
reality in terms that my readers could understand.

In The Nature of Personal Reality, I tried to extend the practical
boundaries of individual existence as it is usually experienced.

I tried to give the reader hints that would increase practical,
spiritual, and physical enjoyment and fulfillment in daily life.

Those books were dictated by me in a more or less straight
narrative style.

In "Unknown" Reality I went further, showing how the
experiences of the psyche splash outward into the daylight,
so to speak.

Hopefully in that book, through my dictation and through
Ruburt's and Joseph's experiences,

The reader could see the greater dimensions that touch ordinary
living, and sense the psyche's magic.

When you are in touch with your psyche, you experience direct
knowledge.

Direct knowledge is comprehension.

When you are dreaming, you are experiencing direct knowledge
about yourself or about the world.

You are comprehending your own being in a different way.

When you are reading a book, you are experiencing indirect
knowledge that may or may not lead to comprehension.

Comprehension itself exists whether or not you have the words —

Or even the thoughts — to express it.

You may comprehend the meaning of a dream without understanding it at all in verbal terms.

Your ordinary thoughts may falter, or slip and slide around your inner comprehension without ever really coming close to expressing it.

The Nature of the Psyche Chapter 3: Session 762, December 15, 1975

The first important step is to realize that your beliefs about reality are just that—

Beliefs ABOUT reality and not necessarily attributes of reality.

You must make a clear distinction between you and your beliefs.

You must then realize that your beliefs are physically materialized.

What you believe to be true in your experience IS true.

To change the physical effect, you must change the original belief—

While being quite aware that for a time physical materializations of the old beliefs may still hold.

If you completely understand what I am saying, however, your new beliefs will—and quickly—begin to show themselves in your experience.

But you must not be concerned for their emergence, for THIS brings up the fear that the new ideas will not materialize,

And so this negates your purpose.

The Nature of Personal Reality, Session 621

The span of a god's love can perhaps equally hold within its
vision the existences of all individuals

At one time in an infinite loving glance that beholds each person,
seeing each with all his or her peculiar characteristics and
tendencies.

Such a god's glance would delight in each person's difference
from each other person.

This would not be a blanket love, a soupy porridge of a glance in
which individuality melted,

But a love based on a full understanding of each individual.

The emotion of love brings you closest to an understanding of
the nature of All That Is.

NotP Chapter 5: Session 774, May 3, 1976 — with Jairon Guerrero Cuesta.

You are dealing with the spacious intellect, the KNOWER. That
'knower' (the inner self) is instantly aware of all of your needs,

And is the portion of the universe that is personally disposed in
your direction,

Because its energies FORM your own person.

That protection always couches your existence.

It means that you live 'in a state of grace.'

When you realize this, then you can accept seeming setbacks, or
seeming contradictions, with a calm detached air,

Realizing that such factors appear as they do only in the light of your present intellectual knowledge—

A knowledge that must be limited to current events—

And that in the larger picture known to you AT OTHER LEVELS, such seeming contradictions,

Or seemingly unfortunate situations, or whatever, will be seen to be to your advantage.

You do not have all the facts, you see, at that intellectual level,

So if you base all of your judgments—

ALL of your judgments—at that level alone, then you can be quite shortsighted.

We are dealing with the psychology of EXPERIENCE, however, so you yourselves alter the situation according to your own reactions.

If you feel threatened by certain situations, and lacking protection,

Then you will take certain steps that might not be taken otherwise,

So your actions are vastly different according to whether or not you REALIZE that you are indeed being protected.

If you build up feelings of threat, then at your level you also react to those.

The protection exists, but in such cases you do not allow yourselves to take full advantage of it.

Dreams, "Evolution," and Value Fulfillment, Vol. 2, Session 922

The self that sits in class is not the self that wonders in a dream state,

And the self that wonders in a dream state is, my dear friends,

Far more educated than the self that sits in the classroom.

The self you call yourself, what does it know?

To whom must it listen?

The self that you call yourself knows relatively little.

It is perhaps 16 years old.

Indeed, the inner identity knows, and the inner identity knows that it knows.

All of you are on a threshold.

Uncounted millions have been at that threshold.

Those of you who would change your world, then I tell you, listen:

For if you would change your world you must listen to the voice within yourself.

You must examine your own dreams.

You must inspect the innermost portions of yourself,

And from this indeed shall you be resurrected.

I am no beady-eyed spirit.

I am no granddaddy longlegs of the spirit world.

I have simply lived before within your system and on your planet.

Unless you have read the material, it does me little good to go deeply into any specificproblems or questions,

Since you will not have the background for this.

The only message I can give you clearly is that you must develop your own abilities.

You must probe into the intuitive self, for you will find much knowledge there.

Books will help you, but the greater knowledge is buried within the layers of the self.

You all have abilities, and you all have liabilities.

Both of these come from past experiences in other lives.

The inner portions of your personality know the details of your past lives.

The abilities that you have now have been developed in past lives.

Those problems which you cannot solve on a psychic and mental level,

You will have to solve in the physical system.

The Early Sessions Book 7 Seth's Lecture to Pat [Norelli's] Boston High School Class March 25, 1967

Now I am emphasizing the issue of hate in this chapter on reincarnation because its results can be so disastrous.

A man who hates always believes himself justified.

He never hates anything that he believes to be good.

He thinks he is being just, therefore, in his hatred,

But the hatred itself forms a very strong claim that will follow him throughout his lives,

Until he learns that only the hatred itself is the destroyer.

I would like to make it clear that there is nothing to be gained, either, by hating hatred.

You fall into the same trap.

What is needed is a basic trust in the nature of vitality,

And faith that all elements of experience are used for a greater good,

Whether or not you can perceive the way in which 'evil' is transmuted into creativity.

What you love will also be a part of your experience in this life and others.

Seth Speaks, Session 550

All of existence and consciousness is interwoven.

Only when you think of the soul as something different, separate, and therefore closed, are you led to consider a separate god –

A personality that seems to be apart from creation.
All That Is is a part of creation, but more than what creation is.

There are pyramid gestalts of being impossible to describe,

Whose awareness includes knowledge and experience of what

would seem to be to you a vast number of other realities.

In the terms of which I am speaking for your benefit, their present might, for example, include the life and death of your planet in a moment of their "time."

Seth Two's existence is at the outside fringes of one such galaxy of consciousness.

When Seth Two speaks,

Ruburt initially is aware of the following:

His consciousness strains upward, following an inner psychic pathway,

An energized funnel, until quite simply it can go no further.

It seems to him that his consciousness goes out of his body through an invisible pyramid whose open top stretches far up into space.

Here he seems to make contact with impersonal symbols whose message is somehow automatically translated into words.

That point actually represents a warp in dimensions,

A place between systems that has far more to do with energy and psychological reality than it has to do with space, for space is meaningless.

I am almost always present as a translator at such times.

My knowledge of both realities is necessary for the communication.

SS 589

Individuals can go from psychologist to psychologist, from self-therapy to self-therapy, always with the same question: 'What is wrong?'

The question itself becomes a format through which experience is seen,

And itself represents one of the main reasons for all limitations, physical, psychic or spiritual.

At one point or another, the individual ceased concentrating upon what was RIGHT in certain personal areas,

And began to focus upon and magnify specific 'lacks.'

With all good intentions, then, various solutions are looked for,

But all based upon the premise that something is WRONG.

If such a practice is continued,

The concentration upon negatives can gradually bleed out into other previously unblemished areas of experience.

Take your break—and mark this session well.

The Nature of Personal Reality, Session 657

Now: All of your so-called pasts exist within you now,

And you can recapture your memories and discover what they are. You are not imprisoned in time unless you believe that you are,

And there is nothing more important than belief.

If you believe that you exist only within the context of this life,

That you are born only to death and annihilation

Then you will not use your freedoms in this existence.

You deny their abilities when they show themselves,

Yet no one forces this bondage upon you but yourself.

To understand your multidimensional self is to use it.

Seth Speaks The Eternal Validity of the Soul

APPENDIX: ESP CLASS SESSION

The Holy Roman Empire united a civilization under one
religious idea,

But the true brotherhood of man can be expressed only by allowing
the freedom of man's thought under the banner of cooperation;

And only this will result in the fulfillment of the species,

With developments of consciousness that in your terms were
latent from the beginning.

The 'Unknown' Reality, Vol. 1, Session 681

Seth on "the Poet and the Artist".

The two of you thought of yourselves specifically as a writer - or
rather a poet – and an artist before our sessions began.

I would like to clear up some important points.

You identified, primarily now, as a poet and an artist because
those designations, up to that time, seemed most closely to fit
your abilities and temperaments.

Ruburt's writing set him apart.

Your paintings set you apart.

These were recognizable, tangible proof of creativity. You therefore identified with elements, characteristics, and traditions that seemed to suit you best.

To some extent you had your own niches, recognizable by society even if they were relatively unusual.

You did not know that there was a deeper, older, or richer tradition - a more ancient heritage –

To which you belonged, because you found no hint of it in your society.

It seemed at different times since our sessions began that there were disruptive conflicts.

For example: Was Rupert a writer or was he a psychic?

Were you an artist, or weren't you?

What about the writing you did - both for our books, and the writing that you sometimes plan to do on your own?

Those kinds of conflicts can only exist in a society in which the entire concept of creativity is segmented,

In which the creative processes are often seen as inner assembly lines leading to specific products:

A society in which the very nature of creativity itself is largely ignored unless it's "products" serve specific ends.

Ruburt was correct in his introductory notes (for Mass Events) today - about the poet's long-forgotten abilities, and his role.

Ruburt has been a poet all of the time in the most profound meaning of that term.

For the poet did not simply string words together,

But sent out a syntax of consciousness using rhythm and the voice, rhyme and refrain

As methods to form steps up which his own consciousness could rush.

Early artists hoped to understand the very nature of creativity itself as they tried to mimic earth's forms.

Poetry and painting were both functional in ways that I will describe in our next book (humorously, elaborately casual), and "esthetic,"

But poetry and painting have always involved primarily man's attempt to understand himself and his world.

The original function of art - meaning poetry and painting here specifically - have been largely forgotten.

The true artists in those terms was always primarily - in your terms again - a psychic or a mystic.

His specific art was both his method of understanding his own creativity and a way of exploring the vast creativity of the universe –

And also served as a container or showcase that displayed his knowledge as best he could.

That is the heritage that both of you follow, and have followed faithfully.

It has an honored tradition.

Also involved is, as Ruburt correctly picked up from me, a group of accomplishments that we will call the psychological arts.

You are involved in those also.

I want you to specifically understand that there is and can be no conflict, for example,

Between your writing and painting, for in the most basic of ways they represent different methods of exploring the meaning and the source of creativity itself.

The sessions I give you, in usual terms, are a new extension of that creativity –

But again, that extension has an ancient heritage.

Your own writing, of course, is art.

It is also a method of perceiving and understanding creativity.

It is a method of learning that redoubles upon itself,

And you are uniquely equipped to discover comprehensions from a standpoint that is most unusual.

Explore, for example, your own feelings towards me:

Whether or not they have changed through the years, how much I seem to be myself, or part Jane, or part Ruburt, or part you, or part Joseph, or whatever.

Realizing that you are in the position you wanted to be [in],

And realizing that your abilities are not in conflict with each other, nor you with them,

Will automatically fulfill and develop all of those abilities, in a new kind of overall creativity that is itself beyond specifics.

Now: When Rupert begins to trust himself, as he has, the physical (arthritic) armor loosens.

The creative abilities become even more available, hence his new creativity,

And the new physical steps he has taken. They all go together.

He believed in the specific nature of the creative self,

So that it would only be trusted in certain areas.

He believed he needed strong mental barriers as well as physical ones, set up against his own spontaneity.

He is beginning to understand that the spontaneous and creative aspects of personality are the life-giving ones.

They can and must be trusted.

He knows now he does not have to slow down, and that relaxation leads to motion.

-DEaVF1, Preface by Seth, Private Session, September 13, 1979, p108 to 110.

If you remember that beneath all, each unit of consciousness is aware of the position of each other unit,

And that these units form ALL physical matter,

Then perhaps you can intuitively follow what I mean, for whatever knowledge man attains,

Whatever experience any one person accumulates,

Whatever arts or sciences you produce, all such information is instantly perceived at other levels of activity

BY EACH OF THE OTHER UNITS OF CONSCIOUSNESS that compose physical reality

—

Whether those units form the shape of a rock, a raindrop, an apple, a cat, a frog or a shoe.

Dreams, "Evolution," and Value Fulfillment, Session 890

The Medicine World Is Slippery Slope

Your medical technology may help you 'conquer' one disease
after another—

Some in fact CAUSED by that same technology—

And you will feel very efficient as you do heart transplants,

As you fight one virus after another.

But all of this will do nothing except to allow people to die, perhaps,

Of OTHER diseases still 'unconquered.'

People will die when they are ready to, following inner dictates
and dynamics.

A person ready to die WILL, despite any medication.

A person who wants to live will seize upon the tiniest hope, and
respond.

The dynamics of health have nothing to do with inoculations.

They reside in the consciousness of each being.

In your terms they are regulated by emotions, desires, and thoughts.

The "Unknown" Reality, Vol. 1, Session 703

You create your physical image and your world.

If anything in that physical image or world needs changing,

The change must first be made in the atmosphere of the inner self.
For this projection of inner into outer is automatic.

Understanding the processes involved is of great benefit.

The physical self SEEMS to react to physical stimuli.

Actually, of course, it is reacting to its own reality, projected outward.

The objects in the physical universe are but symbols to express other realities existing within private realms.

The inner will always be projected outward within your system.

If, for example, a letter comes to you bearing good news, and you react to the letter with high spirits,

Then you should understand that the high spirits existed first,

And created the materialization of the letter within the physical systems,

Through the multilayered and complicated reactions that bind together the physical system.

If an annoying letter arrives and you react to it negatively,

The negative quality preceded the letter and caused it to materialize in your system.

Now you do not force someone to write such a letter, you see.

You broadcast the negative feelings, which were then picked up by whomever was ready to receive them, for their own purposes.

I cannot emphasize too strongly that this is automatic.

The Early Sessions, Book 8, Session 334

When you are in a position of safety, you do not help by pretending that you are not safe,

Or by taking upon yourself the agony of others.

Your reality, when you are safe, is a reality of security.

From that framework you have strength, validity, grace, exuberance—

Additional energy that you can send out to touch the hearts and the realities of other people.

If you become so frightened of realities that are not your own;

If you take upon yourselves tragedies that do not exist in your reality, in your moment;

Then you weaken your position and you weaken the position of those you THINK YOU are helping.

You look about you and you see only hopelessness and helplessness.

YOU ORGANIZE YOUR REALITY ACCORDING TO THE TRAGEDIES OF THE NEWSPAPERS!

Conversations With Seth, Vol. 2, Chapter 20

Now let me give you a brief example of a core belief.

It is a blanket belief: human nature is inherently evil.

This is a core belief.

About it will spring events that only serve to reinforce it.

Experiences—both personal and global—will come into the

perception of a person who holds this belief, that will only serve
to deepen it further.

From all the available physical data of newspapers, television,
letters and private communication,

He or she will concentrate only upon those issues that 'prove'
that point.

Suspicion of others will grow, to say nothing about the individual's
personal distrust.

The belief will reach into the most intimate areas of his or her life,

And finally no evidence will SEEM to be available to disprove it.

Another more personal core belief: 'My life is worthless.

What I do is meaningless.'

Now a person who holds such an idea will ordinarily not recognize
it as an invisible belief.

Instead he or she may emotionally feel that life has no meaning,

That individual action is meaningless,

That death is annihilation;

And connected to this will be a conglomeration of subsidiary
beliefs that deeply affect the family involved,

And all those with whom such a person comes in contact.
In writing down your list of personal beliefs, therefore, leave
nothing out.

Examine the list as though it belonged to someone else.

I did not want to imply that you make a list of specifically negative ideas, however.

It is of supreme importance that you recognize the existence of joyful beliefs,

And take into consideration those elements of your own experience with which you have had success.

I want you to capture that feeling of accomplishment, and to translate it,

Or transfer it, to areas in which you have had difficulty.

But you must remember that the ideas exist first and the experience physically follows.

You make your own reality.

I cannot say this too often.

The Nature of Personal Reality, Session 617

To understand what the larger self is, you must try to imagine yourself in an environment that is not physical.

Not only without physical environment in terms of space and objects

But without the intimate physical environment of the body that now you take so for granted.

Many personalities do not operate in such a manner,

And I am not speaking merely of survival personalities in your terms.

I am speaking in terms of personality gestalts that simply do not operate through matter at all, in your terms,

And whose components are of a psychological variety.

Now you can close your minds to such possibilities,

Or you can open your imagination and inner perceptions and try to perceive them.

You can take a step out of the self that you think you are and the world that you think you inhabit.

Now when your read what I have said, you should have some good ideas for experiments of your own.

Think in terms not only of other personalities,

But of your own personality as it might operate in completely different environments both physical and nonphysical.

As other personalities then have looked into this room,

Then imagine yourself looking into other environments.

Open up your imaginations in this regard

Throw off the shells of habit —

All kinds of habits

In your terms we remember our part in the creation of your universe,

But you are not aware of your part in the creation of other universes into which you also peer.

You are on a journey into awareness.

You are recovering the knowledge and acknowledgment of your own past.

The words you hear are translations.

We do not understand what a room is. We merely use the term.

We peer into a segment of reality.

We did (think) construct it, and we have gone our way.

In your terms, we are very distant.

We have an equivalent of emotions,

But you would not understand them.

You must realize that each reality is unique and precious and a part of the whole.

The whole is contained within any given part lying in the sleep of probability from which it will and already has awakened.

And so will you awaken and so have you awakened

And so even in the trance of physical focus are you already awake to your own greater reality.

You only focus upon a point of ignorance.

Merely turn the focus of your awareness in another direction

And freedom shows itself

And time is seen then as the figurative closed eyelid that deceives you.

In the midst of your dreaming you are awake.

In the midst of your dreaming you are what we are.

You are in other terms, the memory of us,

Yet we are also the memory of you.

I bid you a good evening,

But I want you to watch your conscious thoughts for a different reason this time.

I've told you to watch them in the past to become aware of what you are thinking

And what negative suggestions you are giving yourselves.

But I want you now to watch them to catch your limiting intellectual concepts about your own reality

And what is possible and what is not possible.

For many of these ideas are so a part of your mental furniture

And you do never change the furniture about.

You do not even see it, it is so a part of your mental environment.

So I would like you to listen inward to your own thoughts with this in mind.

You will not open up if you are automatically closing down.

TECS3 ESP Class Session, January 19, 1971 - by Jane Roberts © L. Davies Butts

Man directs his existence through the use of his imagination —

A feat that does distinguish him from the animals.

What connects people and separates them is the power of idea

And the force of imagination.

Patriotism, family loyalty, political affiliations —

The ideas behind these have the greatest practical applications in your world.

You project yourselves into time like children through freely imagining your growth.

You instantly color physical experience and nature itself with the tints of your unique imaginative processes.

Unless you think quite consistently — and deeply —

The importance of the imagination quite escapes you,

And yet it literally forms the world that you experience and the mass world in which you live.

Because man has not understood the characteristics of the world of imagination,

He has thus far always insisted upon turning his myths into historical fact, for he considers the factual world alone as the real one.

A man, literally of flesh and blood, must then prove beyond all doubt that each and every other [human being] survives death —

By dying, of course, and then by rising, physically perceived, into heaven.

Each man does survive death, and each woman (with quiet amusement),

But only such a literal-minded species would insist upon the physical death of a god- man as "proof of the pudding."

A person's private experience happens in the context of his psychological and biological status,

And basically cannot be separated from his religious and philosophical beliefs and sentiments, and his cultural environment and political framework.

All of the issues form together to make a trellis of behavior.

Thorns or roses may grow therein.

That is, the individual will grow outward toward the world, encountering and forming a practical experience,

Traveling outward from his center in almost vine like fashion, forming from the fabric of physical reality

A conglomeration of pleasant or aesthetic, and unpleasant or prickly events.

The vine of experience in this analogy is formed in quite a natural fashion from 'psychic' elements

That are as necessary to psychological experience as sun, air, and water are to plants.

The Individual and the Nature of Mass Events, Session 801

ELIAS: But the intent is a direction that you want to explore within your individual focus.

Your desire is more associated with your personality – you only.

Your intent involves you with your world

And with people and with things,

And your desire is only about you.

In order to become physical, probable events must meet certain conditions, as it were.

They must fall into the proper time and space slots.

There must be a psychological fit also, certain intensities reached in terms of desire, belief, or intent.

By intensity I do not necessarily mean effort, vehement desire, or determined conscious intent.

I mean instead the collection of certain intangible qualities, precisely focused toward physical activity.

The Nature of the Psyche, Session 789

Dreams Came Before Physical Life
And—Life Is A Dream

I am going to end our session, but I have a comment. I have said this before: You are as dead now as you will ever be.

Now, if you understand that remark and think about it you will understand much that is behind what I have said this evening.

[Question:] "Then we are as alive now as we have ever been?"

That is correct - except that in the life in which you are now involved, you are not focusing on the full potential of your vitality.

[Question:]

"Was there a continent of Mu?"

There was.

Now, I tell you to remember your dreams.

In your context I will tell you again not only to remember your dreams,

But to learn to come awake in the middle of them and realize that you can manipulate within them.

You form them.

They are yours, not something thrust upon you in which you are powerless.

[Question. "We are using our existence as the dream?"

What I have said applies to what you just said.

In one context what you call physical reality is a dream,

But in a larger context, it is a dream that you have created.

When you realize that you form it

You come into the memory of your whole self.

And when you realize that you form the events of your life in the same way,

You will learn to take hold of your entire consciousness in whatever aspect it shows itself in this life.

Through all of this, you must realize that you are not powerless.

Remember, also, that this life is a dimension of experience and reality even if it is, in contrast,

A dream in a higher level of reality in which you have your larger consciousness.

Seth Speaks The Eternal Validity of the Soul APPENDIX: ESP CLASS SESSION

Hatred does not exist as a basic psychological structure.

It is, however, the result of psychological manipulation of fear;

And fear is not a basic psychological structure.

The Early Sessions Book 2 Session 75 July 29, 1964

Habitual errors become part of the psychological perspective. Communication between individuals in the psychological perspective is almost exclusively telepathic,

And is picked up early by the young from their parents.

In the beginning, children actually begin their physical construction along lines telepathically received from their parents,

At the same time that they learn their own manipulation in the psychological perspective.

The Early Sessions Book 2 Session 75 July 29, 1964

ELIAS: Your desire is geared in association with your personality in a particular focus,

Therefore, it's very personal to you.

Scientists look for the objective most of all, and clear-cut cause and effect.

They examine what they think of as an impersonal universe.

The universe is however personal first of all.

It is filled with intimate relationships.

It has a subjective rather than an objective basis.

Civilizations do not fall and rise because of weapons, or economies, or technologies.

They rise and fall because of the great sway of emotion and belief.

People do not die of disease.

They die because of emotion and belief,

And because there is subjective rather than objective time for dying.

You live then in a personal universe, in which each being of whatever degree comes personally in contact with space and time,

Alive with meaning,

Alive as a portion of reality that no other being could or can replace.

The Personal Sessions, Book 4, Session 11/19/77

Now before I bid you a fond good evening

Let me tell you that those of you who come to class regularly and gravitate here,

If you have not already discovered this for yourself, are the black sheep of the universe.

You want to go your own way.

You do not want dogma.

You will not be satisfied with hearts and flowers.

It is not an easy way, and all of you know that.

It is past the time for you to be entranced by other personalities including my own.

It is time for you to become entranced with your own personality.

It is time for you to feel independent enough to launch yourselves from your own subjective reality into others;

To emerge, to drop the paraphernalia of all dogma.

Not for new dogma but for new freedom.

Not to substitute one authority for another,

But to allow yourselves the freedom to recognize that the prime authority is All That Is

That resides within you and that speaks with your own voice.

These realities, because of their continuing effects within your system, and their actual transformation of it,
Should be studied thoroughly, for much can be gained in this way.

Like transformations are made by events in your universe upon the dream universe.

Often, again, the dream universe possesses concepts which will, someday, completely transform the history of your field;

But a denial of such concepts as actualities or possibilities within reality, holds these back,

And put off breakthroughs that are sorely needed.

Such developments would mean the releasing and availability of added energy into your field,

That would have endless possibilities in all directions.

Ideas and concepts are nonphysical actualities that attract unaligned energy, and direct and concentrate it.

The dream world exists more closely in that spacious present of which the inner self is so aware.

It is not as involved with camouflage constructions as your own universe,

And its actions are somewhat limited within its own framework.

It might be said then, that in many ways the dream universe

depends upon you to give it expression, in the same manner,

That you also depend upon it to find expression,
Although in this case you have other outlets, and it has few.

The impact of any given dream has physical, chemical,
electromagnetic, psychological and psychic repercussions.

These are also actual and continuing,

And they not only represent a part of your environment in all of
these cases,

But they affect most deeply the ordinary channels of everyday life.

The type of dream, or the types of dreams experienced by any
individual, is determined by many factors.

I am speaking now of the dream experience as it occurs, and not
of the remnant of it that his ego allows him to consciously recall.

As an individual creates his physical image and environment
according to his abilities and defects, and in line with his
expectations and subconscious and inner needs,

So does he create his dreams; and these interact with the outer
environment which he has created.

However, with the ego at rest the individual may allow
communications and dream constructions through, past the ego
barrier, in such a manner that he becomes in some ways free.

If for example, his present expectations are faulty, when the ego
rests he may recreate a time when expectations were high.

The resulting dream will then partially break the circle of poor expectations, with their shoddy physical constructions,

And start such an individual along a more beneficial path.

In other words, such a dream may begin to transform the physical environment through lifting inner expectations.

The Early Sessions Book 3 Session 115 December 16, 1964

The reality, the physical reality, of fire was such a contribution made by the physical universe to the universe of dreams.

Physical man, observing fire, dreamed of it, thereby immeasurably enriching the universe of dreams.

His discovery in the physical universe of domesticating fire was another such contribution to the dream universe.

The universe actively loves itself and all of its parts.

The world loves itself and all of its parts.

It is not true that energy is neutral or indifferent.

Energy is active, positive, propelled by what can almost be called an instantaneous pleasure with itself and its characteristics.

Despite all concepts to the contrary, energy is indeed at its basis, love.

WTH Part One: Chapter 3: March 20, 1984

Now the weapons and the destruction are the obvious things that you see.

The counterparts are not so evident, and yet it is the counterparts that are important.

The self-discipline learned, the control, the compassion that finally is aroused,

And the final and last lesson learned,

The positive desire for creativity and love over destruction and hatred.

When this is learned the reincarnational cycle is finished.

TES9 Session 452 December 2, 1968

ECS4 ESP Class Session, June 15, 1971

It is theoretically possible, for example, for any of you to disperse your consciousness and become a part of any object in the room –

Or to fly apart, to disperse yourself out into space - without leaving your sense of identity.

This is not practical in your terms,

Yet many of you do it to gain refreshment while you are sleeping.

Consciousness by its very characteristics carries the burden of perception.

This is the kind of consciousness you are used to thinking of.

You cannot imagine it without perception in your terms,

And yet consciousness can be vital and alive without your idea of perception.

The last part of that sentence is important.

Seth Speaks The Eternal Validity of the Soul. APPENDIX: ESP CLASS SESSION

And in that once again, your perception, which creates your reality,

Is very influenced by your experiences and your experiences are influenced by what you pay attention to.

Therefore, with those two factors, that definitely colors your perception of any subject.

Now; that doesn't mean that your perception can't change, and it doesn't mean that your perception is absolute.

But it does mean that regardless of those two factors,

Your perception is your reality at any given point.

Elias: Now, my dear scientific friend over there:

Atoms and molecules, minute as they may appear to you, also carry their burden of consciousness and responsibility.

Yet there is a portion of consciousness that can joyfully perceive in a manner that is not dictated by its nature;

It can playfully perceive all creative aspects of its being, without responsibility.

In one manner of speaking the very air about you sings with its own joyful consciousness.

It does not know the same kind of burden of consciousness that often oppresses you.

You are so frightened of death, in your terms, that you dare not turn your consciousness off for one second;

For you fear that if you do indeed, who will be there to turn it back on again.

[Question:] "Is the whole entity involved in this dispersion of consciousness, or just the portion of it we know now?"

It is the way that galaxies form. It is the way that the universe expands, and it is the way that entities form.

Now, that is your answer. Chew that one over for a while.

I am pleased because you are thinking this evening, all of you –

That is what I want you to do.

Ideas have no reality unless you make them your own.

Make friends or enemies of them.

Fight with them or love them but use and experience them, not only with your intellect

But with your feelings.

Seth Speaks The Eternal Validity of the Soul

APPENDIX: ESP CLASS SESSION... TUESDAY, JANUARY 5, 1971 —The Individual and the Nature of Mass Events Part Two: Chapter 4: Session 829, March 22, 1978

You are a part of All That Is—of all the nature that you know and experience, of the world that you know,

And even a part of the world that you know that you do not like. If you rip off the wing of a fly, you are yourself less.

If you purposefully, now, or with malice, step upon an ant,

Then to the extent of your malice you step upon yourself all unknowing.

Violence will always be used creatively,

BUT IF YOU DO NOT UNDERSTAND THIS—

And at your present rate of development you do not—

Then any violence is violence against yourself.

This applies to each of you, for when you think in terms of violence you think in terms of malice or aggression.

Despite all man does, he cannot really work any destruction—

But while he BELIEVES in destruction, then to that extent he minimizes what he is, and must work harder to use creativity.

Dreams, "Evolution," and Value Fulfillment, Vol. 2, Session 933 Notes

A modern Western physician—granted, with the greatest discomfiture—

Will inform his patient that he is about to die,

Impressing upon him that his situation is hopeless,

And yet will react with scorn and loathing

When he reads that a voodoo practitioner has put a curse upon some innocent victim.

In your time, medical men, again with great superiority, look at primitive cultures

And harshly judge the villagers they think are held in the sway of witch doctors or voodooism;

And yet through advertisement and organization, YOUR doctors impress upon each individual in your culture

That you must have a physical examination every six months or you will get cancer;

That you must have medical insurance because you WILL become ill.

In many instances, therefore, modern physicians are inadequate witch doctors who have forgotten their craft—

Hypnotists who no longer believe in the power of healing,

And whose suggestions bring about other diseases that are diagnosed in advance.

You are told what to look for;

You are as cursed—far more—as any native in a tiny village,

Only you lose breasts, appendixes, and other portions of your anatomy.

The doctors follow their own ideas, of course,

And in that system they see themselves as completely justified— as humane.

In the medical field, as in no other, you are faced directly with the full impact of your beliefs,

For doctors are not the healthiest, but the least healthy.

They fall prey to the beliefs to which they so heartily subscribe.

Their concentration is upon disease, not health.

The Nature of Personal Reality, Session 659

These inborn leanings or attitudes can roughly be translated as follows:

1. I am an excellent creature, a valuable part of the universe in which I exist.

2. My existence enriches all other portions of life, even as my own being is enhanced by the rest of creation.

3. It is good, natural, and safe for me to grow and develop and use my abilities,

And by so doing I also enrich all other portions of life.

Next: I am eternally couched and supported by the universe of which I am a part,

And I exist whether or not that existence is physically expressed.

Next:
By nature, I am a good deserving creature, and all of life's elements and parts are also of good intent.

And next: All of my imperfections,

And all of the imperfections of other creatures, are redeemed in the greater scheme of
the universe in which I have my being.

Those attitudes are inbred in the smallest microscopic portions of the body

A part of each atom and cell and organ,

And they serve to trigger all of the body's responses that promote growth and fulfillment.

You Were Born Loving

Infants are not born with an inbred FEAR of their environment, or of other creatures.

They are instead immersed in feeling that their needs will be met, and that the universe is well-disposed toward them.

They feel a part of their environment.

They do not come into life with feelings of rage, or anger, and basically they do not experience doubts or fears.

The inborn leanings and attitudes that we have been discussing could IDEALLY remain with you for the rest of your life,

Leading you to express your abilities, and finding fulfillment as your knowledge expands through experience.

The same feelings and beliefs should also IDEALLY help you die with a sense of safety,support and assurance.

While these inbred psychological supports never leave you entirely,

They are often diminished by beliefs encountered later in life,

That serve to undermine the individual's sense of safety and well-being.

The Way Toward Health, January 27, 1984 4:08 Friday - by Jane Roberts © L. Davies

But
You are born loving. You are born compassionate.

You are born curious about yourself and your world.

Those attributes also belong to natural law.

You are born knowing that you possess a unique, intimate sense of being that is itself,

And that seeks its own fulfillment, and the fulfillment of others.

You are born seeking the actualization of the ideal.

You are born seeking to add value to the quality of life,

To add characteristics, energies, abilities to life that only you can individually contribute to the world,

And to attain a state of being that is uniquely yours, while adding to the value fulfillment of the world.

NOME, Ch 9, S862

ELIAS: Because stress trumps everything.

ANN: Mm.

ELIAS: In that, let me say to you that there are two systems in your body that affect everything in your body,

Everything, literally, and that would be your circulatory system and your nervous system.

And stress is an expression of your nervous system,

And therefore it affects every aspect of your body.

Everything. Even your teeth.

ANN: Wow.

Therefore, in that, it's ultimately important to look at that and address to that,

And to recognize that when you move in directions of expressing constant stress – and don't be fooled,

I am expressing that directly to him –

In the idea that you're not always working

Or you're not always expressing that stress.

Don't fool yourself.

It's become so automatic and so familiar that you don't even recognize when you're doing it,

AND it's one of those situations in which it's so familiar that you wouldn't recognize it until it's not there.

ELIAS:

Because it's so important to you

And it's so much a part of your life that you look for it.

And in that, it's not that you're simply moving in a direction of wishful thinking.

There's a difference between knowing that anything is possible

And then looking for that magic in everything,

Which is what you do,

And an individual that is not looking for magic in everything

But is simply wishful thinking

ANN: Ah. Okay. Got ya.

ELIAS: —

Who doesn't actually want to DO anything.

And this is a significant difference also, is that there are some people that are wishful thinking,

And in that, they don't want to implement any actions.

They don't want to do anything.

They want magic to simply appear.

That that's part of their definition of magic,

Is that it should simply appear from nowhere and from nothing.

Therefore, they aren't actually doing anything that is magical.

I have told you that if you do not like the state of your world,

It is yourselves that you must change, individually and en masse.

This is the only way that change will be effected.

Here Seth stared at Carl and said,

If your generation or any generation effects a change, this is the only way it will be done.

It is wrong to curse a flower and wrong to curse a man.

It is wrong not to hold any man in honor, and it is wrong to ridicule any man.

You must honor yourselves and see within yourselves the spirit of eternal vitality.

If you do not do this, then you destroy what you touch.

And you must honor each other individual also, because in him is the spark of eternal vitality.

When you curse another, you curse yourselves, and the curse returns to you.

When you are violent, the violence returns.

I speak to you because yours is the opportunity [to better world conditions] and yours is the time.

Do not fall into the old ways that will lead you precisely into the world that you fear.

When every young man refuses to go to war, you will have peace.

As long as you fight for gain and greed, there will be no peace.

As long as one person commits acts of violence for the sake of peace, you will have war.

Unfortunately, it is difficult to imagine that all the young men in all of the countries will refuse to go to war at the same time.

And so you must work out the violence that violence has wrought.

Within the next hundred years that time may come.

Remember, you do not defend any idea with violence.

There is no man who hates but that that hatred is reflected outward and made physical.

And there is no man who loves but that that love is reflected outward and made physical.

The Seth Material, Chapter 18

ELIAS:

Outside of physical realities, which incorporate that aspect of separation

Because it's necessary

Because you're creating physical manifestations.

Anything physical creates an element of separation,

And the more you have, the more you create physically,

The more separation there is

And the more separation you perceive as, in a manner of speaking, normal – because that's what you know.

It's a matter of the more physical manifestations you create or the more complex your physical reality is,

Not only the more separation you create

But you create a more complex perception,

Which is weaving in more and more separation.

But outside of physical realities, there is none of that.

There is no perception.

There is no creation of physical manifestations

And therefore there is no separation of essences.

You always recognize one package of psychological reality as 'you.'

In basic terms you are always arriving by a kind of instantaneous mail into that package, however.

You are unknowingly immersed in and a part of pure energy, being newly created in each moment,

So that the energy of your atoms and molecules and of your physical universal system is being replenished at every conceivable moment.

Your psyche is being drawn back into itself, into All That Is,

And 'out of itself' into your individuation, in psychological pulses of activity.

The Nature of the Psyche, Session 787

The progression through the centuries would be far more noticeable if you knew all the facts.

There is one aspect here that I have not previously mentioned:

Man was not allowed to play with the more dangerous toys until certain evidence was given that he had gained some control.

This does not mean that he could not have destroyed the world he knew.

It simply meant that such destruction was not inevitable.

You do not give a child a loaded gun if you are certain he is going to shoot himself or his neighbor.

Now:

The weapons and destruction are the obvious things that you see.

The counterparts are not so evident, and yet it is the counterparts that are important:

The self-discipline learned, the control, the compassion that finally is aroused, and the final and last lesson learned—

The positive desire for creativity and love over destruction and hatred.

When this is learned, the reincarnational cycle is finished.

This is some of the most important material that I have given you,

For you have wondered about the purpose (of consciousness within this system),

And have been able often only to see one small speck of time and space.

The Seth Material, Appendix, Session 452

You have an ego because you are conscious.

The ego is a responsive part of yourself.

It is not a stupid relative to be shunted out of the way.

And yet, you look at it constantly and you say:

"You stupid thing, you know nothing. Out you go.

Let my pure unconscious well up and give me the answers.

And so, your life operates according to your belief.

And, since you believe you do not have the answers,

It does not seriously occur to you to listen to yourself.

You listen to your animus or your anima or your shadow.

But, try listening to the self that you are, in all your remarkable unity.

And then, the answers ARE. And, they are a part of you.

And, for heaven's sake, do not look so serious.

When you read Oversoul Seven, then identify yourself with "Seven"

And have some fun with yourselves, for a change.

And, when you are thinking of finding the answers to the universe,

Do not expect groans and sadness and deep shadows of any kind.

Listen to a raindrop as it falls.

And, listen within yourselves to your own gentle voice.

And, smile at yourselves -- with yourselves.

Seth Audio Collection #41 December 12, 1972

The spacious present does not contradict the existence of durability,

But durability does not imply the existence of a future as you conceive it.

The spacious present, while existing spontaneously,

while happening simultaneously, still contains within it qualities of duration.

TES2 Session 44 April 15, 1964

In certain terms, science and religion are both dealing with the idea of an objectively created universe.

Either God 'made it,' or physical matter, in some unexplained manner, was formed after an initial explosion of energy,

And consciousness emerged from that initially dead matter in a way yet to be explained.

Instead, consciousness FORMED matter. As I have said before, each atom and molecule has its own consciousness.

Consciousness and matter and energy are one,

But consciousness INITIATES the transformation of energy into matter.

In those terms, the 'beginning' of your universe was a triumph in the expansion of consciousness,

As it learned to translate itself into physical form.

The universe emerged into actuality IN THE SAME WAY,

But to a different degree, that any idea emerges from what you
think of as subjectivity into physical expression.

Dreams, "Evolution," and Value Fulfillment, Vol. 1, Session 882

Some people do not question their religious beliefs but accept
them as fact.

Others find it comparatively easy to recognize such inner
assumptions when they appear in a religious context

But are quite blind to them in other areas.

It is far simpler to recognize your own beliefs in regard to religion,
politics, or similar subjects,

Than it is to pinpoint your deepest beliefs about yourself

And who and what you are — particularly in relationship with
your own life.

Many individuals are completely blind to their own beliefs about
themselves and the nature of reality.

Your own conscious thoughts will give you excellent clues.

Often you will find yourself refusing to accept certain thoughts
that come to your mind

because they conflict with other usually accepted ideas.

The Nature of Personal Reality Part One: Chapter 2: Session 614, September 13, 1972

Many people believe fervently that with approaching age they
will meet a steady, disastrous deterioration

In which the senses and the mind will be dull,

And the body, stricken with disease, will lose all of its vigor and aging.

Many young people believe such nonsense,

And therefore THEY SET THEMSELVES UP to meet the very conditions they fear.

The mind grows wiser with age WHEN IT IS ALLOWED TO DO SO.

There is even an acceleration of thought and inspiration,

Much like that experienced in the adolescent years, that suddenly brings a new understanding to the aged individual,

And provides an impetus that should help the person to achieve greater comprehension

A comprehension that should QUELL all fears of death.

The Way Toward Health, Chapter 5, April 9, 1984

If you will think this sentence over, then you will realize,

That those who worship do no real honour to the object of their worship.

For upon that object, they place all of their hopes, all of their dreams, all of their inadequacies, and all of the responsibility for their lives;

And even a god - a sane god - would refuse to accept such worship.

The god would understand also the nature of the universe,

And the nature of playful creativity,

And would know that such a worship is - at it's base now, at it's base —

A denial of the very vitality of life.

When the old answers and the old organizations no longer have
any meaning to the individual;

When he can find reflected in the official answers none of his
own questions;

Then the individual rises up from within itself;

And, as once this civilization was born, so shall others be born in
the same way.

And so always, from within itself does the race then go within its
psyche for newer revelations;

Newer in that they are fresher to the source of itself —

They have not been worn away by distortions

And so in-turned by organizations that their meaning has
become lost.

Conversations with Seth, 25th Anniversary Edition, book one, chapter one, by Susan M Watkins, (C)

Religion's Not All Bad In The Bag Of Framework 2

The exterior religious dramas are of course imperfect representations of the ever- unfolding interior spiritual realities.

The various personages, the gods and prophets within religious history –

These absorb the mass inner projections thrown out by those inhabiting a given time span.
Such religious dramas focus, direct, and, hopefully, clarify aspects of inner reality that need to be physically represented.

These do not only appear within your own system.

Many are also projected into other systems of reality.

Religion per se, however, is always the external facade of inner reality.
The primary spiritual existence alone gives meaning to the physical one.

In the most real terms, religion should include all of the pursuits of man in his search for the nature of meaning and truth.

Spirituality cannot be some isolated, specialized activity or characteristic.

I want to point out that faith is not all that unusual, but a prime element in your life.

You can have faith that you will be ill.

This should be obvious, because for example there are healthy people also, with no evidence of any disease,

Who have utter faith that disease is hidden within them, or swiftly approaching.

It is, therefore, quite to everyone's advantage that Framework 2 is not neutral.

Faith in a creative, fulfilling, desired end, sustained faith, literally draws from

Framework 2 all of the necessary ingredients,
All of the elements however staggering in number, arranges all the details, and then inserts into Framework 1

The impulses, dreams, chance meetings, motivations, or whatever is necessary so that the desired end

Then falls into place as a completed pattern.

You must begin somewhere, so you state your purpose clearly in Framework 1.

Then you have the faith that the event will be brought to pass.

Your own creative, abilities are instantly mobilized in that direction.

Your behavior in Framework 1 must automatically change.

The ways and the means, however, cannot be questioned,

For they will come about from a greater source of knowledge than you consciously possess.

I am trying to give you some kind of an overall picture so that you can make your own helpful comparisons, and understand more thoroughly what is involved.

Often I will use examples that do not involve health,

For you can apply them to health yourselves even more effectively,

For you will make your OWN connections.

The entire pattern of your lives is taken into consideration in Framework 2.

There is no need for bargaining.
Ruburt does not have to fear that he must give up some creativity for physical freedom,
FOR THE TWO GO HAND IN HAND.

Framework 2 contains all the dreams, plans, and thoughts of all human beings of any time.

THERE, the spacious present is operative.

THERE, it makes no difference if you have had an undesirable physical condition for a day or a lifetime.

THERE, you are not impeded by the past.

If your beliefs in Framework 1 make you assign great power to the past, then you impede your progress.

I have said many times that spontaneity knows its own order, and I am speaking of true spontaneity.

I say this because often anger, for example, may seem spontaneous—

And may be—but is more often the explosive, finally forced expression of reactions long withheld or repressed.

True spontaneity however comes directly from Framework 2,

And behind it are endless patterns of orderliness and complexity that are beyond your conscious Framework 1 comprehension.

The small instance of Ruburt's doing the dishes this morning is a case in point –

And THAT emerged as the result of those abilities mentioned in our last session.

This morning, for the first time in well over a year, at the very least, Jane spontaneously decided to do the dishes after breakfast WHILE STANDING UP AT THE SINK.

Such an impulse, followed, will lead to its own performance the means will be given.

Before, Ruburt's fear prevented him from even acknowledging many such impulses to act.

Ruburt's assessment of your dream and its conditions is another case in point.

The inner organizations immediately trigger all the necessary actions required, from Framework 2.

This applies to any issue – but again, your creative abilities, used on behalf of Ruburt's physical condition will give him a normally cooperating body.

Each improvement is to be considered as a significant piece of a puzzle being put together,

Even though you may not see any connection between one improvement or another.

Again, you should not double check at every moment.

As Ruburt's Cézanne simply came out of nowhere, so will his
complete flexibility.

It is not simply that in Framework 2 there is no resistance to
creative, fulfilling, natural, life-seeking desires,

But that the medium of Framework 2 itself automatically adds
its own MAGNIFICATION to them,
So that ONCE YOU GET ROLLING, so to speak, the acceleration
is spectacular, in whatever issue is involved.

(We've already had hints of this.)
The entire Cézanne book was inherent in the first page.

Ruburt's faith and habits allowed the initial impulse its freedom,

And that impulse, expressed, carried within it the means of its
own fulfillment, and the book unfolded.

The Personal Sessions, book 4, Deleted Session October 24, 1977 - by Jane Roberts © L. Davies Butts

The value climate of psychological reality can be likened to an
ocean in which all consciousness has its being.

There are multitudinous levels that can be plunged into with
various life forms, diverse and alien,

But nevertheless interconnected and dependent one upon the other.

TES2 Session 45 April 20, 1964

You always know what you are doing, even when you do not
realize it.

Your eyes know it sees, though it cannot see itself except through
the use of reflection.

In the same way the world as you see it is a reflection of what you are, a reflection not in glass but in three-dimensional reality.

You project your thoughts, feelings, and expectations outward, then you perceive them as the outside reality.

When it seems to you that others are observing you, you are observing yourself from the standpoint of your own projections.

Seth, Nature of Personal Reality

Physically speaking, man's 'purpose' is to help enrich the QUALITY of existence in all of its dimensions.

Spiritually speaking, his 'purpose' is to understand the qualities of love and creativity,

To intellectually and psychically understand the sources of his being,

And to lovingly create other dimensions of reality of which he is presently unaware.

In his thinking, in the quality of his thoughts, in their motion, he is indeed experimenting with a unique and a new kind of reality,

Forming other subjective worlds

Which will in their turn grow into consciousness and song,

Which will in their turn flower from a dream dimension into other ones.

Man is learning to create new worlds.

In order to do so he has taken on many challenges.

Dreams, "Evolution," and Value Fulfillment, Vol. 1, Session 901

You are being allowed freedom within limits.

The human race is a stage through which various forms of consciousness travel.

The ideals keep the race pointed in beneficial directions.

Thoughts and emotions form the basis.
You learn by seeing these turn into physical reality.

You may be killed by what you have created.

If so the lesson is doubly learned.

Before you can be allowed into systems of reality that are more extensive and open,

You must first learn to handle energy, and see, through physical materializations,

The concrete result of thought and emotion.

As a child forms mud pies from dirt, so you form your civilization out of thoughts and emotions,

And then see what you have created, and you must deal with it on its terms.

In other systems energy is more directly felt, more extensive.

Consciousness has much more freedom in its utilization.

The lessons must be properly learned before such responsibility.

It is not that you must be taught not to destroy, for destruction does not actually exist.

It is that you must be taught and trained to create responsibly.

The Early Sessions, Book 9, Session 446

Only true compassion and love will lead to an understanding of the nature of good,

And only these concepts will serve to annihilate the erroneous and distortive concepts of evil.

The simple fact is that as long as you believe in the concept of evil,

It is a reality in your system, and you will always find it manifested.

Your belief in it will, therefore, seem highly justified.

If you carry this concept through succeeding generations, through reincarnations, then you add to its reality.

Seth Speaks, Session 550

Your scientists seem to have the strange idea that you can UNDERSTAND a reality by destroying it;

That you can perceive the life mechanism of an animal by killing it;

Or that you can examine a phenomenon best by separating yourself from it.

So, often you attempt to examine the nature of the brain in man by destroying the brains of animals,

By separating portions of the animal brain from its components, isolating them,

And tampering with the overall integrity of both the animal in question and of your own spiritual processes.

By this I mean that each such attempt puts you more out of context, so to speak, with yourself and your environment, and other species.

Period.

While you may 'learn' certain so called facts,

You are driven still further away from any great knowledge, because the so called facts stand in your way.

You do NOT as yet understand the uniqueness of consciousness.

The "Unknown" Reality, Vol. 1, Session 701

As I have said before, your thoughts are reality.

They directly affect your body.

It seems that you are highly civilized people because you put your ill into hospitals where they can be cared for.

What you do, of course, is to isolate a group of people who are filled with negative beliefs about illness.

The contagion of beliefs spreads.

Patients are obviously in hospitals BECAUSE THEY ARE ILL.

The sick and their doctors both work on that principle.

Stimuli pertaining to health is effectively blocked in such organizations.

The ill are gathered together and denied all of their normal and natural conditions,

Including the compensating motivations that ALONE would

sometimes be enough to RESTORE HEALTH if given time.

This isolation would be unfortunate enough without the application of drugs meant to help, but often given without understanding.

Loved ones are permitted to visit the sick on but certain occasions, so those who wish them well in the strongest terms, who are closest to them and who love them,

Are efficiently prevented from exerting any natural constructive behavior.

For all practical purposes the ill are put into prison.

They are forced to concentrate upon their condition.

All of this applies quite apart from any other dehumanizing effects, such as overcrowded conditions, the denial of human privacy, and often the negation of dignity.

The individual is made to feel powerless, at the mercy of doctors or nurses

Who often do not have the time or energy to be personable,

Or to explain his [or her] condition in terms that he can understand.

The patient is therefore forced to transfer his own sense of power to others,

Which further deepens his misery;

This in turn reinforces the sense of powerlessness that initiated his condition.

Furthermore, the natural elements of sun, air, and earth are refused him.

The stability of familiarity is withdrawn.

Now with your set of beliefs you are indeed more or less obligated to go to hospitals in severe conditions.

I am not saying here that many doctors and nurses do not try their best to promote healing, and certainly healings occur –

But they do so DESPITE the system and not because of it.

In many cases the belief of a DOCTOR in a person who is ill revives him and re-arouses his own belief in himself.

The patient's confidence in the DOCTOR will then reinforce the entire medical procedure, and he may THEN be filled with faith in his recovery.

But as there are natural healing processes within animals, so there are in your race.

Illnesses usually represent un-faced problems, in your terms,

And these dilemmas embody challenges meant to lead you to greater achievement and fulfillment.

Because body and mind operate so well together, one will attempt to cure the other, and will often succeed if left alone.

The organism has its own beliefs in health that are unconscious on your part.

No one who decides upon death is saved from it by the medical profession, however.

On deeper levels the quite normal desire for survival requires that the individual leave his or her body, in your terms, at one time or another.

When that period arrives the person knows it, and the great vitality of the spirit no longer wants to be encased by a suffering physical body.

Yet here the medical profession often takes care to see that every technological advance is brought to bear to force the self to remain within its flesh, when naturally soul and flesh would part.

There are normal interlocking mechanisms that prepare the self for death, even chemical interactions that make this easier physically - bursts of acceleration, in your terms, to propel the individual easily out of the body. Drugs can only hamper this.

Certain kinds of medications can indeed help, but those given in your hospitals simply drug the consciousness out of its own understanding, and inhibit the body mechanisms that make for an easy transition.

In your prisons you do the same thing, of course, isolating groups of people with like beliefs - denying them all natural stimuli so that a greater: contagion of similar beliefs ensues.

You separate such people from the normal contact of their loved ones, and all usual conditions for growth or development.

The Nature of Personal Reality, session 661 - by Jane Roberts © L. Davies Butts

Beliefs Are The Wankers Best Friend

You create BELIEFS as you go along, in your terms.
Behind all of your BELIEFS is a reality of your being in this moment.
And this moment is eternal and unending.
When I say that, I do not mean that it is completed as it is forever.
I mean that it is endlessly creative and never finished – eternally
never finished,
But forever growing as you yourselves are.
And as I have told you before, you are indeed gods couched in
creature-hood.
Now, I will let you digest that and enjoy the vitality and energy of
your own being!
Transcript Narration:
(Larry related to Jane what Seth had said.
Rick said that if there is a reality beyond our BELIEFS, we can
change it.)
Seth (To Rick): Now. You are real. You exist.
You have BELIEFS about your existence.
You have BELIEFS about YOUR OWN existence.
Behind all the BELIEFS is your existence.
Your existence is the reality.
The answer then, the BELIEFS and the questions, are within the
reality that you are,
And you will explain them to yourself as your experience changes.
Jeff Asks:
"Is there a plane without BELIEFS and questions as we know them?"
Seth (To Jeff): There are realities in which, in your terms,
questions do not exist as such,
In the way that a tree grows outward an inch at a time.
The growing an inch at a time, in your world, is a question.
In the world of the tree it is not a question but a growth.
And that is my answer to you.
THE TREE BELIEVES THERE IS A SPACE THROUGH WHICH
IT CAN GROW, and that is an answer to you.
And I am deliberately leaving loopholes through which you can

jump for yourselves –

And do so gallantly with some daring!

Rick Asks: "When you say that behind all your BELIEFS is my existence,

Is my existence perhaps something like the BELIEFS of another aspect of my personality,

Or like the BELIEFS of All That Is - do you know what I mean?

Seth (To Rick):

Do you know what you mean? YOU EXIST BECAUSE YOU BELIEVE THAT YOU EXIST.

Barrie Asks: "What if he didn't believe that?"

Seth (To Barrie, Jovially):

It would be 'Good-Bye, Ricky!'

But there is a certain portion of Ricky that is aware of his constant existence in flesh or out of it

And that part cannot be tricked by Ricky's BELIEFS.

Barrie Asks: "Does that part have its own BELIEFS?"

Seth (To Barrie): That part EXISTS.

Barrie Asks: "Then that part would be beyond BELIEFS, like what we were talking about before."

Seth (To Barrie): I did not say it was beyond BELIEFS.

Now, you must all do some thinking on your own and look to the great god self within you,

Instead of toward the great Seth!

Seth (Session 645)

I would like you to recognize your own BELIEFS in several areas.

YOU MUST REALIZE THAT ANY IDEA YOU ACCEPT AS TRUTH IS A BELIEF THAT YOU HOLD.

Few BELIEFS are intellectual alone.

When you are examining the contents of your conscious mind,

You must learn, or recognize, the emotional and imaginative connotations that are connected with a given idea.

As you examine the contents of your conscious mind,

It may seem to you that YOU HOLD SO MANY DIFFERENT BELIEFS AT DIFFERENT TIMES THAT YOU CANNOT

CORRELATE THEM.

They will, however, form into clear patterns.

You will find a grouping of core BELIEFS about which the others gather.

If you think of these as planets, then your other ideas orbit about them.

There may be some 'INVISIBLE BELIEFS,'

And there may be one or two INVISIBLE CORE BELIEFS.

These, following the analogy, would be hidden behind the other brighter, more obvious "planets,"

And yet would show their presence through their effects upon your relationships with all of the other visible core BELIEFS in your planetary system.

Questions you cannot seem to answer as you study your own ideas, for example

May lead you to suspect the existence of such INVISIBLE CORE BELIEFS.

Let me emphasize that they are consciously available.

You can find them through the approaches mentioned earlier working from your feelings

Or by beginning with the BELIEFS that become most readily available.

Seth (Session 618):

A CORE BELIEF IS INVISIBLE ONLY WHEN YOU THINK OF IT AS A FACT OF LIFE, and not as a BELIEF about life.

You must become aware of your own structures.

Build them up or tear them down,

But DO NOT ALLOW YOURSELF TO BECOME BLIND TO THE FURNITURE OF YOUR OWN MIND.

Seth (Session 617):

I expect that by now my readers have at least begun to examine their BELIEFS,

And perhaps obtained a glimpse of some INVISIBLE ONES THAT HAD BEEN ACCEPTED BEFORE AS DEFINITE ASPECTS OF REALITY.

Seth (Session 846):

Religion and science both loudly proclaim their search for truth,
although they are seemingly involved in completely opposing
systems.
THEY BOTH TREAT THEIR **BELIEFS** AS TRUTHS, with
which no one should tamper.

They search for beginnings and endings.

Seth (Session 613):

Basically you create your experience through your **BELIEFS**
about yourself and the nature of reality.

Seth (Session 614):

Your environment is the physical picture of your thoughts,
emotions and **BELIEFS** made visible.
Since your thoughts, emotions and BELIEFS move through
space and time,
You therefore affect physical conditions separate from you.

Seth (Session 615):

There are no accidents in cosmic terms, or in terms of the world
as you know it.
Your **BELIEFS** grow as surely in time and space as flowers do.
When you realize this you can even feel their growing.

Seth (Session 621):

Your BELIEFS automatically attract the appropriate emotions.
They reinforce themselves through imagination;
And at the risk of repeating myself, because this is so important:
Imagination and feeling follow your **BELIEFS**.
It is not the other way around.

Seth (Session 642):

You cannot will yourself to be happy while believing that you
have no right to happiness, or that you are unworthy of it.
You cannot tell yourself to release aggressive thoughts if you
think it is wrong to free them,
So YOU MUST COME TO GRIPS WITH YOUR BELIEFS IN ALL
INSTANCES.

Seth (Session 771):

The child is not born a sponge, however, empty but ready to soak up knowledge.

IT IS ALREADY SOAKED IN KNOWLEDGE.

Some will come to the surface, so to speak, and be used consciously.
Some will not.

I am saying here that to some extent the child in the womb is aware of the mother's **BELIEFS** and information,

And that TO SOME EXTENT it is "programmed" to behave in a certain fashion,

Or to grow in a certain fashion as a result.

In greater terms, positive and negative have little meaning,

For the physical experience is meant as a LEARNING one.

In your system of reality, YOU ARE LEARNING what mental energy is, and how to use it.

YOU ARE LEARNING responsibility—the responsibility of any individualized consciousness.

YOU ARE LEARNING to handle creative energy;

And since you are still in the process of doing so, you will often misdirect it.

YOU ARE LEARNING how to form reality from your own beliefs,

While having at the same time the freedom to choose those beliefs—to choose your mental state.

You are not your consciousness.

It is something that belongs to you and to the soul.

YOU ARE LEARNING to use it.

YOU ARE LEARNING to be co-creators.

YOU ARE LEARNING to know yourselves. At the rate you are going, it will take you some time.

YOU ARE LEARNING to handle the energy that is yourself, for creative purposes.

In physical reality YOU ARE LEARNING that your thoughts have reality,

And that you create the reality that you know.

YOU ARE LEARNING to use the creative energy of which you are a part,

And you are indeed quite isolated, so you cannot do much harm, in your terms.

In this existence YOU ARE LEARNING to handle the inexhaustible energy that is available to you.

You are consciously aware of certain events, and unconsciously aware of much more

That in one way or another YOU ARE LEARNING to bring into conscious focus.

YOU ARE LEARNING to be gods as you now understand the term.

YOU ARE LEARNING now, in a three dimensional context, the ways in which your emotional and psychic existence can create varieties of physical form.

YOU ARE LEARNING to BE as completely as possible.

In one way, YOU ARE LEARNING to create yourselves.

YOU ARE LEARNING how to transform the imaginative realm of probabilities into a more or less specific, physically experienced world.

In your particular camouflage universe, YOU ARE LEARNING energy transformation.

YOU ARE LEARNING to use your consciousness to become conscious co-creators of your own reality.

In rational, intellectual terms alone, and using the terms the way [they are] usually used,

YOU ARE LEARNING a lot from someone who has no reality,
And that is a good trick on your part.
Finding yourselves is something else.

MAN IS LEARNING TO create new worlds.
In order to do so he has taken on many challenges.

From Seth Speaks; The Nature of Personal Reality; The Seth Material; The Individual and the Nature of Mass Events; Dreams, "Evolution," and Value Fulfillment, Vol. 1; Conversations With Seth, Vols. 1 & 2SI

In each life you are meant to check the exterior environment in order to learn your inner condition. The outer is a reflection of the inner.

You are meant to understand the nature of your inner self, and to manifest it outward.

As this is done, the exterior circumstances should change for the better as the inner self becomes more aware of its own nature and capabilities.

Theoretically, then, in each life you would become stronger, healthier, wealthier, and wiser, but it does not work that way, for many reasons.

As mentioned earlier, many personalities adopt different kinds of experiences, focusing upon development in certain specific areas, and ignoring other perhaps for a series of lives.

No consciousness has the same experiences or interprets them the same,

And so each individual utilizes reincarnational opportunities in his own way.

Sex changes, for example, are necessary.

Some individuals alternate their sex in each succeeding life.

Others have a series of female lives and then a series of male lives, or vice versa,

But the entire reincarnational framework must involve both sexual experiences.

There are certain characteristics inherent in energy itself,

Quite aside from any that you ascribe to it,

Since of course to date you do not consider energy conscious.

Once again, in terms of your equations, energy and consciousness and matter are one.

And in those terms—in parentheses: (the qualifications are necessary)—

Consciousness is the agent that directs the transformation of energy into form and of form into energy.

All possible visible or invisible particles that you discover or imagine—

Meaning hypothesized particles—possess consciousness.

They are energized consciousness.

Dreams, "Evolution," and Value Fulfillment Volume 1 Chapter 2: Session 884, October 3, 1979

Now, the message of the Christ entity was, in religious terms:

"You are all children of God, the sinner as well as the saint."

Indeed, according to the original Christ thesis, while a man could sin, no man was identified as a sinner.

He was not identified with his failures or limitations but, instead, with his potential.

The Christ entity knew the vitality, power, and strength of myths.

That vitality allows for different readings, of course.

And, through man's changing development, he reads his myths differently.

Yet, they serve as containers for intuitional knowledge.

Christ's thesis was inserted into a Jewish tradition dealing deeply with guilt.

And, the new thesis was meant to temper that tradition and to spread beyond it.

Instead, while carrying the belief in man's potential,

Christianity smothered the thesis beneath a slag heap of old guilt.

Guilt can be used to manipulate people, of course.

And, it is a fine tool in the hands of government, religion, science, or any large organization that wants to retain its power.

Christ dealt with myths, once again, potent ones that stood for inner realities.

Christ clothed those realities in colorful stories geared to peoples understanding.

I am using the name here, Christ, as one person for the sake of discussion, for that entity touched many lives, each leaping into a kind of super-reality as it joyfully played its part in the religious drama.

The message was "Do not condemn yourself or others",

For Christ well knew that self-righteous condemnation of the self or of one's neighbors served to darken the door through which man might view his own potential and its greater source.

The Christian concept of heaven with its riches, God and his bounty, the source of nature itself, all of this, in our terms, was a symbolic structure describing in storybook terms the attributes and characteristics of Framework 2.

In our terms, All-That-Is exists in Framework 2 as elsewhere.

But, Framework 2 represents the source of your known physical reality.

From it flow all of the known facts of your world.

Christ hoped to show that you survived death psychically and spiritually, that you "returned" to the father in heaven.

Literal minds, looking for evintial proof, would insist that the physical body itself must rise, ascending, hence the related stories, the misinterpretation of data.

"Ask, and you shall receive." Christ well knew that that statement was indeed true.

But, men who condemned themselves, who considered themselves sinners, would not know what to ask for, except punishment to relieve their guilt.

Hence he stressed time and time again that each person was a child of God.

He also stressed the importance of a childlike belief, knowing that the adult mind was apt to question:

"How and when and in what manner can my request be granted?"

The words "Let thy will be done" represented excellent psychological understanding.

For according to Christ's teachings as originally given,

God the father represented the source or parent of the self, who was by nature free from the self's ignorance or lack of understanding at any given time

And who would know better than the known self those experiences that would fulfill the self's hopes, dreams, and potentials.

In this way, with the words spoken, "Let thy will be done", the self could free itself from its own misconceptions and attract from Framework 2 benefits

That it might otherwise not be knowledgeable enough to request.

A portion of each person dwells in Framework I and Framework 2.

Understand that Framework 2 is a psychic or spiritual or mental structure.

In deepest terms, of course, it is not a place.

It is, if you prefer, a spiritual landscape of far greater resources than the one you know.

It brings forth the world of your experience in that world. And so, it is your source also.

"Let thy will be done" meant Let me follow those greater dictates of my inner nature.

Even without all of the distortions, that formula worked for centuries in large measure.

The God, the source, was put outside of nature, however, finally becoming at last too remote.

And, the story itself became frayed at the edges as man tried to tie intuitive truths to objective fact.

To be a child of God was to trust in your own worth.

You could admit failings, transgressions of one kind or another without identifying yourself, say, with failure.

The child of God would automatically find salvation.

And, everyone was a child of God.

When Christ said "Believe in me, and you will be saved", he meant Believe in your relationship to God, in that you are his son, as I am, and you will surely be saved.

Again, he spoke in religious terms, for those were the terms of the times.

This knowledge, however, of the innate goodness of the self literally gives the individual the inner support necessary for the exercise of man's fullest potentials.

January 9, 1978, Personal Sessions Book 4

Health Begins In The Mind

ELIAS: Health is a matter of function.

Health is how you function in the most optimal capacity for you, and what is the most natural for you.

Because everyone is different, and therefore the optimal functioning for each person is different.

But that would be the expression of health, is functioning.

Therefore, the functioning of your mental capacity,

The functioning of your emotional capacity,

The functioning of your physical capacity.

That is health.

Well-being is perception, outlook and your state of mind.

Therefore, the maintenance of yourself, your being.

Therefore, the wellness of your being.

In this, it is a matter of balancing both of those factors together.

And when you don't, one or the other will express some type of dysfunction.

And it, expressing some type of dysfunction, is your signal, your communication to yourself that you're not expressing that balance

And you're not maintaining both of those.

Which is the reason that people create injuries and illnesses or they create depression or they create anxiety.

In this, you create expressions of one or the other to alert you

That you're not balanced and that you're not maintaining health AND well-being.

And they very much move in harmony with each other.

God does not exist apart from or separate from physical reality,

But exists within it and as a part of it, as he exists within and as a part of all other systems of existence.

Seth Speaks Session 560

The complete physician would be a person who learned to understand the dynamics of being, the soul-body relationship—

One who was healthy in his or her own body.

Unhappy people cannot teach you to be happy.

Sick ones cannot teach you to be well.

Psychiatrists have a high suicide rate.

Why do you think they can help YOU live happily, or add to your vitality?

Physicians are NOT the healthiest of men by far.

Why do you think they can cure you?

The sick doctor does not know as much about health as an 'uneducated, untrained,' but healthy person—

And I am speaking in quite practical terms.

The person who is healthy understands the dynamics of health.

In your framework it seems that his or her understanding can be of little practical value to you if you are, for instance, unhealthy.

But a true medical profession would be, literally, a HEALTH PROFESSION.

It would seek out people who were healthy

And learn from them how to promote health, and not how to diagram disease.

A true healing, or health profession, would deal intimately with the POWERS of the psyche in healing the body,

And with the interrelationship among the desires, beliefs, and activities of the conscious mind and its effects upon the cellular behavior.

The 'unknown' reality. Unknown or not, it is what you are working with.

The "Unknown" Reality, Vol. 1, Session 703

(Apropos of this question, in ESP class eight days later Seth had this to say about Charles Darwin and his theory of evolution:)

[Darwin] spent his last years proving it, and yet it has no real validity.

It has a validity within very limited perspectives only;

For consciousness does, indeed, evolve form.

Form does not evolve consciousness.

All consciousness does, indeed exist at once, and therefore it did not evolve in those terms.

It is according to when you come into the picture,

And what you choose to observe and what part of the play you decide to observe.

It is more the other way around, in that evolved consciousness forms itself into many different patterns and rains down on reality.

Consciousness did not come from atoms and molecules scattered by chance through the universe

Or scattered by chance through many universes.

Consciousness did not arrive because inert matter suddenly soared into activity and song.

The consciousness existed first and evolved the form into which it then began to manifest itself.

Now, if you had all been really paying attention to what I have been saying for some time about the simultaneous nature of time, and existence,

Then you would have known that the theory of evolution is as beautiful a tale as the theory of biblical creation.

Both are quite handy, and both are methods of telling stories, and both might seem to agree within their own systems,

And yet, in larger respects they cannot be realities.

No - no form of matter, however potent, will be self-evolved into consciousness,

No matter what other bits of matter are added to it.

Without the consciousness, the matter would not be there in the universe, floating around, waiting for another component to give it reality, consciousness, existence, or song.

(A class member: "Every bit of matter already has consciousness?"

Indeed, and the consciousness came first, you are quite correct.

I thank you for bringing up the matter.

There are many ways of bringing up matter.

Remember that each segment of life is motivated by value fulfillment,

And is therefore always attempting to use and develop all of its abilities and potentials,

And to express itself in as many probable ways as possible, in a process that is cooperatively correction: in a process that takes into consideration the needs and desires of each other segment of life.

The very existence of certain kinds of viruses provides safety against many other diseases, whether or not those viruses even exist in an active manner.

It is obvious, of course, that the overall physical stability of the earth is possible because of the ever-occurring storms, "natural disasters," and other seeming calamities.

Yet such events promote the earth's great, bountiful food supplies, and serve to redistribute the planet's resources.

Period.

In the same fashion, diseases also, in the overall picture, promote the health and well-being of life in all of its aspects.

Value fulfillment operates within microbes and nations, within individual creatures and entire species,

And it unites all of life's manifestations so that indeed creatures and their environments are united in an overall cooperative venture —

A venture in which each segment almost seeks to go beyond itself in creativity, growth, and expression.

In a smaller, individual framework, each man and woman, then, is motivated by this same value fulfillment. Period.

You will shortly see how some diseases are caused by the detriments set up against value fulfillment, often because of fears, doubts, or misunderstandings — and how other diseases may actually lead to instances of value fulfillment that are misread or misinterpreted.

I also want to stress here that all aspects of life experience not only sensations but emotional feelings. Therefore, there is a kind of innate gallantry that operates among all segments of life — a gallantry that deserves your respect and consideration.

You should have respect, then, for the cells of your body, the thoughts of your mind, and try to understand that even the smallest of creatures shares with you the emotional experience of life's triumphs and vulnerabilities.

I bid you, then, another fond good afternoon.

MAY 6,1984 4:23 RM. SUNDAY The Way Toward Health

Seth in response to a statement from a class member:

There is nothing wrong with self-love.

Class Member: "Unless you believe that it is binding you?"

Seth Responds: Unless you believe that it is binding you,

And unless you do not understand the beauty and miracle of yourself.

If you believe that you are a beast and no better than a beast and you have a poor opinion of beasts, [then] indeed you will find self-love a horrendous barrier.

If you understand the beauty and miracle and spirituality of your flesh and of any beast or the smallest fly or ant, then self-love becomes a benediction

That the universe gives you and that you, as a portion of the universe, give yourself.

Seth (ESP Class, 6-26-73)

Jane Roberts (C) L.Davies Butts

Now. Think in terms of energy being action.

Energy is action. It must act and move.

It constantly seeks to know itself, and to expand.

It cannot remain static.

Its survival is dependent upon change.

Its very permanency is determined by its nature, and its nature demands constant change.

Energy or action is composed of an infinity of itself, and yet, forever acting upon itself, it forms forever new portions of itself.

Each action causes another.

Now until we have done more talking you will simply have to take my word, for the sake of our discussion—

Our one-way discussion—that any action or energy possesses consciousness seeking to know itself, Therefore;

Acting within itself it forms new consciousnesses that are individual and independent,

And yet connected to every other consciousness.

The purpose is the expansion of consciousness itself,

And this automatically leads to the knowledge that every consciousness is connected to every other,

And that any harm to one is harm to all.

Time simply does not exist as a series of moments.

This is a three-dimensional illusion.

Therefore, in actuality no one life is lived before nor after another.

Action acts spontaneously.

In three-dimensional existence you must speak of reincarnation in terms of continuous lives, for it seems to you as if there is indeed a past, present and future.

Imagine then action or energy which is conscious, exploding into bloom like some gigantic cosmic flower, spontaneously, instantaneously, and intuitively.

You however would view this in slow motion,

So that eons of time would seem to have passed.

And yet energy or action, which is consciousness, is always changing,

And the shape of the flower and the blossom would constantly change.

Energy can never be lost but only change its form.

The consciousness therefore would never be destroyed in reality.

The most minute blossom within it would experience only an almost instantaneous change of form, and all of this would transpire in the breath of an instant.

The individual petals would merely change, as the personalities of men change in what seems like a series of before and after reincarnations.

And no memory, you see, would ever be lost, and nor is any memory lost.

The personality that you have now is simply the flower of the moment,

Not realizing that it has the knowledge of its own past histories; and all of this would be but one cosmic flower.

Energy constantly renews itself.

The various flowers could then be compared to the various

dimensions through which action and consciousness know their own reality.

The expansion of consciousness automatically leads you to understanding and compassion.

TES8 Session 357 July 31, 1967

All personal contact with the multidimensional God, all legitimate moments of mystic consciousness, will always have a unifying effect.

They will not, therefore, isolate the individual involved,

But instead will enlarge his perceptions until he will experience the reality and uniqueness of as many other aspects of reality of which he is capable.

He will feel, therefore, less isolated and less set apart.

He will not regard himself as being above others because of the experience.

On the contrary he will be swept along in a gestalt of comprehension in which he realizes his own oneness with All That Is.

As there are portions of reality that you do not consciously perceive,

And other systems of probability of which you are not consciously aware,

So also are there aspects of primary godhood that you cannot at this moment comprehend.

There are, therefore, probable gods, each one reflecting in its way the multidimensional aspect of a prime identity

So great and dazzling that no one reality form or particular kind of existence could contain it.

I have tried to give you some idea of the far-reaching creative effects of your own thoughts.

With that in mind, then, it is impossible to imagine the multidimensional creativities that can be attributed to All That Is.

The term "All That Is" can be used as a designation to include all of those probable gods in all of their manifestations.

It is easier perhaps for some of you to understand the simple stories and parables of beginnings of which I have spoken.

But the time has come for mankind to take several steps further, to expand the nature of his own consciousness by trying to comprehend a more profound version of reality.

You have outgrown the time of children's tales.

When your own thoughts have a form and reality,

When they have validity even in other systems of reality of which you are unaware,

Then it is not difficult to understand why other systems of probabilities are also affected by your own thoughts and emotions –

Nor why the actions of the probable gods are not affected by what happens in other dimensions of existence.

Now if you are looking for simple definitions to explain the psyche, I will be of no help.

If you want to experience the splendid creativity of your own being, however,

Then I will use methods that will arouse your greatest adventuresomeness,

Your boldest faith in yourself,

And I will paint pictures of your psyche that will lead you to experience even its broadest reaches, if you so desire.

The psyche, then, is not a known land.

It is not simply an alien land, to which or through which you can travel.

It is not a completed or nearly complete subjective universe already there for you to explore.

It is, instead, an ever-forming state of being,

In which your present sense of existence resides.

You create it and it creates you.

The Nature of The Psyche, Chapter 1: Session 755, September 8, 1975 - by Jane Roberts © L. Davies Butts

The state of grace is a condition in which all growth is effortless,

A transparent, joyful acquiescence that is a ground requirement of all existence.

Your own body grows naturally and easily from its time of birth,

Not expecting resistance but taking its miraculous unfolding for granted;

Using all of itself with great, gracious, creatively aggressive abandon.

You will die in a state of grace whether or not special words are used.

You were born into a state of grace, therefore.

It is impossible for you to leave it

You share this blessing with the animals and all other living things.

You cannot 'fall out of' grace, nor can it be taken from you.

You can ignore it.

You can hold beliefs that blind you to its existence.

You will still be graced but unable to perceive your own uniqueness and integrity,

And blind also to other attributes with which you are automatically gifted.

The Nature of Personal Reality, Session 636

It would be silly for a violet to wonder why it was not a grape.

You have certain natures, then, that are your own.

It is somewhat beside the point to wonder why your natures are as they are.

You have always been loners, in reincarnational terms and otherwise.

Suggestion, so-called, is little understood.

The word perhaps is a poor one. Yet to an important extent your world runs by suggestion.

Suggestion is simply an impetus to act in given directions.

Your social, political, religious, economic and medical areas of life are all built upon certain assumed suggestions that people agree to accept as standards of behavior.

The word "standards" is important, for in certain terms through such "obedience", through such compliance,

They are given recognizable patterns into which their most personal experience can flow.

There are given recognizable patterns through which their experience with others, and with the community can flow.

They are given certain more or less predictable frameworks in which to experience their lives.

Those experiences may at times be quite jarring, tragic, frightening,

But they will happen within a framework provided by the accepted suggestions of the society.

People may question the precepts,

But generally speaking they live and work within organizational frameworks,

Each one ruled by various assumptions or suggestions.

Students go to school, patients go to doctors, criminals go to jail.

Experience, then, is largely programmed in that respect, so that you know where you belong.

Your experience, no matter how joyful, bizarre or frightening, can find a category.

Few people STRAY from those frameworks,

And few creative people, even of high quality, operate outside of the accepted disciplines, schools, and organizations.

Because of your natures, to a far greater extent than most, you and Ruburt have strayed in such a fashion.

Because of your natures, you are seeking answers to the most difficult problems of LIFE AND DEATH ALIKE, on your own, so to speak.

This is because your natures require it.

You WANT to do it.

At the same time, you provide a new group of suggestions, an alternate way for others.

In the meantime, however, you have no cozy categories in which to place your experience.

In a way everything is new.

This of course requires on your parts energy, self-reliance, faith in what you are doing, and a certain stubbornness.

At the same time, you are everywhere surrounded by the suggestions of your culture.

The Personal Sessions [Deleted], Aug 27, 1977, Book 4,

by Jane Roberts © L. Davies Butts

At each moment, from the most microscopic levels the body in one way or another is ascertaining a constant picture of its position within physical reality.

That picture is composed of millions of ever-changing smaller snapshots, as it were—or moving pictures is better—determining so many conditions, positions and relationships that they could never be described.

You end up with a predominating picture of reality in any given moment—one that is the result of the activity of psychological, biological, and electromagnetic stratus.

One picture is transposed upon the others, and calculations made constantly, so that all of the components that make up physical existence are met, and intersect to give you, life.

Spontaneously, with the process just mentioned, millions of pictures are being taken also of the probable actions that will—or MAY—be needed, in your terms,

In the moment immediately following, from microscopic action to the motion of a muscle, the driving of a car, the reading of a book, or whatever.

The Magical Approach, Session Six

The God myth enabled man to give his higher so-called instincts an objectivity,

And the God concept represented and still represents a link with the inner self.

Now. As far as hard facts are concerned,

There is no God as mankind has envisioned him,

And yet God once existed as mankind now envisions him.

Now. This absolute, ever-expanding, instantaneous psychic gestalt, which you may call God, if you prefer,

Is so secure in its existence now that it can constantly break itself down and rebuild itself.

If there is no white-haired, kind old Father God to hear [your prayers]

Then there is instead the initial and ever-expanding energy that forms everything that is,

And of which every human being is a part.

If you prefer to call this supreme and absolute psychic gestalt God,

Then you must not attempt to objectify him in terms of material,

For he is the nuclei of your cells, and more intimate than your breath.

There is, then, truly no beginning or end,

Because we are speaking in terms of an expansion that has nothing to do with space or time,

An evolution in dimensions of which you and your kind have not yet even dreamed.

As an idea expands, changing a world but taking up no space,

And unperceived by your scientific instruments,

So does the ultimate and instantaneous absolute gestalt,

Which you may if you prefer call God, exist and expand.

The Early Sessions Book 2 Session 81 August 26, 1964

Now unless you come to terms with your own doubts about yourselves then you will have no idea what faith is

And when I use the word faith, I am not speaking in religious terms.

When you look at your physical reality and see what it is this does not take faith, it is a simple matter of physical perception.

When, however, you begin to have glimpses about the nature of reality and realize that you are more than you know that you are now,

Then it takes faith to bring that inner image close to some actuality, in your terms.

You are all hampered, in other words, by doubts.

Now your physical perceptions operating alone are often responsible for these doubts for you think you are all that you can see of yourselves,

Or you think your life is all that you presently perceive of it,

And so if you trust in your physical senses alone then you must, indeed, be filled with doubts for you know, instinctively,

That you are more than the self that you are presently able to materialize or to give expression to.

If you judge yourself according to the physical self that you know, then you must be filled again by doubts

Because again instinctively, you know that you are more.

Now when you begin to sense the interior invisible self then in physical terms you begin to act upon what you call faith.

Belief in that which is not at this point physically real.

Faith, however, is not believing in an unreality,

It is believing in realities that you cannot, at this point physically, perceive.

It is banking on those portions of your own personality that you feel but cannot see in the ordinary mirror.

It is banking on the invisible self that, as yet you have not been able to actualize in physical reality.

Now each of you in your own way, particularly in the dream state, are intimately acquainted with this invisible portion of yourselves.

Now in world's terms, you can be a realist and you can say, I am the self that you see and smell and touch.

I am the self that I see in the ordinary mirror and that is all, or you can realize that the mirror only captures a small portion of your entire image.

That there is far more that is not seen by the mirror, and it is not seen by other eyes

And you can choose to bank upon those abilities that you know are inherently your own.

Now these are your abilities as members of what you now call, simply, the human race.

They are inherent abilities that belong to consciousness no matter what form it adopts.

You can look in the mirror and take your image for granted

And brush your teeth and stare at yourself and think, I am a
sorry picture, indeed,

Or I am quite a beautiful thing and smile, but in either case you
are taking it for granted that only physical perceptions are real.

Your criterion for physical reality is physical materialization.

You have been brought up to accept that as criteria for existence
and yet each of you instinctively knows that you are far more
than this,

And those of you here realize it quite well and so you are driven
to other than physical means.

You are driven to find the reality of yourselves beneath the reality
that you know

And to do this you must work through the reality that you know
and a self that you know.

To believe that there is something there to work for is faith.

To realize that there is more of yourself than you can physically
perceive is faith.

The Early Class Session, book 3, ESP Class Session, February 2, 1971 - by Jane Roberts © L. Davies Butts

You Can't visually see energy, but you can develop that more fully

And you can allow yourself to actually see energy moving,

And in that, you can apply that vision within your interactions
with physical individuals also.

Which can be beneficial, for if you allow yourself to visually SEE
other individuals' energies.

And I will express to you, my friend, this is in actuality quite significant and important,

In recognizing that solidity is not necessarily an indicator of real,

It allows you to more effectively recognize how real energy is

And what it does –

That this is an expression that does not incorporate solidity, but it moves and it generates.

And in that, many expressions are created THROUGH energy,

But it is another example of things being created by non-things,

Which is a fine example of actually what you are.

For you are in essence a non-thing,

But you are a thing, for you have manipulated energy in a manner that allows you to create a physical manifestation.

It is the same with ANY of your imagery and your reality:

Whether it contains solidity or not is not the indicator of whether it is real.

Energy is a powerful expression.

And as you continue, you can actually allow yourself to visually SEE the energy, which you have previously.

Pastly, you have allowed yourself at times know it is being projected and manipulated,

It can allow you a greater understanding of what another individual is doing beyond what they are saying

And beyond even what they may be physically engaging.

The Tender Trap: Thinking You Had No Input In Your Birth

For many times individuals, as you are aware yourself, think they are engaging doing in one direction, and in actuality they are doing in a different direction.

They think they are projecting their energy in one manner, and in actuality their energy is being projected in a different manner.

Elias

The cooperative aspects of consciousness construction form the whole fabric of your material universe.

A subdivision of primary construction can be called the distortive mirror construction,

Which would include of course the physical construction of another physical being in birth.

This distortive attempt to re-create the self once more on the physical plane, and to insure self-continuity within that plane,

Is the basis for the divergence of physical types and characteristics.

Such a creation, or re-creation, is obviously impossible.

The distortions are so great that the attempt is foredoomed.

It is, nevertheless, attempted, and is a necessary physical adjunct to constructions in your field.

I have explained birth, at least briefly.

The new human being is obviously not either the father or the mother,

And yet is obviously a construction formed by each from physical matter belonging to each.

Yet the physical matter of the born infant contains NONE of the SAME physical matter

Which was received initially from the parents.

The original matter has completely disappeared,

To be replaced by other matter as the consciousness of the infant slowly constructs

about itself its growing awareness of ITSELF into physical matter.

The parents, therefore, give definite parts of their own physical matter to initiate the infant's construction

And yet it is not this particular matter which grows.

Call the particular matter given by the parent's x and y.

When the child is born, it does not contain anywhere within it these particular portions of matter called x and y.

It would appear that the matter had changed.

Instead, the matter has vanished, in ways I have explained earlier.

Do you recall?

No particle of matter is the same in the born infant,

That was contained in either the fetus or earlier in the sperm or egg.

I am going into all this for a reason.

Leave this for a moment, and consider a seed, a grass seed.

You say that grass grows from a seed, but the grass is not the seed.

The material of the grass is not the material of the seed.

From experience you know that the seed will often precede grass.

As usual, this is putting things backward.

The grass contains NO particle of matter that is identical in the seed.

Here you see clearly the difference between value fulfillment and what you call growth.

In your physical field value fulfillment consists of the development of the ability of the immaterial to express itself within the physical field.

Growth is the erroneous conception that begins with the distortive idea of continuous physical matter, durable in time.

And as you know instead, matter is the simultaneous expression of consciousness.

Matter has little, really no, durability in itself,

And is merely the instantaneous form taken by consciousness as it projects itself in the physical field.

Grass is common. it is supposed to grow from seed,

Yet again no particle of matter is the same in grass or seed.

Seed does not grow into grass. Acorns do not grow into trees.

Children do not grow into adults.

In all instances, no particle of matter is the same in the so-called grown version, and the initial construction.

Matter does not grow. I cannot make this too plain.

There is obviously something identical, and some continuity between the child and the adult, but it is not matter.

Consciousness, according to its ability, projects itself into the physical plane, and through value fulfillment it constructs its image.

It must work according to its ability to do this.

It must first get a foothold, so to speak; hence or seed.

As the consciousness attains its foothold it projects more effectively.

It dispenses with its atoms and molecules, or matter, almost instantaneously, as you know.

The atoms and molecules appear and disappear.

Their place is taken by others, so quickly that YOU do not know the constant coming and going.

The form that consciousness takes in the field of matter is determined by its own strength and capacity.

Consciousness forces its way into matter.

You should see, then, that though you call a particular portion of grass one blade of grass, the matter that composes it is not static or permanent.

And it is not a particular physical object growing, since the matter that composes it is neither static or permanent.

YOU say the matter that composes it steadily changes, but this is not the case.

The apparent continuity is a result of your inability to perceive the actual atoms that compose matter as they appear and disappear.

Because grass appears where seed has been sown, you have leaped to the conclusion that the matter of the seed grows from the matter of which they are composed, and that grass grows from the actual matter of the seeds.

Again, there is NO continuity in the matter that composes the seeds, and the matter that composes the grass.

What you have instead is the value fulfillment of the consciousness behind matter, as it expands and expresses itself in various forms.

Since you can more or less count upon the appearance of grass seed, preceding grass, all this may seem making much over nothing, but it is very important, as you will see latter.

It is not matter that has continuity, and it is not matter that dictates the form.

Now that we have gone into the nature of matter as it pertains to grass, you will understand my next analogy more clearly.

Consider a lawn. Obviously this is an arbitrary designation for utility's sake.

Of itself, the matter of grass does not form itself into a lawn.

You merely designate certain portions of grass and call it a lawn.

This is the same sort of thing you do when you designate certain portions of matter as blades of grass.

Lawns do not come from grass.

That is, grass does not grow into a lawn. Do you follow me?

AND NEITHER THEN DO SEEDS GROW into grass.

You perceive certain matter as blades of grass, as you perceive the matter of grass as lawn.

You can see clearly that the matter of grass in a lawn is not the same.

Then understand also that the matter within one blade of grass is not the same.

You call a floor a floor. Matter may be added to the floor in the form of paint or varnish, yet you still call the floor the floor.

Paint may be added to a house, and paint may disappear from a house through weathering, and you still call a house a house.

You call yourself yourself, though the color of your hair may change, and indeed the adult bears any resemblance to the child.

Form simply cannot be a characteristic of matter, since matter can be proven to come and go, while form in many cases remains recognizable.

This will be a vital point in later discussions.

You must, and will, learn to look at things in a new way, and many implications will arise from tonight's discussion that will carry us further along our way.

You will indeed see clearly that matter is created simultaneously, and has no duration,

But is completely and almost instantly replaced by other matter,

And that identity and continuity are not characteristics of matter, but must be found in other places.

Unless you realize you are free, you cannot use your freedom!

Unless you realize that the life force is manifest now in every atom of your being, then you cannot form the physical reality that you want to form.

For instead, you form physical pictures that are replicas of your fears.

I have said this often in class:

You have been given the most awesome gift of all—the gift to create from your own thoughts and desires.

The Early Class Sessions, book 2, ESP Class Session, February 3, 1970 - by Jane Roberts © L. Davies Butts

You were born into a state of grace.

It is impossible for you to leave it.

You will die in a state of grace whether or not special words are spoken for you, or water or oil is poured upon your head.

You share this blessing with the animals and all other living things.

You cannot "fall out of" grace, nor can it be taken from you.

The state of grace is a condition in which all growth is effortless, a transparent, joyful acquiescence that is a ground requirement of all existence.

Your own body grows naturally and easily from its time of birth, not expecting resistance

But taking its miraculous unfolding for granted;

Using all of itself with great, gracious, creatively aggressive abandon.

NoPR Part One: Chapter 9: Session 636, January 29, 1973

Man's dreams have always provided him with a sense of impetus, purpose, meaning, and given him the raw material from which to form his civilizations.

The true history of the world is the history of man's dreams, for they have been responsible in one way or another for all historic developments.

Dreams,"Evolution," and Value Fulfillment Vol 1 SESSION 890 - December 19, 1979 - (C) L. Davies Butts

Remember, even false beliefs will seem to be justified in terms of physical data, since your experience in the outside world is the materialization of those beliefs.

So you must work with the raw material of your ideas, even while your sense data may tell you that a given belief is obviously a truth.

To change your experience or any portion of it, then, you must change your ideas.

Since you have been forming your own reality all along, the results will follow naturally.

The Nature of Personal Reality, Session 615

As to what I love, I find that question itself has many complications.

I love the inquiring consciousness in whatever form it may appear.

This is the simplest, most direct and spontaneous answer that I could possibly give.

In the spacious present, units of consciousness form a psychic gestalt with a purpose behind their grouping; for instance, say, to create our individual realities.

The units of consciousness (CUs) within the psychic gestalt emanate Electromagnetic

Energy (EE) units, which are built up in response to emotional intensities.

Both CUs and EE units while always in the spacious present, also underlie matter.

The entryway into physical matter is the ATOM, and it still resides outside physical reality in the spacious present,

While being within it at the same time—which is true of everything, of course, including us.

The atom is the materialization of the energy of the combination of the CUs and EE units; and atoms are aware of their existence.

No particles smaller than the atom—which of course includes sub-atomic particles—can kick off the creation of physical reality.

The atom is the definitive threshold into physicality.

Atoms in physical reality are undifferentiated.

That is, each of our physical realities is a sea of atoms, and none is named body or cloud or wave, or even space,

Until we, the consciousness of self, want to materialize, say, a rock.

Then a grouping of atoms forms the rock from the sea of undifferentiated atoms.

Since we blink in and out of physical reality millions of times a second, with everything terminated on the blink out and re-initiated on the blink in, all our camouflage reality goes out and then back in with us, INCLUDING THE ATOMS.

And with each new iteration, everything is newly assembled.

Therefore, our rock would be created from a wholly different set of undifferentiated atoms (but some of which could have been part of it previously, too).

And that is why physical reality is AFTER THE FACT.

There is NO continuity to it other than what the CONSCIOUSNESS OF SELF brings through its beliefs, including the beliefs (root assumptions) of time, space and matter.

Another thought here is the love of continuing creation, which is continually formed by, through, and because of inquiring consciousness.

It, inquiring consciousness, is as you know always individualized, and it is because of this amazing diversity that so many forms are possible.

Everything that is, is a materialization of aware, individualized, inquiring consciousness;

And to love this is a personal, almost all-encompassing discipline and devotion.

I say discipline because whenever, individualized inquiring consciousness expresses itself in form, it not only expresses its spontaneity; and this is not contradictory:

But even while expressing its spontaneity, it disciplines it.

Form always implies a discipline.

The love of individualized inquiring consciousness has always been my strength, and the source of my energy.

Early Sessions, book 3, session 110, page 162, by Jane Roberts (C) L. Davies Butts

All That Is: Now That's A Quiz

All That Is is not done and finished.

Everything within your three-dimensional system occurs simultaneously.

Each action creates other possibilities of itself, or other actions from the infinite energy of the universe, which itself is never still.

The answer is that the whole is more than the sum of its parts.

All That Is simultaneously and unendingly creates itself.

Only within your particular frame of reference does there seem to be a contradiction between action that is simultaneous and yet unending.

This has to do mainly with the necessary distortions arising from your time concept and the idea of duration;

For duration to you presupposes existence continued within a time framework - predisposing to beginnings and endings.

Experience existing outside of that reference is not dependent upon duration in your terms.

There is no "perfect ending," no completed perfection beyond which further experience is impossible or meaningless.

All That Is is a source of infinite and unending simultaneous action.

Everything happens at once, and yet there is not beginning and end to it in your terms, so it is not completed in your terms at any given point.

Ideally by following your impulses you would feel the shape, the impulsive shape (as Ruburt says) of your life.

You would not spend time wondering what your purpose was,

For it would make itself known to you as you perceived the direction in which your natural impulses led

And felt yourself exert power in the world through such actions.

Again, impulses are doorways to action, satisfaction,

The exertion of natural mental and physical power, the avenue for your private expression –

The avenue where your private expression intersects the physical world and impresses it'

NoME Ch8, session 857

Earlier I compared your thoughts to viruses.

Think of them now as living electromagnetic cells, differing from the physical cells in your body only in the nature of their materialization.

Your thoughts direct the overall functioning of your body's cells, even though you do not consciously know how those cells operate.

That work IS unconscious.

Each physical cell is in its way a miniature brain, with memory of all of its personal experiences

And of its relationship with other cells, and with the body as a whole.

In your terms this means that each cell operates with an innate picture of the body's entire history—past, present, and future.

Now this picture is ever-changing and mobile.

An alteration in just one cell is instantly noted by the body consciousness (the combined consciousnesses of the cells), and the future effect perceived.

This information is used together with all other data from the body, and a prediction made.

This body prediction is then assessed, and on more levels than it is possible for me to explain.

Briefly, the picture is "shown" in the invisible arena where flesh and spirit meet.

This arena is not a place, of course, but an inner state of gestalt consciousness.

The state is brought about through certain interactions that occur deep within the body.

Magnetic structures are formed.

They are created on a physical level through certain activations of the nerves in which the normal patterns are jumped, so to speak, and images are formed.

The nerves and the cellular structures at their tips take pictures.

These are all assembled and used to form the larger picture of the body's condition.

These are not images as you think of them but highly coded information,

electromagnetically imprinted, that would not appear as images to the physical eye.

In any case they cannot be perceived except by the body.

But this procedure is so far superior to anything that you know that the body, therefore, actually takes precognitive pictures of its future condition—

As if the body situation at the time were projected into the future.

This predictive picture is then set against two models.

First it is checked against the body's ideal standard of health in its individual case —its own greatest fulfillment.

Then it is checked against the image of the body sent to it by the conscious self.

Correlations are made instantaneously.

In an organizational framework that would certainly be envied by the most advanced technological concern, communications spring back and forth with great rapidity.

The body makes whatever changes are necessary in order to bring the two images in line with the present corporeal condition.

The Nature of Personal Reality, Session 632

You are all portions of your own higher identity, your own multidimensional selves.

Now these selves know how to heal, and in the dream state they will indeed do so if you allow them to.

You carry many of your misconceptions into certain areas of your dream reality and even there you close many doors.

Each of you automatically heal yourselves day by day, as you know. Cells die and are born.

You renew your bodies every seven years, all without your conscious knowledge.

You use the energy of the universe to heal yourselves constantly,

But you have very definite conceptions of how this healing can take place and what is possible and what is not possible.

You expect the cells of your body to be replaced.

You expect your image to continue day by day, although the physical matter of your image today has not one atom or molecule within it that was a portion of your image ten years ago.

The bodies that you had ten years ago are dead and gone, and you never missed them, and you do not feel dead.

You feel very alive, indeed.

These things you take for granted but you form your own image, and you form them in consistent belief with those ideas that you have.

And if you believe that you have a bad gall bladder, for example,

And if you do not discover the reasons behind the difficulty you will faithfully reproduce that faulty gall bladder with every new formation of your physical image.

And it does not occur to you that as your body is completely transformed within each seven years, so there is no reason at all to reproduce it each time with the old ailment.

You can, indeed, heal yourselves but you must realize that you can do so in order to do it yourself effectively.

There is, unfortunately, a great difference between theory and practice, as you should know, in the field of medicine.

And therefore, because I tell you that you can heal yourself, I also tell you that there are some difficulties in the way,

And those difficulties are those ideas that you have in your heads that prevent you from using your own abilities.

There is not one of you present in this room who cannot contact your own entity and have that entity heal your physical being, for it can use its abilities quite freely.

It does not have your present hang-ups.

It does not think it is fat, it does not think it has a bad neck.

It does not think it has a bad foot.

It can erase your difficulties as easily as you can erase a mistake on a painting, easily and swiftly and beautifully and well.

Now, to some extent, all of you take advantage of these abilities or you would not have physical bodies to begin with.

They simply would not last that long, in your terms.

But when you cannot do this for yourself, and when your own misconceptions hold you back from using your own abilities,

Then there are others who can reawaken your own energies and direct them to your advantage;

Who can meet you and speak with you when you are in more auspicious states than the one you usually call conscious—

When you are at your most creative and alert, in other words, when you are asleep.

These others can then speak to you and communicate with you, illuminate you as to the reasons behind your difficulty and help you erase that difficulty.

I want each of you to understand, however, that you have these abilities and you use them.

When you cut your finger the flesh is made new.

This is done automatically by a portion of yourself that is not conscious but is very vital and very real.

You are kept alive as you listen to me and yet you do not understand what keeps your body alive and functioning.

This is taken care of by the inner self and if you trust it, it will keep you in excellent health.

Whenever you doubt it then you have need of doctors and nurses and it is good to have them if there is no other place to turn.

There are many personalities, however, who understand your difficulties

And who sympathize with them and who help you when you call upon them and such is the healer upon whom you have called.

You are responsible for your health as well as for your illnesses.

You form your physical body according to your inner conception of what you are at any given time.

The word psychosomatic, therefore, is misleading to some extent.

Now, if I may say so, you have beautiful eyes (to Louise). You create them yourself. You are responsible, therefore, for them.

They represent a portion of you that you are materializing in physical reality with great success.

Is that, then, psychosomatic working backward?

([Louise:] "It could be, but I am not aware of things.")

You are aware of your body as you know it, and you form it, but this you do not yet realize.
Therefore, the point I am trying to make is that you form your own illnesses

And your own physical defects but you also form your entire physical being,

And the good points of your physical image are also your own work.

You can get rid of all the illness when you realize that you have the habit of creating and drawing.

ESP CLASS SESSION, NOVEMBER 10, 1970

I have said this before: If you were able to focus your attention upon the dissimilarities, merely those that you can perceive but do not,

Then you would be amazed that mankind can form any idea of an organized reality.

I look now between the two of you. When the others look at our friends here on the fancy blue couch, they see a picture of true organization.

There is an individual there, and an individual there, with space between.

The picture is equalized. It appears perfect and organized.

However, the space between our two friends is not vacant.

You think of it as vacant because you do not perceive what is there.

The picture appears to be very organized.

As soon as you realize that the picture is not complete, however, then you must begin to ask new questions,

And the old idea of the perfect organization is gone.

Now: As you know, you do not perceive the atoms and molecules that swim about the room,

Nor those that fill the space between our two friends, nor the forces— the field forces— that exist.

The couch seems to unite them since they sit upon it. And what do they sit upon?

Emptiness that you perceive as solidity.

Now without your particular physical senses you would not perceive the couch as solid.

Consciousness that has different perceptive mechanisms than your own is unaware of our now famous blue couch.

YOU make the organization.

YOUR thoughts perceive an organization.

You enforce the organization, and indeed create it.

Seth Speaks, Appendix, ESP Class Session, 6-23-70

A great painting of a battle scene, for example, may show the ability of the artist as he projects in all its appalling drama the inhuman and yet all-too-human conditions of war.

The artist is using his abilities. In the same way, man is using his abilities, and they are apparent when he creates a real war.

The artist who paints such a scene may do so for several reasons, because he hopes, through portraying such inhumanity, to awaken people to its consequences,

To make them quail and change their ways; because he is himself in such a state of disease and turmoil that he directs his abilities in that particular manner;

Or because he is fascinated with the problem of destruction and creativity, and of using creativity to portray destruction.

In your wars you are using creativity to create destruction, but you cannot help being creative.

Illness and suffering are not thrust upon you by God, or by All

That Is, or by an outside agency.

They are by-products of the learning process, created by you, in themselves quite neutral.

On the other hand, your existence itself, the reality and nature of your planet,

The whole existence in which you have these experiences, are also created by you, using the abilities of which I have spoken.

Illness and suffering are the result of the misdirection of creative energy.

They are a part of the creative force, however.

They do not come from a different source than, say, health and vitality.

Suffering is not good for the soul, unless it teaches you how to stop suffering.

That is the purpose.

SS 580

Fairy Tales Create Quite The Scene In A Illusionary Dream

The emergence of action within a time scheme is actually one of the most important developments connected with the beginning of your world.

The Garden of Eden story in its most basic sense refers to man's sudden realization that now he must act within time.

His experiences must be neurologically structured. This immediately brought about the importance of choosing between one action and another, and made acts of decision highly important.

This time reference is perhaps the most important within earth experience, and the one that most influences all creatures.

Free will operates in all units of consciousness, regardless of their degree — but it operates within the framework of that degree.

Man possesses free will, but that free will operates only within man's degree — that is, his free will is somewhat contained by the frameworks of time and space.

He has free will to make any decisions that he is able to make.

This means that his free will is contained, given meaning, focused, and framed by his neurological structure.

He can only move, and he can only choose therefore to move, physically speaking, in certain directions in space and time. That time reference, however, gives his free will meaning and a context in which to operate.

Dreams, "Evolution," and Value Fulfillment, sess. 904 - February 27, 1980

Now, Seth does not 'dig' worship.

For one thing, Seth understands worshippers. And, when one understands worshippers, one does not dig worship!

If you will think this sentence over, then you will realize, that those who worship do no real honor to the object of their worship.

For upon that object, they place all of their hopes, all of their dreams, all of their inadequacies, and all of the responsibility for their lives;

And even a god - a sane god - would refuse to accept such worship.

The god would understand also the nature of the universe, and the nature of playful creativity,

And would know that such a worship is - at its base now, at its base - a denial of the very vitality of life.

For All That Is endows creatures with a latent capacity for the greatest kind of creativity.

And a creature who says, "Save me, Oh Lord, and hear my voice!

Look upon my iniquity and save me from my sin, and rule Thou my life which Thou hast indeed given me," says really,

Oh, Lord, thou hast given me no capacity for reason, no free will, no power, no authority, and no goodness;

And since Thou hast wronged me of all the holy virtue, then

Thou might as well protect me, for I have no abilities of my own, and Thou hast made me without honor.

Therefore, it is Thy duty to preserve the poor world upon which indeed Thy mighty foot is placed!

So, Seth does not dig worship.

But worshippers have to face the god that they believe they are worshipping.

For they are saying,

"You have made an inferior product - a flawed image.

I am despicable, and therefore, although I adore you and I say,

"Yea, though I travel through the valley of death, et cetera", and though I 'say', I adore you, Oh Lord!" what I 'mean is',

I hate you because you have created me an inferior creature, and therefore I will make you pay - for my iniquities, Oh Lord, are yours.

How can I be good when Thou hast made me evil?

How can I hold up my head in the universe, when Thou hast made me flawed?

Therefore, do I crawl upon my knees to show you that I cannot stand upright before

Thee, for Thou hast made me flawed!

Such worshippers take it for granted that the product of God is poor - from an inadequate factory - a poor cosmic assembly line.

Ford calls back it's products if they are flawed, and so such worshippers say,

Oh Lord, call back humanity, for we are flawed!! And, no one answers, so it seems.

When the old answers and the old organizations no longer have any meaning to the individual;

When he can find reflected in the official answers none of his own questions;

Then the individual rises up from within itself; and, as once this civilization was born, so shall others be born in the same way.

And so always, from within itself does the race then go within its psyche for newer revelations;

Newer in that they are fresher to the source of itself - they have not been worn away by distortions and so in-turned by organizations that their meaning has become lost.

So you arise out of yourselves individually, and out of the heart of your psyche; and so shall the civilization also emerge out of its mass psyche.

'Conversations with Seth', book one, chapter one, by Susan M Watkins © - 25th Anniversary Edition

People who can ignore the physical evidence of wars will triumph.

You are the power of God manifested.

You are not powerless. To the contrary, through your being, the power of God is strengthened, for you are a portion of what He is.

You are not simply an insignificant, innocuous clump of clay through which He decides to show Himself.

You are he manifesting as you. You are as legitimate as He is.

If you are a part of God, then He is also a part of you.

And, in denying your own worth, you end up denying His as well.

I do not like to use the term "He", meaning God, since All-That-

Is is the origin of not only all sexes but of all realities, in some of which sex, as you think of it, does not exist.

Affirmation is in the spontaneous motion of the body as it dances.

Many churchgoers who consider themselves quite religious do not understand the nature of love or affirmation

As much as some bar patrons, who celebrate the nature of their bodies and enjoy the spontaneous transcendence as they let themselves go with the motion of their beings.

True religion is not repressive, as life itself is not.

When Christ spoke, he did so in the context of his times, using the symbolism and vocabulary that made sense to a particular people in a particular period of history, in your terms.

He began with their beliefs and using their references tried to lead them into freer realms of understanding.

With every translation, the Bible has changed its meaning, being interpreted in the language of the times.

Christ spoke in terms of good and bad spirits because these represented the people's beliefs.

In their terms he showed them that "bad" spirits could be vanquished.

But, these were, then, symbols accepted as realities by the people, sometimes for quite "normal" diseases and human conditions.

The very term, "Love your neighbor as yourself", was an ironic statement, for in that society no man loved his neighbor but distrusted him heartily. Much of Christ's humor has been lost, therefore.

In the Sermon on the Mount, the phrase "the meek shall inherit the earth" has been grossly misinterpreted.

Christ meant: "You form your own reality. Those who think thoughts of peace will find themselves safe from war and dissension.

They will be untouched by it. They will escape and, indeed, inherit the earth.

Thoughts of peace, particularly in the middle of chaos, take great energy. People who can ignore the physical evidence of wars and purposely think thoughts of peace will triumph. But, in your terminology the word "meek" has come to mean spineless, inadequate, lacking energy.

In Christ's time, the phrase about the meek inheriting the earth implied the energetic use of affirmation, of love and peace.

Session 674 The Nature of Personal Reality

Let us make a clear distinction here:

Your conscious beliefs direct the flow of unconscious processes which bring your ideas into physical reality,

So while your thoughts cause your experience, you are NOT consciously aware of how this takes place.

The Nature of Personal Reality, session 640, Page 188 - Jane Roberts

Mental associations are living things.

They are formations of energy assembled into invisible structures, through processes quite as valid and complicated as the organization of any group of cells.

Comparing them with cells, they are of briefer duration, generally speaking.

But your thoughts form structures as real as the cells.

Their composition is different in that no solidity is involved in your terms.

As living cells have a structure, react to stimuli and organize according to their own classification, so do thoughts.

Thoughts thrive on association.

They magnetically attract others like themselves,

And like some strange microscopic animals they repel their 'enemies,' or other thoughts that are threatening to their own survival.

Using this analogy, your mental and emotional life forms a framework composed of such structures,

And these act directly upon the cells of your physical body.

The Nature of Personal Reality, Session 633

Time Begins And Ends Now

The universe will begin yesterday.

The universe began tomorrow.

Both of these statements are quite meaningless.

The tenses are wrong, and perhaps your time sense is completely outraged.

Yet the statement:

The universe began in some distant past, is in basic terms, just as meaningless.

Whenever science or religion seeks the origin of the universe, they search for it in the past.

The universe is being created NOW. Creation occurs in each moment, in your terms.

The illusion of time itself is being created NOW.

It is therefore somewhat futile to look for the origins of the universe by using a time scheme that is in itself, at the very least, highly relative.

Your NOW, or present moment, is a psychological platform.

Dreams, "Evolution," and Value Fulfillment, Vol. 1, Session 882

Some waking states, of course, come very close to sleep states.

These blend one into the other so that the rhythm often goes unnoticed.

These gradations of consciousness are accompanied by changes in the physical organism.

In the more sluggish periods of waking consciousness there is a lack of concentration,

A cutting off of stimuli to varying degrees, an increase in accidents, and generally a lower body tone.

Now: This extended period, given to waking consciousness without rest periods,

Builds up chemicals in the blood that are discharged in sleep.

But in the meantime they make the body sluggish and retard conscious concentration.

The long sleep period to which you are accustomed then does become necessary.

A vicious circle then is formed.

This forces over-stimulations during the night, increasing the body's work,

Making it perform continuously over an extended time physical purifications

That ideally would be taken care of in briefer periods of rest.

The ego feels threatened by the extended "leave of absence" it must take,

(It) Becomes wary of sleep, and sets up barriers against the dream state.

Many of these are highly artificial.

Seth Speaks Part One: Chapter 8: Session 533, June 1, 1970

Seth sat back in the chair and rocked back and forth, eyes closed,
for several minutes before continuing.

As long as you believe in aggression and in force, in this country,

You elect persons who believe in aggression and in force

And who react to it, and so do the people in all the other nations.

Unfortunately, you equate aggression with strength,

So you are afraid to elect a peaceful man.

And all the other countries feel the same,

So they are afraid to put into power, by whatever means,
peaceful men.

So your world situation is the result of your individual beliefs,
en masse.

Now, when individually you believe in peace, and when you no
longer believe that good is weak and evil is powerful,

Then on a countrywide basis, you will put people in power who
believe in the active nature of peace.

And again, there is no other answer.

I am, basically, as you are, independent of flesh.

But in your terms, and in your terms alone, you have
issue--physical issue,

That must deal with the time and the place that you have created.

And as long as you believe that you must fight for peace, you will lose your issue.

In greater terms, you know quite well that you cannot annihilate a consciousness.

And all of those who die in war know that they will die in war ahead of time.

But still, in physical terms, all that must be worked out,

For the very point of physical existence is that you realize that your thoughts become matter while you are here,

And matter can be vulnerable.

And so through direct experience you learn what happens when you let thoughts and feelings of aggression have full play.

I have said this in my book [The Nature of Personal Reality].

An artist may create a warscape,

And you can look at it, and it may be a masterpiece. But you are multidimensional creators!

And when you create a warscape, the brushstrokes suffer, for

You Are the brushstrokes.

And the guns are real, and the wounds are real.

But it is an excellent representation--an excellent multidimensional creative endeavor!

If you do not like the landscape, then you change the brushstrokes.

You wipe out the oil. You create a new painting.

"Conversations with Seth," by Susan Watkins. Chapter Twelve.

Scientists realize that the atmosphere of the earth has a distorting effect upon their instruments.

What they do not understand is that their instruments themselves are bound to be distortive.

Any material instrument will have built-in distortive effects.

The one instrument which is more important than any other is the mind (not the brain) the meeting place of the inner and outer senses.

The mind is distributed throughout the entire physical body and builds up about it the physical camouflage necessary for existence on the physical level.

The mind receives data from the inner senses and forms the necessary camouflage.

The brain deals exclusively with camouflage patterns, while the mind deals with basic principles inherent on all planes.

The brain is, itself, part of the camouflage pattern and can be interpreted and probed by physical instruments. The mind cannot.

The mind is the connective. It is here that the secrets of the universe will be discovered, and the mind itself is the tool of discovery.

You might say that the brain is the mind in camouflage.

Now I found intermission highly amusing. The conditions of which I have been speaking are one thing. As far as the effect of weather upon the moods of individuals, we do have something else.

For the weather is created by you, on a subconscious level.

The weather, at any given time, is a direct physical interpretation of the inner mass mind.

You do indeed react, but you have already created the conditions, you see, and you then react to these in both psychic and physical ways.

The inner state of each individual mind is projected outward.

The inner state causes chemical changes in the physical body.

Chemicals are thrown outward into the atmosphere. Hormones are released of particular varieties.

Very definite and unique electrical changes occur in the skin, which change on a mass level the atmosphere at any given unit.

All of these conditions merge to create the peculiar weather with its innumerable and constant changes.

These exterior conditions then affect the individual physical structures and individuals react to the peculiar conditions which they have themselves created.

The process is constant.

The weather causes psychic activities, to some extent assassinations and accidents.

On the other hand, the atmosphere was originally mental and the weather originates from this mental level.

Now, I will tell you. In many ways, you are children.

And because you do not understand the truths and have not reached or understood the connections, it does not mean that the truths do not exist.

And you must work towards them and use your mind to do so. It will not lead you astray. You can trust it. It will help you arrive at some questions.

You are playing games with yourselves. You are using your mind, but you are not using it correctly. You are using it to mask the true questions.

You are setting up a game of checkers - one part of you is playing one game, and another part is playing another game.

And I will have more to say to you. I have told you time and time again in class, and I tell you all again. And Ruburt has told you: YOU FORM YOUR OWN REALITY.

You form the world that you know ~ and you form your own image.

And there is no justification for violence. Now the words sound simple. None of you has fully accepted them except as they apply to others.

You must apply them to yourself. You must look within yourself and then apply these truths, and learn from them. They are not theoretical ideas. They are realities.

You operate in accordance with these truths whether you realize it or not.

It is not enough to listen ~ you must look within yourself.

It is not enough to play games. It is not enough to squint at yourself to look at one motivation to accept partially.

Do you want to know what freedom is? Then I will tell you.

Freedom is the inner realization that you are an individual. That you do create your reality, that you do have the freedom. And the joy and the responsibility of forming the physical reality in which you live.

Then you can change the reality. Then you are free to move.

Then you are free to misplace violence. and you are free from it.

You are not free when you say: The idea works for everyone but me - but my symptoms are caused by something else.

And when I am violent, different rules apply. Everyone else forms their own physical reality but not me.

My reality is caused by heredity or environment. Every other nation, every other people form their own violence and are responsible for their own miserable condition.

But my people they are right! Any problems that they have are caused by other agencies beyond them.

Then you are not facing yourselves individually or as a people.

You are meant to look at your physical condition, not to compare it against what you want, and what is good ~ and change the inner self accordingly.

Any evils in the world are symptoms of your own inner disorders and are meant to lead you to cure them.

There is a beauty and a strength and a joy in looking within yourselves and a freedom from bondage. And I hope that when I am finished with you all, you will taste some of that joy and freedom.

You will not get it from a book. You will not get it like your chocolates (indicating the box on the table) wrapped up in a merry box.

You will not get it by making exceptions. You will not get it by saying: I am the exception to the rule! You will not get it by running away from yourself.

You will find this joy and this freedom by learning to look inward and by realizing that you create ~ the reality that you know.

Your successes and your failures alike you have yourselves created.

If you would but understand this is the truth that would make you free.

Now, I will say this over and over again. I will say it simply and I will repeat it time and time again until you understand intuitively what I mean.

And I will say it in many ways.

AND AGAIN I WILL TELL YOU: THE ENERGY THAT IS BEHIND AND WITHIN ME NOW. THAT ENERGY IS AVAILABLE TO ALL OF YOU. AND RESIDES WITHIN THE

SELVES OF WHICH YOU ARE COMPOSED. YOU HAVE ACCESS
TO IT. IT IS YOU WHO HAVE DENIED THE KNOWLEDGE.
AND IT IS YOU WHO CLOSE YOUR EYES.

ELIAS: Yes. It is dependent upon the individual, for there is an
involvement of each individual's beliefs and their own energy,
and how they are manipulating energy and how they are
configuring that energy.

Although you may create in dis-eases similarities, as your
physicians can label certain dis-eases and the cellular function
may be created quite similarly, but the reason that it is created is
very individual.

ELIAS: Yes. And you generate waves of energy quite consistently,
and in those waves of energy, there are collectives that create
quite similarly.

Generally, it begins with one individual that creates some new
idea and they share that idea with other individuals, be it's what
you term to be good or bad, and it gains popularity, for other
individuals agree.

And the more individuals that agree, the more energy is generated
with that subject, and then it creates a mass expression.

ELIAS: Which can be in the form of a dis-ease. An individual may
invent the idea and create the distortion of cells within their
body consciousness

And create this dis-ease, and may share that information with
other individuals and they become frightened.

And if they become frightened, they are agreeing with the other
individual that has created the dis-ease, and that generates the
possibility that they may also.

These are examples of your suggestibility. Many individuals concern themselves with appearance and weight.

An individual may invent an idea of how to alter weight quickly and share that with other individuals, and if they agree, it gains energy and it becomes a new trend.

Now, I speak to you somewhat harshly, and yet all of you know that what I say is true.

You must look inward and apply these truths.

It does no good to look outward and apply them to others. You must take the first step and take ~ responsibility for yourself. . . and then you have the freedom to change it.

If you do not accept the responsibility, then you do not have the power to change.

The power to change is within you.

Remember that you only perceive a portion of your own reality.

Do you realize the implications if you make no effort to realize your own reality and to probe into it and to explore it and to understand it?

How do you think you can understand the nature of reality if you do not make an attempt to see the truths that are within yourself?

Then why do you expect other truths to be given to you? Words are but symbols!

Words are not truths.

You must seek through the words for the reality that they represent.

And you must seek within yourselves for the reality that you represent.

There is no security in ignorance, there is only fear!

Know Thy Self Inside And Out

You are but symbols of yourselves.

I can tell you how to meet your own identities.

And I have told you, but no one can make you look into yourselves.

I can look within you and beyond you into the selves that you really are.

I can see your potentials and your abilities and your promise. . .

And you could see your own potentials and promise if you would open your inner eyes, if you would look within yourselves.

Each consciousness, regardless of its physical form, is filled with creativity, and joy, and possibilities. . . each is unique.

You are at a certain level of development or you would not be here. Because you are at this level of development, you are ready and able to use your abilities more.

You are able to look within yourselves. There is nothing stopping you but you. And it is for this reason that I speak severely with you this evening.

You have no idea of the discovery that is possible for you.

You can change your physical existence as you know it. And you can do it tomorrow morning. You have the ability to do this.

Until you realize that you have this ability, you are powerless.

When you realize and accept the fact that you form your physical reality, you can change it instantly. . .

That is your freedom. I cannot give it to you,
but you can take it. . . and I challenge you to do so.

It is yours for the taking... freedom of action. . . it is yours, accept it.

It brings with it not only responsibility, but joy. . . such as you
have never known.

It is yours this instant. You have only to accept it.

Now, you have your kindergarten class. Your children play with
wooden blocks and they make houses.

You play with mental blocks and you make worlds.

You encourage your children in their creativity, and when they
make errors and when you see that their houses will not stand,
you do not kick the blocks aside in ire.

You try, instead, to explain how the blocks must be placed one
upon the other, or you smile at their childish efforts.

When the child does not understand what you are saying, you
tell him again... and again. . . and you tell him in different ways.

You realize that the child must understand the truths. You
explain the truths as you know them. . . the best that you can.
You tell stories and parables.

And you speak in words that are familiar.

And you use baby talk when necessary.

Baby talk in that you do not speak exactly as you would speak to
an adult.

And the baby talk is not obvious. And so I hope the baby talk (here) is not obvious!

It is time for you all to understand the material as I have given it, to use your mind.

You have been in this class long enough to pass now beyond kindergarten.

It is time for you to challenge your own mind and your own intuition.

I shall cease speaking to you as kindergarten children, and I shall expect that you will cease thinking like kindergarten children.

Now, imagine this. Within you, there are sounds, colors, sights that stretch backward into infinity.

Faces face this room; your eyes look out upon physical reality.

Imagine, however, that you have innumerable faces, for our analogy.

And that these faces look out into other realities quite as varied and quite as real. For this is indeed the case.

You can close your physical eyes and focus upon these other realities in which you also have your existence. And you can learn to manipulate in physical reality the better, because you understand your full potential.

I challenge you to open your inner eyes, to use your minds, to use your inner intuitions.

I challenge you to be yourselves, and it is the greatest challenge that could be given you and it is the only way that you will learn

Again, my words are symbols.

The inner part of you will respond to the symbols. I can only begin to hint at the freedom available to you if you will but open your eyes.

You must act. You can easily open within yourselves those channels to creativity. You can use these.

You can attain a true sense of identity. You have only a shadowy understanding of what the world means.

When I see the shadows that you accept as yourselves, and when I see the brilliant and free identities that you are, then it is impossible for me not to speak to you in such a manner.

You must begin to change the reality that you know. These ideas must go through you and outward to others.

You cannot take yourselves as exceptions. There is a purpose for each one of you.

It is your own purpose and it is up to you to fulfill it,

And it necessitates the full use of all your abilities, your mental abilities, and your intuitional abilities.

You must demand the most of yourselves, for some of you will be involved later in asking others to demand the most of themselves and you must serve as examples.

You are meant to teach other classes, but you must develop your own abilities to do so.

Truths must be translated so that you can understand them.

"A chat with Seth" features unpublished transcripts from Jane Roberts' ESP classes held in the early seventies. Jane Roberts (C) L. Davies Butts

Listen To Your Self

Listen to yourself and ask yourself what is your name.

If you were alone in the middle of the universe, surrounded by darkness and someone said, some voice out of the ether, "What is your name?"

What would you answer?

So I ask you, What is your name, each of you?

My name is nameless. I have no name. I give you the name of Seth because it is a name and you want names.

You give yourself the names and you have taken names because you believe names are important.

Your existence is nameless. It is not voiceless, but it is nameless.

The names you take are structures upon which you hang your image.

One thousand years hence what will your names mean, and one thousand years before this moment, what did your names mean, and what have those names to do with your experience?

You are what you are, and what you are is nameless.

What you are cannot be uttered and no letter or alphabet can contain it.

Yet now you need words and letters and names and objects.

You want magic that will tell you what you are.

Deena: "May I ask a question?"

Seth answered jovially: You may indeed. I may not answer but you may ask!

As Deena started to state her question, Seth reached for Jane's glass and interrupted Deena quite good naturedly.

I am drinking Ruburt's wine. It is not as good as brandy, but I am drinking it because beggars cannot be choosers!

Deena: "OK, the question is, in terms of accepting names because we think we need them, it seems like some people have masculine names and some people have feminine names.

I thought originally that I had understood that on other levels there really wasn't a masculine or feminine, so why."

Because they fit in with your beliefs.

Deena: But there really is no such thing.

That was a statement!

Deena: That was a question.

Male and female are biological focuses through which you experience what you think of as physical reality.

It is a focus, like light is a focus.

Deena: "But in terms of an entity name, if that goes beyond physical reality, why have masculine or feminine?"

Because entity names still fit in with your beliefs that you need names.

As you believe that you cannot speak to me unless I have a name, so I am Seth.

Rick: "Is this the entity's beliefs or our belief?"

Your belief.

Paula: "Seth, why do you represent yourself as masculine?"

Because it was the easiest way that Ruburt would relate to me,

And also because it was the easiest way that energy, ancient energy, could be explained within the framework that you and others could understand.

Sumari, you see, is the other side of the same picture and so all must be taken together – as each of you has many aspects.

Ruburt simply operates as a transparent window into other realities more effectively than you because of training, in your terms, in this life and others –

And because of an exquisite stubbornness.

You each, in your own way, are doing your own thing. And each of you are nameless.

That does not mean that you do not have an identity.

It simply means that a name has nothing to do with your identity, and that entity names are a means and a step along levels of belief that you can use.

I told Ruburt from our earliest sessions that he could call me Seth. I never said, "My name is Seth," for I am nameless.

I have had too many identities to cling to one name!

But you think your names define you, and you are afraid to depart from them.

And you think that your physical existence defines you, and you think the moment defines you, and you think that your beliefs define you.

ESP Class, 4-17-73

Let me take this moment to state again that there are no devils or demons, except as you create them out of your belief.

As mentioned earlier, good and evil effects are basically illusions. In your terms all acts, regardless of their seeming nature, ARE a part of a greater good.

I am not saying that a good end justifies what you would consider an evil action.

While you still accept the effects of good and evil, then you had better choose the good.

I am saying this as simply as possible. There are profound complications beneath my words, however.

Opposites have validity only in your own system of reality. They are a part of your root assumptions, and so you must deal with them as such.

You are being taught, and you are teaching yourselves to handle energy,

To become conscious co-creators with All That Is,

And one of the 'stages of development' or learning processes includes dealing with opposites as realities.

In your terms, the ideas of good and evil help you recognize the sacredness of existence, the responsibility of consciousness.

Seth Speaks, Session 587

The reincarnating personality enters the new fetus according to its own inclinations, desires, and characteristics, with some built-in safe guards.

However, there is no rule, then, saying that the reincarnating personality must take over the new form prepared for it either at the point of conception, in the very earliest months of the fetus's growth

Or even at the point of birth.

The process is gradual, individual, and determined by experience in other lives.

It is particularly dependent upon emotional characteristics - not necessarily of the last incarnate self,

But the emotional tensions present as a result of a group of past existences.

Seth Speaks Session 556

Thoughts and emotions directly activate the mechanics of physical matter, alter and transform it, maintain it, and also destroy it.

The beginning of your physical universe occurred when conscious energy directed enough of its attention in what was generalized dimension,

To spark the formation of physical properties.

The creation was just that. The first explosion of psychic energy in an un-generalized dimension sparked the birth of specifics.

Before this the generalized dimension was simply nonexistent, a vacuum, which consciousness had not yet filled.

Since consciousness or action can never fully materialize itself, there are literally infinities of such nonexistent areas from which new dimensions can spring.

Consciousness or action forms all realities. What is not simply represents a possibility which consciousness may bring to life.

Consciousness then formed out of itself a new dimension which was the physical one.

The formation, the explosion, of energy, shattered consciousness into an infinity of parts,

Each with all the abilities in here within consciousness itself.

From itself, therefore, and of itself, consciousness gave birth to its new dimension of experience,

And then experienced what it had created, further extending itself and in turn bringing forth further possibilities of development.

Consciousness therefore continually creates and maintains itself, and this includes the physical materialization,

The properties of the dimension, and yet basically there is no difference between the creator in these terms and the created.

Nor between inner reality, which forms physical matter, and physical objects themselves,

For the atoms which are manipulated to form objects are

themselves a portion of consciousness, and alive in those terms.

They respond to emotional and psychic directives as the physical body responds to light.

All of this talk about consciousness and action does not mean that consciousness is without identity.

You could not appreciate nor understand, nor can I, the nature of identity as it is known in the overall.

What we know of identity represents fragments and splinters that we call ourselves.

These are part however of the prime identity.

The splinters are possessed of individuality, and such units will never be dissolved.

They are still but a portion of prime identity, and without them, prime identity could not know itself

Nor act upon itself nor develop its own abilities or potentials.

Now in the same way that consciousness originated the physical dimension,

You as portion of consciousness continue to maintain and create it anew.

Your source of energy is that first creation, in which consciousness focused, where before it had not.

You also then know and develop yourselves through your own creations,

And you automatically create and maintain your physical environment in the same manner that you breathe.

Your physical image and your physical environment are both materialized extensions of your inner selves.

The physical body itself however has much more to do with the maintenance of environment than is realized,

For you use it so that your environment becomes almost like a second body, extending outward from the first, through which you express your inclinations and characteristics.

There are intricate complications that arise as environmental elements merge and mix with those of others.

You can see here the formation of nationalistic characteristics on a mass level.

This is constant creation. The initial creation provided the energy, the dimension, of possibility itself,

But every particle of consciousness will always attempt to express itself within as many possibilities as possible.

The inner self therefore creates the physical body and the land upon which it moves.

Bear in mind also that as individuals, you are creating new dimensions through which consciousness can know itself,

Both in physical experience and within other systems.

As a part of consciousness other systems are not closed to you,

But as physical organisms, other systems are closed to you.

TES8 Session 338 May 1, 1967

From The Inner Self The Soul Sings

True spirituality is a thing of joy and of the earth, and has nothing to do with fake adult dignity.

It has nothing to do with long words and sorrowful faces.

It HAS to do with the dance of consciousness that is within you, and with the sense of spiritual adventure that is within your hearts.

That is the meaning of spirituality; and as I have told you before,

If I could I would do a merry dance about the room to show you that your vitality is not dependent upon a physical image.

It is not dependent upon your youth. It is not dependent upon your body.

It rings and sings through the universe, and through your entire personality. It is a sense of joy that makes all creativity probable.

So do not think you are being spiritual when you are being long faced, and do not think you are being spiritual when you berate yourself for your sins.

The seasons within your system come and go.

The sun falls upon your face whether you think you are a sinner or a saint.

The vitality of the universe is creativity and joy and love, and THAT is spirituality.

And that is what I shall tell the readers of my book.

Your will is your intent.

All of the power of your being is mobilized by your will, which makes its deductions according to your beliefs about reality.

Each of you use your will in your own way. Each of you have your own way of dealing with challenges.

The will operates according to the personality's beliefs about reality, so its desires are sometimes tempered as those beliefs change.

Many people never learn to apply the power of the will at all.

The "Unknown" Reality, Vol. 2, Session 713

If you are convinced that your world is not safe, then it seems sensible to protect yourself in questionable areas by expecting the worst, so that you will be prepared.

Unfortunately, such expectations are disadvantageous.

They have, however, a strong basis in your society, from childhood up.

Wear a sweater or you'll catch a cold. A simple enough suggestion it seems, a preventative measure.

Yet, in that innocent remark lies the assumption that a cold can be expected, rather than a normal state of health.

There are all kinds of like suggestions, all meant as 'preventative measures.

AND:

Whenever you reinforce the idea of threat, defense must be built up.

Some threats are realistic and some are not.

If you concentrate upon your daily, natural, prime events, you will not live under a constant sense of threat.

If you worry about probable future threats, you lose some of that natural safety

And if you do that, as a matter of course, you not only lose that safety,

But you project threats into the future.

The first quote from The Personal Sessions, Book 3, Session 1/19/76 The second quote from The Personal Sessions, Book 3, Session 9/10/1977

Earlier in this book I mentioned alternate presents on several occasions, and reincarnational lives are indeed alternate presents.

There is interaction between you and your reincarnational selves constantly. There is, as your friend Sue Watkins said, "constant action across the board."

Those [so-called 'past' selves] are not dead, in other words.

Your understanding of this must be limited because you automatically think in terms of one life experience at a time, and in linear patterns of development.

In your terms, a reincarnational self can be aware of your environment, and interact sometimes through your own relationships.

Certain "present happenings" can, indeed, spark such interactions.

In quite other terms, however, the reincarnated personality, while interacting with or through you,

Can still be having other kinds of experience at other levels.

Because time is open-ended, as you think of it,

You can also affect what you would think of as past reincarnational selves, and at times react in and to their environment.

You would usually do this in the dream state, but this is often accomplished just below the level of waking consciousness

And is blotted out by you as you go about your daily business.

Strong emotional associations can often trigger such responses.

Reincarnation, as it is usually explained, in terms of one life before another, is a myth;

But a myth enabling many to partially understand facts that they would otherwise dismiss –

Insisting as they do upon the concept of continuity of time.

Seth Speaks The Eternal Validity of the Soul APPENDIX: Session 595

Christ was the symbol of man's emerging consciousness, holding within himself the knowledge of man's potential.

His message was meant to be carried beyond the times, but this interpretation is often not made.

There are indeed lost gospels, written by men in other countries in that time, relating to

Christ's unknown life, to Sessions not given in the Bible.

The messages were given in other terms, but again they reflected the affirmation of the self and its continued existence after physical death.

Regardless, Christ's message was one of affirmation.

Christ as you think of him was simply saying that you form your own reality.

He tried to rise above the idea-systems of those times, yet even he had to use them,

And so the connotations of sin and punishment distorted the message given.

Now: the message of the Christ entity was, in religious terms "You are all children of

God—the 'sinner' as well as the saint."

Indeed, according to the original Christ thesis, while a man could sin, no man was identified as a sinner.

Christ's message was that each man is good inherently, and is an individualized portion of the divine —

And yet a civilization based upon that precept has never been attempted.

The vast social structures of Christianity were instead based upon man's "sinful" nature

Not the organizations and structures that might allow him to become good,

Or to obtain the goodness that Christ quite clearly perceived man already possessed.

Christ, as you know, was a common name, so when I say that there was a man named

Christ involved in those events, I do not mean to say that he was the biblical Christ.

His life was one of those that were finally used to compose the composite image of the biblical Christ.

Christ, as you understand him historically to be, spoke in parables and symbols.

Men often took him literally, but his message was that the spirit of God was within each person.

In terms of the symbolism, each person being a child of the father who dwelled in heaven.

But heaven meant an inner reality for Christ, not an exterior one.

For centuries, priests of one kind or another have been put in charge of "reading God's messages,

And interpreting them to the rest of mankind, just as in later times.

The scientists have been put in the position of interpreting man's own world to him—

In terms quite as esoteric as those of any religion.

The Christ drama is a case in point, where private and mass dreams were then projected outward into the historical context of time,

And then reacted to in such a way that various people became exterior participants —

But in a far larger mass dream that was then interpreted in the most literal of physical terms.

Your Christ figure represents, symbolically, your idea of God and his relationships.

Christ tried to return man to nature.

In a manner of speaking, again, there was no one Christ, historically speaking,

But the personage of Christ, or the entity, was the reality from which the entire dramatic story emerged.

Christ dealt with myths, once again—potent ones that stood for inner realities.

Christ clothed those realities in colorful stories gear to people's understanding.

I am using the name here, Christ, as one person for the sake of discussion for that entity touched many lives, each leaping into a kind of super-reality as it joyfully played its part in the religious drama.
The message was, "Do not condemn yourself or others," for Christ well knew that self- righteous condemnation of the self

Or of one's neighbors served to darken the door through which man might view his own potential and its greater source.

Now, you have been given the free will because the spirit of Christ is within you, this does not mean that you do not have free will.

The spirit of Christ gives you the life to do with it what you choose.

My message to the reader will be:

Basically, you are no more of a physical personality than I am, and in telling you of my reality I tell you of your own.

When the historical Christ "died," Paul was to implement the spiritual ideas in physical terms, to carry on.

He lingered after Christ, [just] as John the Baptist came before.

John and the historical Christ each performed their roles and were satisfied that they had done so.

Paul alone was left at the end unsatisfied, and so it is about his personality that the future Christ will form.

Matter Comes From Consciousness
Not The Other Way Around

No particle of matter is the same in the born infant, that was contained in either the fetus or earlier in the sperm or egg.

I am going into all this for a reason. Leave this for a moment, and consider a seed, a grass seed.

You say that grass grows from a seed, but the grass is not the seed.

The material of the grass is not the material of the seed. From experience you know that the seed will often precede grass.

As usual, this is putting things backward. The grass contains no particle of matter that is identical in the seed.

Here you see clearly the difference between value fulfillment and what you call growth.

In your physical field value fulfillment consists of the development of the ability of the immaterial to express itself within the physical field.

Growth is an erroneous conception that begins with the distortive idea of continuous physical matter, durable in time.

And as you know instead, matter is the simultaneous expression of consciousness.

Matter has little, really no, durability in itself, and is merely the instantaneous form taken by consciousness as it projects itself in the physical field.

Grass is common. It is supposed to grow from seed, yet again no particle of matter is the same in grass or seed.

Seed does not grow into grass.

Acorns do not grow into trees.

Children do not grow into adults.

In all instances, no particle of matter is the same in the so-called grown version, and the initial construction.

Matter does not grow. I cannot make this too plain.

There is obviously something identical, and some continuity between the child and the adult, but it is not matter.

Consciousness, according to its ability, projects itself into the physical plane, and through value fulfillment it constructs its image.

It must work according to its ability to do this. It must first get a foothold, so to speak; hence our seed.

As the consciousness attains its foothold it projects more effectively.

It dispenses with its atoms and molecules, or matter, almost instantaneously, as you know.

The atoms and molecules appear and disappear.

Their place is taken by others, so quickly that you do not notice the constant coming and going.

The form that consciousness takes in the field of matter is determined by its own strength and capacity.

Consciousness forces its way into matter.

You should see, then, that though you call a particular portion of grass one blade of grass, the matter that composes it is not static or permanent,

And it is not a particular physical object growing, since the matter that composes it is neither static or permanent.

You say that the matter that composes it steadily changes, but this is not the case.

The apparent continuity is a result of your inability to perceive the actual atoms that compose matter as they appear and disappear.

Because grass appears where seeds have been sown,

You have leaped to the conclusion that the matter of the seeds grows from the matter of which they are composed, and that grass grows from the actual matter of the seeds.

Again, there is absolutely no continuity in the matter that composes the seeds, and the matter that composes the grass.

What you have instead is the value fulfillment of the consciousness behind matter, as it expands and expresses itself in various forms.

Since you can more or less count upon the appearance of grass seed, preceding grass, all this may seem making much over nothing, but it is very important, as you will see later.

It is not matter that has continuity, and it is not matter that dictates the form.

Now that we have gone into the nature of matter as it pertains to grass, you will understand my next analogy more clearly.

Consider a lawn. Obviously this is an arbitrary designation for utility's sake.

Of itself, the matter of grass does not form itself into a lawn.

You merely designate certain portions of grass and call it lawn.

This is the same sort of thing you do when you designate certain portions of matter as blades of grass.

Lawns do not come from grass. That is, grass does not grow into a lawn. Do you follow me here?

ELIAS: I would say that that is an excellent beginning.

And what I would say to you, my friend, is to recognize that this is something that masters have in common.

It doesn't matter what they master, but that in becoming more aware, what they initially begin to do is connect with everything that is.

You term that to be nature, but it's bigger than nature.

Nature is perhaps the beginning of it, which would include the elements, but it's more than that.

It's everything. It's your entire universe and beyond. It's knowing that you are interconnected

And that that interconnectedness is greater than you even realize, and that there's so much more to it than you necessarily realize.

And I would say to you, my friend, that this is the beginning of it.

And I would very much encourage you to continue in that

direction because I would express the encouragement to you of paying attention while you're outside, to how much you ARE connected with everything.

Everything is a part of you and you are a part of all of it. And it reaches so far beyond your immediate environment or your environment as a whole.

And in that, that will lead you even more in a direction of recognizing that contentment,

Because it will lead you in the direction of realization of who and what you are.

I have expressed from the onset of this forum that you are glorious beings.

For the most part, almost no one believes me.
(Both laugh)

And almost everyone in their head, if not in words, argues with me. And in that, it's because you don't remember and you don't recognize just how glorious you genuinely are.

And in this, you are bright beings and very diverse beings.

And I would say that the more you can simply be and experience yourself as connected with everything, the more you will recognize just how glorious you are.

Because everything around you is glorious, and if everything around you is glorious and you are a part of it all, then you must be also.

Therefore, all of what is occurring in your world is purposeful and is an element of the Shift.

What is significant and important is allowing yourself the ability to be aware of what you want

And what you are generating in your individual experiences

That is contributing to the manner in which you want your world to be –

Which is an element that many individuals have not quite grasped yet,

That the actions that they incorporate in their mundane life, in their everyday comings and goings and interactions and actions,

Are a projection of energy that is contributing to a collective energy.

And in that, if the individual is incorporating satisfaction and comfort and directedness in their experience,

They are contributing to lessening the trauma that is being experienced and they are contributing to that widening of awareness.

If an individual is generating fear and protection

And conflict and argumentativeness and stubbornness or defense,

Or not incorporating responsibility for themselves, they are contributing an energy of more conflict and more trauma.

They may express to themselves and to other individuals that they disagree with violence

Or that they disagree with a war, or that they disagree with the methods of a terrorist,

But in generating absolutes in association with their own expressions

And being defensive or protective or generating conflicting
expressions in their own interactions,

They are contributing to the very expressions that they express
they do not agree with.

Elias

Seth on "Grace"; NOPR.
The state of grace is a condition in which all growth is effortless,

A transparent, joyful acquiescence that is a ground requirement
of all existence.

Your own body grows naturally and easily from its time of birth,

Not expecting resistance but taking its miraculous unfolding for
granted;

Using all of itself with great, gracious, creatively aggressive
abandon.

You were born into a state of grace, therefore.

It is impossible for you to leave it. You will die in a state of grace
whether or not special words are spoken for you, or water or oil
is poured upon your head.

You share this blessing with the animals and all other living
things. You cannot "fall out of" grace, nor can it be taken from
you.

You can ignore it. You can hold beliefs that blind you to its existence.

You will still be graced but unable to perceive your own uniqueness and integrity,

And blind also to other attributes with which you are automatically gifted.

Love perceives the grace in another.

Like natural guilt, the state of grace is unconscious in the animals.

It is protected. They take it for granted, not knowing what it is or what they do,

Yet it speaks through all their motions and they dwell in the ancient wisdom of its ways.

They do not have conscious memory, again, but the instinctive memory of the cells and organs sustains them.

All of this applies in degrees according to the species,

And when I speak of conscious memory I am using words that are familiar to you —

I mean a memory that can at any time look back through itself.

The dog does not recall joyful appreciation of his own state of grace from a past, nor anticipate a recurrence in any future.

With the large freedom provided by the conscious mind, however,

Man could stray from that great inner joy of being, forget it, disbelieve in it, or use his free will to deny its existence.

The splendid biological acceptance of life could not be thrust or forced upon his emerging consciousness, so to be effective, efficient, to emerge in the new focus of awareness,

Grace had to expand from the life of the tissue to that of the feelings, thoughts and mental processes.

Grace became the handmaiden of natural guilt, then.

Man became aware of his state of grace when he lived within the dimensions of his consciousness as it was turned toward his new world of freedom.

When he did not violate, he was aware of his own grace.

When he violated, it fell back into cellular awareness, as with the animals,

But he felt consciously cut off from it and denied.

NoPR Part One: Chapter 9: Session 636, January 29, 1973

When you are fairly happy and content in your daily life, you can be said to be in a state of grace.

On those occasions when you feel at one with the universe, or come upon an exceptional experience in which you seem to go beyond yourself,

You can be said to be in a state of illumination, and this has many degrees and levels.

In any such state your physical health benefits, generally speaking, though there may be some beliefs blocking in that direction.

NoPR Part Two: Chapter 10: Session 638, February 7, 1973

If you misinterpret the myths, then you may believe that man has fallen from grace and that his very creature hood is cursed,

In which case you will not trust your body or allow it its "natural" pattern of self- therapy.

Because you have free will you have the responsibility and the gift, the joy and the necessity, of working with your beliefs

And of choosing your personal reality as you desire.

I told you earlier (in the 636th session in Chapter Nine) that you cannot fall out of a state of grace.

Each of you must intellectually and emotionally accept it, however.

NoPR Part Two: Chapter 12: Session 648, March 14, 1973

Seth (ESP Class, 11-18-73):

Transcript Narration: Class discussions had ranged over a wide variety of subjects including last week's dreams, class dreams, out-of-body experiences and beliefs.

Jane had read a portion from Seth's new book. After the second class break, Wade was wondering if a previous statement of Seth's, in which he said to run from anyone who told you he had the truth,

Was in any way a contradiction with what Seth was saying in his book about beliefs.

Seth joined the class discussion speaking first to Wade:

When a man tells you,

My reality and my version of it is the only truth then run from it.

When he says, 'I have the truth and no one else has it' then run from him.

When he says, 'I hold the truth and you certainly do not have it then run from him.

I am telling you that you have your own truth –

That you make your own reality, and that is the truth.

You make your reality! When the meaning of those words really dawns upon you, you will yell back at me saying, I knew it all along.

It is so simple. Why did you make so much of it? In the meantime, however, it is not so apparent and so I say it again and again.

The self is not limited –

That gives you room to make your own truths and your own realities.

The self has no boundaries.

You can be yourself, experience yourself

And not be lost in the universe and still go beyond the boundaries that you now accept.

You form your own reality. You form your own reality according to your beliefs. There is no one truth.

So I cannot give you truth and any man -- or ghost or spirit -- who offers it to you in a pill or a potion or an idea, run from him.

For when he says, 'This is the truth,' he is saying that everything else is not truth,

And he is limiting your vision and your reality and structuring your trip.

Susan: "How can you say there is no truth except what one believes to be the truth? Is that the truth?"

This is not what I have said, and I will leave it to you when you examine the transcript, to see the difference.

There is no one truth. You are a truth.

Marjorie: "Except that you create your own reality."

Seth: You are a truth!

Rick: "Then, that you create your own reality is a belief."

Marjorie: "Then the fact that you create your own reality – what does truth mean?"

Seth: Ask yourself the question and tell me what answer you come up with

For you are already structuring your answer,

And all of your questions thus far are indeed structured through your beliefs about the word "truth.'"

Mary Jo: "When you say that the self is not limited and we find that difficult to absorb, is that because our system of beliefs creates realities that don't allow ourselves to manifest in an unlimited way?"

Seth: To some extent indeed, but also you have chosen the reality in which those beliefs exist as mass ideas.

Mary Jo: "Then our reality is that our self is limited so it becomes limited."

Seth: Until you realize that it is not limited.

Bob: "What about when you are working with the whims of others, as in music or something, working with the whims of others.

You have to make an impression on others. It calls for a certain power over them or power to communicate."

Seth: Now, when you are thinking in terms of power over.

Bob: "Not necessarily power over, but you've got to influence them in some way."

Seth: There is power to and not the power over.

There is the power to live, and the power to die, and the power to love, and the power to hate.

You have no power over anyone.

When you think that you do, then you are fooling yourself because if you have power over another,

Then another has power over you, and your beliefs become meaningless.

Tam: "Aren't there forces against you though?"

Seth: The only forces against you are those forces in yourself that you believe to be against you.

Tam: "Jane was talking before about her belief about work."

Seth: Those are beliefs that Ruburt held.

They were not forces working against Ruburt. And indeed, for some time Ruburt utilized those same beliefs quite well.

You can all utilize various beliefs quite well for a time.

Sometimes you do not realize that you carry them too far.

They are not negative beliefs, and many of the beliefs that hamper you now are not negative beliefs.

They are simply beliefs that are not working for you in the way that you want at this time in your reality.

At another time they might be quite handy.

Mary Jo: "Do you mean you wouldn't have them if you hadn't used them at some time or other?"

Seth: I do, indeed. They are ingredients.

The ingredients that you use to form your reality.

If you put too much salt in the cake, it may be a lousy cake,

But there is nothing wrong with salt!

Now, I will see to it that Ruburt reads to you a chapter of my book,

And then I hope to see you put the ideas in the book into practice

In forming your own reality and exuberantly trying out experiments with the reality that you have.

First, start with the goodies, not the problems.

Richard: "What would be the first step?"

Seth: If there is one thing I would have you do this week,

It is the same thing I would have you do up to now:

To realize emotionally, and not just intellectually, that you form
your reality.

Now look about you then this week in all the areas of your activity;

Your work, your personal relationships, your health, your joys
and your pains,

And see if you can find the connections between your beliefs and
your experience.

Examine your life and your consciousness in that way.

Feel the unrestricted energy that flows through you in some
directions and that is inhibited in others.

You each have an excellent laboratory in which to work— the
laboratory of your own consciousness.

Now, you should also have help in the dream state, and you can
indeed request it.

There are those, however, who seek goblins in each ray of light!

Bill: "You just said that if you wanted help you could ask for it.

You just ask yourself?"

Seth: And you believe that you will receive it.

Bill: "Well, I think I believe that.

Seth: There is no question that you can ask to which you do not have an answer.

Now if you believe that, each of you, then the answers to your own questions will be given to each of you.

But you must believe that the answers are there, and that you can indeed receive them.

You cannot say, Well, I will see if this works, but I am such an ass it probably will not work for me or,

It is so difficult to remember my dreams that I probably won't, but I will tell myself that I will,

And then give yourself a good suggestion!

You have already given yourself suggestions.

So you end up with counter-suggestions, one saying, 'I will remember my dreams and get the answer to my question, the other saying,

I will never remember my dreams, and I do not have the answers.

You make your own reality— Your dreaming reality, your waking reality

And all realities in which you have existence.

Death Is A Change In Dimensional Focus

There are no accidents.

Your joys come from you and your successes and your failures or what you think of as failures.

Tom: "Earlier in the evening we were talking about death and certain things that people went through in the final stages of this level of consciousness.

How does that effect different people? If a person has a violent death does that affect them on another level of reality differently than a person who has a peaceful and happy death?"

Seth: You are always dealing with individuals so the answer cannot be given in those terms.

But a person who chooses a violent death chooses that method, for example, over a lingering illness for his own reasons.

Susan: "Is one more beneficial than the other?"

Seth: Not at all.

Susan: "Why does one want to experience suffering?"

Seth: According to the person's beliefs.

Tom: So we shouldn't be that upset or affected by that type of situation?"

Seth: Now, some of this is in my book;

But many people would rather go out in a blaze of glory, whether it be gory or not,

Rather than lie in a hospital room.

Others would much prefer to lose their memories of this life, in your terms,

And step out quietly.

Some people prefer a life of excitement and danger and near-death;

Others much prefer a quiet life with books.

One is not better than the other. They each are.

Tom: "The question I have that I'm leading up to is that in this life right now, at my age, I have a certain attitude about dying.

Will that attitude that I have, the type of death that I want, stay with me? I don't want a violent death."

Seth: If you do not want a violent death, you will not have one--if you believe that you will not have a violent death.

If you think that you do not want a violent death because you believe that you will have one, that is another matter.

By Jane Roberts © Davies

As you read the words upon this page, you realize that the information that you are receiving is not an attribute of the letters of the words themselves.

The printed line does not contain information. It transmits information.

Where is the information that is being transmitted then, if it is not upon the page?

The same question of course applies when you read a newspaper, and when you speak to another person.

Your actual words convey information, feelings, or thoughts.

Obviously the thoughts or the feelings, and the words, are not the same thing.

The letters upon the page are symbols, and you have agreed upon various meanings connected with them.

You take it for granted without even thinking of it that the symbols — the letters — are not the reality — the information or thoughts — which they attempt to convey.

Now in the same way, I am telling you that objects are also symbols that stand for a reality who's meaning the objects, like the letters, transmit.

The true information is not in the objects any more than the thought is in the letters or in words.

Words are methods of expression.

So are physical objects in a different kind of medium.

You are used to the idea that you express yourselves directly through words.

You can hear yourself speak them. You can feel the muscles in your throat move, and if you are aware,

You can perceive multitudinous reactions within your own body — actions that all accompany your speech.

Physical objects are the result of another kind of expression. You create them as surely as you create words.

I do not mean that you create them with your hands alone, or through manufacture.

I mean that objects are natural by-products of the evolution of your species, even as words are.

Examine for a moment your knowledge of your own speech, however.

Though you hear the words and recognize their appropriateness,

And though they may more or less approximate an expression of your feeling, they are not your feeling, and there must be a gap between your thought and your expression of it.

The familiarity of speech begins to vanish when you realize that you, yourself, when you begin a sentence do not know precisely how you will end it, or even how you form the words.

You do not consciously know how you manipulate a staggering pyramid of symbols, picking from them precisely those you need to express a given thought. For that matter, you do not know how you think.

You do not know how you translate these symbols upon this page into thoughts, and then store them, or make them your own.

Since the mechanisms of normal speech are so little known to you on a conscious level, then it is not surprising that you are equally unaware of more complicated tasks that you also perform — such as the constant creation of your physical environment as a method of communication and expression.

It is only from this viewpoint that the true nature of physical matter can be understood.

It is only by comprehending the nature of this constant translation of thoughts and desires — not into words now, but into physical objects — that you can realize your true independence from circumstance, time, and environment.

Seth Speaks Chapter 5 Session 523, April 13, 1970 Jane Roberts © L. Davies

And neither then do seeds grow into grass. You perceive certain matter as blades of grass, as you perceive the matter of grass as lawn.

You can see clearly that the matter of grass in a lawn is not the same. Then understand also that the matter within one blade of grass is not the same.

You call a floor a floor. Matter may be added to the floor in the form of paint or varnish, yet you still call the floor the floor.

Paint may be added to a house, and paint may disappear from a house through weathering, and you still call a house a house.

You call yourself yourself, though the color of your hair may change;

And indeed the adult bears little resemblance to the child.

Form simply cannot be a characteristic of matter, since matter can be proven to come and go, while form in many cases remains recognizable.

This will be a vital point in later discussions. You must, and will, learn to look at things in a new way, and many implications will arise from tonight's discussion that will carry us further along our way.

You will indeed see clearly that matter is created simultaneously, and has no duration, but is completely and almost instantly replaced by other matter, and that identity and continuity are not characteristics of matter, but must be found in other places.

This has been a most fruitful session, and I will close it unless you have questions that you want to ask me.

("I guess I have none, for a change.
I felt that Jane might enjoy the extra time off.)
Then I shall say good evening.

Perhaps I shall accompany you to your house Saturday, though I refuse to do Ruburt's cleaning for him.

Let me tell you that only now, with this material, will we really begin our leap into real understanding of things as they are. My congratulations, both of you. You have hereby completed the preliminary lessons of our course; and I mean preliminary.

This is the material without which no deep understanding could ever be achieved. It marks the first important step in your development and understanding, and I will give you an A.

The Early Sessions, book 2, Session 71 July 15, 1964 - by Jane Roberts © L. Davies Butts

Seth: Hate Is Like A Summer Storm

When you do not express it, then you dam it up.

And you can express it against yourself in terms of physical symptoms, or in your relationship with others.

But if you realize it is nothing to be frightened of, then you are free of it. Hate is, as I have said before, like a summer storm.

When you let it go, it lets forth energy and rain that heals the earth. It is turned into quite constructive framework— it is good and natural.

Sky would never think of holding back its storm—again, it has better sense.

Do not fear negative thoughts.

That simply adds to what you consider negative energy. Where would the world be without thunderstorms, and even floods, and hurricanes, and earthquakes?

That is how the earth changes and renews itself. To deny your emotions, any of them, is denying the aspect of your own reality, and it is, literally, impossible.

Let it go and no one will be hurt. The universe is not afraid of your hatred. It can hold it easily.

Each individual has their own built-in defense and energy, and your hatred, directed even against them, will not hurt them.

The Seth Audio Collection Vol 1, selection 1 - Excerpt J - by Jane Roberts © L. Davies Butts

It means the further expansion of the concept of identity:

You would not only be aware of the you that you have always known, in the same way that you are now,

But a deeper sense of identity would also arise.

UR1 Section 2: Session 692 April 24, 1974

Instead, consciousness formed matter.

As I have said before, each atom and molecule has its own

consciousness.

Consciousness and matter and energy are one,

But consciousness initiates the transformation of energy into matter.

In those terms, the "beginning" of your universe was a triumph in the expansion of consciousness,

As it learned to translate itself into physical form.

The universe emerged into actuality in the same way,

But to a different degree, that any idea emerges from what you think of as subjectivity into physical expression.

The consciousness of each reader of this book existed before the universe was formed (in your terms)—

But that consciousness was un-manifested.

Your closest approximation—and it is an approximation only—of the state of being that existed before the universe was formed is the dream state.

In that state before the beginning, your consciousness existed free of space and time, aware of immense probabilities.

This is extremely difficult to verbalize, yet it is very important that such an attempt be made.

Your consciousness is a part of an infinitely original creative process.

I will purposely avoid using the word "God" because of the connotations placed upon it by conventional religion.

I will make an attempt to explain the characteristics of this divine process throughout this book. I call the process "All That Is."

All That Is is so much a part of its creations that it is almost impossible to separate the "creator from the creations,"

For each creation also carries indelibly within it the characteristics of its source.

DEaVF1 Chapter 1: Session 882, September 26, 1979

I am not assigning human traits to energy. Instead, your human traits are the result of energy's characteristics—

A rather important difference.

DEaVF1 Chapter 2: Session 884, October 3, 1979

We Are The Probabilities We Experience

STORIES OF THE BEGINNING, AND THE

MULTIDIMENSIONAL GOD

History as you think of it represents but one thin line of probabilities, in which you are presently immersed.

It does not represent the entire lifetime of your species or the catalogue of physical activities, or begin to tell the story of physical creatures, their civilizations, wars, joys, technologies, or triumphs.

Reality is far more diverse, far richer and unutterable than you can presently suppose or comprehend.

Evolution as you think of it and as it is categorized by your scientists, represents but one probable line of evolution, the one in which, again, you are presently immersed.

There are, therefore, many other equally valid, equally real evolutionary developments that have occurred and are occurring and will occur, all within other probable systems of physical reality.

The diverse, endless possibilities of development possible could never appear within one slender framework of reality.

With splendid innocence and exuberant pride, you imagine that the evolutionary system as you know it is the only one, that physically there can be no more.

Now, within the physical reality that you know there are hints and clues as to the nature of other physical realities.

There are, latent, within your own physical forms other senses, unused,

That could have come to the front but in your probability did not.

Now, I have been speaking of earthly development, realties therefore clustered about earthly aspects as you know them.

No evolutionary line is a dead one.

Therefore, if in your system it disappears, it emerges within another.

All probable materializations of life and consciousness have their day, and create those conditions within which they can flourish, and their day, in your terms, is eternal.

I am speaking now, in this chapter, mainly about your own planet and solar system, but the same applies to all aspects of your physical universe.

You are aware, then, of only one specific, delicately balanced but unique portion of physical existence.

You are not only creatures of corporal being, forming images of flesh and blood, embedded in a particular kind of space and time;

You are also creatures rising out of a particularized dimension of probabilities, born

From dimensions of actuality richly suited to your own development, enrichment and growth.

SS 559

The inner self is embarked upon an exciting endeavor;

In which it learns how to translate its reality into physical terms.

The conscious mind is brilliantly attuned to physical reality, then,

And often so dazzled by what it perceives that it is tempted to think physical phenomena is a cause, rather than a result.

Deeper portions of the self always serve to remind it that this is not the case.

When the conscious mind accepts too many false beliefs, particularly if it sees that inner self as a danger, then it closes out these constant reminders.

When this situation arises the conscious mind feels itself assailed by a reality that seems greater than itself, over which it has no control.

The deep feeling of security in which it should be anchored is lost.

The false beliefs must be weeded out so that the conscious mind can become aware of its source once again, and open to the inner channels of splendor and power available to it.

The Nature of Personal Reality, Session 615

Now.

Desire, wish and expectation rule all actions, and are the basis for all realities.

Within All Other Is, then, the wish, desire and expectation of creativity existed before all other actuality.

Some of this discussion is bound to be distorted, because I must explain it to you in terms of time, as you understand it.

TES9 Session 427 August 7, 1968

Jim H.: "Didn't you say earlier, referring to the woman who was born in a minority race, that her challenges had been set up by a previous personality, in our terms?"

By the whole self.

The decision was made when that previous personality had returned to the whole self for a period of reevaluation.

You must realize, again, that we are speaking of divisions for convenience's sake, where none really exists.

At the same 'time,' so to speak, that this personality is born into a minority race,

In a completely different era it may be born rich, secure and aristocratic.

It is searching out different methods of experience and expansion.

Do you follow me?

Jim H.: "I understand. I thought you probably meant the challenges had been set up by the whole self."

Indeed. Remember, this is your entire identity of which we are speaking.

It is only you who are presently aware of but one portion of it; and this portion you insist upon calling yourself.

You are the self who makes these decisions.

Bert C.: "What recourse would the poor individual who was born with all of these seemingly insurmountable handicaps have, were she to say consciously, at the ego level,

I just don't want any of this. I would have much preferred to have been born aristocratic?"

The inner self realizes, however, that potentials are present that would not necessarily be present under other circumstances—

Abilities that can not only help the present personality but other individuals, and even society at large.

You forget your home so that you can return to it enriched.

Seth Speaks, Appendix, Feb. 9, 1971

Children understand the importance of symbols, and they use them constantly to protect themselves –

Not from their own reality but from the adult world.

They constantly pretend,

And they quickly learn that persistent pretending in any one area will result in a physically-experienced version of the imagined activity.

The child carries with him or her the impetus and supporting energy provided at birth from Framework 2,

And he knows intuitively that desires conducive to development 'happen' easier than those that are not.

The child is innately honest.

When he gets sick, he intuitively knows the reason why,

And he knows quite well that he brought about the illness.

Parents and physicians believe, instead, that the child is a victim,
FOR NO PERSONAL REASON,

But indisposed because of elements attacking him –

Either the outside environment or something working against
him from within.

The child may be told: 'You have a cold because you got your feet
wet.' Or:

You caught the cold from Johnny or Sally.

He may be told that he has a virus, so that it seems his body itself
was invaded despite his will.

He learns that such beliefs are acceptable.

Mother's little man or brave little girl can then stay at home, for
example,

Courageously bearing up under an illness,

With his or her behavior condoned.

Gradually it becomes easier for the child to accept the parents'
assessment of the situation.

Little by little the fine relationship, the precise connections
between psychological feelings and bodily reality, erode.

He is therefore a victim, and his sense of personal power is eroded.

The Individual and the Nature of Mass Events, Session 824

When you are proficient you will not be swept willy-nilly into other stages of consciousness as you sleep but will be able to understand and direct these activities.

Consciousness is an attribute of the soul, a tool that can be turned in many directions.

You are not your consciousness.

It is something that belong to you and to the soul.

You are learning to use it.

To the extent that you understand and utilize the various aspects of consciousness,

You will learn to understand your own reality, and the conscious self will truly become conscious.

You will be able to perceive physical reality because you want to, knowing it to be one of many realities.

You will not be forced to perceive it alone, out of ignorance.

SS 575

The physical self SEEMS to react to physical stimuli.

Actually, of course, it is reacting to its own reality, projected outward.

The objects in the physical universe are but symbols to express other realities existing within private realms.

The inner will always be projected outward within your system.

If, for example, a letter comes to you bearing good news, and you react to the letter with high spirits,

Then you should understand that the high spirits existed first.

And created the materialization of the letter within the physical systems,

Through the multilayered and complicated reactions that bind together the physical system.

If an annoying letter arrives and you react to it negatively,

The negative quality preceded the letter and caused it to materialize in your system.

Now you do not force someone to write such a letter, you see.

You broadcast the negative feelings, which were then picked up by

Whomever was ready to receive them, for their own purposes.

I cannot emphasize too strongly that this is automatic.

The Early Sessions, Book 8, Session 334

"GOD"
He is not human in your terms, though he passed through human stages;

And here the Buddhist myth comes closest to approximating reality.

He is not individual but energy gestalt.

This absolute, ever-expanding, instantaneous psychic gestalt, which you may call God if you prefer, is so secure in its existence

That it can constantly break itself down and rebuild itself.

Its energy is so unbelievable that it does indeed form all universes;

And because its energy is within and behind all universes, systems and fields, it is indeed aware of each sparrow that falls.

These connections between you and ALL-THAT-IS can never be severed.

And its awareness is so delicate and focused that its attention is indeed directed with a prime creator's love to each consciousness.

Consciousness, seeking to know itself, therefore knows you.

You as a consciousness, seek to know yourself and become aware of yourself as distinct individual portion of ALL-THAT-IS.

You not only draw upon this overall energy but you do so automatically since your existence is dependent upon it.

Each consciousness, is therefore, cherished and individually protected.

This portion of overall consciousness is individualized within you.

The personality of God as generally conceived is a one dimensional concept based upon man's small knowledge of his own psychology.

What you prefer to think of as God is, again, an energy gestalt or pyramid consciousness.

It is aware of itself as being, for instance as you, Joseph. It is aware of itself as the smallest seed.

This portion of ALL-THAT-IS that is aware of itself as you, that is focused within your existence, can be called upon for help when necessary.

This portion is also aware of itself as something more than you.

This portion that knows itself as you, and as more than you, is the personal God, you see.

Again: this gestalt, this portion of ALL-THAT-IS, looks out for interests and may be called upon in a personal manner.

Prayer contains its own answer.

And if there is no white-haired kind old Father-God to hear,

Then there is instead the initial and ever-expanding energy that forms everything that is.

And of which each human being is a part.

This psychic gestalt may sound impersonal to you, but since its energy forms your person, how can this be?

If you prefer to call this supreme psychic gestalt God, then you must not attempt to objectify him, for he is the nuclei of your cells and more intimate than your breath.

You are co-creators. What you call God is the sum of all consciousness.

And yet the whole is more than the sum of its parts.

There is constant creation.

There is within you a force that knew how to grow you from a fetus to a grown adult.

This force is a part of the innate knowledge within all consciousness,

And it is a part of the God within you.

THE SETH MATERIAL

All events are real.

You only experience some events or certain portions of events and call these physical.

Now, scientists also use terms like 'electron trap.'

And so, in your reality in a certain way you form certain traps, certain openings through which your thoughts can become real.

Your beliefs form such traps or channels, ATTRACTING certain thoughts to actuality.

There is an inner sequence of events.

That is, there is an inner order to your existence

That is immeasurably rich and varied.

And because of this you have free will.

You have indeed a multitudinous variety of events to choose from as you make up the script of your life.

So from your beliefs and ideas and with the mental and psychic energy at your disposal,

You ATTRACT certain events into becoming, in your terms, and therefore physically materialize them.

But about your existence are also a multitudinous variety of probable events

Events that you have not, in your terms, as yet chosen to make real.

And we will resume dictation. Give us a moment. Core beliefs are those about which you build your life.

You are consciously aware of these, though often you do not focus your attention upon them.

They become invisible, therefore, unless you become aware of the contents of your conscious mind.

To become acquainted with your own ideas and beliefs you must walk among them, symbolically speaking, without blinders.

You must look through the structures that you have yourself created, the organized ideas upon which you have grouped your experience.

To see clearly into your own mind, you must first of all un-structure your thoughts,

Follow them without judging them, without comparing them to the framework of your beliefs.

Structured beliefs collect and hold your experience, packaging it, so to speak.

And so when you look at a given experience that seems like another,

You put it into the same structured package, often without examination.

Such beliefs can hold surprises;

When you lift up the cover of one you may find that it has served to hide valuable information that did not belong there.

An artificial grouping of ideas, like paper flowers, can be collected about a standard core belief.

The core belief, because of its intensity and because of your habits, will often tend to attract to itself others of a like nature.

They will hang on.

If you are not accustomed to examining your own mind,

Then you can allow separate growths of this kind to form about a belief until you cannot distinguish one from the other.

This can develop to such an extent that all of your experience is seen only in relationship to this idea-growth.

Data that seems unrelated to this core belief is then not assimilated but thrown into the corners of your mind, unused.

And you are denied the value of the information.

Usually when you look into your conscious mind you do so for a particular reason, to find some information.

But if you have schooled yourself to believe that such data is not consciously available,

Then it will not occur to you to find it in your conscious mind.

If furthermore your conscious data is strongly organized about a core belief,

Then this will automatically make you blind to experience that is not connected with it.

A core belief is invisible only when you think of it as a fact of life,

And not as a belief about life;

Only when you identify with it so completely that you automatically focus your perceptions along that specific line.

NoPR Chapter 3: Session 618, September 28, 1972

Class Session, July 21, 1970 Seth:

I am glad to see so many friends here this evening and as usual, I have a message for you and, as usual, I want you to do something.

I want you to watch your own conscious thoughts.

You let them escape you half the time.

You do not realize what you are thinking.

Now, you blame many of your difficulties upon subconscious reaction.

And you think particularly in your weak moments that you have no control.

You let the thoughts of your mind chatter on.

But you are not aware of what you are thinking.

You do not stop and check your thoughts.

You think, for example, I feel poorly or this hurts,

Or you think this is a cruddy world I am in sometimes.

As I have told you often, your body reacts to your thoughts.

Now, it does no good to take ten minutes a day and give yourself
good suggestions and say,

I am brave, I am strong, I am healthy and young and rich.

And spend the rest of the time saying to yourself,

I am poorly, I am getting old, and I feel sore, or it is a cruddy world.

Therefore, often you allow these thoughts to take all of your
conscious attention.

You are hypnotizing yourself.

You would not think of going to a hypnotist and having him tell
you that you are getting sicker by the moment

Or the world was getting cruddier by the moment.

Or that your arm or foot or head or toe or ear would hurt more
and more with each breath you took.

You would have the man up to be hung.

And think such an affair an evil thing indeed, and yet you do this
to yourselves often.

And then you say with all blind innocence, why does this come
about, why am I sick

Or why am I sore or why am I caught in this cruddy universe.

And yet you do not change your own thought.

You use suggestion in the same way that you read a paragraph from a book that you think you should read perhaps for five minutes,

But then allow your own thoughts to take over completely and it seems to you that you have no control.

Now you are not using the control that you have.

None of you are helpless to change events, to change your health or your reality at this moment.

No one is responsible for your own conscious thought but yourself.

Now you may have built up poor habits of thought, but you can recognize this and change them.

Every time you say I am helpless, and I am slipping into chaos,

Whether you get laughs or not, or whether you say it humorously or not,

You are indeed pushing yourself further into the chaos you are creating with every breath you take

Because you make no effort to change the nature of your thoughts.

And this is what you must do, exert your own control.

On the one hand you "believe" that you form your own reality,

And on the other you believe that things will most likely go wrong unless you do something to stop them;

And this is the most conventional world view that forms the

experience of, say, the newspaper world.

In general, however, you are tying the highest faculties of your consciousness to goals that are at least unbecoming to them,

And because you have still accepted the tenets of conventionalized beliefs.

You cannot serve two masters at any one time with hopes of doing justice to either,

And you only confuse yourselves.

It is the mixture of consciousness with which you form your events that causes the difficulty.

The acquisition of your house is on its own a creative achievement almost purely a side effect of your creativity.

But the ideas you have projected upon it belong to that other level of consciousness

That erode the joy and accomplishment that should be connected with it.

In one area, that of money, Ruburt is fairly free, finally.

You consider taxes as a symbol of the creator's support of the mass world

That is, you feel forced to contribute to a world with which you do not agree.

You feel that that world threatens you, and yet you must support it.

But the threat – and you must try to understand me –

The threat does not exist in that world, but only in your beliefs toward it.

You are in that world of threat only according to the degree of power you allow it to have over you.

Now, these are words of the profoundest wisdom, from the fountains of your own psyches, as well as from my own knowledge.

And against those words you should judge your own actions, so that you do not react to threatening situations,

Whose validity exists only at a level of consciousness which you must learn to dismiss.

You can learn to dismiss it. –

Not as a reality to which others may not give acquiescence, but one that you realize is basically powerless.

You can no longer afford to serve two masters.

You have shut off your own psychic experiences, as to some extent Ruburt has,

Because of the dual purposes mentioned earlier, and the dual sets of beliefs.

Some of these beliefs did not confront you earlier, you see, for you were not in a position to confront them.

Your ideas about houses, for example, did not bear fruit until you had one.

You did not either, incidentally have to confront your negative beliefs about taxes until you were lucky enough,

And creative enough, to find yourself in a position where you need pay a considerable amount.

You could have chosen to remain poor, and hence avoid the difficulty.

You have a clash of beliefs, some hangers-on, in other words, but those hangers-on are troublesome,

For they are precisely those that prevent you from utilizing techniques with which you are quite familiar,

That could vastly enrich your situation.

You keep trying to justify yourselves in the normal world, with the people that you meet.

You work long hours, you both over-insist, so people will not think you lazy –

Or, worse, imagine that you are having fun or enjoying your situation.

You are not having much fun right now, and partially for that reason.

You are often working longer hours for the same reason, and enjoying it less, as the saying goes.

You want other people to think you are working as hard as they are, or harder.

You do not want them to think that your money came easily, which in a way it did.

At the same time, you say how good it would be to just take a job and come home when

it was finished –

a self-deception.

You know better.

January 10, 1977, Personal Sessions, Book 3

Sensing your Greater Being:

Your intents and concerns, your interests, your needs and desires, your characteristics and abilities,

Directly influence our material, for they lead you to it to begin with.

You want to make the material workable in your world - a natural and quite understandable desire:

The proof is in the pudding, and so forth.

Yet of course you are also participators in an immense drama in which the main actions occur outside of your world,

In those realms from which your world originated.

And you are, foremost, natives of those other realms, as each individual is; as each being is.

Those realms are far from lonely, dark, and chaotic.

They are also quite different from any concept of nirvana or nothingness.

They are composed of ever-spiraling states of existence in which different kinds of consciousnesses meet and communicate.

They are not impersonal realms, but are involved in the most highly intimate interactions.

Those interactions exist about you all the while,

And I would like you in your thoughts to aspire toward them, to try to stretch your perceptions enough

So that you become at least somewhat aware of their existence.

These frameworks, while I speak of them separately, exist one within the other, and each one impinges upon the other.

To some extent you are immersed in all realities.

In a strange fashion, and in this particular case [to Rob],

Your conflict with your notes had to do with a sense of orderliness aroused by the need to assemble facts.

If you can, try to sense this greater context in which you have your being.

Your rewards will be astonishing.

The emotional realization is what is important, of course, not simply an intellectual acceptance of the idea.

Ruburt wanted material on this book, and that is well and good.

The book is important. The book has its meaning in your world,

But I do not want you to forget the vaster context in which these sessions originate.

This kind of information can at least trigger responses on your part,

Increasing still further the scope of knowledge that you can receive from me.

In your world knowledge must be translated into specifics,

Yet we also deal with emotional realities that cannot be so easily deciphered.

In this session, in the words I speak - but more importantly in the atmosphere of the session –

There are hints of those undecipherable yet powerful realities that will then, in your time,

Gradually be described in verbal terms that make sense to you.

There is more, but it will have to wait simply because it is not presently translatable.

According to the impact of this session,

Your own comprehensions and perceptions will bring other clues, either in the waking or the dream state.

Keep your minds open for them, but without any preconceived ideas of how they might appear.

Ruburt's own development triggers certain psychic activity that then triggers further growth.

He has been participating in his library, for example, whether or not he is always aware of it.

The Individual and the Nature of Mass Events Chapter 3: Session 818, February 6, 1978.

It is past the time for you to be entranced by other personalities including my own.

Now before I bid you a fond good evening let me tell you that those of you who come to class regularly and gravitate here,

If you have not already discovered this for yourself, are the black sheep of the universe.

255

You want to go your own way. You do not want dogma. You will not be satisfied with hearts and flowers.

It is not an easy way, and all of you know that.

It is past the time for you to be entranced by other personalities including my own.

It is time for you to become entranced with your own personality.

It is time for you to feel independent enough to launch yourselves from your own subjective reality into others;

To emerge, to drop the paraphernalia of all dogma.

Not for new dogma but for new freedom.

Not to substitute one authority for another,

But to allow yourselves the freedom to recognize that the prime authority is

All That Is that resides within you

And that speaks with your own voice.

TECS4 ESP Class Session, June 15, 1971

The beliefs of course will be accepted by you not as beliefs, but as reality.

Once you understand that you form your reality, then you must begin to

Examine these beliefs by letting the conscious mind freely examine its own contents.

NoPR Chapter 2: Session 616, September 20, 1972

Seth: There is no penance!

You are here to develop.

You do learn the consequences of your thoughts and actions, and you face them.

But there is no penance!

And I tell you this: there is no guilt.

And I tell you: there is no guilt.

You learn the consequence of your action and you face the consequence of your action.

You create the idea of guilt.
And when you believe in guilt, then you create the penance in accordance to how strongly you believe in the guilt.

ESP CLASS SESSION, OCTOBER 14,1969 - by Jane Roberts (C) L. Davies Butts

There is no man that hates but that hatred is reflected outward and made physical.

And there is no man that loves but that that love is not reflected outward and made physical.

TECS1 ESP Class Session, March 12, 1968

Free will could not exist without the nature of probabilities, or without the rich choices available to you.

There are an infinite number of interior events, but you choose which ones in your reality to make real –

The accidents that do not happen, the accidents that do, the encounters that happen in your world, and those that do not.

You choose these and your physical system is the MECHANISM of that creativity.

The nerves and the messages that leap between them bring about your reality as you physically perceive, from an immense data of interior events, those that will be physically experienced.

Seth (ESP Class, 11-13-73): Seth (ESP Class, 11-13-73): from Seth quotes, by

Jane Roberts (C) L. Davies Butts

Now, let me say something to you in this, that I don't generally engage in this direction because it is so easily distorted in relation to metaphysic beliefs, but:

Every Thing Is An Expression Of Consciousness

Everything incorporates energy.

Energy is an actual thing, and energy is expressed and created by consciousness.

It is a thing that is created from no-thing.

Now; in that, there is an expression that is not actually a thing but it can be produced into a thing, which is identified as vibration—

Vibration qualities.

Now; energy is a force, in a manner of speaking, similar to electricity.

It is a physical force.

Vibration, or vibrational qualities, are the direction that is used in relation to energy.

Vibration is a directing expression;

Therefore, it determines the direction of energy, and it can be used in any form of direction.

Therefore, it can be inward, it can be outward, it can be manifest, it can be simply projected—

It can be expressed in countless, countless manners.

An excellent example of that would be color or music.

These are energy expressions that are coupled with vibrational qualities

That make them truths,

Because of the vibrational quality and how that energy is being directed.

With some energies, some energies are flexible

And therefore can be incorporated with vibrational qualities in many different capacities,

Which then allows them to be expressed in any area of consciousness, which then designates them as a truth.

What has this to do with (chuckles) what you were discussing?

You expressed that one example of this individual expressing

That if they are generating a certain energy that someone else can come to them with something dysfunctional,

And that if the individual is expressing directing their own energy in a particular manner,

That the other individual will leave differently.

Now, let me express to you, there is a difference between creating someone else's reality—which you don't—

And influencing reality, which you do.

And, as I have expressed many times previously, you all automatically express a type of automatic cooperation in certain capacities,

Which is the reason that you create shared expressions.

Therefore, you see basically the same trees as hundreds of other people.

You see the same buildings in your community—or practically the same buildings—

As thousands of people in your community.

This is because you cooperate with each other in relation to how you influence each other.

Now; in that, people do this constantly.

You are constantly influencing each other and allowing that to happen.

And you don't have to have an objective agreement to do it,

Because you have that automatic agreement, for the most part, simply by participating in physical focus with each other,

In a physical reality with each other.

Therefore: in that, in certain situations, individuals may be in a particular expression, a particular situation,

And they may not be comfortable

And they may not be happy and they may not want to be there, such as a psychiatric facility.

And in that, they also are automatically, IN that facility, wanting someone to help them.

Therefore, in that, they don't have to be objectively asking for help;

The factor that they are unhappy, uncomfortable and don't want to be there is in itself somewhat of a request for help.

Now, in that, another individual—such as this individual—

Could actually walk into that environment and could actually adjust the vibrational quality of the energy that they themselves are expressing,

And could conceivably adjust the vibrational quality of the energy around them that they themselves are engaging.

Now, in that, they are not necessarily directly engaging any specific individual.

They are not creating the reality of any other individual, and they are not creating the choices of any other individual.

But they could actually conceivably, through that action of changing the vibrational quality of the energy in that atmosphere,

They could be influencing other people in that environment,

And those people might accept that change of the vibrational quality of the energy, and it could affect them dramatically.

It is possible, because the vibrational quality is simply a direction;

It creates a direction for the energy.
Elias email 8-8-2021

Because All That Is contains within itself such omnipotent, fertile, divine creative characteristics,

All portions of its subjective experience attained dimensions of actuality impossible to describe.

The thoughts, for example, of All that Is were not simply
thoughts as you might have,

But multidimensional mental events of superlative nature.

Those events soon found that a transformation must occur.

If they were to journey into objectivity—

For no objectivity of itself could contain the entire reality of
subjective events that existed within divine subjectivity.

Only in that context could their relative perfection be maintained.

Yet they had yearned before the beginning for other experiences,

And even for fulfillments of a different nature.

They sensed a kind of value fulfillment that required of them the
utilization of their own creative abilities.

They yearned to create as they had been created, and All That Is,
in a kind of divine perplexity, nevertheless realized that this had
always been its own intent.

All That Is realized that such a separation would also allow you
to bring about a different kind of divine art,

In which the creators themselves created, and their creations
created,

Bringing into actuality existences that were possible precisely

Because there would seem to be a difference between the creator
and the creations.

All That Is is, therefore, within each smallest portion of consciousness.

Dreams, "Evolution," and Value Fulfillment Volume 1 Chapter 2: Session 884, October 3, 1979

The exterior religious dramas are of course imperfect representations of the ever- unfolding interior spiritual realities.

The various personages, the gods and prophets within religious history - these absorb the mass inner projections thrown out by those inhabiting a given time span.

Such religious dramas focus, direct, and, hopefully, clarify aspects of inner reality that need to be physically represented.

These do not only appear within your own system. Many are also projected into other systems of reality.

Religion per se, however, is always the external facade of inner reality.

The primary spiritual existence alone gives meaning to the physical one.

In the most real terms, religion should include all of the pursuits of man in his search for the nature of meaning and truth.

Spirituality cannot be some isolated, specialized activity or characteristic.

Exterior religious dramas are important and valuable only to the extent that they faithfully reflect the nature of inner, private spiritual existence.

To the extent that a man feels that his religion expresses such inner experience, he will feel it valid.

Most religions per se, however, set up as permissible certain groups of experiences while denying others.

They limit themselves by applying the principles of the sacredness of life only to your own species, and often to highly limited groups within it.

At no time will any given church be able to express the inner experience of all individuals.

At no time will any church find itself in a position in which it can effectively curtail the inner experience of its members. –

It will only seem to do so.

The forbidden experiences will simply be unconsciously expressed, gather strength and vitality,

And rise up to form a counter projection which will then form another,

Newer exterior religious drama.

The dramas themselves do express certain inner realities,

And they serve as surface reminders to those who do not trust direct experience with the inner self.

They will take the symbols as reality. When they discover that this is not so, they feel betrayed.

Christ spoke in terms of the father and son because IN YOUR TERMS at that time, this was the method used.

The story he told to explain the relationship between the inner self and the physically alive individual.

No new religion really startles anyone, for the drama has already been played subjectively.

What I have said, of course, applies as much to Buddha as it does to Christ:

Both accepted the inner projections and then tried to physically represent these.

THEY WERE MORE, however, than the sum of those projections.

This also should be understood.

Mohammedanism fell far short.

In this case the projections were of violence predominating.

Love and kinship were secondary to what indeed amounted to baptism and communion through violence and blood.

In these continuous exterior religious dramas, the Hebrews played a strange role.

Their idea of one god was not new to them.

Many ancient religions held the belief of one god above all others.

This god above all others was a far more lenient god, however, than the one the

Hebrews followed.

Many tribes believed, quite rightly, in the inner spirit that pervades each living thing.

And they often referred to, say, the god in the tree, or the spirit in the flower.

But they also accepted the reality of an overall spirit, of which these lesser spirits were but a part.

All worked together harmoniously.

The Hebrews conceived of an overseer god, an angry and just and sometimes cruel god.

And many sects denied, then, the idea that other living beings beside man possessed inner spirits.

The earlier beliefs represented a far better representation of inner reality,

In which man, observing nature, let nature speak and reveal its secrets.

The Hebrew god, however, represented a projection of a far different kind.

Man was growing more and more aware of the ego, of a sense of power over nature.

And many of the later miracles are presented in such a way that nature is forced to behave differently than in its usual mode.

God becomes man's ally against nature.

The early Hebrew god became a symbol of man's unleashed ego.

God behaved exactly as an enraged child would, had he those powers,

Sending thunder and lightning and fire against his enemies, destroying them.

Man's emerging ego therefore brought forth emotional and psychological problems and challenges.

The sense of separation from nature grew. Nature became a tool to use against others.

Sometime before the emergence of the Hebrew god these tendencies were apparent.

In many ancient, now-forgotten tribal religions, recourse was also made to the gods to turn nature against the enemy.

Before this time, however, man felt a part of nature, not separated from it.

It was regarded as an extension of his being, as he felt an extension of its reality.

One cannot use oneself as a weapon against oneself in those terms.

In those times men spoke and confided to the spirits of birds, trees, and spiders,

Knowing that in the interior reality beneath, the nature of these communications was known and understood.

In those times, death was not feared as it is in your terms, now, for the cycle of consciousness was understood.

Man desired in one way to step out of himself,

Out of the framework in which he had his psychological existence, to try new challenges,

To step out of a mode of consciousness into another.

He wanted to study the process of his own consciousness.

In one way this meant a giant separation from the inner spontaneity that had given him both peace and security.

On the other hand, it offered a new creativity, in his terms.

During break I went over a few questions about the relationships between the three members of the Christ entity –

John the Baptist, Jesus Christ, and Paul.

Now: At this point, the god inside became the god outside.

Man tried to form a new realm, attain a different kind of focus and awareness.

His consciousness turned a corner outside of itself.

To do this he concentrated less and less upon inner reality.

And therefore began the process of inner reality ONLY AS it was projected outward into the physical world.

Before, the environment was effortlessly created and perceived by man and all other living things, knowing the nature of their inner unity.

In order to begin this new venture, it was necessary to pretend that this inner unity did not exist.

Otherwise the new kind of consciousness would always run back to its home for security and comfort.

So it seemed that all bridges must be cut, while of course it was only a game because the inner reality always remained.

The new kind of consciousness simply had to look away from it to maintain initially an independent focus.

I am speaking here in more or less historic terms for you.

You must realize that the process has nothing to do with time as you know it, however.

This particular kind of adventure in consciousness has occurred before, and in your terms will again.

Perception of the exterior universe then changed, however, and it seemed to be alien and apart from the individual who perceived it.

God, therefore, became an idea projected outward, independent of the individual, divorced from nature.

He became the reflection of man's emerging ego, with all of its brilliance, savagery, power, and intent for mastery.

The adventure was a highly creative one despite the obvious disadvantages, and represented an "evolution" of consciousness

That enriched man's subjective experience, and indeed added to the dimensions of reality itself.

To be effectively organized, however, inner and outer experience had to appear as separate, disconnected events.

Historically the characteristics of God changed as man's ego changed.

These characteristics of the ego, however, were supported by strong inner changes.

Seth Speaks, session 587 JULY 28, 1971, 9:17 P.M. WEDNESDAY by Jane Roberts © L. Davies Butts

All That Is creates its reality as it goes along.

Each world has its own impetus, yet all are ultimately connected.

The true dimensions of a divine creativity would be unendurable for any one consciousness of whatever import.

And so that splendor is infinitely dimensionalized.

Worlds spiraling outward with each 'moment' of a cosmic breath; with the separation of worlds, a necessity;

And with individual and mass comprehension always growing at such a rate

That All That Is multiplies itself at microseconds.

Building both pasts and futures and other time scales you do not recognize.

Each is a reality in itself, with its own potentials.

And with no individual consciousness, however minute, ever lost.

DEaVF2 Chapter 10: Session 933, August 7, 1981 Seth (ESP Class, 11-13-73):

All Experiences Are Real In A Believable Kind Of Way

In this value system the black races are feared, as, basically, the
aged are feared.

The blacks are considered the primitives.
To them are assigned creative musical abilities, for example, but
for a long time these were "underground" activities:

They gave birth to acceptable musical productions but were not
admitted themselves into the concert halls of the respectable nation.

In your society therefore the black race has represented what
you think of as the chaotic, primitive, spontaneous, savage,
unconscious portions of the self.

The underside of the "proper American citizen.

The blacks were to be oppressed then on the one hand, and yet
treated indulgently as children on the other.

There was always a great fear that the blacks as a race would
escape their bounds — given an inch they would take a yard —
simply because the whites so greatly feared the
nature of the inner self.

And recognized the power that they tried so desperately to strangle
within themselves —

NoPR Chapter 13: Session 651, March 26, 1973

You were born with an in-built recognition of your own goodness.

You were born with an inner recognition of your rightness in the
universe.

You were born with a desire to fulfill your abilities, to move and act in the world.

Those assumptions are the basis of what I will call natural law.

You are born loving.

You are born compassionate.

You are born curious about yourself and your world.

Those attributes also belong to natural law.

You are born knowing that you possess a unique, intimate sense of being that is itself, and that seeks its own fulfillment, and the fulfillment of others.

You are born seeking the actualization of the ideal.

You are born seeking to add value to the quality of life,

To add characteristics, energies, abilities to life that only you can individually contribute to the world.

And to attain a state of being that is uniquely yours, while adding to the value fulfillment of the world.

All of these qualities and attributes are given you by natural law.

You are a cooperative species, and you are a loving one.

Your misunderstandings, your crimes, and your atrocities, real as they are, are seldom committed out of any intent to be evil.

But because of severe misinterpretations about the nature of good, and the means that can be taken toward its actualization.

Most individual people know that in some inner portion of themselves.

Your societies, governments, educational systems, are all built around a firm belief in the unreliability of human nature.

You cannot change human nature.

Such a statement takes it for granted that man's nature is to be greedy, a predator, a murderer at heart.

You act in accordance with your own beliefs.

You become the selves that you think you are. Your individual beliefs become the beliefs of your society, but that is always a give-and-take.

Shortly we will begin to discuss the formation of a better kind of mass reality —

A reality that can happen as more and more individuals begin to come in contact with the true nature of the self.

Then we will have less frightened people, and fewer fanatics.

And each person involved can to some extent begin to see the "ideal" come into practical actualization.

The means never justify the ends.

NoME Chapter 9: Session 862, June 25, 1979 - by Jane Roberts (C) L. Davies Butts

And so, each of you, in your own way, attempt to live your lives excellently;

To rise above levels of yourselves that disappear as you attempt new versions of excellence.

Excellence! There are no standards but your own!

You cannot compare yourself against others.

For your own abilities are like no others, and dimensions of your own greatness cannot fit in the standards of others.

But you know what excellence means within yourself, and it means truth to the heart of yourself.

There are some things that you know it means.

It means not lying.

It means not lying to yourself;

Not being afraid to use your own abilities;

Not being afraid to be the excellent self that you are.

Excellence does not mean false humility.

It does not mean inflated, artificial pride that sets you apart from all others, for you cannot set yourselves apart from all others.

You are, because of your nature, apart from all others, and everlastingly unique—while everlastingly a part of all others.

In the terms that you understand, excellence means not lying to yourself.

It means do not shop-lift [which a few class members had been joking about]—it is not funny.

It means when you steal objects, you steal ideas, and you do not know what belongs to you and what does not.

It means you are playing around with other peoples' integrity instead of your own.

And you are not willing to stand there and say, This is mine!

Excellence means that in your relationships, you face each other honestly, and do not pretend.

It means that you do not use excuses. It means that you do not hide your abilities from yourself.

[It] means that you take advantage of your abilities.

And do not deny them.

And that you expect things of yourself.

And do not look to others for their answers;

And that you do not dribble away your energy.

Seth in Class December 18, 1973 - Jane Roberts (C) L. Davies Butts

Seth: Forget your problems and they will go away.

That almost sounds like the babbling of a child or an idiot.

It certainly sounds Unintellectual, like wishful thinking of the most sentimental variety.

Mothers tell children to forget their troubles.

The children, not realizing how dumb their poor mothers really are, often do just that.

And discover that their problems do indeed disappear.

If you worry about the world, you can somehow perhaps save it—
or so many people think.

If you DON'T worry about the world, you are considered unfeeling,
and it certainly seems ridiculous to imagine that the world can
somehow take care of itself.

And even remedy whatever damage it seems man has done to it.

But no: it seems that worrying will get you someplace.

It provides impetus, and so it does—by promoting further problems.

You are used to thinking, however, that worry is an acceptable
method of showing concern for private or public affairs.

The best thing you can do for yourself, or your loved ones, or the
world, is to stop worrying.

And hence release all of the negative thoughts therein generated.

All consciousness of whatever extent feels love, though it may
not know the verbal designation, for that is the basis of all existence.

And, there is no existence when you try to separate feeling from
reality or consciousness from its experiences.

1971.04.13 (ESP: EC3)

Seth: Remember, therefore, that your own vitality is without bounds.

That it is ever new.

That it sweeps through your own frame as easily and as naturally
as the energy sweeps through this form.

That you have only to accept it and acknowledge it. And, again that the vitality of life is not quiet.

It is not adult. It is not dignified. It is!

All the alleyways down which you have traveled have openings.

Any disasters that you have worked upon yourselves have openings.

Any energy that you need to direct to any part of your physical image is yours for the asking.

Any thought that you have is creative.

When you listen, do not only listen but feel.

And, within the energy of this voice feel, therefore, the energy within yourselves, within your spirits and your tissues.

For, you are now presently dwelling within tissue which you have also formed.

Know, therefore, your own exaltation and your own energy and your own strength.

Feel within yourselves that confidence and power.

And, draw upon it as you go about your daily way.

And, feel it within you. For, it comes easily.

As easily and miraculously as a flower grows or as a hair grows out of your skull or as a thought rises from your brain.

That energy resides within you.

That energy is your own. Your own divinity rests within it.

The bridgeways that you form (and that all of you know) are made of this vitality.

In silence it grows and is nurtured.

But, it is not of itself quiet.

It is vigorous. And, it is not afraid of quiet. It forms you. Get on good terms with it.

And, do not deny it.

I ask you to identify with the power behind this voice and to feel it within your very cells.

For, it is your own power, your own energy, your own knowledge and the divinity from which you have sprung and which is a part of each of you.

The voice that answers is your own.

Then listen to it with love and understanding.

July 6, 1971 Early Class Sessions, Book 4

(With much amused irony:) The foolhardy, the brave, the utterly courageous, might even take a step further, and imagine that whatever problem is involved no longer exists.

Or to pretend that it will go away, for in any case it is not as bad as I thought.

Some other more courageous souls might decide to balance their input.

And if the news is bad to turn their attention to the joys of the day, which are indeed immediately present.

Now: I can't—nor would I want to—turn you into children again.

You Can Only Be Reached From The Inside

But you have a natural optimism, both of you—

A creature optimism, with which all are innately equipped.

That natural optimism is a power in the individual and in the world.

It believes in triumph, in pleasant, unpredictable surprises, in unexpected solutions, joyful occurrences.

It is like the child's anticipation of Christmas Eve, and it is biologically ingrained.

There is a point where all realities intermingle.

It can only be reached from the inside.

Many of the questions you have asked cannot be answered in the manner in which you have asked them.

The ideals of which you speak are your protection, built-in survival mechanisms that warn of danger, invisible fences like psychic signs saying beware.

Abundance is all around you. It is the sun! It is the rain!

Now you think of those things as natural and good.

But wealth, in whatever terms you happen to translate it, is also a part of your natural world and translation.

And so for you to feel free to accept one portion of nature and not the other is not a good belief.

You ARE! Your being IS! You are a portion of All That Is.

Therefore, you have a right to abundance as the flower has to the sun.

In human terms there are many kinds of abundance, and they are all yours.

You must realize that you do not have to rationalize your existence.

Because you ARE, you have a right to the abundance of nature in whatever way it is transformed or translated for you.

Cassette One, audio transcript, by Jane Roberts © L. Davies Butts

Now: It is easy to live—so easy that although you live, rest, create, respond, feel, touch, see, sleep, and wake, you do not really have to try to do any of those things.

From your viewpoint they are done for you.

They are done for you in Framework 2—

And further discussions of Framework 2, incidentally, will be inter-wound throughout our present book.

Your beliefs often tell you that life is hard, however, that living is difficult, that the universe, again, is unsafe, and that you must use all of your resources—

Not to meet [life] with anything like joyful abandon, of course, but to protect yourself against its implied threats;

Threats that you have been taught to expect.

But your beliefs do not stop there.

Because of both scientific and religious ones, in Western civilization you believe that there are threats from within also.

As a result, you forget your natural selves, and become involved in a secondary, largely imaginary culture:

Beliefs that are projected negatively into the future, individually and en masse.

People respond with illnesses of one kind or another, or through exaggerated [behavior].

LIVING IS EASY. It is safe and reliable because it is easy.

note, session 893 - DEVF - by Jane Roberts (C) L. Davies Butts (DEVF = Dreams, "Evolution" and Value Fulfillment)

I have said, again, much of this before—

But this is an update.

Neither of you do yourselves service by worrying about Ruburt's condition.

WORRYING that it might worsen in the future, or in your old ages, or by stressing its negative aspects.

You might each secretly believe that such worrying will frighten Ruburt enough "to make him do something.

And that is hardly the case—for worrying always increases stress.

Whenever possible, minimize the impediments in your minds.

Now Ruburt has started doing that.

At least keep in mind what I have said, for it is true.

TO THE EXTENT that you forget the problem, it will vanish.

Physically, Ruburt is improving, as you can see—but he used a stimulus of fear —

The fear that otherwise he might be bedridden.

Whenever he remembers Framework 2 there are sudden, significant improvements.

I want him to imagine a box.

And each day simply to imagine he puts into it a sheet of paper that says Of course I walk normally.

Do it as a joke, or whatever.

Roberts, Jane. The Personal Sessions: Book Five of the Deleted Seth Material, DELETED SESSION NOVEMBER 29, 1978 9:07 PM WEDNESDAY © L. DAVIES BUTTS

In your realm of reality, there is no real freedom but the freedom of ideas.

And there is no real bondage except for the bondage of ideas.

(NoME Chapter 7: Session 855, May 21, 1979)

Value fulfillment combines the nature of a loving presence. —

A presence with the innate knowledge of its own divine complexity.

With a creative ability of infinite proportions that seeks to bring to fulfillment even the slightest, most distant portion of its own inverted complexity.

Translated into simpler terms, each portion of energy is endowed with an inbuilt reach of creativity that seeks to fulfill its own potentials in all possible variations—

And in such a way that such a development also furthers the

creative potentials of each other portion of reality.

In physical reality, if you will forgive me, life is the name of the game

And the game is based upon value fulfillment.

That means simply that each form of life seeks toward the fulfillment

And unfolding of all of the capacities that it senses within its living framework.

Knowing that in that individual fulfillment, each other species of life is also benefited.

Individually and globe wide, value fulfillment is in a fashion the purpose of all events.

The impetus that drives the wheels of nature, so to speak.

Value fulfillment is the reason behind the existence of all systems, and of all experience within your field.

There was always a great fear that the blacks as a race would escape their bounds
— given an inch they would take a yard —

Simply because the whites so greatly feared the nature of the inner self.

And recognized the power that they tried so desperately to strangle within themselves.

NoPR Chapter 13: Session 651, March 26, 1973

We ask you in the most scandalous manner possible, to realize one thing:

That you are good, that you are blessed, and that there is nothing
wrong with you.

(ESP Class, 6-4-74) - by Jane Roberts (C) L. Davies Butts

It is the tension between the search for fulfillment or perfection
and the actual performance possible in the physical world

That promotes creative arts, as they are understood.

The inner problems that you encounter are always constructive—

Challenges leading you toward greater fulfillment.

In the three-dimensional reality in which your ego has its main
focus, becoming presupposes arrival, or a destination

An ending to that which has been in a state of becoming.

But the soul or entity has its existence basically in other dimensions.

And in these, fulfillment is not dependent upon arrivals at any
points, spiritual or otherwise.

The word "perfect" holds many pitfalls.

In the first place it presupposes something completed and done
beyond change.

And so beyond motion, further development, or creativity.

You must not expect to be perfect.

Your ideas of perfection mean a state of fulfillment beyond which
there is no future growth,

And no such state exists.

Value Fulfillment always implies the search for excellence—not perfection, but excellence.

You can only advance the cause of mankind and the cause of your brethren by helping yourself and knowing yourself. And fulfilling your own abilities—

When you are yourself in your own shining uniqueness.

And you are, if you but realize it.

Then you help others to become in awareness what they really are.

But if you believe you must sacrifice yourself to others, then you distort the truth within you.

For there is no sacrifice involved,

But the fulfillment of your being that brings out in each of the people that you know, the fulfillment of their being.

Far from beliefs being embedded in the so-called unconscious, they are relatively speaking more plastic there.

Beliefs are strongest at precisely the point of conscious impact upon the physical environment.

The belief, any belief, is a conscious formation of ideas that are accepted as physical truth.

The energy for the beliefs comes from other levels, of course.

Without the energy the beliefs would wither.

TPS2 Session 664 (Deleted Portion) May 21, 1973

Now there is a reason why these lessons must be learned in just this way.

Elementally there is only creativity.

Destruction is merely the changing of form.

A cloudburst or a tornado knows nothing of destruction.

This same energy encased within a human form is something else.

There are different kinds of creativity, then, to learn.

And a specialization in energy is focus and feelings that did not exist for it earlier;

Millions of molecules momentarily united with the living consciousness.

Filled with primal energy, now learning love, and forming highly sensitive psychic patterns—

Electrical charges that now form emotions instead of clouds;

The innocent chaos of undifferentiated personality that exists behind the highly specified and truly sophisticated mechanism of one thought.

And all of this before an individual is born within your system.

In terms of time this is behind us all.

Little wonder that psychic battles wage.

And yet beyond your system there are refinements impossible to describe.

And further developments more miraculous than those that have gone before.

And through all of this, the entity formed from this massive chaos retains its identity, the knowledge of its pasts, and continues to grow in creativity.

TES9 452

Impulses Lead Us To Our Truth

Value fulfillment means that each individual, each entity, of whatever nature, spontaneously, automatically seeks those conditions that are suited to its own fulfillment.

And to the fulfillment of others.

You are born loving.

You are born compassionate.

You are born curious about yourself and your world.

Those attributes also belong to natural law.

You are born knowing that you possess a unique, intimate sense of being that is itself.

And that seeks its own fulfillment, and the fulfillment of others.

You are born seeking the actualization of the ideal.

You are born seeking to add value to the quality of life,

To add characteristics, energies, abilities to life that only you can individually contribute to the world.

And to attain a state of being that is uniquely yours,

While adding to the value fulfillment of the world.

Value fulfillment is a psychological and physical propensity that exists in each unit of consciousness.

Propelling it toward its own greatest fulfillment in such a way that its individual fulfillment also adds to the best possible development on the part of each other such unit of consciousness.

The individual person is also involved in an ever-continuing process to increase the quality of life as it exists at all levels of personal experience.

Reality is so constructed that each individual seeking such fulfillment does so not at the expense of others, but in such a way that the quality of life is increased for all.

This sense of value fulfillment benefits not only the individual, but its species, AND ALL OTHER SPECIES.

Each species or life form "realizes" that its own fulfillment adds immeasurably to the existence of all other forms.

In a way impossible to explain, the fly and the spider are connected, and aware of the connection.

Not as hunter and prey, but as individual participants in deeper processes.

Together they work toward a joint kind of value fulfillment, in which both are fulfilled.

The insects also appreciate flowers' profusion of color, and also for esthetic reasons.

I am saying, therefore that even insects have an esthetic sense, and again, that each creature, and each plant, or natural entity, has its own sense of value fulfillment— seeking the greatest possible fulfillment and extension of its own innate abilities.

All species are motivated by value fulfillment; in which each
seeks to enhance the quality of life for itself

And for all other species at the same time.

That characteristic of value fulfillment is perhaps the most
important element in the being of All That Is.

And it is a part of the heritage of all species.

Value fulfillment operates within microbes and nations, within
individual creatures and entire species.

And it unites all of life's manifestations.

Every object that you perceive—

Grass or rock or stone—even ocean waves or clouds—any physical
phenomenon—

Has its own invisible consciousness, its own intent and emotional
coloration.

Each manifestation of consciousness comes into being with an
inner impetus toward value fulfillment.

Civilization is dependent upon the spontaneity and fulfillment of
the individual.

Your civilization is in sad straits—

Not because you have allowed spontaneity or fulfillment to
individuals, but because you have denied it.

And because your institutions are based upon that premise.

Value fulfillment of each and every element in life relies upon those spontaneous processes.

And at their source is the basic affirmative love and acceptance of the self, the universe, and life's conditions.

If you go with your being, spontaneously, you will find fulfillment in all of your ways.

Going along with your nature automatically brings value fulfillment and fortunate events, for your intents, abilities, and needs work naturally together.

Impulses are meant to help you create your reality.

They are meant to help you move through belief systems.

They are meant to help you find your best fulfillment and not only your private best fulfillment:

But you are, through your impulses, led to situations where your best improvement also aids the species and all species—

When you listen, when you trust your impulses. And I am talking about your private, innocuous, everyday impulses, also.

Our impulses are good.

Left alone they'd lead us naturally toward self-fulfillment.

Impulses arise in a natural, spontaneous, constructive response to the abilities, potentials, and needs of the personality.

They are meant as directing forces.

Luckily, the child usually walks before it is old enough to be taught that impulses are wrong.

And luckily the child's natural impulses toward exploration, growth, fulfillment, action and power are strong enough to give it the necessary springboard —

Before your belief systems begin to erode its confidence.

When I speak of impulses, many of you will automatically think of impulses that appear contradictory or dangerous or "evil"—

And that is because you are so convinced of the basic unworthiness of your being.

You have every right to question your impulses, to choose among them, to assess them, but you must be aware of them,

Acknowledge their existence, for they will lead you to your own true nature.

Change alone allows for the possibility of identity within any universe,

For without change there can be no value fulfillment, no experience, and no identity.

Development comes not from a series of actions strung out along a single line, one before the other in lengthwise fashion.

Instead, development is largely a matter of value fulfillment, which is achieved through the perspectives of actions,

Through traveling within any given action, and following it and changing with it.

Within you is the ability to change your ideas about reality and about yourself,

And to create a personal living experience that is fulfilling to yourself and others.

You are what you are, and you will be more.

Do not be afraid of change, for you are change,

And you change as you sit before me.

All action is change,

For otherwise there would be a static universe,

And then indeed death would be the end.

What I am is also what you are:

Individualized consciousness.

Change with the seasons, for you are more than the seasons.

You form the seasons.

They are the reflections of your inner psychic climate.

You change constantly.

And All That Is, or in your terms, God,

Is not a static being but always creative and always changing.

So do not put yourself at a particular level of experience and stay there,

Allow yourself growth and freedom.

Allow yourself, therefore, the flexibility of change in whatever you do.

Allow yourself the flexibility of motion, for what you set up today, you may want to change tomorrow.

Your reasoning as you now use it, however, deals primarily with reality by dividing it into categories,

Forming distinctions, following the laws of cause and effect –

And largely its realm is the examination of events already perceived.

In other words, it deals with the concrete nature of ascertained events that are already facts in your world.

On the other hand, your intuitions follow a different kind of organization, as does your imagination –

One involved with associations, an organization that unifies diverse elements.

And brings even known events together in a kind of unity that is often innocent of the limitations dictated by cause and effect.

The Nature of Personal Reality

Session 640

What exists physically exists first in thought and feeling.

There is no other rule.

You have the conscious mind for good reason.

You are not at the mercy of unconscious drives unless you consciously acquiesce to them.

Your present feelings and expectations can always be used to
check your progress.

If you do not like your experience, then you must change the
nature of your conscious thoughts and expectations.

You must alter the kind of messages that you are sending
through your thoughts to your own body, to friends and associates.

Seth/Jane Roberts, The Nature of Personal Reality

Session 609

Now. There is, and this will certainly seem a contradiction in
terms, there is nonbeing.

It is a state, not of nothingness in your terms,

But a state in which probabilities and possibilities are known,
anticipated, but blocked from all expression.

Dimly, through what you would call a history, hardly remembered,
there was such a state.

It was a state of agony in which the powers of creativity and
existence were known,

But the ways to produce them were not known.

This is the lesson that All That Is had to learn, and that could not
be taught.

This is the agony from which creativity originally was drawn,
and in reflection is still seen.

All That Is, in your terms, retains memory of that state, and it serves as a constant impetus toward renewed creativity.

Each self, as a part of All That Is therefore also retains memory of this state.

It is for this reason that each portion of All That Is,

Each most minute consciousness, is endowed with the impetus toward survival, change, development and creativity.

It is not enough that All That Is, as a primary consciousness gestalt, desires further being,

But, that every portion of it also carry this determination.

Yet the agony itself was used as a means.

And the agony itself served as an impetus, strong enough finally

So that All That Is initiated within itself the means to be.

All That Is therefore knows the agony of what you would call not being.

Not being, in other terms, is impossible.

It is being without the means of expressing being.

Now, every portion of consciousness is imbued with innate knowledge towards the means of expression and creativity.

If, and this is impossible, all portions but the most minute last unit of All That Is were destroyed,

All That Is could still continue

For within the smallest portion is the innate knowledge of the whole.

All That Is protects itself therefore, and all that is has, and is, and will create.

TES9 426

Whenever you concentrate upon "what can happen" negatively, you literally cut down your options, Inhibit your own and life's abundance.

You feel unsafe and ill-at-ease.

The Personal Sessions Book 3 Session 766 (Deleted Portion) February 17, 1976

This first state of agonized search for expression may have represented the birth throes of All That Is as we know it.

There existed, and clearly, the possibilities of creation as we know it, but the means were not known.

Pretend then that you possessed within yourself the knowledge, the sight, of all the world's masterpieces in sculpture and art, that they throbbed and pulsed as realities within you,

But that you had no physical apparatus, no knowledge of how to achieve it;

That there was neither rock, nor pigment, nor source of any of these,

And you ached with the yearning to produce them –

And this, on an infinitesimally small scale, will perhaps give you, as an artist,

Some idea of the agony and the impetus that was felt.

And each self is endowed with the agony and the impetus, for it is a fabric from which

All That Is made itself.

And all that you know. Perhaps now you can understand why it is so difficult to try to explain matters to you in terms that you can understand.

All That Is loves all that it has created, down to the least,

For it realizes the dearness, and the uniqueness of each consciousness

Which had been wrest from such a state and at such a price;

And it is triumphant and joyful at each new development taken by each consciousness,

For this is an added triumph against that first state, and an added security against that first state,

And it revels and takes joy in the slightest creative act of each of its issue.

It, of itself and from that state, has given life to infinities of possibilities.

From its agony it found the way to burst forth in freedom,

Through expressing and in doing so gave existence to individualized consciousness that forever continues the process.

Therefore, it is rightly jubilant.

The connections between you therefore and All That Is can never be severed.

And its awareness is indeed so delicate and focused that its attention is directed with a prime creator's love to each consciousness.

I have been sent to help you.

And others have been sent through the centuries of your time,

For as you develop you also form new dimensions

And you will help others.

Each individual is innately driven by a good intent,

However, distorted that intent may become.

Or however twisted the means that may be taken to achieve it.

NoME Chapter 9: Session 860, June 13, 1979

Beliefs Form Cultural Systems

Now: in The Nature of Personal Reality we discussed the nature of private beliefs.

Someday there can be a book called The Nature of Cultural Reality.

To some extent Ruburt is beginning to move in that direction now, in Psychic Politics—

Particularly with his codicils.

First of all, of course, you do choose the culture into which you are born.

The belief system is like a mental and spiritual climate.

To some extent or another each individual alive alters that climate,

So that even if there were no revolutions there would be constant change, sometimes gradual and sometimes sudden.

People's beliefs DO form the cultural system, which then exerts its influence upon the individual.

The cultural system is not imposed however from some outside source,

And it is not biologically predetermined.

It has its biological aspects, of course;

But war, for example, is not a biological culmination of an aggressive instinct.

Since it is formed by beliefs held by natural creatures, culture is, as Ruburt states, as natural as your physical environment.

Once you are born into a particular time and country, you DO grow up in an almost invisible

But definite environment of concepts, assumptions.

And predetermined ideas that serve as a basis from which your own individual beliefs spring.

There is a constant give-and-take between any individual and his cultural system.

The entity and its time are not separate. They are one.

Basically time is simply psychological experience, regardless of the lapses between perception of the manner of perception.

The entity is its own experience.

Time could be thought of as the tissues of the entity.

These would be ever-changing.

In our analogy, the projected image would seem to float, including ever-different stars and planets within its boundaries.

Your own time structure would be very minute in this picture.

Now the moment points could also represent various personalities belonging to the entity— portions of its own consciousness that it sends upon the journeys of exploration and discovery.

It is as if the nuclei of a cell could travel through itself.

The boundaries of the entity would be imaginary, taking in as many moment points as the entity felt it could handle.

Now. Some personalities can be a part of more than one entity.

This is something I do not believe we have discussed before.

The entities, being action, always shift and change.

There is nothing arbitrary about their boundaries.

The personalities have the same freedom.

Like fish, they can swim to other streams. Within them is the knowledge of all their relationships.

Any personality may become an entity on its own.

This involves a highly developed knowledge of the use of energy and its intensities.

As atoms have a mobility, so do psychological structures in their own way.

They move through the value climate of psychological reality as freely as atoms move through your time.

Value fulfillment corresponds to your time in that area.

TES9 429

The Seth portion of me has been intimately connected with you both, and so, in that respect, have I.

This is closely related to the definition of a personality energy essence, from which, of course, all personalities spring.

The voice became even more powerful.

There is a peculiar corner within Ruburt's personality, also deflected into your own, that allows him rather clear access to informational channels most difficult to reach from your system.

During this session, and at this moment, the contact is particularly good.

There is also access to energy far beyond that which is usually experienced.

Ruburt sensed this in the past, and feared to open these channels until he felt himself suitably ready.

There exists what could almost be compared to a psychological and psychic warp in dimensions,

And that corner of Ruburt's personality is an apex point at which communication and contact can take place.

Then, to Rob's surprise, Seth told him to end the session.

Rob was to follow the procedure given, recently, to end my trance.

Seth said, This evening you have reached somewhat beyond the personality by which I usually make myself known to you. Even if I continue to speak, end the trance.

Roberts, Jane. The Seth Material (pp. 266-268). New Awareness Network, Inc.. Kindle Edition. © L. Davies Butts

Illness in many ways is a learned response, and it follows patterns set up in the system having to do with memory *banks*, though we shall find a better word here.

Habitual illness will follow the lines of learned response and memory.

Definite molecular substructures are formed biologically in response to inner electrical charges.

The inner electrical charges are not a part of the physical system as such, you see.

But they act within the physical structure, forming then definite changes in the RNA patterns.

There was some question in the article about long-term and short-term memory.

Now basically the original intensity of the charge determines its duration in your time structure.

The intensity of particular charges can completely reorganize the personality structure through changes in the RNA formations.

Previous life memories, existing electronically and magnetically, may carry such intense charge that they superimpose themselves in the present physical structure,

And form memory patterns quite alien to those of the present ego personality.

TES7 Session 295 October 19, 1966

The ego is an offshoot of the conscious mind, so to speak.

The conscious mind is like a gigantic camera with the ego directing the view and the focus.

Left alone, various portions of the identity rise and form the ego, de-group and reform,

All the while maintaining a marvelous spontaneity and yet a sense of oneness.

The ego is your idea of your physical (and mental) image in relation to the world.

Your self-image is not unconscious, then.

You are quite aware of it, though often you reject certain thoughts about it in favor of others.

False beliefs can result in a rigid ego that insists upon using the conscious mind in one direction only, further distorting its perceptions.

Often you quite consciously decide to bury a thought or an idea that might cause you to alter your behavior, because it does not seem to fit in with limiting ideas that you already hold.

Listen to your own train of thought as you go about your days.

What suggestions and ideas are you giving yourself?

Realize that these will be materialized in your personal experience.

Seth/Jane Roberts, The Nature Of Personal Reality, Chapter 2

The soul is open-ended

It is not a closed spiritual or psychic system.

I have tried to show you that the soul is not a separate, apart-from-you thing.

It is no more divorced from you than — God is.

There is no need to create a separate god who exists outside of your universe and separate from it,

Nor is there any need to think of a soul as some distant entity.

God, or All That Is, is intimately a part of you.

"His" energy forms your identity.

And your soul is a part of you in the same manner.

In larger terms, my soul includes my reincarnational personalities, Seth Two, and probable selves.

I am as aware of my probable selves, incidentally, as I am of my reincarnational existences.

Your concept of the soul is simply so limited.

I am not really speaking in terms of group souls, though this interpretation can also be made.

Each "part" of the soul contains the whole —

A concept I am sure will startle you.

As you become more aware of your own subjective reality you will therefore, become familiar with greater portions of your own soul.

When you think of the soul as a closed system you perceive it as such,

And close off from yourself the knowledge of its greater creativity and characteristics. —

Seth Speaks Chapter 22: Session 589, August 4, 1971

Consciousness Is The Action Of Energy

ELIAS: I do not alter the body consciousness. I do not manipulate the functioning of the body consciousness, other than to manipulate the physical function of speaking.

But any other function of the body consciousness is being directed by Michael's subjective awareness.

The objective awareness is removed, and a significant portion of the subjective awareness is removed also.

But there is enough of the subjective awareness maintained to continue to be instructing the functioning of the body consciousness.

I am projecting energy.

I do not think, and I do not perceive, for those are objective mechanisms, and I do not incorporate an objective awareness.

Therefore, I am manipulating energy in a manner that allows me to configure energy to connect with you through speech along with energy.

Therefore, in association with Michael's body consciousness, I do not experience what it is doing, so to speak, or how it is functioning.

Therefore, whatever Michael has created in physical manifestations continue to be expressed, but I am not experiencing them;

Therefore, they do not necessarily translate into an objective expression during the energy exchange.

Are you understanding?

Now; I would also express that building this new foundation requires different materials.

You are very accustomed to using the materials of comparing.

These materials are not effective with this new foundation.

They crumble, and they do not allow you to build a structure that will stand.

Therefore, it is important that you generate new materials to build with.

And in doing so, it is important that you begin to notice what materials are at your

disposal and what you are already generating, what resources you already have.

In this, it is also a matter of each time you present yourself with the encounter of the old material of comparing, that you set it aside;

That you recognize it and acknowledge it and you express to yourself,

No, this material is not effective for building this structure.

Therefore, I will set this aside.

There are beneficial uses for comparing, but not in your experience thus far.

Your uses of comparison have served to confuse you and discount you.

Therefore, we are not entirely discarding the expression of comparing, but we are definitely setting it aside and not using it.

Therefore, temporarily it can be a decoration in your construction site.

ANON: Well, I get it. But what do I do instead?

ELIAS: What do you do instead? You draw upon the resources that are available to you

That you are not accustomed to drawing upon, —

Which are what you do accomplish, what you do like about yourself.

ELIAS: Just as an individual would incorporate tools of a hammer or a saw to build a structure, you also incorporate tools to build the structure of you.

To make it firm, to develop it, and to construct it in the most aesthetically wondrous manner that you can imagine.

And the manner in which you begin to do that is to use those tools of what you like about you, concentrating your attention upon that –

NOT concentrating upon and generating an importance with what you do not like, which is very familiar.

It is very familiar to you to discount yourself and to focus upon what you do not like,

Or what is different, or what you perceive to be wrong or bad.

What is significant in building this new structure is to focus upon what you DO like and enhance that.

Use it. Express it. Rather than placing it upon a shelf and perhaps glancing at it occasionally

But never actually engaging it and never actually using it—

Remove it from that shelf, dust it off and use it.

ELIAS: And in this exercise, in relation to using your new tools –

Or rather, your old tools that are dusty and that you may be re-engaging now –

Your new exercise is to generate a quest to discover what all those tools are.

What are all those tools that you incorporate that are sitting upon your shelf that are collecting dust?

What is it that you like about you? –

ALL of the aspects that you like about you, regardless of what it is.

It may be that you like the manner in which you organize your table when you set it to express a meal.

Or you like that you will stop in certain moments and pet your cat. You like that about yourself.

You like different aspects of yourself for different reasons,

But what is important is that you begin to SEE all those aspects of yourself that you like,

That you have merely occasionally glanced upon throughout the years

And that are almost unrecognizable for they are encased in so much dust upon that shelf that perhaps you may be feather-duster-in-hand rather than a sword.

You shall yield your mighty feather duster, and you shall approach that shelf and you shall be dusting off all of those objects of what you like about you.

Your medical technology may help you 'conquer' one disease after another—

Some in fact CAUSED by that same technology—

And you will feel very efficient as you do heart transplants, as you fight one virus after another.

But all of this will do nothing except to allow people to die, perhaps, of OTHER diseases still 'unconquered.'

People will die when they are ready to, following inner dictates and dynamics.

A person ready to die WILL, despite any medication.

(Emphatically:) A person who wants to live will seize upon the tiniest hope, and respond.

The dynamics of health have nothing to do with inoculations.

They reside in the consciousness of each being. In your terms they are regulated by emotions, desires, and thoughts.

Seth/Jane Roberts, The "Unknown" Reality, Vol. 1, Session 703

Once you wholeheartedly accept life on life's terms, then you may indeed find what you are after, but not while you insist upon it as a condition for continued existence in this life.

You have no right to set such terms any more than a flower
would insist upon sunny ground

And a preferred spot within the garden as a prerequisite for its
own existence.

You are pouting. You are quarreling, and in so doing you cut
yourself off from the joy and vitality that do make life
worthwhile living.

Your own purpose can and will make life a daily pleasure when
you let your conditions go.

You forget what you do have - physical health and vitality.

You forget your intellect, which is a good one, and your intuitions.

Many are not blessed with these.

You cannot pervert them by trying to force them to serve purposes
that you have set up as a condition of existence.

You must live in the faith that your purpose is and will be fulfilled,
Is being fulfilled and will be fulfilled.

You must live in the faith that you have such a meaning and purpose,
or you would not be here.

TES9 440

Dreams Make Your World Go Round

In other words, a dream allows the inner self to view itself within the spacious present.

Now, chemically the physical body does need to dream.

That is, dreaming is a necessity if the physical body is to survive.

This is the result of certain chemical reactions and chemical necessities, chemical excesses that build up during the days, inciting the mental dream mechanism.

Without dreams the outer camouflaged self would lose all touch with inner realities,

Or would be in danger of thus denying its own heritage;

And therefore the physical body is so constructed that excess chemicals must be discharged and transformed into human action, or the physical mechanism would be clogged with poisons.

TES3 Session 93 September 30, 1964

Each probability system has its own set of "blueprints," clearly defining its freedoms and boundaries, and setting forth the most favorable structures capable of fulfillment.

These are not inner images of perfection,

And to some extent the blueprints themselves change, for the action within any given system of probabilities automatically alters the entire picture, enlarging it.

The blueprints are actually more like inner working plans that can be changed with circumstances, but to some extent they are idea-lizations, with a hyphen.

As an individual you carry within you such a blueprint, then;

It contains all the information you require to bring about the most favorable version of yourself in the probable system that you know.

These blueprints exist biologically and at every level –

Psychically, spiritually, mentally.

The information is knit into the genes and chromosomes,

But it exists apart, and the physical structures merely represent the carriers of information.

In the same fashion the species en masse holds within its vast inner mind such working plans or blueprints.

They exist apart from the physical world and in an inner one,

And from this you draw those theories, ideas, civilizations, and technologies which you then physically translate.

The Unknown Reality, Volume One, Session 696 - by Jane Roberts © L. Davies Butts

All viruses of any kind are important to the stability of your planetary life.

They are a part of the planet's biological heritage and memory.

You cannot eradicate a virus, though at any given time you destroy every member alive of any given strain.

They exist in the earth's memory, to be recreated, as they were before, whenever the need arises.

The same applies of course to any animal or plant considered extinct.

Only an objectively tuned consciousness like man's

Would imagine that the physical eradication of a species destroyed its existence.

NoME Chapter 6: Session 840, March 12, 1979

Now I tell you this to clear the air, and show you that your conditions will not be met while you hold them as conditions.

Only when you accept life and do not hold conditions.

Now. Practically speaking, you must stop insisting upon male-female personal love as the condition of existence.

You must accept life on its own terms with the faith that your life now has a meaning and a beauty and a purpose.

You can do this, and I know that you can do it. Then you will begin to see the meaning in your life that has always been there, and the purpose and joy that you have not been able to fill.

Men and women have joyfully honored and loved the evening.

And the dawn, and listened to the heart-pulse within them,

With a blessing and a joy who have not had one-hundredth of your blessings

Or one third the reason to look forward to another day,

And they have fulfilled themselves and brought joy to others.

They accepted life on its own terms, and in so accepting it they were filled with a grace, a grace that comes from giving life all that you have.

Personality Is An Ever-Changing Thing

Your basic personality in this life is open.

You are trying to close it.

It reaches out to all kinds of people over and beyond sexual lines,

And you are attempting to hold it in bounds.

You feel the need for a great love, but you have the great love and do not realize it.

You are trying to make it safe. You are trying to hide yourself in one man's arms.

You can reach both sexes, particularly in your teaching, and in this way you have gifts for both, and they are spiritual and psychic gifts.

You do not understand them yet so you turn this great love inward, and try to narrow it down, and fasten it upon one individual who will then reciprocate –

And you do not basically care who this individual is.

Instead your love is very wide and deep.

It can aid many people, for it is un-generalized and vast, and it will bring you much satisfaction and pleasure as it helps others.

But you must not insist on any one condition as a prerequisite for existence.

I am not saying that you will not have what you want, again,

But as long as you hold the wish as a condition of existence you will not.

TES9 440

It is no coincidence that Ruburt does not possess a scientific vocabulary, though he does possess a scientific as well as intuitive mind.

The very attempt to describe reality in scientific terms, as they are currently understood, pays, my dear friend, undue tribute to a vocabulary that automatically scales down greater concepts to fit its rigors.

In other words, such attempts further compound the problem of considering a seemingly objective universe,

And describing it in an objective fashion.

The universe is

And you can pick your terms —

A spiritual or mental or psychological manifestation,

And not, in your usual vocabulary, an objective manifestation.

There is presently no science, religion, or psychology that comes close to even approaching a conceptual framework that could explain, or even indirectly describe, the dimensions of that kind of universe.

Its properties are psychological, following the logic of the psyche, and all of the physical properties that you understand are reflections of those deeper issues.

Again, each atom and molecule and any particle that you can

imagine possesses, and would possess, a consciousness.

Unless you accept that statement at least as a theory upon which to build, then much of my material would appear meaningless.

The Nature of Mass Events, Chapter 7: Session 855, May 21, 1979 - by Jane Roberts (C) L. Davies Butts

Events are materialized in your time from their origins in no time, then.

There is no end in those terms to the source or supply of probabilities, therefore no time is not a static, completed cosmic storehouse.

It is being continually added to. Each event that you form from any given set of probabilities automatically gives rise to new probabilities.

The nature of any given probable action does not lead to any particular inevitable concluding act.

Probabilities expand in terms of value fulfillment.

One given act does not necessarily then lead to act B and C,

And hence to a concluding action. Instead it has offshoots in infinite directions,

And these offshoots have offshoots.

Sessions on the creative dilemmas and the sessions dealing with relative non being will help you here.

"Outside" in quotes of the realities of which I am aware and others are aware, there are systems that we cannot describe.

They are massive energy sources, cosmic energy banks, who

make possible the whole reality of probabilities.

TES9 438

No methods will work if you are afraid of your own impulses, or
of the nature of your own being.

Most of you understand that All That Is is within you—

That God is within creation, within physical matter,

And that "He" does not simply operate as some cosmic director
on the outside of reality.

You must understand that the spiritual self also exists within the
physical self in the same fashion.

The inner self is not remote, either —

Not divorced from your most intimate desires and affairs,

But instead communicates through your own smallest gesture,
through your smallest ideal.

This sense of division within the self forces you to think that
there is a remote, spiritual, wise, intuitive inner self,

And a bewildered, put-upon, spiritually ignorant, inferior
physical self, which happens to be the one you identify with.

Many of you believe, moreover, that the physical self's very
nature is evil.

That its impulses, left alone, will run in direct opposition to the
good of the physical world and society

And fly in the face of the deeper spiritual truths of inner reality.

The inner self then becomes so idealized and so remote that by contrast the physical self seems only the more ignorant and flawed.

In the face of such beliefs the ideal of psychic development, or astral travel, or spiritual knowledge, or even of sane living, seems so remote as to be impossible.

You must, therefore, begin to celebrate your own beings,

To look to your own impulses as being the natural connectors between the physical and the nonphysical self.

Children trusting their impulses learn to walk, and trusting your impulses, you can find yourselves again.

NoME Chapter 10: Session 872, August 8, 1979

It must be realized that the physical conditions are NOT permanent, but ever-changing.

To imagine otherwise is to become hypnotized by the physical symbols.

Each day should be considered a new day.

Ruburt (Jane) should not think for example:

"I have had these symptoms for such and such a time."

This reinforces the idea of permanency.

The day should be considered as a psychic rebirth.

Seth/Jane Roberts, The Early Sessions, Book 8, Session 334

The Early Sessions, Book 8, Session 334

Dying is a biological necessity, not only for the individual,

But to insure the continued vitality of the species.

Dying is a spiritual and psychological necessity, for after a while the exuberant, ever- renewed energies of the spirit can no longer be translated into flesh.

Inherently, each individual knows that he or she must die physically in order to survive spiritually and Psychically.

The self outgrows the flesh.

SESSION 801, The Individual and the Nature of Mass Events - By Jane Roberts © L. Davies Butts

The concept of reincarnation itself clearly shows the change of sexual orientation, and the existence of a self that is apart from its sexual orientation, even while it is also expressed through a given sexual stance.

To a good extent, sexual beliefs are responsible for the blocking-out of reincarnational awareness. Such "memory" would necessarily acquaint you with experiences most difficult to correlate with your current sexual roles.

Those other-sex existences are present to the psyche unconsciously. They are a portion of your personality. In so specifically identifying with your sex, therefore, you also inhibit memories that might limit or destroy that identification.

The Nature of the Psyche: Its Human Expression; Chapter 5: Session 773, April 26, 1976, Jane Roberts ©

2011 Laurel Davies-Butts

Now, in those terms, you are the power of God manifested.

You are not powerless.

To the contrary, through your being, the power of God is strengthened, for you are a portion of what He is

You are not simply an insignificant, innocuous clump of clay through which He decides to show Himself.

You are he manifesting as you. You are as legitimate as He is.

If you are a part of God, then He is also a part of you.

And, in denying your own worth, you end up denying His as well.

I do not like to use the term "He", meaning God, since All-That-Is is the origin of not only all sexes

But of all realities, in some of which sex, as you think of it, does not exist.

1973.07.02 Sess. 674: NOPR

There is no such thing as a cat consciousness, basically speaking, or a bird consciousness.

In those terms, there are instead simply consciousnesses that choose to take certain focuses.

NoME Chapter 6: Session 840, March 12, 1979

What you are learning is a technique for self-development.

You cannot use it, therefore, to attain those things that do not pertain to your own self-development

And the techniques will not help you get something that you were not meant to have

Nor that you have before decided as an entity that you should not have.

Nevertheless, the facts remain that your own inner self

And your own entity has given you challenges that you have accepted.

Now you know these challenges; subconsciously you are aware of them.

There must be an open-minded, an openhearted attitude here.

You must not try to use what you have learned in a narrow, limiting way.

This hampers your own development.

It closes your eyes to many possibilities that will be important to you.

It is natural, perhaps, to want to use what you have learned,

This information, as a technique to achieve what you at any particular time think desirable, a particular person, a particular thing.

But what is important is the inner development.

If this is taken care of, it will automatically lead you to the person that is best for you

And to the circumstances that will help you develop.

To insist that a specific individual or a specific goal be attained through these methods is limiting.

There must always be the acknowledgment that you do not consciously as yet realize the depths of yourself, —

The goals you have set and the challenges.

And this material should be used to open up your inner horizons
—
And to lead you in those directions toward which your inner self has already set you.

If you then egotistically, say

—No—

This particular situation is what I want,

Then you may be blocking the inner direction which has been meant for you.

The Early Sessions, Book 8, Session 403

Now: in the most basic manner, each person and creature possesses faith, whatever its degree or nature.

Without it, there would be no family groups, animal or human, or civilizations or governments.

It may seem that the retribution of law holds societies together and keeps, for example, criminal elements down.

So that you have operating processes that insure more or less stable living conditions.

The laws, however, are necessarily based upon man's faith that those laws will indeed be largely followed.

Otherwise the laws would be useless.

You go on faith that there will be a tomorrow.

You operate on faith constantly, so that it becomes indeed an almost invisible element in each life.

It is the fiber behind all organizations and relationships,

And it is based upon the innate, natural knowledge possessed by
each new creature—

The knowledge that it springs from a sustaining source,

That its birth is cushioned by all the resources of nature,

And that nature itself is sustained by the greater source that gave
IT birth.

You cannot be alive, without faith, yet faith can be distorted.

There is faith in good, but there is also faith in evil.

In usual terms faith takes it for granted that a certain desired
end will be achieved, even though the means may not be known.

In usual terms, again, there is no direct evidence, otherwise you
would have no need for faith.

When you fear the worst will happen, you often are showing
quite real faith in a backward fashion—

For with no direct evidence before your eyes of disaster,

You heartily believe it will occur—you have faith in it.

That is, indeed, misplaced faith.

I want to point out that faith is not all that unusual,

But a prime element in your life.

You can have faith that you will be ill.

This should be obvious, because for example there are healthy people also,

With no evidence of any disease,

Who have utter faith that disease is hidden within them, or swiftly approaching.

It is, therefore, quite to everyone's advantage that Framework 2 is not neutral.

Faith in a creative, fulfilling, desired end, sustained faith, literally draws from

Framework 2 all of the necessary ingredients,

All of the elements however staggering in number, arranges all the details,

And then inserts into Framework 1 the impulses, dreams, chance meetings, motivations, or whatever is necessary

So that the desired end then falls into place as a completed pattern.

You must begin somewhere, so you state your purpose clearly in Framework 1.

Then you have the faith that the event will be brought to pass.

Your own creative, abilities are instantly mobilized in that direction.

Your behavior in Framework 1 must automatically change.

The ways and the means, however, cannot be questioned, for they will come about from a greater source of knowledge than you consciously possess.

I am trying to give you some kind of an overall picture so that you can make your own helpful comparisons, and understand more thoroughly what is involved.

Often I will use examples that do not involve health, for you can apply them to health yourselves even more effectively, for you will make you OWN connections.

Someone may plan an airplane trip.

Everything will be arranged. The last detail taken care of.

The person may take great precautions to see that the plane is not missed.

Persons may have been contacted to care for the house during the time of absence.

Children may have been sent to camp, neighbors assigned to care for pets, and every logical situation cared for.

Let us say that this particular plane may well crash, and in fact does.

After all of this person's planning, hard work and effort, at the last moment everything seems to go wrong.

Nothing seems right.

The children do not leave for camp in time.

One of the animals runs away.

A ticket is lost. Our individual comes down with indigestion, or a headache.

Lo and behold--for while everything seems so poorly, our

friend's life is being saved, for he misses his plane.

Later he wonders what happened, that his life was saved, and his plans altered at the last moment.

Our friend wanted to live and had faith that he would.

In spite of his own conscious lack of knowledge, he was brought to operate according to the information available in Framework 2, though he was not aware of it.

He lost his ticket--a stupid error, it seemed.

The lives and events of all those involved with his trip

The neighbors, the children, and so forth—

All of those issues were arranged in Framework 2,

So that while the events seemed most unpleasant, they were highly beneficial.

If our friend learned of the plane crash, he saw this only too well

If he never learned of the plane crash,

And did not have faith in the beneficial nature of events,

Then he might simply remember the entire affair as highly unpleasant, stupid, and even think that it was another example that he could do nothing right.

The entire pattern of your lives is taken into consideration in Framework 2.

There is no need for bargaining.

Ruburt does not have to fear that he must give up some creativity for physical freedom,

FOR THE TWO GO HAND IN HAND

.

Framework 2 contains all the dreams, plans, and thoughts of all human beings of any time.

THERE, the spacious present is operative.

THERE, it makes no difference if you have had an undesirable physical condition for a day or a lifetime.

THERE, you are not impeded by the past.

If your beliefs in Framework 1 make you assign great power to the past, then you impede your progress.

I have said many times that spontaneity knows its own order,

And I am speaking of true spontaneity.

I say this because often anger, for example, may seem spontaneous

And may be.

But is more often the explosive, finally forced expression of reactions long withheld or repressed.

True spontaneity however comes directly from Framework 2,

And behind it are endless patterns of orderliness and complexity that are beyond your conscious Framework 1 comprehension.

And THAT emerged as the result of those abilities mentioned in our last session.

Such an impulse, followed, will lead to its own performance the means will be given.

Before, Ruburt's fear prevented him from even acknowledging many such impulses to act.

Ruburt's assessment of your dream and its conditions is another case in point.

The inner organizations immediately trigger all the necessary actions required, from Framework 2.

This applies to any issue—but again, your creative abilities, used on behalf of Ruburt's physical condition will give him a normally cooperating body.

Each improvement is to be considered as a significant piece of a puzzle being put together, even though you may not see any connection between one improvement or another.

Again, you should not double check at every moment. As Ruburt's 'Cezanne' simply came out of nowhere, so will his complete flexibility.

Seth, The Personal Sessions, Deleted. Book 4, pages 71-73. by Jane Roberts (C) L. Davies Butts

You do not set conditions upon life.

This is the greatest lesson that anyone can learn. Basically, basically, there is no other, for this one includes all others.

Vitality and joy and creativity move through you all spontaneously if you do not set up barriers in terms of preconceptions and conditions,

And all your desires will be met, but never when you set them up as conditions for your existence.

The life that is within you knows only these terms:

Continued un-predetermined development, expansion;

It will not flow in predetermined patterns or demands.

It can fulfill you and others, and bring you un-imaged fulfillment,

But never when you attempt to force it to follow certain directions.

Who are you to threaten vitality and life?

The Early Sessions Book 9 Session 440

The Art Of Consciousness

All creatures of whatever degree have their own appreciation of esthetics.

Many such creatures merge their arts so perfectly into their lives that it is impossible to separate the two:

The spider's web, for example, or the beaver's dam—

And there are endless other examples.

This is not 'blind instinctive behavior' at all, but the result of well-ordered spontaneous artistry.

Art is not a specifically human endeavor, though man likes to believe that this is so.

Art is above all a natural characteristic.

I try to straddle your definitions—

But flowers, for example, in a fashion see themselves as their own artistic creations.

They have an esthetic appreciation of their own colors—

A different kind, of course, than your perception of color.

But nature seeks to outdo itself in terms that are most basically artistic, even while those terms may also include quite utilitarian purposes.

The natural man, then, is a natural artist.

In a sense, painting is man's natural attempt to create an original

But coherent, mental yet physical interpretation of his own reality—

And by extension to create a new version of reality for his species.

You are still learning. Your work is still developing.

How truly unfortunate you would be if that were not the case!

There is always a kind of artistic dissatisfaction that any true artist feels with work that is completed, for he is always aware of the tug and pull,

And the tension, between the sensed ideal and its manifestation.

In a certain fashion the artist is looking for a creative solution to a sensed but never clearly stated problem or challenge,

And it is an adventure that is literally unending.

It must be one that has no clearly stated destination, in usual terms.

In the most basic of ways, the artist cannot say where he is going, for if he knows ahead of time he is not creating but copying.

The true artist is involved with the inner workings of himself with the universe—

A choice, I remind you, that he or she has made, and so often the artist does indeed forsake the recognized roads of recognition.

And more, seeing that, he often does not know how to assess his own progress, since his journey has no recognizable creative destination.

By its nature art basically is meant to put each artist of whatever kind into harmony with the universe,

For the artist draws upon the same creative energy from which birth emerges.

Roberts, Jane (2012-06-02). Dreams, "Evolution," and Value Fulfillment, Volume One - by Jane Roberts

Thoughts and images are formed into physical reality and become physical fact.

They are propelled chemically.

A thought is energy.

It begins to produce itself physically at the moment of its conception.

Mental enzymes are connected with the pineal gland.

As you know them, body chemicals are physical,

But they are the propellants of this thought-energy, containing all the codified data necessary for translating any thought or image into physical actuality.

They cause the body to reproduce the inner image.

They are sparks, so to speak, initiating the transformation.

Chemicals are released through the skin and pore systems, in an invisible but definite pseudo-physical formation.

The intensity of a thought or image largely determines the immediacy of its physical materialization.

There is no object about you that you have not created.

There is nothing about your own physical image that you have not made.

The initial thought or image exists within the mental enclosure [as explained in earlier sessions].

It is not yet physical. Then it is sparked into physical materialization by the mental enzymes.

This is the general procedure.

All such images or thoughts are not completely materialized in your terms, however.

The intensity may be too weak.

The chemical reaction sparks certain electrical charges, some within the layers of the skin.

There are radiations then through the skin to the exterior world, containing highly codified instructions and information.

The physical environment is as much a part of you, then, as your body.

Your control over it is quite effective, for you create it as you create your fingertip.

Objects are composed of the same pseudo-material that radiates outward from your own physical image,

Only the higher intensity mass is different.

When it is built up enough, you recognize it as an object.

At low intensity mass it is not apparent to you.

Nerve impulses travel outward from the body, invisibly along these nerve pathways in much the same manner that they travel within the body.

The pathways are carriers of telepathic thoughts, impulses, and desires that travel outward from any given self, altering seemingly objective events.

In your system of reality, you are learning what mental energy is,

And how to use it.

You do this by constantly transforming your thoughts and emotions into physical form.

You are supposed to get a clear picture of your inner development by perceiving the exterior environment.

What seems to be a perception, an objective concrete event independent from you, is instead the materialization of your own inner emotions, energy, and mental environment.

The Seth Material Chapter Ten

Imagine Cancer Cells Being Neutralized With An Imaginary Wand

Many cancer patients have martyr-like characteristics, often putting up with undesirable situations or conditions for years.

They feel powerless, unable to change, yet unwilling to stay in the same position.

The most important point is to arouse such a person's beliefs in his or her strength and power.

In many instances these persons symbolically shrug their shoulders, saying. What will happen, will happen,

But they do not physically struggle against their situation.

It is also vital that these patients are not overly medicated, for oftentimes the side effects of some cancer-eradicating drugs are dangerous in themselves.

There has been some success with people who imagine that the cancer is instead some hated enemy or monster or foe, which is then banished through mental mock battles over a period of time.

While the technique does have its advantages, it also pits one portion of the self against the other.

It is much better to imagine, say, the cancer cells being neutralized by some imaginary wand.

Doctors might suggest that a patient relax and then ask himself or herself what kind of inner fantasy would best serve the healing process.

Instant images may come to mind at once,

But if success is not achieved immediately, have the patient try again, for in almost all cases some inner pictures will be perceived.

Behind the entire problem, however, is the fear of using one's full power or energy.

Cancer patients most usually feel an inner impatience as they sense their own need for future expansion and development, only to feel it thwarted.

The fear that blocks that energy can indeed be dissipated if new beliefs are inserted for old ones –

So again we return to those emotional attitudes and ideas that automatically promote health and healing.

Each individual is a good person, an individualized portion of universal energy itself.

Each person is meant to express his or her own characteristics and abilities.

Life means energy, power, and expression.

Those beliefs, if taught early enough, would form the most effective system of preventative medicine ever known.

Again, we cannot generalize overmuch,

But many persons know quite well that they are not sure whether they want to live or die.

The overabundance of cancer cells represents nevertheless the need for expression and expansion

- the only arena left open –

Or so it would seem.

Such a person must also contend with society's unfortunate ideas about the disease in general,

So that many cancer patients end up isolated or alone.

As in almost all cases of disease, however, if it were possible to have a kind of 'thought transplant' operation, the disease would quickly vanish.

Even in the most dire of instances, some patients suddenly fall in love, or something in their home environment changes,

And the person also seems to change overnight - while again the disease is gone.

Session 5/11, Page 273

The soul can be described

As a multidimensional, infinite act, each minute probability being brought somewhere into actuality and existence;

An infinite creative act that creates for itself infinite dimensions in which fulfillment is possible.

Seth Speaks Part Two: Chapter 16: Session 565, February 1, 1971

The integrity of any intuitive information depends upon the inner integrity of the person who receives it.

Expansion of consciousness, therefore, requires honest self appraisal, an awareness of one's own beliefs and prejudices.

It brings a gift and a responsibility.

All who wish to look within themselves, to find their own answers, to encounter their own appointment with the universe,

Should therefore become well acquainted with the intimate workings of their own personality.

Such self-knowledge is in itself highly advantageous, and in one way is its own reward.

It is impossible, however, to look inward with any clearness if you are unwilling to change your attitudes, beliefs, or behavior,

Or examine those characteristics that you consider uniquely your own.

You cannot examine reality without examining yourself, in other words.

You cannot hold encounters with All That Is apart from yourself,

And you cannot separate yourself from your experience.

You cannot use truth.

It cannot be manipulated. Whoever thinks he is manipulating truth is manipulating himself.

You are truth. Then discover yourself.

Seth Speaks, Session 596 - by Jane Roberts (C) L. Davies Butts

Now, these facts do not deny the validity of the soul,

But instead add to it immeasurably.

The tapestry of your own existence is simply such that the three dimensional intellect cannot behold it.

These probable selves, however are a portion of your identity or soul,

And if you are out of contact with them it is only because you focus upon physical events and accept them as the criteria for reality.

From any given point of your existence however, you can glimpse other probable realities, and sense the reverberations of probable actions beneath those physical decisions that you make.

Some people have done this spontaneously, often in the dream state.

Here the rigid assumptions of normal waking consciousness often fade, and you can find yourself performing those physically rejected activities, never realizing that you have peered into a probable existence of your own.

SS 565

Time—A Highly Specialized Illusion

Now to some extent, to some large extent, time as you know it with its continual moments is a highly specialized illusion, even within your physical system.

Your own race is the only one who plays with any facility.

Other myriad life forms have nothing to do with it at all.

You merely transpose your values upon them.

They do not experience time as you do.

This does not mean that they are not advanced enough to understand the reality of your time.

They do not share the illusion.

Almost all animals, plants, birds, insects, rocks and trees perceive according to intensities.

The intensity of an experience is their present;

But in many ways that I will not explain to you at this point, their present is of wider duration than yours.

This does not necessarily mean that they perceive more of the past and future within their present than you do, for they do not in those terms.

But in terms of quality and value fulfillment there is greater duration and the "moment," is more intensely perceived.

Be reminded here that they are not concerned with moments in your terms.

Each experience is highly intense, however.

The organism responds to an acute degree. This applies to both birds and rocks,

Though there is a large scale of difference between the extremes.

TES9 433

Humility is pride in your part of All That Is.

It is joyful recognition of the cooperative plan that you hold in the structure of being.

It is not a cringing voice that says, "I am nothing!

I bow down before the gods of the universe, or before any god!

True humility says, "I am a joyous portion of All That Is,

And I recognize the joy of my being as a portion of All That Is.

And I am thankful, in this life, for the rain that falls,

And for the rays of energy that pervade my being,

And for the seasons that come and go.

And I am thankful for the wisdom that dwells within the cell of my smallest toe,

And all the miraculous being of my skin

That seems to keep me within myself

And yet connects me with all else in the universe.

And so I rejoice in my uniqueness and in my part of all reality.

That is what humility is.

It is a recognition that you exist within nature and not apart from it,

That you come to this existence interwoven with it –

Not as a conqueror walking upon the face of the earth for all other creatures and beings to obey him.

This ESP class session is unpublished...1972.09.19

You form the fabric of your experience through your own beliefs and expectations.

The truth set forth by Seth teaching is centered on "beliefs creates reality".

In order to let us know more clearly what is meant by Your beliefs form your reality,

Seth metaphorically stated that the specific material world can be called "Framework 1,"

And the spiritual world of consciousness can be called "Framework 2".

"Framework 1" is like the TV programs we watch, and "Framework 2" is a spiritual studio.

The process of creation is the realization of the spiritual world into the concrete world.

All the images in the world have the image of intention in Framework 2

Before they are manifested into the material reality in
Framework 1.

So, how exactly does the inner Belief manifest into the outer Reality?

Seth says that, just like matter has the smallest unit Atom, the
so-called belief, that is consciousness,

It also has the smallest consciousness.

The basic unit of consciousness "CU's" (units of consciousness)
is neither concrete nor fixed,

But it has the infinite properties of expansion, development,
organization, etc.

The unit of consciousness is conscious energy.

They operate in the form of Particles or Waves.

Regardless of the mode of operation, the consciousness units can
perceive their own existence.

Everything in the universe originates from a consciousness unit.

It is the first being.

When the mind prepares to form reality, the unit of
consciousness is strengthened,

And explosive sparks are excited from within, thereby beginning to

Explode into a process of materialization.

After that,

The unit of consciousness became what was called the EE unit (Electromagnetic Energy Unit),

Which also took a step closer to the physical reality.

Just like consciousness units, EE units also operate as "fields," waves

Or particles, but they are closer to matter than consciousness units.

The EE unit is the "magnetic field" or "energy field" as the saying goes.

After the EE unit is formed, they will combine in their own way and gradually form matter.

However, there are countless subtleties before becoming the smallest particles of matter.

The formation of the EE unit into matter is one of the greatest and mildest selection processes

Through which the atoms and molecules of the material world are created.

The frequency of vibration of the unit of consciousness is very different from that of matter.

The unit of consciousness moves faster than the speed of light,

But when the unit of consciousness approaches the structure of matter,

The frequency of vibration slows down.

In other words, the electron is slow and bulky compared to the EE unit,

And so is the unit of consciousness compared to the EE unit.

From the unit of consciousness, the unit of EE to the formation of material reality,

It is the specific process of Belief creates reality.

All things in the world are born following this procedure.

So, is it possible to run out of the unit of consciousness, or energy of the source?

Seth reassures us that there is no one in the world who has been allotted a ration of energy and will die when it is used up.

On the contrary, everything is always a constant supply of energy to everyone,

And life can be recreated in every moment if people live with passion and have positive and joyful thoughts.

This is the law of creation, and the mystery of creation.

NoPR Chapter 2: Session 614, September 13, 1972

When your scientists examine them, for example, they do not examine the nature, say, the essence of an atom.

They only explore the characteristics of an atom as it acts or shows itself within your system.

Its greater reality completely escapes them.

Seth Speaks Session 567

The nature of matter itself is not understood.

You perceive it at a certain stage.

Using your terms now and speaking as simply as possible there are other forms of matter beyond those you see.

These forms are quite real and vivid, quite physical, to those who react to the particular sphere of activity.

In terms of probabilities, therefore, you choose certain acts, unconsciously transform these into physical events or objects, and then perceive them.

But those unchosen events also go out from you and are projected into these other forms.

Now the behavior of atoms and molecules is involved here, for again these are only present within your universe during certain stages.

Their activity is perceived only during the range of particular vibratory rhythms.

When your scientists examine them for example, they do not examine the nature, say, of an atom.

They only explore the characteristics of an atom as it acts or shows itself within your system.

Its greater reality completely escapes them.

You understand that there are spectrums of light.

So are there spectrums of matter.

Your system of physical reality is not dense in comparison with some others.

The dimensions that you give to physical matter barely begin to hint at the varieties of dimensions possible.

Each of you is couched now in the natural world,

And that world is couched in a reality from which nature emerges.

The psyche's roots are secure, nourishing it like a tree from the ground of being.

The source of the psyche's strength is within each individual—

The invisible fabric of the persons' existence.

Nature is luxurious and abundant in its expressions.

The greater reality from which nature springs is even more abundant,

And within that multidimensional experience no individual is ignored, forgotten, dismissed, lost, or forsaken.

NotP Chapter 11: Session 800, April 4, 1977 - by Jane Roberts © L. Davies Butts

Because of the energy he is given by [some], he will have a certain consciousness of his own,

But a mock devil has no power or reality to those who do not believe in his existence, and who do not give him energy through their belief.

He is, in other words, a superlative hallucination as mentioned earlier,

Those who believe in a hell and assign themselves to it through their belief can indeed experience one,

But certainly in nothing like eternal terms.

No soul is forever ignorant.

Now those who have such beliefs actually lack a necessary deep trust in the nature of consciousness, of the soul, and of All That Is.

They concentrate upon not what they think of as the power of good, but fearfully upon what they think of as the power of evil.

Seth Speaks Part Two: Chapter 17: Session 568, February 22, 1971

The inner reality of the message was told in terms that man at the time could understand, in line with his root assumptions.

Development unfolds in all directions.

The soul is not ascending a series of stairs, each one representing a new and higher point of development.

Instead, the soul stands at the center of itself, exploring, extending its capacities in all directions at once, involved in issues of creativity, each one highly legitimate.

The probable system of reality opens up the nature of the soul to you.

It should change current religion's ideas considerably.

For this reason, the nature of good and evil is a highly important point.

Seth Speaks Part Two: Chapter 17: Session 568, February 22, 1971

There is no penance! You are here to develop.

You do learn the consequences of your thoughts and actions,

And you face them.

But there is no penance!

And I tell you this: there is no guilt.

You learn the consequence of your action

And you face the consequence of your action.

You create the idea of guilt.

And when you believe in guilt,

Then you create the penance in accordance to how strongly you believe in the guilt.

When your precious psychologists walk out of their bodies

And when your psychologists put on the type of personality performance

That I can put on—

then I will listen to them when they tell me about the ego and subconscious.

When their theories are broad enough to explain telepathy and clairvoyance and out-of-body realities, then I will listen to them and to their theories.

Their ego and their subconscious and their superego and their id leads

Them no further than a worm that wiggles in the grass

And is dead forever tomorrow,

Even the worm has more reality than they are willing to assign to one human consciousness.

All you have to do is swing the flashlight in other directions.

You must momentarily, for now, shift the focus of the flashlight.

And when you shift it, the direction in which you are used to looking will momentarily appear dark,

But other images and realities will become available to you.

There is nothing to prevent you from swinging the flashlight back.

And when you learn what you are doing, when you learn what you are doing— then you will learn how to hold the flashlight stationary and still illuminate all these other areas.

And these whole other areas represent human personality and all its potentials.

The Early Class Sessions Book 1 ESP Class Session, October 14, 1969

All of the issues form together to make a trellis of behavior.

Thorns or roses may grow therein.

That is, the individual will grow outward toward the world, encountering and forming a practical experience, traveling outward from his center in almost vine like fashion,

Forming from the fabric of physical reality a conglomeration of pleasant or aesthetic, and unpleasant or prickly events.

The vine of experience in this analogy is formed in quite a natural fashion from psychic elements that are as necessary to psychological experience as sun, air, and water are to plants.

I do not want to get too entwined in this analogy, however;

But as the individual's personal experience must be seen in the light of all of these issues,

So mass events cannot be understood unless they are considered in a far greater context than usual.

The question of epidemics, for example, cannot be answered from a biological standpoint alone.

It involves great sweeping psychological attitudes on the part of many,

And meets the needs and desires of those involved.—

Needs which, in your terms, arise in a framework of religious, psychological and cultural realities that cannot be isolated from biological results.

I have thus far stayed clear of many important and vital subjects, involving mass realities,

Because first of all the importance of the individual was to be stressed,

And his power to form his private events.

Only when the private nature of reality was emphasized sufficiently

Would I be ready to show how the magnification of individual reality combines and enlarges to form vast mass reactions.

Such as, say, the initiation of an obviously new historical and cultural period;

The rise or overthrow of governments;

The birth of a new religion that sweeps all others before it;

Mass conversions;

Mass murders in the form of wars;

The sudden sweep of deadly epidemics;

The scourge of earthquakes, floods, or other disasters;

The inexplicable appearance of periods of great art or architecture or technology.

A Quick Look At The Psychological Platform Of Death

At death, to those who so believe in these symbols

The guides take on the guises of those beloved figures of
Christian saints and heroes.

Then with this as framework,

And in terms that they can understand, such individuals are told
the true situation.

Mass religious movements have for centuries fulfilled that
purpose, in giving man some plan to be followed.

It little mattered that later the plan was seen as a child's primer,
a book of instructions

Complete with colorful tales, for the main purpose was served
and there was little disorientation.

In periods where no such mass ideas are held, there is more
disorientation,

And when life after death is completely denied, the problem is
somewhat magnified.

Many, of course, are overjoyed to find themselves still conscious.

Others have to learn all over again about certain laws of behavior,

For they do not realize the creative potency of their thoughts or
emotions.

Such an individual may find himself in ten different
environments within the flicker of an eyelash, for example, with

no idea of the reason behind the situation.

He will see no continuity at all,

And feel himself flung without rhyme or reason from one experience to another,

Never realizing that his own thoughts are propelling him quite literally.

I am speaking now of the events immediately following death, for there are other stages.

Guides will helpfully become a part of your hallucinations, in order to help you out of them, but they must first of all get your trust.

At one time--in your terms--I myself acted as such a guide; as in a sleep state Ruburt now follows the same road.

The situation is rather tricky from the guide's viewpoint, for psychologically utmost discretion must be used.

One man's Moses, as I discovered, may not be another man's Moses.

I have served as a rather creditable Moses on several occasions—

And once, though this is hard to believe, to an Arab.

The Arab was a very interesting character, by the way, and to illustrate some of the difficulties involved, I will tell you about him.

He hated the Jews, but somehow he was obsessed with the idea that Moses was more powerful than Allah

And for years this was the secret sin upon his conscience.

He spent some time in Constantinople at the time of the Crusades.

He was captured, and ended up with a group of Turks, all to be executed by the Christians, in this case very horribly so.

They forced his mouth open and stuffed it with burning coals, as a starter.

He cried to Allah, and then in greater desperation to Moses, and as his consciousness left his body, Moses was there.

He believed in Moses more than he did Allah,

And I did not know until the last moment which form I was to assume.

He was a very likable chap, and under the circumstances I did not mind when he seemed to expect a battle for his soul.

Moses and Allah were to fight for him.

He could not rid himself of the idea of force,

Though he had died by force, and nothing could persuade him to accept any kind of peace or contentment, or any rest, until some kind of battle was wrought.

A friend and I, with some others, staged the ceremony, and from opposite clouds in the sky Allah and I shouted out our claims upon his soul-

While he, poor man, cowered on the ground between us.

Now while I tell this story humorously, you must understand that the man's belief brought it about, and so to set him free, we worked it through.

I called upon Jehovah, but to no avail, because our Arab did not
know of Jehovah - only of Moses –

And it was in Moses he put his faith.

Allah drew a cosmic sword and I set it afire so that he dropped it.

It fell to the ground and set the land aflame.

Our Arab cried out again. He saw leagues of followers behind

Allah, and so leagues of followers appeared behind me.

Our friend was convinced that one of the three of us must be
destroyed,

And he feared mightily that he would be the victim.

Finally, the opposing clouds in which we appeared came closer.

In my hand I held a tablet that said: Thou shalt not kill.

Allah held a sword.

As we came closer we exchanged these items, and our followers
merged.

We came together, forming the image of a s-u-n and we said:
"We are one."

The two diametrically opposed ideas had to merge or the man
would have had no peace,

And only when these opposites were united could we begin to
explain his situation.

Seth Speaks, Chapter 9: Session 536, June 22, 1970, by Jane Roberts (C) L. Davies Butts

Seth withdrew. During break, Florence brought up the question
of the will of God—

Whether God has control over what happens to us, etc. Seth
suddenly spoke:

No stimuli is ever accidental.

No stimuli is ever accidental.

I repeat the sentence so you can understand it.

You are never controlled.

God is creativity and he creates creativity or other creators.

Creativity of necessity, because of its nature, leads to further
development and existence—to further creations.

Control leads to rigidity, nonexistence and the negation of all.

In the terms that are usually used, perfection would be death
and annihilation,

For it presupposes an end beyond which no progress is possible.

Creativity always knows that further development always lies latent.

New possibilities grow constantly from the heart and spirit.

To control is to court rigidity.

No God knows the word or the meaning of control,

Nor does he exert control as far as his abilities are concerned, for
it would lead to dead alleys,

And spirituality would go and leave him dried up as a fruit pit.

It is not my ego that remains, for I have shed egos as a snake
sheds skin.

It is my identity that remains and it is your identity that remains.

Freedom knows its own control, but not the kind you are thinking of.

Spontaneity, indeed, has its own discipline and is never applied
from without.

It is the other side of the coin.

There is no such control, then.

Spontaneity knows its own direction and the god is not fearful.
Control is a result of fear.

The Early Class Sessions Book 1, Session 10/22/1968 pages 89, 90 - By Jane Roberts © L. Davies Butts

I bid you my greetings, and I simply point out to you that you
identified yourself here as a young lady with a disease.

The first words you spoke identified yourself as a person with a
disease.

Your self-image is too involved in the disease that has a name
that has been given it.

"NOW HEAR ME!" Seth boomed, his voice roaring out the
autumn windows.

You have your own name—assert it in the joy of your being!

And if you want to live in vitality and joy,

Then your name is more important than any name of any group of symptoms,

For they have not the kind of reality that you have!

And your glowing integrity identifies you here,

So, then accept the vitality of your being, given you in this space

And in this time,

And do not accept instead the name of a disease in which you lose, it seems, identity and strength.

Do not quail before vocabulary!

Your integrity and your beauty and your strength identify you here,

And identify you for all time.

Therefore, do not look wan!

And forget thoughts of tragedy that are spelled out, and assert the vitality of your being!

Now, if you decide to leave this world, that is your right, and go in joy and vitality,

Seth was telling Cora. But go because you know YOU decide to leave,

And not as the victim of a disease that has been given a name.

If you decide that you want to live, then live in your full glory and strength,

But make up your mind, and do not allow yourself to be victimized.

If you want to die, then why do you want to die?

Know the reasons, and go because you have made up your mind,

And go with strength and vitality, making your own decisions—

But not as a victim, and not in tragedy, and not wan!

If you decide to live, then tell yourself you want to live

And know the reasons,

And your body will repair itself in joy and glory,

You are NOT a victim!

Conversations With Seth, Volume II", Chapter 11, by Susan M. Watkins ©

Human beings, and all creatures for that matter, have a strong inner impetus leading to action and expression.

If anything impedes this natural smoothness and coordination,

Then ALL aspects of expression are in one way or another impeded.

The cells and organs and muscles and bones all grow by expressing the natural, innate expression characteristic of their kinds.

There is a spontaneous order that directs their motions

And leads them ever onward to further expression and fulfillment.

Truly great artistic, creative, athletic and social abilities are inherent within each human individual.

Each person has the capacity, then, to be a genius ON MANY LEVELS.

These abilities may largely lay latent now—

But they are nevertheless part of the human heritage.

At the present time they may only represent distant ideals,
against which mankind measures itself,

Yet many of them can indeed be realized in the world as it is,

If only people become more aware of their expressive capabilities
so that the main direction of their lives are expressive rather
than Repressive.

The Personal Sessions, book 7, Deleted Session December 16, 1983 - by Jane Roberts © L. Davies Butts

Dream locations do not exist like physical objects in your head.

How could your small skull hold a replica of a cement building,
for example,

Even though the skull might be a rock head?

You need not take that remark personally, Joseph.

I couldn't resist making it, however.

These dream locations are realities.

They do exist, even though they do not exist in space as you
know it,

And certainly they do not take up space in the skull.

There would be no room for anything else.

As a brief byline here,

Even in reincarnation for example, an ego who experienced a

Civil War life is now aware of another

Who may have experienced life in the year three thousand.

Within the earthly cycle, such knowledge is not transmitted to
the physical brain, but it is always known.

It follows then that I am aware of the other Seth personality, and
he of me.

Because of your time misconceptions you make serious errors
whenever you attempt any predictions into life after death,

Or life within other systems than you own.

It is most difficult for you to conceive of an ego who experiences
events not in serial form.

When any contact is attempted in so-called mediumistic situations,

Then it is expected that the survival personality will "remember,"
events as you do;

But events no longer exist in that way.

The associative processes determine not only which events have
meaning, but also the "order."

An event happening say in 1948, of great importance to the sitter,

May no longer have any meaning to the survival personality.

Now.

If such is the case with personalities so closely allied with your own,

Then you can perhaps understand how alien your idea of time is to personalities that have never existed within your physical system.

They are used to experiencing events not in any time sequence. Instead moment points are experienced fully,

Developments opening simultaneously, and "events" are recognized as psychic and psychological happenings

Not necessarily connected with any exterior circumstances.

In some systems therefore exterior camouflage is not needed.

TES9 430

The basis for all experience is depth perception, and value fulfillment.

The self organizes data basically in a manner that psychology has not found.

The organization of such data is not simply the result of pre-adulthood tendencies, inclinations or experience.

Such tendencies are highly colored by previous existences,

By past lives, and this prehistory, existing as the electromagnetic property of the whole self,

Is the blueprint which is followed by the structure of the chromosomes.

That information, you see, will never be found in physical terms.

If such past memories are consciously recovered, as they have been,

The closed mind of the academic psychologist will not see what he has,

But will suppose the overworked imagination responsible.

A fully developed psychology will not exist until reincarnation is accepted as a fact.

Now, there is an overall personality pattern that is characteristic of each

Whole self, of which the reincarnated selves each give evidence.

There are particular and unique overall goals and abilities

That the whole self strives for through these existences.

Any psychology worthy of the name must take this inner motivation into consideration.

The study of dreams has been held back immeasurably because past-life memories have been stubbornly ignored.

Reincarnational material usually discusses various existences as occurring one before the other.

I emphasize strongly once more that the concept of continuity in terms of time is highly erroneous.

The Early Sessions, book 7, Session 312 January 16, 1967 - by Jane Roberts (C) L. Davies Butts

Illness and suffering are the results of the misdirection of creative energy.

They are a part of the creative force, however.

They do not come from a different source than, say, health and vitality.

Suffering is not good for the soul,

Unless it teaches you how to stop suffering.

That is its purpose.

Seth Speaks Session 580 - by Jane Roberts © L. Davies Butts

If you believe firmly that your consciousness is locked up somewhere inside your skull and is powerless to escape it,

If you feel that your consciousness ends at the boundary of your body, then you sell yourself short, and you will think that I am a delusion.

SS Part One: Chapter 1: Session 511, January 21, 1972

The destination is within you. You do not have to go any place to get that destination;

And it is only when you think that that destination lies elsewhere that you allow yourself to go astray.

Your identity is within you and do not look for it in others.

This is perhaps the strongest point of my message to you this evening,

The one I would have you take to heart.

When you realize that your own identity is within you will not spend energy seeking to find yourself in others.

Others cannot give you a sense of worth; this is your own.

Any lack is your own lack.

I may perhaps deal with more specific issues this evening.

But I will not discuss them until these points have been made.

TES8 Session 403 March 16, 1968 - by Jane Roberts (C) L. Davies Butts

Without dreams the whole self would have no way of holding its various manifestations together,

And the so-called conscious present personality would soon falter.

Imagine if you will now a band of men, some in cars with the high beams of the headlights gleaming,

So that some generalized conditions can be seen;

And some with low beams showing only the road that the automobiles directly pass.

The men can be compared to personified areas of the subconscious, with partial vision of existing conditions.

Another man in an airplane above sees the whole landscape, and through radio communicates to those below about those conditions which they cannot perceive.

The man in the airplane, then, can be compared to the inner self,

Sending messages to other areas of the subconscious, whose energies and focus are necessarily used in limited fashion.

Only in this case the man in the airplane, instead of a radio message,

Would radio directly into the mind mechanism of the men below,

A dream drama in the coded symbols which would be interpreted automatically by the men below.

Now. The conscious self responds without knowing it, often changing course and direction, to these dreams of which he is often not aware.

The ego, the conscious ego, the so-called conscious self, is only the front man in the front lines,

Supported by multitudinous areas or portions of himself that he does not know,

And whose messages come to him only through the correspondence of dreams.

TES3 Session 93 September 30, 1964

Love Has Tons Of Expressions And Characteristics

You must first love yourself before you love another.

By accepting yourself and joyfully being what you are, you fulfill
your own abilities.

And, your simple presence can make others happy.

You cannot hate yourself and love anyone else.

It is impossible.

You will, instead, project all the qualities you do not think you
possess upon someone else, do them lip service,

And hate the other individual for possessing them.

Though you profess to love the other,
You will try to undermine the very foundations of his or her being.

When you love others, you grant them their innate freedom

And do not cravenly insist that they always attend you.

There are no divisions to love.

There is no basic difference between the love of a child for a parent,

A parent for a child, a wife for a husband, a brother for a sister.

There are only various expressions and characteristics of love.

And, all love affirms.

It can accept deviations from the ideal vision without condemning them.

It does not compare the practical state of the beloved's being

With the idealized perceived one that is potential.

In this vision, the potential is seen as present.

And, the distance between the practical and the ideal forms no contradiction, since they coexist.

Now, sometimes you may think that you hate mankind.

You may consider people insane, the individual creatures with whom you share the planet.

You may rail against what you think of as their stupid behavior,

Their bloodthirsty ways, and the inadequate and shortsighted methods that they use to solve their problems.

All of this is based upon your idealized concept of what the race should be –

Your love for your fellow man, in other words.

But, your love can get lost if you concentrate upon those variations that are less than idyllic.

When you think you hate the race most, you are actually caught in a dilemma of love.

You are comparing the race to your loving idealized conception of it.

In this case, however, you are losing sight of the actual people involved.

You are putting love on such a plane that you divorce yourself from your real feelings

And do not recognize the loving emotions that are the basis for your discontent.

Your affection has fallen short of itself in your experience

Time Is A Wiff In A Cloud Of Smoke

Because you have denied the impact of this emotion, for fear that the beloved (in this case the race as a whole) will not measure up to it.

Therefore, you concentrate upon the digressions from the ideal.

If, instead, you allowed yourself to free the feeling of love that is actually behind your dissatisfaction,

Then it alone would allow you to see the loving characteristics in the race that now escape your observation to a large degree. Session 674

You must understand that in any way your situation,

And any that you know of physical reality, is highly artificial.

It is the mass creation formed by your inner ideas.

The time concept is but one example, and it is responsible for many of your most cherished misconceptions.

You must form ideas into physical materialization in order to recognize the force behind the ideas you are learning to use and understand.

However, such materializations are only necessary at certain levels.

The time scheme appears valid only within that framework.

When an idea no longer needs physical materialization, then the time concept is useless.

Intensity of experience and value fulfillment takes time's place.

Developments open, in your terms, at once.

Organization of inner events is managed according to the inner interests of the various personalities

And the intensities with which any given event is experienced.

In your terms then, a future event would exist before a past event.

Do you follow me?

Therefore, you are hampered in your attempt to understand personalities who do not exist within your system,

For identity is not therefore structured in any kind of a time sequence,

And what you call memory flies out the window.

An entity does not "remember" when a portion of it existed within your system.

In its time that portion simply is.

The time concept leads then to a limited idea, for you cannot conceive of an identity without memory of the past in your terms.

This is also responsible for the fact that it is difficult to understand how one personality, while retaining its individuality, can be a portion of more than one entity,

And we will have more to say on that. TES9 430

Talent Is A Self-Created Thing

This is not dictation. Now. Contrary to most thought on such matters,

No one is given a particular amount of talent that must then be used.

Talent does not come in quantities.

Instead people have varying abilities to use any of an infinite number of channels,

Any one of which in your terms leads to an inexhaustible source.

The channels by their nature will translate and shape creative energy with their unique dimensions.

You are not given 800 or 5,000 milligrams of talent.

You are given your own nature,

Certain portions of it naturally tuning in to what in your case you could call the channel of art.

You sense its great dimensions, the richness of its complexity.

You are particularly attuned to it.

Your knowledge of form now can work for you automatically,

Serving to give structure to those ideas which will come to you freely and clearly.

Your own "psychic abilities" now give you easy access to inspiration.

You must forget the idea as you have it,

That your painting must serve to work out problems.

In that framework you set problems.

You wanted to express ideas in paintings that do not come in youth,

And to merge a particular kind of understanding with a particular kind of form.

You had an existence in which your art matured early, as Josef in Ruburt's Seven.

You dealt with emotion unrestrained by discipline,

And with the feelings of a young man.

Josef was not able to paint anything worthwhile past the age of 40, and he turned to a land-owner's province.

You wanted to express now the fuller inspirations that come later, and with an exquisite sense of form that Josef never learned.

The sense of form incidentally will, mark my words, emerge in a new way for you,

But even the information given that so upset you had its purpose in your whole plan.

His "success" was no success to him.

The illumination that makes great paintings, again, has nothing to do with time.

A man may work for nearly a century and not attain it, or it may come tomorrow afternoon.

The image therefore of yourself standing with the knowledge of the unspoken,

The unexpressed, on the verge of new expression.

The painting on the verge then of coming alive.

TPS2 Deleted Session December 4, 1972

You do not understand the dimensions into which your thoughts drop for they continue their own existence,

And others look up to them and view them like stars.

Now I am telling you that your own dreams and thoughts and mental actions appear to the inhabitants of other systems

Like the stars and planets within your own,

And those inhabitants do not perceive what is within and behind the stars in their own heavens.

Though they probe their own universe, they will not wander into your reality.

They will only perceive the shape and form that your own mental acts, thoughts and dreams take within their own system.

This is some material that we have not given you,

Lest the implications lead you to thoughts of insignificance.

But you are not simply receivers, you are also givers.

As your own universe was formed by entities that you do not presently understand,

So the discards of your own consciousness form realities

For entities that are scarcely aware of your existence.

TES9 45

Again, as mentioned earlier, an individual can be so certain that death is the end of all, that oblivion, though temporary, results.

In many cases, immediately on leaving the body there is, of course, amazement and a recognition of the situation.

The body itself may be viewed, for example,

And many funerals have a guest of honor amidst the company —

And no one gazes into the face of the corpse with as much curiosity and wonder.

SS Chapter 9: Session 536, June 22, 1970

That point is not in the past unless you abjectly decide to acquiesce to worn-out beliefs that no longer serve you.

NoPR Chapter 22: Session 676, July 9, 1973 - by Jane Roberts (C) L. Davies Butts

To the question, What is time?

The following answer might quite rightly be given:

Time is an apple. Time is no apple.

Time is a worm in an apple. Time is a worm not in an apple;

And yet such definitions will be absolutely meaningless to most people,

For they can only think of time in terms of days or hours,

And they do not think of time as experience itself,

Or quite simply, being.

And yet such definitions are far more near the truth than those that have to do with measurements.

There are no measurements of any kind.

Reality, of itself, forms an apple.

Your perception of the apple enables you to see it piecemeal.

The apple is time. It is an event.

It is the so-many-odd days or months that have gone into its production in your terms, or years that have gone into production of the tree.

It is as much an event of time as it is an event of space.

Here I am merely using your terms to make the point.

There are such natural things as apples, you see.

There are no natural things such as minutes, or hours.

These are concepts imposed upon reality,

But this does not make them real in themselves.

An individual, and I am speaking in your terms now, again to make a point:

An individual is the 60 or 70-odd years of his earthly existence, as much as he is the 150-odd pounds that he may be.

Now unless you have questions we will end the session.

My last remarks were meant to clear up if possible some of the misconceptions that you have concerning your own time concept.

Keep in mind that the concept is only valid within your present circumstances, however.

TES9 430

The more "civilized" man becomes, the more his social structures and practices separate him from intimate relationship with nature —

And the more natural catastrophes there will be, because underneath he senses his great need for identification with nature;

He will himself conjure it into earthquakes, tornadoes, and floods,

So that he can once again feel not only their energy but his own.

NoPR Chapter 18: Session 665, May 23, 1973

There is a short-circuiting process in which even good intentions are distorted and turned to other purposes.

That which is feared is feared so strongly and concentrated upon so intensely that it is attracted rather than repelled.

The approach should not be fear of war

But love of peace; not fear of poor health

But concentration upon the enjoyment of good health;

Not fear of poverty,

But concentration upon the unlimited supplies available on
your earth.

Desire attracts but fear also attracts.

Severe fear is highly dangerous in this respect and in this context.

Many of your dreams are like the tail end of a comet:

Their real life is over, and you see the flash of their disappearance
as they strike your own mental atmosphere and explode in a
spark of dream images.

They are transformed, therefore, as they travel through your own
psychological atmosphere.

The resulting structure of the dream suits your reality and no other:

As this intrusive matter falls, plummets, or shifts through the
levels of your own psychological atmosphere,

It is transformed by the conditions it meets.

The Nature of the Psyche Chapter 8: Session 786, August 16, 1976

Now. All of this does not mean that personalities within other
systems do not construct their own kind of time structures,

But in all of these cases the personalities realize quite well that
the structures are
adapted for the sake of organization of experience.

They do not suppose any given time system to have any reality of
its own.

Such systems do not use the consecutive structure of your own however.

In much the same manner materializations of a kind may be utilized,

But the personalities do not give the materializations any reality outside of themselves.

They know the origin of images.

It is rather difficult for those who have not been in your system to understand that you give time and images a reality of their own,

As if they existed apart from you.

Form does not necessarily presuppose the existence of images.

Form is not dependent upon mass.

This comes close to what I am trying to tell you.

In your time system the growth of mass seems to be dependent upon continuity of moments.

Time has nothing to do with form, however.

The personality who sometimes speaks, (Seth's larger entity), can change form at will.

He was never imprisoned by believing that one personality existed within one form.

To your way of thinking he would change form according to his mood;

As he thinks, he is.

His development began in your terms in such ancient times that
for all intents and purposes you could say

That in terms of value fulfillment he was so far advanced as to be
alien entirely.

TES9 432

Most of these probable systems, returning to our earlier discussion,
are open.

You simply do not realize that this is the case.

In your system it seems as if you have chosen one course,

One main line of probabilities, and that is the end of it.

On other existence however you choose other probabilities.

Now your own system is relatively closed, in that within it as a
rule only one ego predominates,

And you think of yourself as that ego.

In other systems this is not necessarily the case.

The time system within them is entirely different than your own.

In these the inner self is aware of itself as more than one ego.

The inner self can play more than one role at once, consciously
in other words.

Simply as an analogy,

It would be as if within physical reality you lived,

Say, the life of a rich man of great talent,

The life of a poor man with entirely different talents,

And the life of a mother and career woman.

You would be aware of yourself in each of these three roles, and find qualities being developed in each of the separate lives.

Again this is an analogy, for in several respects it could lead you astray if you took it too literally.

In such a system there would be no breakup of time for example, since time does not exist in the same manner.

You would not spend for example part of a day as one personality and part another. This will all be explained in good time.

TES9 438

You have a fine, strong and worthwhile purpose, but you will not fulfill it well while you rail against what you do not have,

And ignore the abilities and gifts and blessings that you do have.

You will not discover the purpose and meaning of your life when you insist that it follow certain consciously predetermined roads, And while you concentrate upon what you do not have.

This saps your energy and dulls your intuitions.

You are indeed obsessed with the idea of marriage, and with male love,

But as Joseph mentioned this is but a symptom.

Underneath is the real cause,

And this basic cause is behind all those that I have previously given you, in your own background.

You are not accepting life on life's terms as an individual.

You are demanding that it behave in certain ways,

And take courses that you have consciously set upon,

And you are refusing to gladly accept life as life, as its own reason and cause within you.

This idea that you must find a man that will love you and you alone, is a cover to hide this deeper refusal to accept life on life's terms.

There is a cultural aspect here that you do not realize, and that you would consider beneath you.

It is a superficial concept, as if your individuality, merit and worth, are only activated if you have a strong sex, love or married relationship.

Your survival, your unique abilities, and your purpose, exist quite apart from these.

They can exist with these, but they cannot exist if you insist that such a relationship is the condition upon which you will accept existence.

You are saying "Unless existence meets my terms, I will not exist,"

And no one has the right to so set themselves against their own innate vitality and the joy of life that is within them.

The Early Sessions Book 9 Session 440

True self-knowledge is indispensable for health or vitality, and this means in every instance.

The recognition of the truth about the self means that you must first discover what you think about yourself subconsciously.

If this is a good image, build upon it.

If it is a poor one, recognize it as simply the opinion of the subconscious

And not as a definite truth.

TES8 Session 340 May 10, 1967

For of real love, you know very little;

Of real understanding, you know very little;

But you will learn and you are learning and learning itself is discovery and joy.

TECS2 ESP Class Session, May 5, 1970

Seth: Honey and vinegar are cheap; Self-knowledge is dear but far more valuable.

Such inner remedies and such real remedies do not come in packages

And you cannot pick them up at the supermarket,

And they are not herbs to be eaten for breakfast

Though these will serve as an in-between measure

And there is nothing wrong with in-between measures.

But if you want to get at the real knowledge of yourself

And at the real reason for symptoms, then there are ways of doing so

And I have given them to you.

TECS2 ESP Class Session, July 21, 1970

True spirituality is a thing of joy and of the earth and has nothing to do with fake adult dignity.

It has nothing to do with long words and sorrowful faces.

It has to do with the dance of consciousness that is within you

And with the sense of spiritual adventure that is within your hearts.

That is the meaning of spirituality.

TECS2 ESP Class—From an Earlier Session (Note: Attached to June 23, 1970 ESP Class Session.)

Again, it behooves you to deny your true feelings in order to be spiritual — which is not true spirituality.

SS Appendix: ESP Class Session: Tuesday, January 12, 1971

Seth about one of his many lives:

Though I yelled at my children and screamed sometimes in rage against the elements,

I was struck through with the magnificence of existence,

And learned more about true spirituality than I ever did as a monk.

SS Chapter 22: Session 589, August 4, 1971

Seth on Rob's mother:

Because of her own actions and stress laid upon what was right and proper at the expense of true feelings.

Your mother is quite shrewd however, and has grown these years.

In the past she would have been quite able to face and handle everyone's honesty, and honesty would have been far kinder.

So the true love and compassion goes crying, while you are forced to express an exterior love and compassion many times.

TPS2 Session 603 January 10, 1972

True love allows one to perceive the sublime uniqueness of the beloved.

TPS2 Deleted Session February 16, 1972

True self-pride allows you to perceive the integrity of your fellow human beings

And permits you to help them use their strengths.

Many people make a great show out of helping others, for example,

Encouraging them to lean upon them. They believe this to be a quite holy, virtuous enterprise.

Instead they are keeping other people from recognizing and using their own strengths and abilities.

NoPR Chapter 21: Session 674, July 2, 1973

When you try to be spiritual by cutting off your creature-hood

You become less than joyful, fulfilled, satisfied natural creatures,

And fall far short of understanding true spirituality.

NoPR Chapter 11: Session 642, February 21, 1973

The potentials of the true self are so multidimensional that they cannot be expressed in one space or time.

Any person who loves another recognizes the infinite potential within that other person.

That potential needs infinite opportunity;

The true self's reality needs an ever-new, changing situation,

For each experience enriches it and therefore, enhances its own possibilities.

UR1 Section 3: Session 695 May 6, 1974

Now, facts may or may not give you wisdom.

They can, if they are slavishly followed, even lead you away from true knowledge.

Wisdom shows you the insides of facts, so to speak,

And the realities from which facts emerge.

UR2 Section 4: Session 709 October 2, 1974

A true teacher allows you to learn from yourself.

UR2 Appendix 16: (For Session 711)

all quotes by Jane Roberts © L. Davies Butts

Now some personalities from one system aid other personalities within other systems,

But highly developed personalities, those in your terms so far advanced, will set for themselves the task of aiding an entire civilization;

Of assisting the development of a new system,

And sometimes initiating the existence of that system.

I have told you that there is much that I do not know,

And for practical purposes there is much that is not known.

Now you are aiding in the development of those consciousnesses

That compose the cells and molecules within your own bodies.

They learn from you almost through a process of osmosis.

Dimly through many cycles of such activities, they become aware of the existence of conceptual thought.

At the same time, they support you.

The capsule comprehension within them will evolve more and more toward the direction of conscious endeavor.

Each will itself learn to organize larger portions of energy.

It is difficult to put this into words that you will understand.

They are incipient and latent personalities.

This does not mean however that they will all materialize within your own system,

But they do represent in your terms the future inhabitants of your system.

The Early Sessions Book 9 Sessions 432

I am what I am, interpreted through your reality.

To some extent, I am like a particularly vivid, persistent, recurring dream image, visiting the mass psyche,

Only with a reality that is not confined to dreams —

A dream image that attains a psychological fullness

That can seem to make ordinary consciousness a weak apparition by contrast, psychologically speaking.

You may say if you wish that I am a dream image lacking even an image —

But if so, then each individual whose life is changed by my words must question:

"What is a dream?"

In the same way that my personality exists without physical manifestation, so does your own.

The difference is that you are not consciously aware of what you are doing, but I am.

The Nature of the Psyche Chapter 9: Session 790, January 3, 1977

Time To Use All Those Inner Senses

Many individuals become confused in relation to the subject of perception, for they generate the idea that perception is

What you THINK about:

What you THINK about a situation,

What you THINK about your body,

What you THINK about yourself,

Or an action, or your surroundings.

But in actuality,

That is NOT a description of perception at all,

For perception engages ALL of your senses.

It is actually what you use to create your reality.

This is the tool that you engage that creates EVERYTHING in your reality.

Therefore, in relation to perception, whatever it is that you perceive, your senses will validate.

Elias

INNER VIBRATIONAL TOUCH

Think of the Inner Senses as paths leading to an inner reality.

The first sense involves perception of a direct nature—

Instant cognition through what I can only describe as inner vibrational touch.

Imagine a man standing on a typical street of houses and grass and trees.

This sense would permit him to feel the basic sensations felt by each of the trees about him.

His consciousness would expand to contain the experience of what it is to be a tree—

Any or all of the trees.

He would feel the experience of being anything he chose within his field of notice:

people, insects, blades of grass.

He would not lose consciousness of who he was, but would perceive these sensations somewhat in the same way that you now feel heat and cold.

Jane: This sense is much like empathy, but far more vital.

Seth says that we can't experience these Inner Senses in their full intensity now,

Because our nervous systems can't handle that much stimuli.

PSYCHOLOGICAL TIME

Psychological Time is a natural pathway that was meant to give an easy route of access from the inner world to the outer, and back again,

Though you do not use it as such.

Psychological Time originally enabled man to live in the inner and outer worlds with relative ease.

As you develop in your use of it, you will be able to rest within its framework while you are consciously awake.

It adds duration to your normal time.

From its framework you will see that physical time is as dreamlike as you once thought inner time was.

You will discover your whole selves, peeping inward and outward simultaneously, and know that all divisions are illusion.

PERCEPTION OF PAST, PRESENT, AND FUTURE

If you will remember our imaginary man as he stands upon a street, you will recall that I spoke of his feeling all of the unitary essences of each living thing within his range, using the first Inner Sense.

Using this third sense, this experience would be expanded. If he so chose, he would also feel the past and future essence of each living thing within his range.

THE CONCEPTUAL SENSE

The fourth Inner Sense involves direct cognition of a concept in much more than intellectual terms.

It involves experiencing a concept completely.

Concepts have what we will call electrical and chemical composition [as thoughts do].

The molecules and ions of the consciousness change into [those of] the concept, which is then directly experienced.

You cannot truly understand or appreciate any living thing unless you can become that thing.

You can best achieve some approximation of an idea by using Psychological Time [as a preliminary].

Sit in a quiet room. When an idea comes to you, do not play with it intellectually, but reach out to it intuitively.

Do not be afraid of unfamiliar physical sensations.

With practice and to a limited degree, you will find that you can 'become' the idea.

You will be inside it, looking out—not looking in.

Concepts such as I am referring to reach beyond your ideas of time and space.

If you become proficient in the use of the third Inner Sense [perception of past, present, and future] when cognition is more or less spontaneous, then you can utilize the conceptual sense with more freedom.

Any true concept has its origins outside of your camouflage system and continues beyond it.

Unless you use the Inner Senses in this manner, you will only receive a glimmering of a concept, regardless of its simplicity.

COGNITION OF KNOWLEDGEABLE ESSENCE

Remember that these Inner Senses operate as a whole, working together smoothly, and that to some degree the divisions between them are arbitrary on my part.

This fifth sense differs from the fourth [conceptual sense] in that it does not involve cognition of a concept.

It is similar to the fourth sense in that it is free from past, present, and future,

And involves an intimate becoming, or transformation of self into something else.

This is difficult to explain.

You attempt to understand a friend by using your physical senses.

Use of this fifth sense would enable you to enter into your friend.

In its fullest sense, it is not available to you within your system.

It does not imply that one entity can control another.

It involves direct instantaneous cognition of the essence of living 'tissue.' I use the word 'tissue' with caution and ask you not to think of it necessarily in terms of flesh.

All entities are in one way or another enclosed within themselves, yet also connected to others.

Using this sense, you penetrate through the capsule that encloses the self.

This Inner Sense, like all others, is being used constantly by the inner self,

But very little of the data received is sifted through to the subconscious or ego.

Without the use of this sense, however, no man would ever come close to understanding another.

This sense is a stronger version of inner vibrational touch.

INNATE KNOWLEDGE OF BASIC REALITY

This is an extremely rudimentary sense.

It is concerned with the entity's innate working knowledge of the basic vitality of the universe, without which no manipulations of vitality would be possible—

As, for example, you could not stand up straight without first having an innate sense of balance.

Without this sixth sense and its constant use by the inner self, you could not construct the physical camouflage universe.

You can compare this sense with instinct, as you think of it,

Although it is concerned with the innate knowledge of the entire universe.

Particular data about specific areas of reality are given to a living organism to make manipulation within that area possible.

The inner self has at its command complete knowledge,

But only portions are used by an organism.

A spider, spinning its web, is using this sense in almost its purest form.

The spider has no intellect or ego,

And its activities are pure spontaneous uses of the Inner Senses, unhampered and un-camouflaged to a great extent.

But inherent in the spider, as in man, is the complete comprehension of the universe as a whole.

EXPANSION OR CONTRACTION OF THE TISSUE CAPSULE

This sense operates in two ways. It can be an extension or enlargement of the self,

A widening of its boundaries and of conscious comprehension.

It can also be a pulling together of the self into an ever-smaller capsule that enables the self to enter other systems of reality.

The tissue capsule surrounds each consciousness and is actually an energy field boundary,

Keeping the inner self's energy from seeping away.

No consciousness exists in any system without this capsule enclosing it.

These capsules have also been called astral bodies.

The seventh Inner Sense allows for an expansion or contraction of this tissue capsule.

DISENTANGLEMENT FROM CAMOUFLAGE

Complete disentanglement from camouflage comes rarely within your system,

Although it is possible to achieve it, particularly in connection with Psychological Time.

When Psychological Time is utilized to its fullest extent, then camouflage is lessened to an astounding degree.

With disentanglement, the inner self disengages itself from one particular camouflage before it either adopts another set smoothly or dispenses with camouflage entirely.

This is accomplished through what you might call a changing of frequencies or vibrations:

A transformation of vitality from one particular pattern or aspect to another.

In some ways, your dream world gives you a closer experience with basic inner reality than does your waking world,

Where the Inner Senses are so shielded from your awareness.

DIFFUSION BY THE ENERGY PERSONALITY

An energy personality who wishes to become a part of your system does so using this sense.

The energy personality first diffuses himself into many parts.

Since entry into your plane or system, as a member of it, cannot be made in any other manner, it must be made in the simplest terms,

And later built up—sperm, of course, being an entry in this respect.

The energy of the personality must then be recombined.

Jane: What is the point in learning to use the Inner Senses?

Seth spoke about some of the benefits in the recorded session he gave for the college psychology class.

You will not be swallowed by subjectivity.

You will learn what reality is.

What is not understood is that self-investigation initiates states of consciousness with which you are usually not familiar.

Now these can be used as investigative tools.

In the sort of exploration of which I am speaking, the personality attempts to go within itself,

To find its way through the veils of adopted characteristics to its own inner identity.

The inner core of the self has telepathic and clairvoyant abilities that greatly affect family relationships—In your civilization. Now you are not using them effectively.

These are precisely those abilities that are needed now

If there is to be any hope of world communication, then each of you must understand where your potentials are as individual subjective creatures.

Books cannot tell you this.

Even if you discover, through psychoanalysis, where your neuroses lie, you are in very shallow water.

You are still exploring the topmost levels of your personality,

And you do not have the benefit of those altered states of consciousness that occur when you look into yourself in the manner I have prescribed.

There is a condition of consciousness that is more awake than any you have ever known

—A condition in which you are aware of your own waking and dreaming selves simultaneously.

You can become fully awake while the body sleeps.

You can extend the present limitations of your awareness.

Roberts, Jane. The Seth Material, New Awareness Network, Inc. Kindle Edition. © L. Davies Butts

You think of flowers in terms of gentleness, beauty and goodness,

And yet every time a new bud opens there is a great thrust of joyful aggression that is hardly passive,

And a daring and courage that reaches actively outward.

NoPR Chapter 11: Session 642, February 21, 1973

Large masses of people became so convinced of God's eventual vengeance and retribution that they began to plan for it.

The way Toward Health Chapter 14: June 27, 1984

The self tries to solve a particular problem.

In so doing, it may end up with a physical difficulty.

The physical difficulty is meant to remind the personality of the inner problem behind it.

The difficulty will be cleared up when the inner problem is.

Now, if instead, a drug is used to camouflage the ailment or, in your terms, to heal it, to cure it, to get rid of it,

The inner self is in a quandary, for it knows the problem has not been solved, though the symptom has disappeared.

The drug used to cure the body MAY now - MAY in many instances,

Obscure the problem and confuse both the body and the mind.

Another ailment must be taken therefore that will symbolically and quite practically materialize the problem in your reality.

So the patient will get another ailment.

If this ailment is also obscured or 'cured' through the drug, whatever it may be,

Then the inner self is in a further quandary,

And it will continue to try to materialize the problem so that it can be solved.

The communication between the mental, psychic, and physical portions of the being can, in such instances, become obscured.

Now, that does not always apply, for someone with a severe difficulty,

Believing in the effectiveness of your doctors, may be given a wonder drug and believe in it

So that when the symptoms are completely annihilated, he is convinced of the fact of an inner help, and therefore feels secure enough to SOLVE his inner problem.

In such a case, however, he has effectively used the drug to heal his mind and his body.

The drug has not done it.

This does not mean that you cannot take advantage of such drugs.

It DOES mean that when you do, you are operating within a framework of reality that still, to some extent, divides you from the reality of your own being.

Seth/Jane Roberts, ESP Class Session, February 5,

Joy and the spontaneous expression of it will always bring increased strength and resiliency to the personality.

It also brings deep and abiding satisfaction to the subconscious, which is much more joyful than it is given credit for.

The subconscious, for example, the personal subconscious, takes great pleasure in its manipulation of the physical fibers in locomotion.

The expression of joy also makes the ego more resilient, less fearful, less resentful of diverse conditions when they occur.

The emotion itself is an automatic signal that unites the conscious and subconscious in shared experience.

It is, as a rule, lack of knowledge on the part of the ego as to the nature of reality,

And its part in it, and the resulting fear, that often prevents a personality from accepting spontaneous expression of emotions in general.

The capacity to feel is important.

When one fears to experience seemingly unpleasant emotions,
The personality also tends to set up an emotional pattern of
rejection that seriously cuts down, also, not only on the expression
but the very perception of joy.

This sort of communication also comes close to action in a fairly
pure state.

There is also another result of such relative ease of communication
between the ego and the subconscious, in that the subconscious,

Which is listened to and taken into consideration by the ego,
will have relatively little need to make its wishes known in other,
perhaps less pleasant ways.

Illnesses and various minor and major physical symptoms are
often caused as the subconscious tries to speak out, in an effort
to make itself heard by the unheeding conscious mind.

If the conscious mind consults with the subconscious, such
nagging or sometimes explosive efforts will not be needed.

Seth/Jane Roberts, TES4 Session 152 May 5, 1965

Now. There are also those who stay within your system, in your
terms, returning again and again in order to help its development.

Such personalities will concentrate their main activates in such
a way that they can best affect conceptual thought, and bring
about necessary changes.

Many large families are representative of this group. They
appear and reappear in your histories, always as dominant and
significant entities.

Here the family represents an entity who has taken upon itself the nurturing of your civilization.

Knowing intuitively those changes which must come about in your future, they try to bring them about by appearing in your past;

Though to them your future and the past are the same they must still work within probabilities, you see,

And what they are doing is affecting probabilities within your system.

Even your time is basically plastic, though it does not seem so to you.

Such personalities try to affect the feelings and thoughts of a civilization, for these thoughts and feelings will alone bring about events.

Personalities may be born within your system and find that it does not challenge them, or it is not to their liking in any case.

They may leave the system then, sometimes as aborted infants,

But if they grow through childhood the first time, in your terms, then they must work out their development within the system.

You block out the realization of non-time, and accept your ideas of time along with the camouflage structure, for one is dependent upon the other.

Once you accept physical matter as you know it, then the time system is indispensable.

In those projections still within your system, you are still bound by a time relationship, in that it seems to you that perception operates as usual.

Now. Any time structure is an aid, organizing experience along certain lines.

To a large extent it limits perception, and is a protective device.

You are learning to handle perception and experience,

And time gives it to you in slow and small doses.

The doses become larger.

Finally, you can sample experience without these limitations.

Non-time represents the freedom to do so.

You organize experience along your own lines because you have learned now to do so.

You do not misuse experience when you have reached that point.

You understand the basic reality of subjective life.

You will then still organize experience but you will not need artificial aids such as time to lean upon.

You will not need to see thoughts materialized in physical matter, for you will have long since learned that the thoughts and not the matter are the basic reality.

You will be able therefore to dispense with many seemingly permanent mass images, but when you form them you will realize why and how.

It is important that you understand that time puts limitations and barriers in the way of perception.

This does not mean that each individual at such a stage is isolated, nor that he dwells in some universe of his own, for interactions always exist.

In non-time you perceive at your own rate.

You organize experience in your own way.

These experiences however will always involve you with others.

Indeed. You can go far further in such relationships.

The relationships between multidimensional personalities is far more complicated than those you know.

When I use the term "psyche," many of you will immediately wonder about my definition.

Any word, simply by being thought, written or spoken, immediately implies a specification.

In your daily reality it is very handy to distinguish one thing from another by giving each item a name.

When you are dealing with subjective experience, however, definitions can often serve to limit rather than express a given experience.

The Psyche Has Many Names

Obviously the psyche is not a thing.

It does not have a beginning or ending.

It cannot be seen or touched in normal terms.

It is useless, therefore, to attempt any description of it through usual vocabulary,

For your language primarily allows you to identify physical rather than non-physical experience.

I am not saying that words cannot be used to DESCRIBE the psyche,

But they cannot define it.

It is FUTILE to question: What is the difference between my psyche and my soul, my entity and my greater being?

For all of these are terms used in an effort to express the greater portions of your own experience that you sense within yourself.

The Nature of The Psyche, session 755, by Jane Roberts (C) L. Davies Butts

When you are born you possess a group of attitudes toward yourself and toward life.

These allow you to grow with the greatest possible impetus into childhood.

They are also important in every period of your life.

You can see the results in life all about you, though in animals or plants these are experienced as a matter of feelings rather than, say, as thoughts or attitudes.

It may sound very simplistic to tell you that you must have sunny thoughts as well as rays of the physical sun in order to be healthy

—

But sunny thoughts are as biologically necessary to your well-being as are the rays of the sun that shines in the sky.

Even as infants, then, you are predisposed naturally toward certain feelings, thoughts and attitudes

That are meant to insure your healthy survival and emergence into adulthood.

These are actually composed of inbred psychological information as necessary

And vital to your life as the data transmitted by your genes and chromosomes.

Indeed, these inbred, inner psychological predispositions are all-important

If the information carried by your genes and chromosomes is to be faithfully followed.

WTH Chapter 2: January 26, 1984

Dictation. These inborn leanings or attitudes can roughly be translated as follows.

1. I am an excellent creature, a valuable part of the universe in which I exist.

2. My existence enriches all other portions of life, even as my own being is enhanced by the rest of creation.

3. It is good, natural, and safe for me to grow and develop and use my abilities,

And by doing so I also enrich all other portions of life.

Next: I am eternally couched and supported by the universe of which I am a part,

And I exist whether or not that existence is physically expressed.

Next: By nature, I am a good deserving creature, and all of life's elements and parts are also of good intent.

And next: All of my imperfections, and all of the imperfections of other creatures, are redeemed in the greater scheme of the universe in which I have my being.

Those attitudes are inbred in the smallest microscopic portions of the body

— A part of each atom and cell and organ,

And they serve to trigger all of the body's responses that promote growth and fulfillment.

Infants are not born with an inbred fear of their environment, or of other creatures.

They are instead immersed in feelings of well-being, vitality, and exuberance.

They take it for granted that their needs will be met, and that the universe is well-disposed toward them.

They feel a part of their environment.

Birth is experienced in terms of self-discovery,

And includes the sensation of selfhood gently rising and unfolding from the secret heart of the universe.

WTH Chapter 2: January 27, 1984

Whatever your language, you perceive trees, mountains, people, oceans.

You never see a man merge with a tree, for example.

This would be considered a hallucinatory image.

Your visual data are learned and interpreted so that they appear as the only possible results of those data.

Inner vision can confound you, because in your mind you often see images quite clearly that you would dismiss if your eyes were open.

In the terms of which we are speaking, however, the young species utilized what I have called the "inner senses" to a far greater degree than you do.

Visually, early man did not perceive the physical world in the way that seems natural to you.

Data, you say, are stored in the chromosomes, strung together in a certain fashion.

Now biologically that is direct cognition.

The inner senses perceive directly in the same fashion.

To you, language means words. Words are always symbols for emotions or feelings, intents or desires.

Direct cognition did not need the symbols.

The first language, the initial language, did not involve images or words, but dealt with a free flow of directly cognitive material.

A man, wondering what a tree was like, became one, and let his own consciousness flow into the tree.

Man's consciousness mixed and merged with other kinds of consciousness with the great curiosity of love.

A child did not simply look at an animal, but let its consciousness merge with the animal,

And so to some extent the animal looked out through the child's eyes.

NotP Chapter 6: Session 777, May 24, 1976

Entities, if they prefer, and under various conditions, when they become acquainted with others,

May introduce to each other if they so prefer, various portions of their personalities.

Various portions will be able to help each other and to aid in development.

Take for example entity A and entity B.

Self 4 personality of entity A may get along quite nicely with B's self 6.

A's self 2 and B's self 2 may not get along well at all, so the entities will shift to those personalities which have the greatest rapport,

And use them to establish a relationship.

In non-time these portions of the entity exist quite freely, without any time barriers to separate them.

Many such relationships have been established as indeed I speak with you because we get on so well.

I am also familiar with your particular system, and found it emotionally satisfying.

Multidimensional personalities can therefore establish contact at various levels.

Their relationship involves a trust that yours do not have.

They have many areas of agreement open.

Now your physical relationships may or may not have anything to do with personal affiliations after any given existence within your system.

There are mothers and fathers that you have forgotten, and children that you do not know.

Psychically and subjectively the relationships did not take.

You are not burdened with them, nor they with you.

This simply means that you did not spark creative impetus of any kind within each other.

TES9 432

The word "ego" is much bandied about, and in many circles it has a poor reputation.

It is, however, as I use it, a term meant to express the ordinarily conscious directive portion of the self.

It can stretch its capacities, becoming far more aware of inner events than it is normally allowed to do,

But its main purpose is to deal with the world of effects, to *encounter* events.

NoME Chapter 3: Session 822, February 22, 1978

Therefore, in concentrating and focusing your attention upon the difference that you dislike,

And generating the assessment and the perception that this structure is chaotic, you are continuously opposing it.

And, you are opposing yourself in not allowing for your own balance

And not allowing yourself to follow your own guidelines and your own preferences within your own structure.

It is not a matter of fixing what is in place, so to speak, or fixing the design of what has already been created;

It is a matter of you discovering and generating your balance and recognizing what is genuinely important to you—

And not distracting yourself by placing importance upon expressions that are not yours to fix,

And pushing yourself and forcing your energy in the attempt to accomplish the fixing that is not yours to fix.

Excellence is not produced in force;

Excellence is produced in comfort.

When you are comfortable and satisfied within yourself,

And are allowing yourself a free flow of energy and are balanced, you produce excellence.

When you are forcing energy, you create obstacles.

Elias 2006

Hmmm. Ron placed his hands in front of his face, fingertips touching.

In May of 1971, after several hours of class debate on good versus evil and the psychological origins of heaven and hell,

Seth abruptly announced that one of his physical lives had been spent as a minor Pope in 300 A.D.;

Therefore, there was an "authority" present on the subject of heaven and hell.

Amidst the chaotic reaction to this statement,

Seth went on to explain that the rigorous concepts of good and evil are themselves highly distorted,

And when you find such a dilemma where goodness is one thing and evil another,

And both are contrary and separate,

Then you automatically separate them in your minds and in your feelings and in your fantasies.

You do not seem at this point able to realize that what you call evil works for what you call good.,

Seth told a somewhat incredulous class.

Both are part of energy and

You are using energy to form your reality, both now and after this life.

This is because you deal with effects physically, as you see them.

And until you divest yourself of such psychological behaviour,

It will always seem to you that good and evil are opposites

And you will treat them as such in your feelings and in your concepts and in your myths.

At this point, Ron Labadee (the intensely "intellectual" fellow in the playing card incident described in CWS, book 1, chapter 3) sat forward in his chair and interrupted

Arnold Pearson in mid-question.

"Is it ever justified to do evil for the sake of good?" Ron asked.

In the terms of which you ask the question, the answer is no,

Seth answered benignly.

"In other words, Ron continued, in this reality we are faced with decisions.

In that context, is it true that our decisions can be only constructive and good, or destructive and evil?"

Only in the terms in which you ask the question, Seth said.

In larger terms, there is no such thing as destruction;

And your second question does not follow logically from the first one.

If you will look at the script when you receive it (the following week), you will see what I mean.

You ask questions without considering the answers that have been given.

Think of the answers before you form the next question.

"Yes, but I don't necessarily agree with the logic of your answers," Ron said.

I do not NEED you to agree with my logic, Seth replied.

I need you to understand the faulty quality in your own logic, and that must come from yourself and not from me.

"Yes, but ---"

Now, wait, Seth said. Part of this is due to the fact that your form questions

Before you comprehend the nature of the answers that you have received.

Read the script. Find out the answers I have given you, and then form the questions.

"Well, I have a question that I know I'm going to form after I read the script," Ron said,

Oblivious to the glares and groans from those around him.

It is that YOUR response was that MY question was only
meaningful in the terms that I use;

So what I am asking is how do YOU conceive of good and evil in
YOUR reality?"

There is no destruction and there is no evil, Seth answered
emphatically.

But while you believe that there is, then you must act accordingly!

While you believe that to murder a man is to destroy his
consciousness forever,

Then you cannot murder, and in your terms it is an evil.

"Well, Hitler could have used that justification for wiping out six
million Jews!" Ron cried.

He could have indeed, Seth agreed.

Ron was beaming with satisfaction. "Well, then, I disagree with you.

I think that even in the way we look at it now there is destruction
which is evil."

I KNOW that you do! Seth roared.

You live within that reality and while you live within it, you must
deal with it ---

And so you are!"

So, Ron mused, coiling for another pounce,

"Is there such a thing as a moral decision for someone who exists in the next plane of existence?"

As Seth, Jane sipped some wine and placidly returned Ron's gaze.

There are ALWAYS moral decisions, Seth stated.

They involve the use of creativity and development.

They involve the use of spontaneity.

"What system of values do you use to choose in your moral decisions?"

I have told you. My last answer implies that answer.

"In your words, it would be whatever is the most creative in terms of what you want to do."

We will ignore the last part of your sentence and agree with the first part,

Seth answered, grinning impishly. And I shall certainly see to it,

If I have any abilities to do so, that in your next life you are put in the position of answering someone whose mind works exactly as yours does!

"I feel like I've made contact with you very well," Ron said.

Irritation among other class members, with whom Ron rarely talked about anything, was turning the air sharp as daggers.

You have indeed, Seth answered dryly.

However, the intuitive rapport that you need to contact others within your environment is at least to some extent lacking.

Reach out to them with feeling rather than with the guise of probing words.

"I don't necessarily deal with physical entities the same way I'm dealing with you right now," Ron said, rather loftily.

You should learn to!" Seth replied.

I egg --- listen to me --- I egg you on.

It is good for you and good for the class and very good for this one over here,

Seth waved Jane's hand at Florence MacIntyre,

Because you ask questions that she is already thinking of,

And for some reason she has suddenly grown timid about her questions!

Now, continue.

"Well, I was just going to say that no evil can be justified on the basis of the greater good," Ron said.

That is what I told you operates in your reality, and you did not listen to my answer.

When you read the text, it will be simply clarified. In your reality, the stance that you adopt is a necessary one, and you must hold to it.

The fact that is DOES apply only to your system need not presently concern you.

"Hmmm." Ron placed his hands in front of his face, fingertips touching.

"Are there instances in which a spirit from another reality would intervene in this reality,

And we would call it a destructive act but the spirit would say it was creative?" he asked, suggestively,

A thin hint of a smile on his lips.

"Oh, for the love of God!" Arnold exploded, but Seth merely answered.

I do not like your term. Any such intervention would occur only on the part of a personality who was, for the present time, physical:

As the villain in a religious drama would be a creative figure.

But he would exist historically in your time and not, for example, be a ghost whispering in the night.

There are no creatures whispering evil in your ear.

"There are no intervening entities?" Ron repeated.

Not in those terms.

But in the terms that we are all spirits acting out our own inner drama, the term 'spirit' has some meaning?

Ron probed, with one of his few smiles ever.

Sometimes --- but only occasionally --- I think you are catching on! Seth yukked.

There are no forces outside of yourselves that in your terms
cause you to do evil.

Unfortunately, what you think of as good and evil reside within
yourselves and you cannot blame an evil force for the destruction
that runs rampant across the earth.

Again, in these terms, these are your problems,

And no god or devil put them upon you;

And there is no one to blame but yourselves,

Seth said to the rest of the class.

On the other hand, for the seasons and the (flowers), you have
yourselves to thank.

You are learning to use the creative energy of which you are a part,

And you are indeed quite isolated, so you cannot do much harm,
in your terms!

And so that the evil that you think you do is an illusion.

And if you destroy your planet, you will have others to work
with, and those that are destroyed are not destroyed.

You are in a training system.

The mistakes in the long run, and in your terms, will not count,
but they are very real to you at this time.

Ron stayed in class for about 6 months, but without participating,
holding his presence to himself like a weapon,

Relentlessly following Seth's words through every twist and turn of logic, picking up truths and casting them down like imperfect artefacts.

And it was here that Ron lost the real experience of Jane's class.

He wanted answers on a platter, according to his definitions;

Answers that would answer all the questions ever asked and that would erase all the doubts of human existence.

And for that, who could fault him?

Who had not wished for the same?

Yet, as Ron sat there, cold and severe as a brittle wind, you could see that such demands would not work.

You could only ask and ask and probe and discard in your serious scientific garb until you dried up trying.

You had to feel your answers, and the feelings had to rise up out of your own experience,

And fall back into it with warmth and joy and acknowledgement.

But Ron's posture of intellectual criticism was crushing the other portions of his psyche.

On the other hand, whatever obstacles Ron manufactured for himself in the name of intellectual probing seemed like nothing compared to the messes people got themselves into as a result of credulousness –

If only because it was more fashionable to be cynical.

Conversations with Seth, volume 2, 25th Anniversary Edition, chapter 5, "Them As Us - Characters Who Passed Through Class" - by Susan M. Watkins ©

If you sell yourselves short, you will say, 'I am a physical organism and I live within the boundaries cast upon me by space and time.

I am at the mercy of my environment.

If you do not sell yourselves short, you will say,

I am an individual. I form my physical environment.

I change and make my world.

I am free of space and time.

I am a part of All That Is. There is no place within me that creativity does not exist.

The Seth Material, chapter 9 - by Jane Roberts © L. Davies Butts

Your creativity, and your being, -- these are unlimited.

Trust Your Own Creativity

You cannot help but be creative.

You can enjoy your creativity, or you can try to hold it back,

And ask yourself, before you make a move,

What should I do? –

How shall I know that this next act will be correct, or right, or real, or the best for me?

Such thoughts would make any god reel!

Your cells grow without asking themselves whether it is better for them to grow or not.

The flowers do not start first, and think,

Is this a good yard, or a bad yard?

Is this yard in a good neighborhood or not?

Shall I be a violet in a good neighborhood, or a rose in a poor neighborhood? and then try to make a distinction.

Do not try to hamper your own creativity or your own being.

If you trust it - if you trust your own creativity, it will find its own fulfillment.

And, avenues that you have taken that you do not presently understand, avenues that may seem closed,

Will later be seen in an entirely different light, and the patterns will begin to fit into you.

They will make sense, but you must trust yourself.

Trust yourself even if you feel you are making errors,

For, again, it is better to make your own errors, in your terms -- granting that there are no errors –

Than it is to go in a particular direction given to you by another that is not your own, and that seems correct.

Trust the motions of your being.

ESP class 7/23/1974 - by Jane Roberts © L. Davies Butts

While there is a portion of All That Is, that is aware of itself as you, for example, a portion that is indeed focused within your existence, whose energy is directed within you, and to whom you can call for help when necessary, there is also an overall God-Personality that is aware of itself also as something that is more than the sum of its creations.

This is All That Is, in the deepest sense.

I am trying to make this as simple as possible.

The part of All That Is, that is aware of itself as you, is also aware of itself as something more than you.

This portion that knows itself as you and as more than you is the personal god, you see.

Again: This gestalt, this portion of All That Is, looks out for your interests

And may be called upon in a personality manner. But this portion is only a part, itself, of All That Is.

But, you see, even this overall pyramid gestalt is not static.

All or most concepts of a god deal with a static god and herein lies the main theological difficulties.

The awareness and experience of this overall gestalt constantly change and grow.

Again, there is no static god.

When you say, "This is God", then God is already something else.

I am using the term God for simplicity's sake.

All portions of All That Is are constantly changing and enfolding and unfolding.

All That Is, seeking to know itself, constantly creates new versions of itself.

For this seeking itself is a creative activity, and the core of all action.

Consciousness, seeking to know itself, therefore knows you.

You as a consciousness, seek to know yourself, and to some extent or other, you become

aware of your self as a distinct and individual portion of All That Is. You not only draw upon this overall energy, but you do so automatically, for your existence is dependent upon it.

The extent of your realization of this fact is the extent of your freedom or vitality, fulfillment and power.

It should not be forgotten, however, that the ego is also a portion of All That Is,

A highly specialized portion, enabling the inner self to manipulate and interpret particular conditions.

If the ego considers itself as the only self, then you are cut off to a large degree from the vitality and energy available.

The ego's false ideas prevent it from accepting this energy,

But once the ego is aware of its position as a portion of the self, then it should not be shunted aside, but can take its place.

It is sometimes referred to almost as if it stood entirely outside of basic reality. It is, of course, within it also.

Again, the term God is used simply because it is an accepted term for the reality we are discussing.

That which knows itself, which experiences itself within many forms

And yet knows itself as something apart from the total of its sums,

That left-over, unexplainable remnant you see, can be thought of as original action,

original consciousness, prime mover, or consciousness as distinct from its own creations, of which it is also part.

All portions of All That Is do not recognize themselves consciously as All That Is.

But know themselves mainly as individuals, not as the prime gestalt individual.

When realization is reached at the highest level, then All That Is instantly creates new realities,

And to some extent, you see, loses the conscious knowledge of its own identity.

TES7 Session 311 January 11,1967

ELIAS: And as to can you change beliefs? No.

You can change which influences you are engaging with a particular belief,

But it's not a matter of changing beliefs.

You all incorporate all beliefs.

ANN: Because that's—

that is the basis of your reality.

It is a matter of each belief has many different influences,

And yes, you can change which influence of a belief that you are expressing and engaging,

And that's where constructs come into play.

[The inner ego] is the prime identity of the whole present personality.

In many cases, it is the I of your dreams.

It is definitely the I of your creative activity.

It is the I, you see, which survives physical existence, and the physical, physically- oriented ego is only a part of it.

TES6 Session 270 June 22, 1966

Your religions stress sin.

Your medical profession stresses disease.

Orderly sciences stress the chaotic and accidental theories of creation.

Your psychologies stress men as victims of their backgrounds.

Your most advanced thinkers emphasize man's rape of the planet,

Or focus upon the future disaster that will overtake the world,

Or see men once again as victims of the stars.

Many of your resurrected occult schools speak of a recommended death of desire,

The annihilation of the ego, for the transmutation of physical elements to finer levels.

In all such cases the clear spiritual and biological integrity of the individual suffers, and the precious immediacy of your moments is largely lost.

Earth life is seen as murky, a dim translation of greater existence, rather than portrayed as the unique, creative, living experience that it should be

The body becomes disoriented, sabotaged.

The clear lines of communication between spirit and body become cluttered.

The Individual and the Nature of Mass Events, Session 805

Truth contains no distortions, and this material with all my best efforts,

And with yours, of necessity must contain distortions merely in order to make itself exist at all on your plane.

I will never condone an attitude in which either you or Ruburt maintain that you hold undiluted truth through these sessions.

Any material, to exist on your plane, must to some extent don the attire of your plane,

And in the very entry to your plane it must be somewhat distorted.

I must use phrases with which your minds are somewhat familiar.

I must use Ruburt's subconscious to some degree.

If I did not take advantage of your own camouflage system, then you would not be able to understand the material at this time.

Inner data, even this, must make its entry through some distortion.

We must always work together, but you must never consider me as an infallible source.

This material is more valid than any material possible on your plane,

But it is nevertheless to some degree conditioned by the camouflage attributes of the plane.

There must be no rigidity here.

This is a living, vital and valid experiment.

I suggest that all you take a brief break,

And if you are in accord then I will continue for a short time.

However, I want to make it plain that we are certainly not setting
up a new dogma.

By all means take your break.

Session 47 © Laurel Davies

In spite of all problems, the life force operates continually in
each person's life, and can bring about at any time the most
profound, beneficial changes.

The idea is to clear the mind as much as possible from beliefs
that impede the fine, smooth workings of the life force,

And to actively encourage those beliefs and attitudes that
promote health and the development of all aspects of experience.

The Way Toward Health, Chapter 11

I am myself using simple terms here to try and make these ideas
clearer.

In a trance state, Ruburt can contact me.

In a state in some ways similar to a trance, I can contact Seth Two.

We are related in ways quite difficult to explain, united in webs
of consciousness.

My reality included then, not only reincarnational identities but also other gestalts of being that do not necessarily have any physical connections.

The same applies to each reader of this book. The soul is open-ended, therefore.

It is not a closed spiritual or psychic system.

I have tried to show you that the soul is not a separate, apart-from-you thing.

It is no more divorced from you than God is.

Seth Speaks Session 589

In your country, the free enterprise system is immersed in strange origins.

It is based upon the democratic belief in each individual's right to pursue a worthy and equitable life.

But that also became bound up with Darwinian ideas of the survival of the fittest,

And with the belief, then, that each individual must seek his or her own good at the expense of others,

And by the quite erroneous conception that all of the members of a given species are in competition with each other.

The ideal of the country was and is an excellent one:

The right of each individual to pursue an equitable, worthy existence, with dignity.

The means, however, have helped erode that ideal,

And the public interpretation of Darwin's principles was, quite unfortunately, transferred to the economic area,

And to the image of man as a political animal.

This is carried through in economics, politics, medicine, the sciences, and even the religions.

So I would like to reinforce the fact that life is indeed a cooperative venture,

And that all the steps taken toward the ideal must of themselves be life-promoting.

The Individual and the Nature of Mass Events, Session 868

Each person is a vital, conscious portion of the universe.

Each person, simply by BEING, fits into the universe and into universal purposes in a way no one else can.

Each person's existence sends its own ripples throughout time.

The universe is conscious at every conceivable point of itself.

Each being is an individualized segment of the universe;

Then, in human terms, each person is a beloved individual, formed with infinite care and love, uniquely gifted with a life like no other.

The inner ego always identifies with its source-identity as a beloved, individualized portion of the universe.

It is aware of the universal love that is its heritage.

It is also aware of the infinite power and strength that composes the very fabric of its being.

It is of great value, then, that each person remembers this universal affiliation.

Such a reminder can often allow the inner self to send needed messages of strength and love through the various levels, appearing as inspiration, dreams, or simply pure bursts of feeling.

The inner ego draws instant and continuous support from the universal consciousness,

And the more the exterior ego keeps that fact in mind, the greater its own sense of stability, safety, and self-esteem.

The Way Toward Health, Chapter 3, March 19, 1984

When you believe the worst will happen, you must always be on guard.

In your culture people use the term 'intellect' almost like a weapon to protect themselves against impending disaster.

They must be alert for dangers of all kinds.

They begin to collect evidence of danger

So that any other kind of orientation to life seems foolhardy, and to be a realist means in that framework to look out for the worst.

First of all, if you realize that the intellect itself IS A PART OF nature, a part of the natural person, a part of the magical processes,

Then you need not overstrain it, force it to feel isolated,

Or put it in a position in which paranoid tendencies develop.

It is itself supported, as your intuitions are, by life's magical processes.

It is supported by the greater energy that gave you and the world birth.

That power is working in the world,

And in the world of politics, as it is in the world of nature, since you make the distinctions.

The Magical Approach, Session Three

The tragedies of the newspapers are symbols.

Those symbols REPRESENT 'real' tragedies,

But those tragedies do not exist in YOUR moment unless you are participating in them.

Those who are involved in such tragedies feel a sense of hopelessness and the loss of power in the present—

AND YOU DO NOT HELP THEM BY TAKING ON THE GUISE OF HOPELESSNESS!

What I am saying this evening is indeed simplified.

But you must operate from strength, not from weakness.

When you stand upon a firm shore, you can extend your arm to the man who is in quicksand.

You cannot help him by leaping into the quicksand with him, for surely both of you will go down— and he will not thank you!

"Then we're doing that as a nation?" Warren asked.

Individually—as you read your paper, as you watch your television,' Seth replied,

Whenever you look around you and say, 'Other men are fools';

Whenever you look around you and say 'The race is ruining itself—

It IS insane'; you are doing the same thing—

You are jumping into the quicksand, and you cannot help.

Organize your reality according to your strength;

Organize your reality

According to your playfulness;

According to your dreams;

According to your joy;

According to your hopes—

And THEN you can help those who organize their reality according to their fears.

Conversations With Seth, Chapter 20

Only your BELIEFS about the psyche and about the body limit your experience to its present degree.

In dreams you are so 'dumb' that you believe there is a commerce between the living and the dead.

You are so 'irrational' as to imagine that you sometimes speak to parents who are dead.

You are so 'unrealistic' that it seems to you that you visit old houses, long ago torn down,

Or that you travel in exotic foreign cities that you have actually never visited.

In dreams you are so 'insane' that you do not feel yourself locked in a closet of time and space,

But feel instead as if all infinity but waited your beckoning.

If you were as knowledgeable and crafty when you were awake,

Then you would put all religions and sciences out of business,

For you would understand the greater reality of your psyche.

You would know 'where the action is.'

The physicists have their hands on the doorknob.

If they paid more attention to their dreams,

They would know what questions to ask.

The Nature of the Psyche, Session 758

The imagination, of course, deals with the implied universe, those vast areas of reality that are not physically manifest,

While reason usually deals with the evidence of the world that is before it.

That statement is generally true, but specifically, of course, any act of the imagination involves reasoning,

And any [act] of reason involves the imagination.

DEaVF2 Chapter 8: Session 917, May 21, 1980

Now: In greater terms, there was no first Speaker.

Imagine that you wanted to be ten places at once,

And that you actually sent one portion of yourself to each of these ten places.

Imagine that you could scatter yourself in those ten directions,

And that each of the ten portions were conscious, alert, and aware.

You — being the ten of you — would be aware of existence in each of the ten places.

It would be impossible to ask which of the ten arrived first, except to say that all began with the original who decided to visit the ten locations.

So it is with the Speakers, who in the same way do not originate in the locations or in the times in which they may appear.

The original source of the Speaker data is the inner knowledge of the nature of reality that is within each individual.

Speakers are to keep the information alive in physical terms, to see that men do not bury it within and dam it up,

To bring it — the information — to the attention of the conscious.

SS Part Two: Chapter 20: Session 578, April 5, 1971

In reincarnational terms, the Speakers are teaching personalities who reach across the centuries.

Seth commented in Chapter Twenty of Seth Speaks:

The Speakers, more than most, are highly active through all aspects of existence, whether physical or nonphysical, waking or sleeping, between lives or at other levels of reality.

NoPR Part One: Chapter 5: Session 623, October 25, 1972

You cannot appreciate your spirituality unless you appreciate your creature-hood.

It is not a matter of RISING ABOVE your nature, but of evolving from the full understanding of it. There is a difference.

ELIAS: But that would be for you to design.

And this is also associated with this wave, for in being consciousness,

You are continually discovering,

And in a manner of speaking, in your discovery you are also inventing.

For, in many directions that you engage, you are not rediscovering some expression or manifestation or action,

But you are actually expanding and discovering or inventing new.

This is the nature of consciousness, to continuously be expanding;

Therefore, as you continue to invent your stories, this is an expression of that expansion.

You are creating new.

This is the reason that when I am posed with the question do I know all,

I would respond I know what there is to be known already,

But how can you know all when you are continually inventing?

About The Author

There's no denying it. My physical personality was lost in one crazy bad-ass netherworld of misremembering for the first forty- seven years of my life. My inner personality kept getting body-slammed by my physical one while I built my egocentric world. I like to say I was a religious, capitalistic slave, immersed in a vat of distorted values. And here's the thing: that is a realistic description of the physical image I created through years of business conditioning and knee-jerk personal choices.

I was a hard-headed, egotistical college dropout with doctoral -level personality skills. My goal was to sell my way to fame and glory, one shoe at a time. I was a money-hungry young shoe salesman—a shoe salesman willing to do the low-class ego dance for an order. I had the capitalistic brazenness to move up the corporate shoe ladder. My capitalistic persona would always stretch reasonable-ability to its outer limits.

So when I failed a time or two or three, I blamed the system. But I rose from my self-created ashes and got objectively successful again by selling more than one shoe at a time. I was selling container loads of shoes at one time. And once I felt successful, I wanted more power and more recognition.

When I bet it all with a blundering, alcohol-enriched mind I offered my impressive shoe talents to the capitalistic wolves, expecting to become one. But my narrow-minded focus sent me over the cliff of self-discovery.

My physical personality was in free fall, and all my lifelines burned in a fire I made. My reality started to change, and I started to feel another presence within me. My inner personality guided me to the bottom, so I could internally heal my self-imposed wounds.
Once I hit bottom, my physical personality drifted in a mysterious mixture of self-pity and irrelevance. But my inner personality came to the rescue. The energy within my inner personality took over when my mother passed in 1996. And that personality helped me understand the passing of my younger brother, Bob, and my dad, Howard, in 2013. I felt something special during these monumental losses.

It felt like I was standing in a nonphysical stream of understanding, and I felt the pure energy in that understanding. My physical personality followed that stream when I began reading psychology and philosophy books.

I found Rumi quotes in many of those books, so at forty-seven, I bought my first book of poetry. The Essential Rumi by Coleman Barks introduced me to some of his thoughts. Rumi, the thirteenth-century Sufi mystic, is an inner-self shaker. I started to look at the nonphysical part of things because of Rumi. Then

Confucius, Lao Tzu, Buddha, the German poet Rainer Maria Rilke, and the Englishman William Blake gave me their versions of inner personality expressions.

Jesus, Muhammad, Ralph Waldo Emerson, Ernest Holmes, James Allen, and other soul-seekers through the ages all said the same thing. And they all used their inner personalities to say it. By the time I found Japan's Shinkichi Takahashi's work, I was on the edge of a nonphysical bridge. I realized that I'd been on that bridge all my physical life but ignored being there.

I always felt the presence of an agreeable being in my thoughts. But I rarely paid attention to that being until I read Ask and It Is Given as soon as it hit the bookstores. Abraham, the author of the book, is a nonphysical energy personality who expresses commonsense thoughts about the nature of physical life.

In the 1990s, I hit the jackpot when I found the Seth Material. Jane Roberts, the poet and writer, brought the thoughts of nonphysical Seth into my world during my fifties. When Elias and Zurac came into my life in the first decade of the twenty-first century through the internet and a booth at Nashville's Galactic Expo, I realized that these nonphysical personalities' unfiltered messages were helping me forge an unfiltered path on this physical journey.

What I've learned on this journey is that I am here to physically experience my thoughts, emotions, perceptions, and choices. I know now what the sages and the people who used their inner senses in this reality were trying to tell me and everyone else:

Our thoughts and emotions are forms of energy that act like cells when we project them into our reality using a mechanism we call "perception." They are the tools we use to create what we experience physically.

I'm not here to form a group or write sermons about self-responsibility. And I'm not here to act like someone who crossed the self-awareness finish line and is basking in a state of bliss. My physical personality is still physically focused on creating my reality. But I'm increasingly using my inner personality to do it. I live in more than one reality. And I'm just beginning to appreciate what these other realities do for me.

H.T.M.

September 2025